TWO DEAI AND COUNTING...

The Underdog Detective Series

RICHARD SCHWARTZ

Print ISBN 978-0-9970965-0-7
ePub ISBN 978-0-9970965-1-4

First Edition

PRINTED BY ALPHAGRAPHICS OF PEARL, MS

Acknowledgements

Two Dead and Counting has been in the works for a number of years and couldn't have been written without the contributions of many individuals. I want to take a moment to express my appreciation.

First, I want to thank Doctor Katz for his medical input. No crime mystery is complete without a murder or two, and Two Dead and Counting is a killer. (I couldn't resist the pun.) Needless to say, we've had many interesting conversations.

As an attorney, I stay extremely busy. To write this book, I needed the assistance of a special writer. My thanks and appreciation to Wendy Carter for all her efforts and contributions. The second book in The Underdog Detective Series, Pearl River Mansion, is scheduled for release in 2016.

A special thanks to all of my friends and family, and one friend in particular, for your support and patience during the writing of this book.

I also want to thank a local artist, Michael Stiffler, who hand-painted the artwork for the first two book covers. In a world that has gone mostly digital, it is great to see such natural talent.

Most of all, I want to thank you, the reader, for taking this perilous journey with Jack Kendall as he solves his first murder investigation.

Enjoy!
Richard Schwartz

Two Dead and Counting
Reference Chart

(Thad) Thurston Oliver Winchester, III.............*Head Coroner, State of MS*

Anthony Winchester ....*Thad Winchester's nephew*

(Trina) Katrina Oliver.................................. *Anthony Winchester's girlfriend*

Cedric Johnson .... *Attorney*

(Josh) Joshua Royce ....*Cedric Johnson's under-attorney*

Stacy Young... *Joshua Royce's legal assistant*

Dr. Ryan Solver ....*Anesthesiologist*

Jack Kendall.. *Private Detective*

Kevin Thomas .... *Police Chief*

Elyse Dawson.. *Jack Kendall's old girlfriend*

Daniel Steinberg.. *Jack Kendall's best friend*

Christine Steinberg.. *Daniel Steinberg's wife*

Alexa Steinberg... *Daniel & Christine's daughter*

Jon Steinberg ....*Daniel & Christine's son*

Teresa Lindsay.. *Jack Kendall's client*

Alan Lindsay.. *Teresa Lindsay's husband*

Chapter One

Victim Number Two...

Frederick Hernandez thought he had opened his eyes, but it was still pitch black. He tried to move, but he couldn't raise a single limb. Gradually, he realized he was moving.

"Two dead and counting," a woman said with stark disapproval.

He tried to remember where he was, but the abyss beckoned him. He had no concept of time, only a growing anxiety that something was terribly wrong. Exhausted, he drifted off to sleep again.

Seconds later, his gurney shook as it crossed another threshold, jostling him into consciousness.

"I'd hate to see that doc's insurance premium," the woman said.

"Who cares about the doctor?" a man replied. "This guy's got five kids."

Frederick tried to concentrate. Were they talking about him? He had five kids.

A loud voice boomed over an intercom. "Ryan Solver, please report to the Emergency Room. Dr. Solver to Emergency."

Dr. Solver? He knew that name. He tried to move his fingers, but he couldn't find them. He was breathing, but only slow, shallow, infrequent breaths. He felt as if he were drowning, and the darkness threatened to suck him under. He tried to speak, but his mouth wouldn't open, and nothing came out.

"Here's your dead guy," the man announced as the

moving sensation ceased. "Want him on the table?"

"Stick him in the vault. I've got two autopsies to finish before I can start that one."

The word autopsy registered. Terror ricocheted through Frederick's body like a high-voltage electrical shock, causing his heart to jolt and then to flatline.

* * *

Six months later . . .

Trina wrapped her arms around Anthony's waist, laid her head against the back of his black leather jacket, and squeezed as the Harley beneath her zoomed from zero to sixty in a matter of seconds. The excitement in her stomach had less to do with her first time on a motorcycle than it did with being this close to Anthony Winchester. She closed her eyes and allowed herself to smile. It was colder tonight than expected, and since she had left her jacket at work, the warmth of Anthony's body was as welcome as the wind block he provided. It didn't take long to decide that she preferred to travel by car.

Her stomach tensed as they turned onto Old Agency Road. Moonlight pierced the thick, leafy canopy with beams of white shimmering light. She felt a yearning sense of homecoming as they traveled the narrow two-lane stretch of country road, though she had never lived in the upscale area.

Anthony pulled past the guardhouse and up to the security gate of one of the many subdivisions accessed from the Old Agency corridor. She watched him push the numbers, but she already knew them. The homes in this community were huge, each the centerpiece of handsomely manicured, fenced acreage. She counted the driveways, twelve until they turned to the left and approached a stucco fence, which stood in contrast to the wrought-iron barriers that divided most of the ten-acre parcels.

She watched him press the code on the private keypad and waited for the gate to open. He didn't surge forward as she expected but rolled slowly down the serpentine driveway towards the three-story mansion and two-story garage that made up three sides of a large courtyard. Timing it so that the garage would be open as they approached, Anthony took a left in front of the fountain, bypassing the upper half of the circular driveway, and pulled into the garage, parking well away from the sleek, black Jaguar that occupied the primary bay.

"Nice digs," she said as she swung her petite body off the back of the motorcycle. "Why haven't you brought me here before? I thought you lived in a dump or something." She glanced over her shoulder at the only illuminated window in the main house and saw a man wearing a brown bathrobe staring down at them. Thankfully, the garage door closed, blocking his view of them.

"My landlord ain't into me having company, so keep your voice down when we step outside."

"Too late," she said. "He saw us pull in."

"Figures. I can't do anything without him knowing it. I'll catch hell for this tomorrow."

"Want me to leave? I don't want to be the cause of any trouble."

"You're not the problem. I don't know why I put up with his crap!"

"Why don't you move out? Are you stuck in a lease or something?"

"Humph. A lease won't keep me here if I decide to go." He scratched his closely shaved head. "I'm gonna catch it no matter what I do, so we may as well go upstairs." He opened the outside door, grabbed her hand, and led her quickly up the outside staircase to his second-floor apartment.

She refused to look towards the window, but she could feel his landlord's eyes on them as Anthony unlocked the door.

Anthony hung his jacket on the back of the door and headed straight for the fridge. "Jack and Coke?"

"Sure," she said. "Speaking of coke, you got any?"

"I've got something better. Sit down and make yourself comfortable." A few moments later, he handed her a glass and joined her on the sofa. "Here's to a great night."

She touched her glass to his and took a healthy swallow. "Just what I need after a long day."

"I don't know how you do it, looking after sick people every day, but I guess somebody's gotta do it."

"Some days are harder than others, but I like helping people, especially when they don't have anyone else to look after them."

"Ever think about becoming a doctor?"

"Me? Nah. That's too much responsibility. I'm happy being a nurse."

"It's a good thing you are, too, or I would've never met you."

"True, but I don't recommend knife fighting as a strategy for meeting nurses. You could've bled to death. You're lucky someone found you when they did."

"Ahhh, it wasn't that bad."

"Maybe you should hang out with different people," she said.

"Maybe I should hang out with you."

"Maybe you should."

Chuckling, he reached for an intricately carved wooden box, which sat in the center of the coffee table. "I've got an impeccable connection for OxyContin. You can't find anything like this in the U.S. anymore." He set a hand-held mirror, a vile containing white powder, and a razor blade on the coffee table.

"Ooh, that looks promising," she said.

Using a razor blade, Anthony drew four thick lines on the mirror and offered it to Trina. "Here, use this," he said, handing her a one hundred dollar bill from his wallet.

"A Benjamin Franklin. Impressive."

"You treat me good; I treat you good. It's that simple."

"Oh, is that how it works?" She leaned over to snort the powder. "Just how many girls are you good to?"

"That's my business. Now come here and kiss me."

Trina straddled his lap and kissed him until she felt his hands on her hips, rocking her against him. She pushed back. "If you're seeing other girls, it's time for me to go."

"I'm not," he said. "You have my undivided attention." He pulled her forward and held her close.

She kissed him until he loosened his grip, and then she shoved away. "In that case, let's go to the bedroom." Rising to her feet, she took off her shirt and tossed it on the couch. As she unbuttoned her jeans and stepped out of them, Anthony did the same. Unable to wait, they came together for a passionate kiss and sank to the living room floor, entwined and desperate, groping with an abandon that left them well-matched and breathless.

A short while later, when their lusts were sated, Trina tenderly stroked the muscular contours of his chest and smiled. "Anthony, are you awake?"

His body twitched. "Yeah. Come here, Trina. Let me hold you."

She molded herself against his side. "Are you ready to take me home?"

"What? Why don't you stay the night? I like having you next to me."

"I have to work in the morning. I need to go home."

He sighed. "Okay, fine. Let's get you home then."

She frowned at the abrupt change in his tone and the dismissive turn of his back as he rose to his feet and dressed.

"I don't wanna go, but I have to be at work by seven. If we wait till morning, we'll have to fight the traffic, and I'll have to be home early enough to shower and change before I go in."

"No, this is best. It's not a problem."

"Do you have a sweatshirt or something I could borrow? It's cold out there."

"Sure. Hold on." He moved into the bedroom and turned on the light. "Here," he said, tossing her a black pullover. "It's big, but it'll keep you warm."

"Perfect." She pulled the shirt over her head and tugged it into place as she followed him down the stairs. Just before she stepped inside the garage, she looked towards the upstairs window. Seeing his landlord there, she faced him squarely and flipped him off.

* * *

Anthony glared at the window where the lights still burned, knowing that if he waited a few seconds Thad would likely appear, but he didn't wait. He jogged up the stairs, entered his apartment, and slammed the door behind him. He had looked like a complete idiot in front of Trina tonight. He was a grown man. He shouldn't need permission to entertain a guest in his apartment. He poured himself a drink.

A knock sounded at the door.

"You've got to be kidding me." He strode to the door and yanked it open.

"Damned inconsiderate of you to keep me waiting. I have an assignment for you. You work for me, remember?"

Anthony stepped back out of the way.

Thad pulled his robe closer around himself and sat stiffly on the edge of the sofa. "I suppose you have a good reason for breaking my rules."

"Yeah, your rules are stupid. I've lived here almost two years now, and this is the first girl I've ever brought here. I have a right to live my life, you know."

Thad's eyes focused on the wooden box. "I trust she appreciates the quality of your drugs."

"Who wouldn't," Anthony snorted as he sat on the far end of the couch. "Look—"

"No, you look. As long as you live under my roof, the only rights you have are the ones I grant, and I forbade you to have company on my property." He pulled an envelope from his pocket and tossed it towards him on the sofa. "The last thing we need is for someone to find one of these lying around."

"I know. It's just that she's so hot, and I—" Thad raised a brow, halting him in mid-sentence. "It won't happen again."

"See that it doesn't."

"Yes, Uncle," Anthony said, relaxing his shoulders now that the worst was apparently behind them.

Thad set a pill bottle on the coffee table.

Anthony immediately plucked it up. "Where's the other one?"

"You're fortunate to get this. If you disobey me again, I'll terminate our agreement, and you can go back to scrounging in the streets. Have I made myself clear?"

"You have," he said, clenching his jaw to keep from speaking his mind as Thad headed for the door.

"Anthony?" Thad said, turning back.

Anthony rose, rigid with anger. Losing the extra supply of OxyContin would mean half his income for the week, and he could lose his new buyer.

"The girl, what's her name?" Thad said.

"What difference does it make?"

"Her *name*?"

"Trina, not that it's any of your business. I don't ask about your private life."

"What is her last name?"

"I don't know."

"You risked my displeasure for a one-night stand?"

"It's not like that. Trina is respectable. She's a nurse at Union General."

"I don't care what she is. You compromised my privacy! You'll satisfy me, by God, or we're finished!"

"Fine! I'll get her name! Are we done now?"

Thad chuckled. "You remind me more of your father every day. We rarely saw eye-to-eye either, but we were loyal to each other nonetheless. I hope the same proves true for you and me, but that's your decision. Good night."

From the kitchen window, Anthony watched his uncle stride across the courtyard, past the three-tiered Italian fountain, and into the mansion he'd never been inside. "The only person you've ever been loyal to is yourself, you selfish SOB." He drained his glass and poured himself another drink.

That loyalty speech didn't fool him. He and his uncle were using each other. For that reason only, he held his tongue. But one day soon, he'd tell Thurston Oliver Winchester III exactly what he thought of him and his agreement, and a few choice other things besides. He glanced at his watch and wondered if Trina was asleep yet. Deciding not to bother her, he grabbed his keys and headed down the stairs. If nothing else, a long bike ride might soothe his temper and help him sleep.

He jumped on his Harley and raced down the driveway, deliberately shattering the silence. Knowing he had a tendency towards self-destruction, he focused his thoughts on Trina, what it felt like to have her arms wrapped around his waist and her body pressed against his back. There was something very special about her. He felt it.

CHAPTER TWO

It was only eight o'clock in the morning, and every phone line in Cedric Johnson's law practice was ringing. Cedric glanced from his computer to the flashing lights on his multi-line phone system with expectancy. He'd been waiting on a particular call for the past two days.

"Ryan Solver's attorney on line one, sir," Jeanette Augustine informed him via intercom.

Blood instantly throbbed in his temples. "Tell him I'll call back. Get Josh in here, and hold my calls."

"Yes, sir."

Cedric rubbed the top of his completely bald head as a victorious smile spread across his forty-eight-year-old face. The Hernandez case was in the bag; he knew it!

A knock sounded. "You wanted to see me?" Joshua Royce said from the doorway.

"Have a seat," Cedric said, waving him in. He gathered the loose pages of the Hernandez file and slid them into the folder. "Have you seen today's headlines?" He grabbed his reading glasses and pointed to the newspaper, which lay open on his neatly organized desk.

Josh, an enthusiastic third-year attorney, brushed his perfectly styled hair away from his forehead and smiled with genuine pleasure. "Who hasn't? Union General has suspended Dr. Solver's operating privileges and launched a full investigation."

"Yet he practices at Dixie Medical Center," Cedric said.

"Yeah. How can that be?"

"His reputation commands revenue."

"Fortunately for us, so do his lawsuits," Josh chuckled. "Think it'll go to trial?"

"They'd be smarter to limit their exposure."

Josh settled into the chair across from Cedric's desk. "I hope it goes to trial. I'm dying for my first shot at a jury."

"Solver's attorney just called."

"Well?" Josh said.

A smug smile tugged at Cedric's lips. "I didn't take the call."

"You're kidding me. I would've thought you'd dump the President himself to take that call."

"I'm letting them *stew*."

As understanding dawned, Josh grinned. "That's why I'm here. You're the best there is in the State of Mississippi."

"You return the call. If it's an offer, set something up for early next week. I want to wrap this up quickly."

"Will the family settle?"

"We'll help them see that a drawn-out trial isn't in their best interests, and they'll agree because victims want closure."

"Not to mention a million dollars," Josh added with a smirk.

"Exactly so," Cedric agreed with a smirk of his own.

"What about Dr. Solver?"

"It's safer to settle, but either way, with this being his second patient to die, his insurance company is likely to drop him. Even if they don't, his rates will skyrocket. Eventually—"

"He'll have to stop practicing medicine."

"Precisely. Now, go bill somebody. Time is money."

Josh headed for the door, but he turned back. "Cedric?"

Cedric looked up through his glasses.

"Can I lead the settlement meeting? I've memorized the previous case. I know the routine by heart."

Cedric considered his protégé, comparing himself when he was young. Josh was bright but idealistic and naive. "Not this time."

"But I'm ready, Cedric. When are you going to trust me with more responsibility?"

"When the stakes aren't as high, and you learn to hide your emotions. We can't afford to make mistakes. Have patience, Josh. You're making excellent progress, but you aren't yet ready to lead."

"What about the Bennett case? Surely, you trust me to handle a basic car wreck. There's no question of guilt."

"Schedule the depositions. I'll sit in and see how you do. Agreed?"

Josh nodded and let himself out.

Cedric took off his glasses and rubbed his eyes. The Hernandez case . . . Returning to the well a second time was reckless and arrogant. He had intended to address the situation, but now that a settlement loomed, maybe it didn't matter. It would soon be behind them.

Swirling in his chair so that his back faced the room, he logged onto his computer and into his brokerage account, grimacing as he reviewed his stock portfolio for the third time that morning. The market was down for the third day in a row. At best, retirement was five years away.

* * *

"Well?" Stacy said, her honey-blonde, shoulder-length hair bouncing as she followed Joshua Royce into his office. She'd been encouraging him for weeks to ask for more responsibility, and she hoped to hear he had finally done it. As her boss sat behind his desk, she plopped into an armchair and crossed her curvy legs, fully aware that his eyes had shifted to her bare skin.

"Uh, I'm leading the depositions for the Bennett case. Wanna celebrate tonight?"

Stacy rolled her big brown eyes and glanced over her shoulder. "I can't tonight. Besides, you have plans with Elizabeth—your fiancée, remember?"

Josh's flirtatious smile faded. "Yes, I do." He turned his attention to the messy stacks of paperwork that covered his desk and began sorting. "Have you seen my calendar?"

Stacy reached beneath a pile of loose documents and laid it in front of him. "Today's lunch appointment got pushed back to one o'clock, and they want to meet at Tico's. You're buying. You have an appointment with Marshall Butler at ten o'clock tomorrow morning. His file is to your right, on top."

Josh shot her a quick glance. "Thanks. I forgot about the Butler meeting. I doubt anything will come of it, but I'm obligated to hear their spiel anyway."

Stacy frowned. "If you'd do your job and read through their stuff, you'd see that they have something there."

"What do you mean?" he said, scowling at her.

"Less than two weeks before the accident, the Butlers paid a ton of money to replace their entire brake system. After reading through the accident report, and their statements, it seems rather obvious that they rear-ended that truck because their brakes failed. That being the case, the repair facility is at fault, not the Butlers."

Josh raised his brows, which both pleased and annoyed her. She enjoyed showing men that there was more to her than a curvaceous body, yet nothing irritated her more than for a man to assume that because she was attractive—and a country girl to boot—she was probably stupid. Josh didn't know it, but his response would determine whether she continued to work for him. As cute as he was, she wasn't staying anywhere she wasn't appreciated.

"Can you show me the repair receipt?"

"Yeah. I've organized and outlined everything. It's right there in the file." She came around the desk and opened the folder.

"Stacy?"

"Yeah?" she said, flipping through the pages.

"You've probably made the difference in whether or not this family receives justice."

"Face it, Josh. I'm indispensable." She pulled out a stack of paper and laid it on top. "Here you go, their receipts, state-ments, everything." She smiled mischievously and leaned in to straighten his tie. "Anything else I can help you with before I go?"

He grabbed her wrists. "You're a bad influence; you know that?"

She laughed. "Maybe, but you started it by kissing the back of my neck the other day. Desire's a two-way street, you know."

"You desire me? I knew it," he said, smiling victoriously. The telephone rang, startling them apart like two preteens caught kissing. Josh pointed to the door. "Get that, will you, at your own desk?"

Knowing he'd be watching, she winked at him over her shoulder and went to answer the call. Despite being a flirt, she was a damn good assistant, and they both knew it.

* * *

Cedric Johnson glanced at his watch for the tenth time that hour; it was a quarter to seven. The courier was due to arrive in fifteen minutes. Wondering if there was any coffee left, he pushed his chair back and headed for the breakroom. He was good at many things, but waiting wasn't one of them.

The halls of his prestigious law firm were dark and irritatingly quiet. While it suited his purpose tonight, he resented that his employees seldom compelled themselves beyond the bare minimum. He had sacrificed everything to build this practice, including his marriage. He had paid his professional dues, yet his only employee with any real drive was Josh, and he had gone to meet his fiancée for dinner.

Reaching the breakroom, Cedric flipped on the lights. Relieved to see coffee in one of the pots, he reheated a cup in the microwave and returned to his office.

With a sigh, he dropped into his chair and faced his computer. He struck the space bar and pretended to read the Wall Street Journal article before him.

* * *

Stacy watched Josh from his fourth-story office window as he hurried down the sidewalk towards his car. "Elizabeth," she muttered. "Humph." She was completely wrong for him. They had absolutely nothing in common except they both valued money more than happiness. She sighed and turned from the window. She didn't want to have feelings for Josh, but she found herself thinking about him more than she cared to admit. Well, they weren't married yet, and he had given her reason to hope.

She straightened his desk, picked up his empty coffee mug, and switched off the lights. She walked down the east side of the L-shaped hallway, surprised to find it dark. Apparently, she was the last one to leave tonight. She had stayed late to be with Josh, of course, not that they paid her for overtime, and heaven help her if she was ever late in the mornings. She bristled at the injustice of it.

The hallway was creepy with the lights off, and the shadows brought to mind all the horror movies she had watched as a teen, urging her to walk faster. She took the ninety-degree right turn, past the reception desk and elevator, and pushed through the windowed double doors of the breakroom. Someone had left the lights on. As she set the mug in the sink, she was surprised to hear the elevator chime. Thinking that Josh might have forgotten something, she rushed to the door. She was about to pull it open when she saw a tall man, wearing blue jeans, a leather jacket, and a blue bandanna tied around his head, walk past the breakroom door. The light from the room revealed that he carried something small and flat in his hand. An envelope, perhaps?

She stepped back from the window feeling silly for hiding but hoping he hadn't seen her nonetheless. She wondered how he had gained elevator access. It required a passkey after regular business hours. She considered calling Josh but decided against it. After all, what could he do? She pulled on the door but stopped when she saw a shaft of light appear across the hallway floor. She didn't dare turn off the lights in case he noticed when he walked back by. Scowling, she realized her only option was to wait— unless she wanted to confront him, which she didn't.

* * *

"Got anything?" A deep voice said.

It was incredibly difficult not to turn around, but Cedric firmly planted his feet and willed himself not to turn. "No." He waited another thirty seconds before swinging his chair around. He grabbed the silver envelope that was lying on the corner of his desk, sliced it open, and scanned it quickly. Blood surged to his temples, giving him an instant headache. After reading the note a second time, he committed the information to memory and shoved it into the shredder.

He groaned as he thought through the ramifications of the missive, and sweat broke out on his forehead. As he reached into his pocket for an initialed handkerchief, his eyes drifted to the wooden crucifix that hung on the wall in the small space beyond the door. There was no doubt about it. If they didn't slow down, they were going to get caught.

* * *

As Stacy debated her options, the man passed by the door again, sending her back against the wall. She waited a few moments and then peered through the window. She didn't see him, but neither did she hear the elevator chimes signaling its descent. She stayed in position. Then another man passed in front of the window; it was Cedric! Clearly the first man had come to see him, but for all of five seconds?

She waited several agonizing minutes before attempting to leave the relative shelter of the breakroom—minutes spent imagining that the messenger had seen her and was waiting for her to make herself vulnerable. She had tried to reach Josh several times, but he still didn't answer his phone, which meant he was almost certainly with Elizabeth.

Finally, after cupping her hands to the glass and looking down the hallway, she pushed the door open and ran for the elevator. "Yes, officer," she said into her phone. "I'm waiting on the elevator now." Her hands trembled as she waited. "Yes, sir. He was wearing blue jeans, a leather jacket, and had a blue bandanna wrapped around his head."

Finally, the elevator arrived. "Yes, sir. How many police cars are waiting outside, did you say?" Relieved to see that the elevator was empty, she stepped inside and waited for the door to close. When it did, she took a deep breath and tried to calm herself. Upon reaching the bottom floor, she continued her pretend conversation until she had stepped outside the building, and then she made a mad dash for her car.

Once she was safely inside, she laughed at herself, but the truth remained—the messenger was real, and he had delivered an envelope important enough for Cedric Johnson to wait for it himself.

Her mind raced with speculation.

CHAPTER THREE

"Yes!" Daniel Steinberg exclaimed, jumping to his feet as Miami scored a layup off the fast break, increasing their lead over the San Antonio Spurs in the fourth quarter of the playoff finals. "Come on," he urged his curly-haired friend. "Let's bet!"

"They're only down by three," Jack said. "This game is far from over."

"So, bet," Daniel said.

Jack grimaced as a bad pass put the ball back into Miami's hands, allowing them to knock down a clean three-pointer, fouling in the process.

"Yeah, buddy! That's my team!" Daniel cheered.

"We're gonna pull this out," Jack said. "You'll see."

A time-out sent them to a commercial break.

"You may as well admit it," Daniel said. "The Spurs are goin' down! Just like last year."

Jack, an ardent proponent for underdog redemption, took the bait. "How much you wanna bet?"

Daniel's wife, Christine, set a plate of sandwiches on the coffee table in front of the two recliners. "I heard that," she said. "I need a new dishwasher, so don't be betting any money right now. Please?"

Daniel flashed a smile. "Okay, honey, we'll come up with something else, but I could bet the moon right now, and it wouldn't matter. This one's in the bag."

Christine, a natural blonde with shoulder-length hair, leaned in to kiss his cheek. "That's what you always say."

"Better listen to her, Danny Boy. We're gonna trounce you after the break."

Daniel reached for a sandwich. "So, what's the bet?"

Christine settled on to her husband's knee. "I've got an idea."

"Oh, no," Jack moaned. "The last time I lost, I ended up cleaning out your garage."

"And you did such a fine job, too," Christine teased.

"The fence still needs painting," Daniel said.

"My thoughts exactly. As for you, *Danny Boy*," Christine said, mimicking Jack, "If you lose, you go on a stakeout with Jack. He's been begging you to go for as long as I remember."

"I like how you think," Jack said.

"If I lose, and that's a very big if," Daniel countered with a pointed finger, "I'm not wearing a disguise. So you can get *that* idea right out of your head."

Jack's hazel eyes twinkled. "Come on, now. That's the best part of my work. We could do you up with a beard, just like Abe Lincoln."

That earned him the expected glower as Daniel reacted to the long-standing jest that his narrow face and tall, slender build resembled that of the famous president. Jack raised his hands as he saw Daniel about to object. "But I'll settle for a plain, boring, ordinary, stakeout. In fact, I have one planned for tomorrow night. Agreed?" He stuffed the corner of a sandwich into his mouth. "Ummm, I love your tuna salad."

"You're welcome," Christine said, rising from her husband's lap.

"Plain, boring stakeout versus painting the back fence," Daniel said, raising his fist for Jack to strike.

"You're on, buddy," Jack agreed.

Game coverage began again, ending their negotiations.

Christine smiled and shook her head. "Men."

Daniel, his eyes glued to the television, said, "Sweetheart, will you, please—"

"Bring you another beer?" she finished for him. "You

ready, Jack?"

"No!" he said as his team committed a shooting foul that sent Miami back to the free throw line. "I mean, yes. Thanks, Christine." He glanced over at Daniel, who was cheering for his team. "Okay, so that was a setback, but we're about to take over."

"Right. You best go put your overalls on because you're gonna paint my fence this weekend."

Just then, San Antonio intercepted the ball.

"Oh! This game is on, President Lincoln. It's on!" Jack said.

"You didn't just call me that," Daniel said.

"And he scores! Oh, yeah! Did you see that pass? Did you see it?"

"I saw it," Daniel said as Miami took a timeout.

"Whoo hoo!" Jack cheered. For him, at least, the competition in the room was every bit as exciting as the game!

CHAPTER FOUR

As usual, Josh let his gaze peruse Stacy's curvaceous body as she moved around his office. So far, it was just a game between them, but lately he'd found himself thinking about her when he was making love to Elizabeth. He couldn't deny his attraction to Stacy. She was vibrant in a way Elizabeth wouldn't understand. While Elizabeth came from an influential family whose connections would further his career, she made sex seem like a task to be performed rather than a pleasure to be enjoyed. He told himself it didn't matter, but in truth, it left him wanting more.

"I'm telling you, Josh, it was weird," Stacy said as she bent over to file something in the bottom drawer of his cadenza. "What explanation could there be for a ganglord, biker dude comin' in here, after hours, to hand-deliver an envelope? If Cedric goes to that much trouble to hide what he's doing, there has to be a reason."

Joshua's gaze traveled up Stacy's legs, lingering first on the gentle sway of her short white skirt, then on her rounded derrière.

She caught him staring. "Will you get your mind off sex for one damn minute and listen to me?"

Shaking his head as if to clear it, he said, "Okay, I'm listening. What's so important about an envelope?"

"Really, Josh, somethin's not right about this. At first, I thought he might be a destitute relative. You know, picking up money from a rich uncle or something. But if that were the case, he wouldn't be delivering envelopes; he'd only pick them up. Cedric's doing something illegal. I feel it in my bones."

"I highly doubt that," Josh scoffed. "Cedric's one of the brightest, most accomplished attorneys in Mississippi. He doesn't need to resort to underhanded activity to make money. Did they see you?"

"No. I stayed in the breakroom for several minutes after Cedric left, which was right away, I might add. There was no one else in the office. That biker dude was definitely there to see Cedric."

"So, some biker dude delivers an envelope. So what? It's a huge leap to assume Cedric's doing something illegal."

"Tell me something, Josh. When have you ever known Cedric Johnson to stay late for a courier? If it were something important, he'd tell Jannette to wait for it, but wait for it himself? I don't think so."

"Maybe he was an informant."

"Maybe, but it was still weird."

"Okay, I'll take it under advisement. Can we move on now?" he said, his gaze lowering to her chest.

Stacy looked to see if anyone was standing outside the office. When she turned back, she gave him a mischievous smile and lifted her blouse for a quick flash.

Josh's breath caught in his throat. "You're such a tease."

"Maybe I'm not teasing," she said as she tugged her blouse back into place.

"Want to meet for drinks tonight?"

"Why not?" she said. "Your schedule's free for a change."

He knew this wasn't wise. He had a lot to lose, yet he heard himself saying, "All right, but I give you fair warning; I'm gonna push for a romp at your place afterward."

Stacy's eyes danced with pleasure. "Perfect. I'm in need of a good romping. Pick me up at eight."

* * *

Anthony watched attractive women come and go as the shift change progressed at Union General Hospital. Most of them never looked his way, and those who did quickly averted their gaze. He was accustomed to rejection from the sophisticated Southern-misses, whose chief concerns seemed to be their hair and makeup, and landing a husband who could secure their place in the upper echelon of society. No, he preferred spice and adventure. He preferred Trina. When she walked through the sliding glass doors of the hospital lobby and onto the covered sidewalk, he smiled and revved his motor.

Her short, spiky hair showed auburn in the sunlight as she trotted across the circular driveway.

"Hey, what are you doin' here?" she said with a smile.

"I've got a surprise for you. Tell me you're free," he said.

She gave him a sideways look. "I'm not free, but I am reasonable."

He laughed. "Hop on. I'll drop you by your car later on."

"Why not?" she said and climbed on behind him.

As her arms wrapped tightly around his waist, Anthony felt relief. He had gone to a lot of trouble to prepare this surprise. If she had declined, he'd have felt like a complete idiot. Soon they were cruising along a secluded road, past the shimmering lake and bayous of LeFleur's Bluff State Park. He continued to the furthermost campsite, which was located in the woods, near the river, yet within sight of the lake.

"It sure is pretty back here," Trina said as they rolled to a stop. "I didn't even know this was back here."

"I'm glad you like it," he said. "See that tent? That's ours for the next two days."

"Really?" She swung herself off the bike and trotted over to check it out. "What an awesome idea! There's even wood for a fire."

"Yep. There's an ice chest inside the tent. We've got Jack and Coke, and all kinds of good things to eat. I can even grill us up some steaks tonight, if you want."

Trina hooked her thumbs inside the belt loops of her tight blue jeans and smiled. "You, Anthony, are a romantic. Who'd have thought it?"

"Nah, I'm just selfish. We can't stay at your place because

of your roommate, and you know how it is at my place. I just thought it would be nice to have some time to ourselves; that's all. Will you stay with me tonight?"

She rose on tiptoe, wrapped her arms around his neck, and looked into his dark brown eyes. "There's nowhere else I'd rather be."

* * *

The moon slipped behind thick storm clouds, and the wind kicked up a notch. The branch of a large oak tree bounced unexpectedly as Daniel shifted his weight, nearly causing Jack to drop the camera.

"Easy there, buddy," Jack said. "We're trying to stay inconspicuous here."

"Remind me never to bet with you again," Daniel grumbled. "For the life of me, I don't know how Miami lost that game." He tugged his shirt collar up around his ears and tried to steady his lanky frame. "How do you do it? We've been up here nearly two hours."

"It's all about patience, dear boy, and luck," Jack said truthfully. "We know they're in there. Maybe we'll get something soon."

Daniel plucked a leaf from Jack's curly mass of brown hair. "I feel like a pervert. What if we get caught?"

"If we stay quiet, it'll lessen the odds. Hand me the thermos, will ya?"

Daniel tightened his grip on the branch above him while he lifted the thermos off his shoulder. He unscrewed the cap, took a swallow of the steaming coffee, and then handed it to Jack.

A light went on in the upstairs window across the street.

"Bingo," Jack whispered.

After taking a quick sip, he handed the thermos back to Daniel and focused his camera on the window. "Don't close the blinds," he muttered. "Don't close the blinds."

A moment later, a man in a business suit passed in front of the window.

Jack took several rapid-fire shots with last year's state-of-the-art camera. "Good, good. Now you, sweetie pie. Let's get a good shot of you."

Despite his earlier discomfort, Daniel leaned over the branch for a better view. "I can't believe it. Do you know who that is?"

Adjusting the lens with subtle movements, Jack prepared for the next opportunity. "Of course, I do, and these pictures will help me prove it. Be ready with that other lens."

The lights suddenly went out.

"Dang," they said simultaneously.

Someone struck a match, sending candlelight flickering near the window.

"And romance saves the day," Jack said. "Quick, hand me that other lens." The switch took mere seconds.

A woman wearing black lingerie moved within the soft circle of light, giving Jack the opportunity to take several more rapid-fire shots.

"I can't believe this," Daniel said with disgust.

Jack made some subtle adjustments, which allowed him to zoom in to the foot of the bed. To his surprise, the woman stepped directly in front of the window. Soft clicking sounds punctuated the night as his camera captured her curvy silhouette as she lowered the blinds.

"Ah, and it was just getting juicy, too," Daniel complained with insincere interest.

"It usually works like that, thank goodness, but it doesn't matter. We have enough."

"Yeah, too much. I wouldn't want to be her sorry husband."

Jack chuckled. "Knowing the Senator, it's his wife who will be sorry. She has a lot to lose."

"I could never be unfaithful to Christine. She'd kill me!"

"There are very few women as wonderful as Christine. You're a very lucky man."

"Don't I know it? What about Elyse?" Daniel countered. "She seemed pretty swell to me."

"Yeah, too swell. You know how I get. When she started talking about moving in together, I sent her packing." Jack held out his hand for the first lens. "Go ahead. Climb down."

Daniel looked down. "Right."

After several attempts to position himself favorably, he frowned at his best friend. "It didn't look this high from down there."

"I've got my cell phone. Want me to call the fire department?"

"Very funny."

Finally, Daniel lowered himself through the branches and walked down the tree trunk until he hung by his hands. Quiet, he was not; he landed with a thud.

"Hey! What are you doing up there?" demanded an elderly woman as her poodle began barking and tugging on its leash.

It was everything Jack could do not to burst out laughing as Daniel spun around. He knew his friend well enough to know that his face was beat red.

"I'm so sorry," Daniel said. "I, uh, my daughter's cat is up in the tree. I can't seem to get him down."

Gripping his stomach to keep from laughing, Jack produced a soulful meow.

The dog barked louder, and the woman jerked back on the leash. "Stop it, Peppie. Be quiet!"

Keeping a suspicious eye on Daniel, she craned her neck to look into the shadowy tree. "Damn tomcats. He'll come down when he's hungry."

Jack grinned. This was priceless! He was already imagining Daniel's horror at hearing it recounted over drinks at Hal and Mal's Pub.

"I'm sure you're right," Daniel said. "He'll come down when he's ready. May I pet your dog? My mom used to have a dog like this. He's very cute."

"Well," the woman said, suddenly pleased and distracted. "It's up to him. He's a very good judge of character, you know."

Daniel dropped to one knee and held out his hand for Peppie to sniff. The dog licked his fingers and wiggled in pleasure. A crisp streak of lightning flashed across the sky, illuminating Daniel's face as he cast a worried glance up into the tree. Turning to the woman, he said, "Looks like rain. Have a pleasant evening, ma'am."

"Good luck with your cat," she called after him as he stalked down the street. Just as she ventured another look into the tree, thunder cracked and then boomed, making her jump. "Good heavens!" She yanked her dog onto the sidewalk. "Come on, Peppie. We'd best get back."

Lightning flashed again, and it started to rain. Sheltering her parlor-curled hair, she hurried back the way she'd come, tugging Peppie along behind her.

CHAPTER FIVE

It had been the best two days Anthony could remember, but they ended the moment he came home with Thad hounding him about where he'd been, and why he hadn't returned his calls. Seeing him bluster about his apartment might have been comical except that he'd had to tell him Trina's last name to shut him up. He was still fuming over that when he yanked off his headphones and parked his Harley in the shadows near the back corner of a crowded parking lot. He waited for the two men in the silver Toyota Tacoma to enter the bar, and then he put on his black ball cap, tugged the collar of his worn leather jacket higher around his neck, and headed for the entrance. Skirting a group of teenagers who were smoking a joint on the tailgate of a tricked-out Ford, he walked the short distance to Hal and Mal's—one of Jackson's trendiest pubs. He ducked through a set of rustic doors and blinked in the dim light.

A waitress hurried by with a steaming bowl of gumbo. His gaze followed as she walked down the center aisle between the tables. The restaurant was packed. Turning his attention to the bar, he saw that it, too, was busy. He lingered for several seconds, assessing the clientele. People in medical scrubs, business suits, sportsman, rednecks, homemakers, and classy Southern misses were all crowded around tables, and the room buzzed with chatter. As he glanced around, he realized who was missing–the Cajuns and the Creoles. A wry smile tugged at his lips. If they didn't add flavor to a gathering, he didn't know what did. He never thought he'd say it, but he missed New Orleans. He missed the food and the music, especially the talented street musicians who were as much a part of New Orleans as the French Quarter itself. In his mind, compared to New Orleans, Jackson was boring.

As the crowd shifted, Anthony spotted his target, Daniel Steinberg, sitting at a table near the bar. A third man, a hefty red-haired dude, had joined him and his curly-headed sidekick. He watched the trio while he waited for a strategic spot to open up. A few minutes later, a man seated at the bar—directly across from their table—threw money on the counter and prepared to leave. Walking over, Anthony nodded his respect and took the stool, which was also near the television. A golf tournament was in progress.

The burly bartender, a copper-colored redhead, popped the tops off of two imports and set them in front of a middle-aged couple, completely ignoring their inappropriate groping. "I'll start a tab," she said and jotted down their order.

Anthony's gaze fell to the tattooed dagger on the upper swell of her left breast. "Nice tat," he said when she walked over.

"You want somethin' ta drink, or are you just lookin' for trouble?"

He chuckled. "Are you always this rude to your guests?"

"You gonna leave me a bigger tip if I'm nice?"

"I might. Jack and Coke will do."

"The name's Harley, and I'll be looking for that big tip."

"You do that. Nice ta meet you, Harley."

Harley moved down the bar, taking orders and removing empties. Anthony admired tough cookies like her, mostly because he understood that outward indifference sheltered unspeakable pain. He had developed a rough exterior while living on the streets, but he missed the genteel manner in which he had been raised. He pushed those thoughts aside; he didn't like thinking about the years following the accident and how they had changed his life.

Harley delivered his drink and kept moving.

The golf tournament caught his attention as the gallery exploded in applause.

"Whoa, did you see that, lads?" Daniel's red-haired friend

said.

Via instant reply, nearly everyone surrounding Anthony watched Rory McIlroy sink an impressive eagle, which pushed his lead to six.

"Still rooting for your kin folk, I see," the curly-haired man teased. "When are you gonna start supporting team USA? After all, you married an American."

"It's not my fault that the best golfer in the world is Irish."

"That's a matter of opinion," the man replied.

"That's where you're wrong, boyo. It's a matter of rankings."

"He's got you on that one, Jack," Daniel said.

It had been years since Anthony had last played golf, a sport that reminded him of his father. He downed his drink and raised the glass. Harley saw it and nodded. He glanced at his watch; Trina would be off work in another hour. He just wanted to finish his business and get on with his evening.

From his vantage point, he could hear most of their conversation as the men continued to goad each other as only friends could get away with. The curly-headed one, whose name he now knew was Jack, was relating a story and clearly enjoying the limelight.

"I kid you not," Jack said to his friends, "when Daniel landed in front of that little old lady and her dog, I thought we were busted."

Daniel laughed despite turning red. "Thank goodness it was only a poodle," he said.

"I feel for you, lad. When I went on a stakeout with Jack, we were nearly arrested for breaking and entering. I quit makin' bets with him a long time ago."

Daniel cuffed Jack's shoulder. "Gotta give it to him, Erik. The boy does one hell of a catcall. Care to demonstrate, Jackster?"

"Jackster?" Erik hooted. "I haven't heard that name since high school."

Jack, the current target of their humor, said, "Yeah, and if you are smart, it'll be another twenty years before we hear it again. Right, *Mr. Lincoln?*"

Daniel groaned and signaled for another round.

Jack glanced at the TV to watch the replay of a lesser-known contender sinking an impressive birdie from the rough—the opening Anthony had waited for.

"Nice shot, ay?" Anthony said, turning for Jack's reaction.

"He's a great golfer. Despite my friend's misplaced loyalty, I think Watson will win this tournament," Jack said.

"I've got five bucks that say McIlroy keeps the lead," Anthony said.

"Why not?" Jack said. "I'll back the underdog every time. Can I buy you a drink?"

Over the course of the next hour, Anthony drifted in and out of their conversation, gathering information. In the end, McIlroy won by three, and Anthony spent a pleasant evening with Trina.

* * *

Three weeks later . . .

Though no longer falling in torrents, the rainstorm had left the somber crowd wet and shivering beneath the dripping graveside awning. Jack was grateful for the rain because it camouflaged his tears. He could hardly believe it; his best friend, Daniel, was dead. Daniel's death was so unexpected that he wondered if it had surprised God.

When the service concluded, Jack stood back while many of the observers took turns sprinkling dirt onto Daniel's casket. Glancing over his shoulder, he saw a line of people waiting to offer condolences to Daniel's wife, Christine, and their two young children. Christine's mother, Nora, who stood at her side, grabbed her hand for a supportive squeeze. He saw all of this, but none of it seemed real.

Jack was the last to stare down at Daniel's casket where it lay in the cold, wet earth. A wrenching pain gripped his stomach as he contemplated the permanence of death. He glanced back at Christine and the children and wondered how they would manage without Daniel. He was their rock. Daniel was his rock, too. They had talked every day and saw each other several times a week. He couldn't fathom how empty his world would seem without the man who was closer to him than a brother.

Officially, Daniel's death had been ruled an unfortunate accident, a rare surgical casualty. The answers were slow in coming, but he sensed there was more to it than anyone cared to admit.

He scooped up a handful of dirt and sprinkled it over the beautifully carved casket. "Rest easy, buddy. I'll look after Christine and the kids, and I'll find out why this happened. I swear it!" An answering peal of thunder sent people scurrying for their vehicles. "We miss you terribly, and it's only been a few days." He brushed fresh tears from his face and hurried to catch up with Daniel's family.

Although Christine's hat veiled her face, her rigid body spoke volumes. Seeking to comfort her, he stretched his arm around her shoulders, but she pulled away. He knew her well enough to know she was angry though she'd never admit it in front of her children. There'd be time for them to talk later, when the first pangs of grief began to subside, and reality had begun to make itself clear.

"I'll see you at the house," Nora told Christine as she hurried towards her silver Lincoln.

Jack opened the door of Christine's white Acura for her and held the back door for the kids. Alexa, who had just turned nine, crawled across the back seat sullen and sniffling. Jon climbed in after her wearing his father's disgusted expression. Though only seven, Jon was the spitting image of Daniel. Jack leaned in and took hold of his hand. "I'm here for you, little buddy—for all of you."

"But I don't want you, Uncle Jack," Jon said, pulling his hand free. "I want my daddy."

"Jon! You apologize to Jack. He's only trying to help," Christine said.

Alexa leaned against the front seat, crossed her arms, and buried her head.

Jon turned his sorrowful brown eyes upward. "I'm sorry, Uncle Jack. I just want my daddy back."

"It's all right, Jon. I know you miss him. We all do." He tenderly stroked Alexa's head and stepped back into the rain, which was falling, now, in an annoying drizzle.

Christine rolled down her window. "Find out what happened, Jack. No one will tell me anything."

"I will," he said. "You have my word."

"I went through some of Daniel's things last night. I found something you might want," she said as her voice began to quiver. "Remind me to give it to you." She wiped her eyes and drove away.

Despite the chill, the back of Jack's neck flashed hot. He quickly scanned what remained of the disappearing crowd. Though he couldn't prove it, he was sure he wasn't the only one watching the Steinberg family drive away. He pulled up his collar, glanced around again, and headed for his car.

* * *

Hours later, after friends and family had showered Christine and the children with food and sympathy, Jack sat inside his ten-year-old Camry waiting for the lights in Jon and Alexa's rooms to go dark. Once he knew the kids were in bed, he called Christine.

"I don't feel like talking, Jack," she said, sniffing back tears.

"You don't have to say anything. I just want you to know that I meant what I said. I'm here for you and the kids. I can stop by the store, do chores—anything you need."

Christine burst into tears and hung up.

Jack knew he couldn't console her. He couldn't even console himself. He drove home from his best friend's house, as he'd done ten thousand times before, but he was numb. Once he arrived home, he grabbed a six-pack out of the fridge, shuffled into the den, and sank into his comfortable brown recliner. His mind kept returning to the day Daniel told him he intended to have surgery. He shook his head. How many times, over the years, had he teased Daniel about his slightly large nose? About as often as Daniel had teased *him* about his unruly, unpredictable mass of curls, but that didn't make him feel any better. Neither did it help that he'd tried to convince him not to have surgery. According to Daniel, he had opted for the procedure to correct his labored nighttime breathing, and not for vanity's sake, yet he couldn't help questioning himself. Had he not teased Daniel, would he still be alive?

The blank wall above his television became a virtual video screen for countless memories. He heard his breath as he exhaled and finally accepted the truth. Daniel was gone, and he wasn't coming back. By the time he finished his second beer, he had jotted a list of questions to ask Christine. If he was going to investigate, he needed some information. As it stood, he knew nothing of the details surrounding Daniel's surgery, not even the surgeon's name. Deciding to begin his research, he unburied his keyboard, which created yet another unorganized pile in the cluttered room, and logged onto the Internet. After reading through several articles, he concluded that the risk for rhinoplasty was negligible. In fact, no deaths had ever been reported as a direct result of the procedure. So what went wrong?

Well after midnight, Jack sought the comfort of his bed feeling sad, half-drunk, and mentally exhausted.

* * *

"Daniel!" Christine cried as she startled awake from another bad dream. Realizing she was alone in the room, she looked at the clock and saw that it was 2:00 a.m. Her heart still racing, she sat up in the bed and hugged Daniel's pillow to her chest. Burying her face, she cried until she could cry no more. When the tears stopped, she wiped her face and stared blankly into the room. She didn't want to get up, but she was afraid to go back to sleep. Her eyes were swollen, and her nose was stuffy, but she didn't care. She didn't care about anything anymore, except her children, who were sleeping in their rooms down the hall. Thank goodness, she hadn't let them see their father in the casket, she thought for the hundredth time. The horrible image of Daniel lying there, cold and still, haunted her every time she closed her eyes. She'd give anything if her last memory were of him kissing her good-bye that morning, but the Rabbi had insisted that seeing him in the coffin would help her accept the truth. Well, it had, and she hated the truth!

She and Daniel had known each other since the third grade when her family moved into the house next to his. Almost all of her memories included him. She didn't know how to move forward without him. Tears pooled in her eyes again, but she was beyond trying to stop them. What she wouldn't give to talk to him about *this!*

Besides being heartbroken, she was scared. How was she supposed to raise and support two children by herself? How was she supposed to help her children deal with losing their father when all she wanted to do was follow him into death?

No, she couldn't think like this! She forced herself to think about how wonderfully supportive everyone was. She was grateful, but the truth remained. While their kindnesses made the pain easier to bear for brief moments, they each went home to their unchanged lives and left her to deal with the pain. It was her life that was devastated—hers, and the lives of her children. Even as she thought it, she knew that wasn't exactly true. Jack's life had also changed. Daniel's work mates' lives had changed, too, and some for the better, she realized resentfully. Someone would step into Daniel's partnership position at the architectural firm that he had helped to create. The more she thought about it, the angrier she grew. She balled up her fists and struck the pillow repeatedly. "How could you let this happen?" she cried. "I trusted you to keep us safe!"

She wiped her face with the back of her hand. It was hard to accept. The man she loved and had confided in was gone. The person she had slept next to, and planned her future with, was dead. Daniel was dead. How was she supposed to deal with that?

For the first time in her life, she felt gut-wrenching compassion for every woman who had ever lost her husband to death. She had never stopped to think about it before, but it was like losing half of one's self. She promised herself she would never lack compassion again.

"Mama? Can I come in?" Jon said as he opened the door.

Christine sniffed back her tears. "Sure, baby. Come climb in bed with me." She lifted the sheet, and Jon climbed in.

He squirmed into a comfortable position and looked up at his mother with troubled eyes. "Why did God take Daddy?"

Christine swallowed hard. "I don't know, Jon. All I can tell you is that he must know what he's doing. We'll just have to trust in that."

"*You* trust him, Mama. I'm mad."

Christine brushed the soft brown hair that was so very much like Daniel's away from his forehead. "Go to sleep, son. Tomorrow is almost here."

CHAPTER SIX

Sleep didn't come for Jack that night, and morning took its sweet time in arriving. After a quick shower, Jack left his historic neighborhood, with its immaculately restored houses and majestic landscaping, and drove to his favorite morning haunt for coffee. The familiar bell jingled when he stepped inside the quaint country diner. Rich, wafting aromas met him at the door, perking his interest, if not his mood.

Dodging people left and right, he took his place in line. As he glanced around, he saw that the coffee shop bustled like any other day. Daniel had met him here almost every morning for the past five years. Didn't anyone realize that a great man was missing?

When he ordered his *usual*—coffee and an onion bagel with cream cheese—he was surprised to see sympathy in the eyes of the black, heavyset cashier. He glanced at her name tag. Though Edna had worked here for as long as he could remember, they had never spoken beyond a polite greeting. He gave her a weak smile.

"I'm praying for you," she said softly.

Unexpected tears stung his eyes. "Thank you." He took his food and settled at his usual table, near the window. While he spread the cream cheese onto his bagel, his brooding gaze moved around the diner. He saw several regulars and wondered if any of them knew. He tried to focus on breakfast, but he found himself glancing at his phone wishing Daniel would call to say that he was running late, or that some minor family crisis would keep him from coming. No matter how hard he tried, he couldn't accept that Daniel wasn't coming back. He thought about Christine and the children and wondered how he could help them. Daniel was the glue that held everyone together. The thought of never seeing him again was staggering.

Jack closed his eyes to banish his thoughts, but even as he did so, he knew that when he opened them again, Daniel would still be dead. Like everybody else, he had heard that there were stages of grieving, but he'd never imagined how difficult it would be just to get past stage one. If it was like this for him, it frightened him to think what it must be like for Christine.

At half past eight, Jack stepped outside the restaurant gripping a bag of warm bagels. He had several errands to run, but he wasn't going anywhere until he checked on Christine and the kids.

It was a clear, brisk morning. Thinking the cool air would do him good, he decided to leave his car in the parking lot and walk the eight or nine blocks to Daniel's house. Usually too busy to notice, he stopped to watch two young squirrels chase each other around the trunk of a large oak tree. Despite his mood, he smiled. They *were* pretty cute. And then he understood. Like it or not, spring was in the air. Life continued as if nothing tragic had happened—and it hadn't, for the squirrels. The same was likely true for most of the people he passed on the sidewalk, and for the people inside the diner. It was his world that had changed. Even so, spring was in the air for him, too. He could ignore it, in his sorrow, but that wouldn't stop the flowers from blooming or the animals from mating. The cycle of life goes on regardless. He found this truth both comforting and annoying. Leaving the squirrels to their antics, he continued on his way feeling wiser for his contemplation.

It took mere minutes to reach Christine's house but only half a second to lose the benefits of his walk. An expensive sports car sat parked on the slope of Daniel's driveway. Suspicion and envy struck him at the same time. Who would be visiting Daniel's widow this early in the morning and in such a nice car? Instead of going to the back door, as he usually did, he rang the doorbell.

"Jack," Christine said as she opened the door. "I'm so glad you're here. Come in." She grabbed his hand and led him into the kitchen where a well-dressed man of fifty or so sat at the kitchen table sipping coffee. The legal documents littering the breakfast table explained the three-piece suit and expensive watch.

Jack's eyes flashed with outrage.

The man stood with an outstretched hand and a smile that didn't quite reach his eyes. "Johnson," he said. "Cedric Johnson."

In the time it took to shake his hand, Jack's trained eyes had taken in every detail of his surroundings. He could see that Christine had suffered a difficult night. Her hair hung in restless tangles, and dark circles shaded her eyes. Dirty dishes towered high in the sink—very uncharacteristic—and the screen door stood open.

"Jack, Mr. Johnson was telling me—"

"Please," Johnson interrupted. "Call me Cedric."

Christine smiled politely. "Mr. Johnson is an attorney. He says he met Daniel at Hal and Mal's a few weeks back. He saw Daniel's obituary."

Jack searched Cedric's face for recognition. "I don't remember meeting you. Where was I?"

"Daniel didn't include you in on everything, Jack," Christine said.

"Perhaps it's been a bit longer than that. You know how fast time flies," Cedric said.

"Mr. Johnson feels that Daniel's death could have been avoided. He's offering to take action on our behalf."

"What kind of action?" Jack said, furious that anyone would dare come calling the morning after Christine buried her husband. "What type law do you practice, Cedric?"

"Personal injury. I've won several multi-million-dollar verdicts and arranged for countless settlements, all related to M and M. It's my specialty."

Jack nodded as if he knew what M and M stood for. "Christine, I don't think it's wise to sign anything in the state you're in, do you?"

Turning grateful eyes towards Jack, she picked up her coffee mug and headed towards the stairs. "Please, Jack, see him out. I know it matters, but it doesn't matter today. I'm going upstairs to cry for my husband. Good day, gentlemen."

Jack watched her go with quiet admiration, recognizing that even in crisis she had her priorities straight. After her footsteps had faded, he said, "What makes you think Daniel's death could have been avoided?"

Cedric began gathering his files. "I'm not at liberty to say. Are you a family member?"

"A close family friend and a private investigator. I'm conducting my own investigation. If you want Christine as a client, you'll have to work through me."

Tension bounced between the two men like opposing magnets. "I realize the timing is inopportune," the attorney said, "but it's critical that we begin working on this as soon as possible. Come by my office this afternoon, and I'll provide you with information to help you evaluate my firm." He nodded towards the stairs. "There could be substantial money at stake. She needs representation." He handed Jack his card. "I'll make myself available at three o'clock."

Jack followed him into the living room and out to the front porch with an apprehension he couldn't quite name.

Cedric turned piercing eyes on him. "We need to act immediately. If negligence or foul play has occurred, evidence will disappear quickly."

While it registered that Jack might need this man, he didn't intend to ignore the red flags that were waving inside his head. "Perhaps we can be of service to each other, perhaps not. I'll hear what you have to say. See you at three."

Cedric smiled. "We'll get the dirty bastard, don't think we won't."

Jack watched the silver ragtop back down the driveway with renewed envy. He'd always thought he'd be driving a Mercedes by now, living in a fancy house, accepting and rejecting cases at will. Though his career hadn't produced the lifestyle he wanted, he liked his work. That counted for something, he told himself as Cedric Johnson's Mercedes drove out of sight. He returned to the kitchen to find Christine waiting with a hot cup of coffee.

"Thanks for coming to the rescue. I know we need to investigate, but I don't have the heart for it today. I miss Daniel so much; I can't stand it! It doesn't seem real." She took a seat at the table. "I keep waiting for him to barge through the door demanding dinner. Funny how that used to irritate me. Now it's what I long for most."

Having been present on hundreds of occasions when Daniel had done exactly that, Jack felt a sudden twist in the pit of his stomach. Shaking it off, he joined her at the table. "I can only stay a few minutes. I want to check out that attorney before I meet with him this afternoon." He sipped his coffee, which he drank black, savoring the rich, dark blend. "He mentioned money, Christine, but this isn't the time for hasty decisions. We need to proceed with caution." Seeing the tension in her eyes, he changed the subject and his tone. "You found something you wanted me to see?"

"Only a picture I found in Daniel's desk." She reached into a nearby drawer and handed him a photograph.

"Wow. I remember this trip," he said with a smile.

"I miss going out on the lake. I used to worry about the kids, but Daniel was always right there to watch them. He was a wonderful father."

"Yes, he was. He loved you guys very much."

"Do you remember the time you set up your tent in that patch of poison ivy?" she said with a wry twitch of her lips.

"Daniel teased me about that for weeks."

"Those were such happy times."

"Except for the weekend you just mentioned," he said.

Despite her mood, she chuckled. "You should have seen your face the next morning when you realized what you'd done. Daniel laughed so hard he cried."

"Believe me, I remember. I had a rash for at least two

months." Smiling at the picture of him and Daniel standing on the bow of a bright red ski boat, he said, "Didn't one of Daniel's architect buddies buy this boat?"

"Mark worked for Daniel. As far as I know, he still owns it."

Jack pointed to the thin white lines that stretched from their eyes to their ears. "We used to call those racing stripes. We'd water-ski all day, and when the sunglasses came off at night, we'd have racing stripes."

Christine gave him another half-smile. "What I wouldn't give for another weekend at the lake."

He slid the picture across the table. "You keep it or give it to the kids." It suddenly struck him that *he* wasn't a father. Not only was his lifestyle lacking, so was his personal life. Normally, he didn't dwell on such things. He lived his life a day at a time, accepting whatever developed, but Daniel's death made him realize there was no special someone to miss him if something bad happened. Shaking off the unpleasant thought, he stood and opened his arms. Today wasn't about him; it was about Christine and the kids. Daniel would expect him to protect what was his, and he was determined to do that.

Christine fell into his arms and burst into tears. "I can't live without Daniel!"

He felt her body shake with grief and desperately wanted to help, but what could he say? Daniel was gone. He felt much like she did. "Things will work out," he said. "Really, they will." Even as she accepted the comfort he offered, he doubted his words. As far as he knew, Daniel hadn't left any life insurance. The topic had come up from time to time, but Daniel was a procrastinator. If he hadn't gotten around to it, money was going to become an issue soon.

After several seconds of warm human contact, Christine pulled away and tugged a tissue from the box on the counter. "Do you have any idea how hard it is to be strong for my children?" She turned to blow her nose.

The emptiness of his own life still stinging, he said, "No, I don't, but Daniel would be proud of you for holding up so well."

A bitter laugh escaped her. "That's because you don't see me when I'm alone."

Footsteps clomped down the solid oak stairs.

Christine snapped her shoulders erect and quickly wiped her eyes.

"Hey, Uncle Jack!" Jon said as he rounded the corner.

Jack lifted his hand for a quick high-five, which Jon engaged with his typical enthusiasm. "Good to see you, little Jon. Wanna play catch for a few minutes?"

Jon looked at his mother.

She gave him a weak smile. "What a good idea, Jon. Why don't you get your mitt?"

Jon furrowed his brow as he took in her appearance. "That's okay. I thought I'd help you make breakfast. I'm hungry."

Christine turned her back; breakfast was Daniel's job on the weekends. "I'll bet Alexa is hungry, too."

Jack put his hand on Christine's shoulder and gave Jon a conspirator's wink. "Can I help with breakfast while your mom takes a shower? I don't cook much, but I brought some bagels."

"Sure," Jon said. He flung open the refrigerator and handed him the egg carton. "Look, Uncle Jack, we have turkey bacon."

Christine headed for the stairs.

Jon talked his ear off, but he took his cooking assignment seriously. Before long, a surprisingly appetizing breakfast sat steaming on the table.

"Mama, Lexie," Jon called from the bottom of the stairs. "Breakfast is ready."

Jack poured the orange juice, and Jon took his normal place at the table. "Wait for your mom, Jon. You'll want to say grace."

"Nah. I don't say grace anymore."

Christine and Alexa entered the kitchen.

"I heard that, young man. In this house, we give thanks for our blessings."

Another challenge, Jack realized. How was she going to deal with her children's anger when she herself was angry? As Christine and Alexa sat down, Jack's gaze shifted to Alexa's long blonde braids. Little hairs had escaped their pleats in the night, and soft sweet curls framed her face. She was wearing black pants and a black shirt. Coincidence? "Good morning, sweetie," he said. He slid a glass of orange juice across the table.

Alexa looked up with brooding blue eyes and reached for the glass, but she didn't return the greeting.

"Jack," Christine said, "will you say the blessing?"

He grimaced. Daniel always said the family prayer. He had never paid attention to the words.

The children were waiting.

"Okay," he said, searching for something to say. "Bless this food and, uh, thank you for the squirrels. Amen."

Jon shot him a quizzical look but dished up his plate without comment. After a few quick bites, he looked expectantly towards his mother.

She didn't notice, but Jack did. Christine's appetite was nonexistent. She was struggling to eat her food. "Wow, Christine. Didn't Jon make a great breakfast?"

"Yes, Jon, breakfast is wonderful," she said quickly. "Thank you."

That was enough praise for Jon. He reached for another piece of turkey bacon.

As Jack observed Daniel's family, a family who only days before had been happy and chaotic, he grew ever more determined to discover what had gone wrong during Daniel's surgery. If Daniel died because some inattentive doctor didn't do his job, then he intended to hold him accountable.

After breakfast, Jon went into the living room to watch cartoons, Alexa went upstairs, and Jack and Christine set about cleaning up the dishes. "Christine, I need some information. Who did Daniel's surgery?"

Christine tucked her long, sweeping bangs behind her ear with a soapy hand. "His name is Wilson Rawlings. He came highly recommended by our regular doctor. We checked him out. Everything we read was favorable."

"Have you met him?"

She rinsed the dishrag and wiped down the table. "No, but Daniel liked him. Do you really think he's at fault?"

"I don't know," Jack said, "but I intend to find out. Which hospital is he associated with?"

"Union General."

Jack put the last plate into the cabinet. "That gives me a place to start." He kissed her cheek. "I'll check on you later. Call me if you need anything."

"I will."

Jack ruffled Jon's hair as he passed through the living room and out the front door. He still had errands to run before returning home to research Cedric Johnson.

CHAPTER SEVEN

"Good morning, Mr. Johnson," Jannette said as Cedric stomped past her desk, ignoring the messages she tried to hand him.

"Get Josh in here, pronto, and get Gloster on the line. Other than him, hold my calls." Cedric closed himself inside his office and dropped into his chair. Of all the blasted luck, the deceased's family friend is a detective. How did *he* fly under the radar?

Jannette buzzed the intercom. "Gloster on one, sir."

Cedric leaned forward and grabbed the phone. "Hey, Richard, how are you? Can you get me the dirt on a private detective named Jack . . . Jack . . . I can't believe this! I don't know his last name."

Gloster chuckled. "Done that myself, Ole boy. Call me back when you know."

"Thanks," Cedric sneered. "I'll do that." He hung up and searched his pockets. "Humph," he grumbled. He forgot to ask for a business card. Now, he'd have to wait until after their meeting to check him out.

The intercom buzzed again. "Josh is here. Shall I send him in?"

Controlling his irritation, he said, "Yes, and will you bring me a cup of coffee, please?"

Clearly forewarned about his mood, Josh opened the door and entered quietly. He settled into a chair in front of the desk and waited while Cedric concentrated on his calendar. Jannette entered behind Josh and set a steaming mug on the corner of Cedric's desk. She emptied his out-box and quietly left the room, closing the door behind her.

"You wanted to see me?" Josh said.

Cedric finally focused on Josh. "There's a new case in the works, and I need your help. One of the parties is a private investigator. We need to convince him that it's in his best interest to work with us. I've scheduled a preliminary meeting for this afternoon, and I want you in on it." He had trained Josh not to interrupt, so after pausing to sip his coffee, he added, "Take notes on the guy. Write down everything he says. I don't think he'll be a problem, but it's important to make him feel useful instead of adversarial."

"Got it," Josh said. "What's the case about?"

"Another wrongful-death in the medical community."

"Oh, I hate to hear that. You'd think with all the new technology they have, they'd lose fewer lives."

"Another death, another dollar."

"Damn, Cedric. I've never heard you talk like that."

"Get over yourself, boy. People die. That's how the world works."

"We're not talking about somebody dying because it's their time to go. We're talking about someone making a mistake and it costing another man his life. There's a huge difference."

"That's how we get paid, remember? If the world were a rosy place, there'd be no need for lawyers."

"Yeah, I know. You've had more time to grow cynical, I guess, but when I see the families who are left behind after something like this, it gets to me."

"Well, toughen up. Without us, victims wouldn't receive justice or compensation. Now, get back to work, and don't forget about our three o'clock meeting."

* * *

Jack's fingers flew across the keyboard as he searched for articles on Cedric Johnson. One article, in particular, caught his interest, but when he selected it, the computer locked up. He struck the top of his desk with his fist. "Come on! I don't have time for this." He raked his fingers through his unruly hair and, after trying everything he knew to get it to work, rebooted the system. While waiting for the computer to reset, he turned to make some notes. He wanted to learn everything possible about Cedric Johnson before their meeting. No matter how he looked at it, it just seemed sleazy to approach Christine so soon after losing Daniel.

When he was finally back online, he typed in Cedric's name again. Several links appeared. It didn't take long to confirm that he was a successful attorney who specialized in medical malpractice cases. He read several glowing articles, but not all the press was good. Several reports indicated that his law firm was under Federal scrutiny. Fifteen plaintiffs had allegedly pled guilty to false claims against a prominent pharmaceutical company. He read the highlights, but nothing stood out. Class action suits were big business. It wasn't surprising to see accusations leveled against a successful law firm.

Next, he clicked on Johnson's website. It was impressive, to say the least. One section featured testimonials with staggering verdicts. It appeared that Cedric Johnson wasn't afraid to go after the big boys. His cell phone rang. "Hello," he said, his eyes still glued to the screen.

"Is this Jack Kendall?" asked a sultry voice.

He turned from the computer, grabbed a notepad, and stepped through the sliding glass doors and onto the covered patio. "It is. Can I help you?"

"I have some suspicions I'd like to confirm. A mutual acquaintance referred you. Are you accepting new cases?"

"Always," Jack said, regretting the word as soon as it left his mouth. The last thing he needed was to announce to a prospective client that business was suffering. "Where would you like to meet?"

"Your office, this afternoon. Say, five thirty?"

After arranging the meeting, Jack settled back at the computer to see what he might dig up on Daniel's plastic surgeon, Wilson Rawlings. He reviewed several sites but found no complaints or reports of disciplinary action. In fact, Wilson

Rawlings looked incredibly well-credentialed. From what he could tell, his reputation was spotless. Time didn't permit further research, but he jotted a note to check with a physician friend of his, Raymond Sassi, to see if he might know Wilson Rawlings personally. Inside information, when you could get it, often provided the most reliable indicators of a person's character and performance, but as he had learned over the years, when it came to misconduct, it was the least likely who were often the most guilty. If Wilson Rawlings had made a mistake that cost Daniel his life, he intended to hold him accountable.

* * *

Josh tapped his foot and glanced at his watch. Elizabeth had been in the ladies room for fifteen minutes. He knew better than to take a late lunch. If the traffic were bad, he'd likely be late for Cedric's meeting. When she finally emerged, she was texting someone on her phone, clearly unconcerned that she had kept him waiting. "Dammit, Elizabeth, I told you I was in a hurry. Couldn't that have waited?"

She stuffed her phone into her designer handbag and scowled at him. "Don't you cuss at me, Joshua Royce. I'm not an employee you can order around. As much as you do for your boss, you'd think he'd be a little more understanding."

Josh knew better than to reply. He helped Elizabeth into the passenger side of his baby blue BMW and hurried around to the other side. Once the traffic cleared, he pulled onto the street and gunned it.

"Really, Josh, won't you, at least, consider my father's proposal? Working for him would give you a lot more free time. With all the late nights you've been working lately, I would think you'd welcome a shorter workday. He'll probably bring it up at dinner tonight."

Josh put on his sunshades. He was feeling guilty about sleeping with Stacy, and he was afraid Elizabeth might figure it out. "I'll listen to what he has to say, but don't get your hopes up. I've spent years studying to become a lawyer. I'm not interested in changing careers."

Elizabeth smiled and let the subject drop.

In his rush to make up time, Josh weaved in and out of traffic, taking advantage of each opening to surge ahead. He glanced into the rear view mirror and was about to change lanes again when the driver of the pickup truck he was following slammed on his brakes. Josh reacted in time, but the person behind him was also following too closely. She slammed into the back of his car, causing Josh to hit the truck.

"Dammit!" Josh said. "Elizabeth, are you all right?"

"Yes, thank goodness, but your car!"

Pulling themselves together, they got out to survey the damage, which certainly could have been worse. The driver of the pickup truck had also gotten out and was already on the phone.

The Honda Civic, which had rammed into the back of Josh's car, had suffered the worst damage. The driver, a young woman in her early twenties, ran up to Josh and Elizabeth. "Oh, my gosh! I'm so sorry! Please tell me you're all right."

Elizabeth gave her a dirty look.

Seeing it, Josh said, "We're fine. Do you have insurance?"

"I do. I'll get my purse."

While Elizabeth waited for the woman to write down her information, Josh gave his information to the truck driver. Afterward, he called his insurance company, and then the office to let them know he'd be late. Gritting his teeth, he climbed back into his car to wait for the police to arrive.

* * *

Just before three o'clock, Jack into the parking lot of a five-story office complex. He had just gotten out of his car when he noticed a new dent in his bumper. Scowling at it, he said, "When did that happen? Doesn't anyone leave a note these days?" He reached into the back seat for his notepad and spotted Cedric's Mercedes through the window where it sat in the reserved parking section. Further annoyed, he climbed back in and moved his car to the opposite end of the parking lot.

The elevator rose to the fourth floor and opened on the inside of an office space. The sign above the reception desk read, *Law Offices of Cedric K. Johnson.* As he stepped forward, two men wearing suits stepped out of a room and walked down the hallway. Jack glanced down at his tan Docker pants and short sleeved shirt—his typical daily attire. It hadn't occurred to him to change clothes. He didn't own a suit, but he did have some collared shirts and a sports jacket—too late for that now. He approached the young receptionist. "Hi, I'm Jack Kendall. Cedric Johnson is expecting me."

"Oh, yes, Mr. Kendall." She looked down to check her schedule. Not finding his name, she bit her lip and searched again.

Jack smiled. She reminded him of Daniel's daughter, Alexa, who also bit her lip when she was concentrating. "I just met Cedric this morning. Perhaps that's why you don't have a record of our three o'clock meeting."

Relief lit her pretty face. "Thanks. I'll let him know you're here. You said your name was Jack?"

"Jack Kendall. He'll know who I am." Feeling silly for playing up his importance, he turned away from the desk and pretended to peruse the magazine rack. He pulled out the March edition of *National Geographic* and flipped through the pages, but he didn't absorb anything beyond a shallow flash of interesting pictures. He was hoping this meeting would reveal whether Johnson was friend or foe. Ten minutes later, the door leading to the inner offices opened.

"Good afternoon, Mr. Kendall. I'm Jannette Augustine. Mr. Johnson will see you now. Follow me, please."

Jack couldn't help noticing the sway of Jannette's well-rounded hips as he followed her down the hallway and through a set of two-leaved doors, which led to the executive suite. Here, she gestured towards another open door. "He's expecting you." She gave him a condescending smile and sat behind her desk. "Enjoy your meeting, Mr. Kendall."

When Jack stepped forward, he saw Cedric waving to him from behind his desk.

"Come on in, Jack. I'll be right with you," Cedric said.

He took a few hesitant steps and glanced around.

"Brilliant," Cedric said into the phone. "I'll give you a call when I leave the office. What was that?"

Trying to appear uninterested in his conversation, Jack walked over to a large bookcase and picked up a family photograph of Cedric sitting on a bench next to an attractive woman with two young men standing behind them. Nice family, he thought. Their smiles appeared genuine enough. Next, he scanned the books themselves. If the titles were any indication, Cedric Johnson was quite the intellectual. Of course, there was no telling if he'd actually read the classic collection, but it was impressive nonetheless. Framed newspaper articles with copies of impressive checks decorated the walls and bookshelves. One, in particular, drew his attention. The headline read, *Toy Manufacturer Not Having Fun After Yesterday's Verdict.* He scanned through the article and raised a brow. Eighteen million dollars; maybe they *could* get some money for Daniel's family.

"See you then," Cedric said and hung up the phone. He pushed the intercom button. "Jannette, is Josh in?"

"No, sir. He called to say he is running late."

"Very well. Hold my calls."

"Yes, sir."

Cedric stood and stretched out his hand for the second time that day. Jack shook it and winced as Cedric squeezed harder than necessary. So it's like *that*, he thought with amusement. Did Cedric see him as a threat?

"So, Jack. I can call you Jack, can't I?" Cedric said, motioning towards two small sofas that formed an informal sitting area. "Please, sit down. May I offer you something to drink? Bottled water, perhaps?"

"I'm fine, thanks."

Cedric fired the first round. "Did you do your homework before coming here today?"

"Lots of interesting press about you and your law firm. It must have taken courage to build this practice."

"It's a risky business, but rewarding, as you have seen."

"Do I understand correctly that you don't typically engage in initial class-action, but prefer to pick up residual clients after general settlements have been negotiated?"

"That strategy reduces my earnings, but it also limits risk. My primary focus is on individual cases, which brings us to your friend, Daniel Steinberg. I'm sorry for your loss, by the way."

Jack felt as if a sudden weight had struck him in the chest. "Thank you. Daniel was my best friend."

Cedric nodded. "Do you have a business card? I neglected to ask for one this morning."

Feeling somewhat guarded, Jack said, "Sorry, I didn't bring one." He thought he saw irritation in Cedric's eyes, but it vanished quickly.

"Well, then," Cedric said, "let's get down to business. I think there was, at the very least, negligence on the part of Daniel's anesthesiologist, Ryan Solver."

"His anesthesiologist? I've been researching his surgeon, Wilson Rawlings."

"Wilson Rawlings hasn't had any surgical fatalities. Solver, on the other hand . . ."

Jack leaned forward.

"Daniel Steinberg is his third patient-death in a two-year period."

"Three? Why isn't he in jail?"

"The previous cases settled out of court with no admission of guilt."

Jack knew that Cedric was watching him, but he was reeling from the news. If Daniel had known about the previous cases, he certainly wouldn't have used his services, and he'd still be alive today. The thought of Solver getting off again was completely unacceptable. He wanted justice for Daniel's family! He rose to his feet. "If we don't get this guy off the street, someone else may die."

"That's exactly why I went to see Mrs. Steinberg. I'm the best hope she has of winning this case, but we need to file suit immediately. The longer we delay, the greater the risk that someone may tamper with the medical records."

"Why should Christine hire you instead of some other attorney with even bigger checks on his wall?"

"If this case goes to trial, it could drag on for years. You need someone who's prepared to go the distance. Someone who can put this case together and hire expert witnesses. If it goes before a jury, you need someone who can win. I'm the best there is in the State of Mississippi. If you hire anyone else, you're taking a huge risk."

"You said it could drag on for years. Can't we put Solver out of business? The longer he's out there . . ."

"There is another way. A way that doesn't depend upon a fickle jury."

Jack noted the change in Cedric's tone and sat back down.

"Solver's insurance rates are already sky high. Chances are, if he settles this case as he has the other two, it will push him over the edge. If he can't get malpractice insurance—"

"He can't practice medicine," Jack said.

"Either way, we've got a lot of work to do."

"What do you think he'll do?"

"He'll wait to see if we have any evidence before he does anything. Without evidence, we've got nothing."

Jack was beginning to understand the urgency. "How much do you know about Dr. Solver?"

"He graduated from a prestigious medical school on the East Coast. He's published a few scientific papers for the Board of Anesthesiology, and most importantly, he's recently lost his privileges at Union General Hospital. He practices, now, at DMC."

"How much money can you get for Daniel's family?"

"It's too early to guess."

"Where do I fit in?"

Cedric paused. "I want this case, Jack. You can convince Mrs. Steinberg that prosecution will lead to the justice and financial compensation she deserves. In addition, you'll be investigating this case irrespective of a lawsuit. Collaborating clearly makes sense. I'll work on winning our case. You keep me posted on what you find." Cedric eyed him shrewdly. "There will be a lot of press surrounding this lawsuit. Your reputation will benefit from our connection."

"Is that why you want this case—for the publicity?"

"It never hurts, as long as you win. And I do intend to win, Jack. I want to stop Ryan Solver just as much as you do. Sure, I make money on the case, but it serves everyone to get a bad doctor out of practice. Hell, I could get into a car accident and end up with Solver as my anesthesiologist while I'm unconscious and unable to do anything about it."

"I need time to consider our discussion. In the meantime, two things: I want more information about your law firm and a copy of the paperwork you prepared for Mrs. Steinberg."

"Done."

Jack stood. "You're right about one thing; Christine won't hire you unless I recommend it. If we go forward, I expect all correspondence to come directly to me. These are difficult days for Christine and her family. I don't want them unduly upset or disturbed."

"Fair enough." Cedric went to his desk and pushed the intercom button. "Jannette, is Joshua Royce in the building?"

"Yes, sir. He came in a few minutes ago."

"Ask him to join us, please. Oh, and Jannette, have a copy of the Steinberg contract available when we conclude."

A brief knock sounded, and an impressive-looking young man entered Cedric's office. "Sorry to keep you gentlemen waiting," he said. "I was unavoidably detained."

Cedric stepped forward. "Jack Kendall, this is Joshua Royce."

As they shook hands, Jack noted the confidence and intelligence of the young man before him and wondered what it must be like to work under the tutelage of such a successful mentor. He had worked alone for the past twenty-something years, except when he could afford to hire someone to do his filing and whatnot.

"Josh," Cedric said, "educate Jack about our firm. We hope

to represent a friend of his in a wrongful death suit, and we want him feeling comfortable with his choice in counselors."

Josh gave the obligatory response and, suddenly, the meeting was over.

The next thing Jack knew, he was holding Christine's file and following Joshua Royce down the hallway to a stark, masculine-looking conference room. He glanced around before sitting at the long, black conference table, which could easily accommodate twelve. He liked the clean feel of the room, the black and white art on the walls, and the unusual vase in the corner. The entire room screamed success. He compared it to his dark and cluttered office space and decided it was time to upgrade his image.

Joshua Royce draped his jacket over a chair and remained standing. "How can I help you, Mr. Kendall?" His tone revealed an irritation that wasn't apparent in Cedric's office.

"Please, call me Jack. I'm here because a friend of mine died recently during an elective surgery. He left a wife and two young children behind. I want to help them."

"You have my condolences. Look, I could throw all kinds of company stats at you, but the bottom line is you should feel privileged to have Cedric Johnson interested in your case. If there's money to recover, he's the best there is at making sure it gets paid."

"Privileged or not, I have a few questions. How many malpractice cases has Cedric won?"

"Thirty or so."

"Highest single verdict?"

"Twenty-four million."

Jack's eyebrows shot up and, despite the tension, Josh chuckled. "That's a truckload of money. Isn't it, Jack?"

"And how. I wouldn't know what to do with that much money."

"I'd buy a jet," Josh said. "You should see some of these guys who come in here. They fly across the country just to go to dinner."

"It takes all I've got just to walk into McDonalds."

Josh smirked and took a seat at the table.

"How long have you worked for Cedric?"

"He hired me out of law school."

"And when was that?"

"Two years and eight months."

Jack jotted a quick note. "Cedric said this is Dr. Solver's third patient-death. What can you tell me about the previous cases?"

Josh looked surprised and pulled at his tie.

"Is something wrong?"

"Look, Mr. Kendall—Jack, I'm really pressed for time today. I'd prefer to look at the particulars of your case before we discuss the specifics. I'll have my assistant provide you with some general information, and we can set up a conference call for tomorrow afternoon. Is that okay with you, because I really need to be somewhere?"

"Tomorrow's soon enough. Hot date?"

"To be honest, this has been a horrible day. I wrecked my BMW after lunch. I missed the meeting with you and Cedric, and to top it off, I'm locked into a dinner date with my fiancée's parents tonight."

"Ooh. Better you than me," Jack said.

Josh rose from the table with a wry smile and slung his jacket over his shoulder. "I like you, Jack. But just so you know, if you don't become a client of the great Cedric Johnson, you're an idiot."

"Just what I wanted to hear," Jack said. "Good luck at dinner." He made several notes while he waited for Josh's assistant. A few minutes later, she entered the room and placed two thick files on the table.

"I'm Stacy. I'll be back for these in twenty minutes. That should give you plenty of time."

"Thanks," Jack said, appreciating the swing of her short skirt as she headed for the door. Josh definitely had it going on.

She turned back and seemed to scrutinize him from beneath her long lashes. "Make good use of your time, Mr.

Kendall." She flounced out the door and closed it behind her.

Jack wondered about her odd statement and opened the first file. It was a client file, he realized with surprise—a file on Jamal Eli Jackson. The file was divided into sections: Discovery, Motions, Depositions, Defendants, Exhibits, and Settlement. He flipped to the title page. It read, *Jamal Eli Jackson vs. Ryan Bernard Solver, et al.*

A chill rippled through his body. Why in the world would she give him this? It had to be confidential. Was that what she meant by making good use of his time? He pulled out his cell phone and took pictures of several sections of the file. The suit named Union General Hospital, which would explain Solver's sudden move to Dixie Medical Center. He flipped to the settlement section. A soft whistle escaped his lips—1.2 million dollars. This wasn't some huge corporation. This man died in surgery just as Daniel had, and his family received 1.2 million dollars. That would go a long way in assisting Christine and the children.

The title page of the next file read, *Frederick Brown Hernandez vs. Ryan Bernard Solver, et al.* "What in the world is et al?" he mumbled. He turned to the settlement section—1.4 million dollars. If Cedric had negotiated the settlements for both Solver cases, why hadn't he said so? What had upset Josh? He didn't remember what they were discussing at that point in their conversation, but something had changed his demeanor. Was he surprised that Cedric told him about the other cases? He took more pictures. He had just dropped his phone inside his shirt pocket when Stacy returned for the files.

"Have you seen enough?" she said.

"Is there more?"

"You tell me. You're the private investigator."

"Thanks for reminding me," he teased. "Any reason for giving me these particular files?"

"Cedric said you wanted to evaluate his firm. I figured these would help you do that." She picked them up and left the room.

"Hummm," Jack said to himself. Something strange was

going on here.

* * *

Jack was thinking about stopping by O'Malley's for a beer and a quick game of pool when he remembered his appointment. Grumbling, he pulled into the nearest parking lot and turned around. At least he had remembered in time, which wasn't usually the case. He definitely needed more work right now. Since Daniel's death, he hadn't felt like searching out new clients.

After a brilliant job of parallel parking, he stuffed four quarters into the meter and climbed the five steps that led from the curb to the sidewalk, which ran parallel to a row of revitalized office buildings that spanned the entire length of the block. His office was on the corner. After unlocking the security door, he unlocked the solid door and stepped inside his two-room office. His nose wrinkled immediately. "What *is* that?" He flipped on the lights and glanced around for the source of the offending odor, noticing for the first time how marked up the walls were and how desperately the carpets needed cleaning. It was a far cry from the successful decorum of Cedric K. Johnson's office. He added his workplace to his recent list of dissatisfactions.

Unable to tolerate the stench a second longer, he opened all four windows, two of which faced the side street, allowing a cross breeze to flow through. Finding nothing suspicious around his desk, he entered the small adjoining conference room and looked under the table. Seeing nothing there, he checked the trash cans to see if a rolled up bag of rotting fast-food might be the culprit, but he didn't find anything there either. When he opened the bathroom door, the stench drove him back. A small black and white cat lay dead beneath the sink—the unintentional victim of the rat poison he had set out.

"Oh, no," he groaned. "This wasn't supposed to happen." He reached for a paper towel so he could pick up the poor crea-ture, but the roll was empty. Not knowing what else to do, he went to his desk for a piece of typing paper, vowing never to put out poison again.

When he went knelt to pick up the cat, he thought he heard mewing sounds. He opened the cabinets and looked around, but he didn't see any little ones, and he couldn't hear anything now. Crinkling the typing paper, he picked the cat up by its tail, which felt stiff and disgusting, and headed for the front door. When he reached for the knob, he saw a white Mercedes park behind his Camry—his client, he realized with horror. Spinning around, he searched for a place to ditch the cat. Finally, with no other option, he went to a side window, pushed the screen out, and threw the whole thing—paper and all—onto the grass. Leaving the window open, he rushed into the bathroom and grabbed the air freshener. He had just sprayed when the screen door squeaked, and a tall, attractive woman entered his office. She wore dark sunglasses, which set off her blonde, shoulder-length hair to advantage.

"Mr. Kendall?"

"Yes, and you must be . . ." He wondered if she could smell the cat in spite of the spray.

She wrinkled her nose and glanced around. "If you don't remember, that's fine with me. I'd like to discuss your services before I give you my personals anyway."

"I need to wash my hands," he said. "Please, have a seat at the table." When he stepped out of the bathroom, he was relieved to see that she had settled at the conference table, but she didn't look at all comfortable. Thankfully, a stiff breeze fluttered through.

"Forgive the mess," he said lamely. "My best friend just died, and I've been . . ." He was at a loss for words.

"I'm sorry to hear that, Mr. Kendall. If this isn't a good time, I can find someone else."

"Please, call me Jack," he said as he joined her at the table. "To be honest, I could use the distraction. My office is a mess, but I'm very good at what I do."

"Yes, that's what I've heard. You may call me Teresa."

Her fitted white suit, black high-heels, elegant handbag, and huge diamond ring, all labeled her a woman with means, but it was the elegant way in which she carried herself that set her apart from the women Jack knew. She was undeniably first class.

He reached for a legal pad and pulled a pen from his shirt pocket. "How can I help you?"

Teresa gave him a tight smile. "I have reason to believe my husband is seeing someone. This has happened once before, early in our marriage, though he has never confessed to it. Even after twenty-six years of marriage, it remains a painful and unsettled topic between us. I want proof this time."

Jack, a good listener with a casual approachableness that aided him in situations like this, nodded. "Infidelity cases make up the largest part of my practice. I pride myself in obtaining irrefutable proof. What have you observed that makes you suspicious?" The dark tint of her glasses shielded her eyes, but he estimated her age at mid-forties.

"Several things. My husband is a physician and has always worked long hours, but lately he's been going out at odd times. When I ask, he brushes me off. I know my husband, Mr. Kendall. He's feeling guilty about something. I've checked his phone, but the call log is always empty."

Jack recognized the pain and anger that took turns dominating her voice. Feeling that she might need a break, he said, "Would you care for some water?"

She shook her head and laid her sunshades on the table.

He waited for her to continue.

"Sometimes, I hear him talking to someone in a low voice on his cell phone. It's always a short call, and he usually leaves soon after. We argue more lately and . . ." She swallowed hard. "He doesn't seem as interested in sex anymore."

"I understand," he said kindly. "Have you spoken with an attorney?"

Recovering her dignity, she said. "My attorney suggested I speak with you."

"Really? Who's your attorney?"

"I'd rather not say. Tell me, please, how do you go about making a case?"

"Mostly with surveillance and cameras. You can order phone records and tape conversations, but pictures and video are undeniable."

"People Photoshop images all the time," she said.

"You're not paying me for an advertising photo. You're paying me to get photos of him with her. Anything I give you, he won't deny."

Her cat-green eyes hardened. "Fine, then. Get me pictures." She reached into her handbag and laid an envelope on the table.

Jack opened it and saw that it contained basic information about her husband, his routine, and some photographs. Her husband, as distinguished-looking as she was, had black and silver hair and appeared fit and trim. It wasn't difficult to see what might attract another woman. They discussed the financial arrangements and concluded their meeting. Surveillance would begin the following evening, which left his evening free.

After closing up the office, he went around to the side of the building and pushed the screen back into the window frame. He looked towards the street and spotted the trash dumpster. Picking up the crinkled paper, he reached for the cat but then paused. This was wrong.

He jogged to his car and after digging around for several seconds, he took his camping shovel and a dirty T-shirt back to where the cat was lying in the grass. He gently wrapped it in the shirt and carried it into the woods behind the building. There he dug a shallow grave and covered it over. He felt silly for it, but he felt like crying. It had never occurred to him that anything other than mice was getting into his office at night. Had he known, he would've left cat food out instead of poison. And to think that she might have kittens! The least he could do is bury her properly. When the deed was done, he turned on the water spigot and washed his hands. After returning the shovel to his car, he walked down the block to a convenience store and bought kitten chow and two small bowls.

Upon returning to his office, he filled the bowls and set them against the bathroom wall. He listened for several seconds, but he didn't hear any little ones. Having done all he could to make amends, he locked up his office. A cold beer at O'Malley's sounded better than ever—but then he thought about Christine. Thinking the kids would enjoy it, he stopped by a local super-market for a three-foot party sub. While he waited for them to prepare it, it struck him that he and Daniel should be drinking beer and eating pizza in front of the television tonight, with the kids running in and out and Christine calling after them to shut the door, but everything was different now. It was amazing how fast life could turn upside down, and without warning.

Life, he realized, shouldn't be taken for granted.

* * *

"Richard Gloster on line one, sir," Jannette informed Cedric via intercom.

Keeping his eyes on the New York Stock Exchange website, Cedric Johnson felt for his six-line phone and pushed line one.

"Cedric here. What have you got for me?"

"Jack Kendall, age thirty-nine, graduate of Ole Miss, majored in communications. Following in his father's footsteps, he joined the police academy after graduation, completed basic training and was promoted to detective three years later."

"He's a cop?" Cedric said. *This* didn't bode well at all.

"The record shows that soon after Jack made detective, his father, Robert Kendall died in the line of duty. Jack quit the force and went to work for a regional private investigation service where he quickly worked his way into a senior position. Five years later, he left to open his own detective agency where he's been ever since. May I ask why you're inquiring?"

Cedric laid his glasses on the desk. His heart was pounding. "Nothing important. He's a friend of a new client. I just wondered if his detective skills might be useful."

"Not bloody likely," Gloster said with a chuckle, "unless your client's been cheating. The majority of Kendall's clients hire him to track down cheating spouses. I wouldn't count on much help if I were you."

"Good work, Richard. I can always count on you."

"My pleasure, Ole Boy. Give me a bigger challenge next

time."

"I'll try," Cedric said. "Say hello to your wife for me."

An uncomfortable silence followed.

"Gloster?" Cedric said.

"My wife passed, remember? You came to the funeral."

"Damn careless of me, Richard. Of course, I remember."

"Think nothing of it," Gloster said. "Good luck with your case."

"You're a good man, Richard. I appreciate you." Cedric hung up without another thought of his insensitive faux pas. He was much more concerned with the unease in the pit of his stomach. Despite Gloster's words, he wasn't convinced that Jack wasn't a threat. He glanced at the crucifix but quickly looked away. He didn't like feeling guilty, which was a constant struggle in his profession. When he first got into law, he was an idealist like Josh, but the years had slowly changed him. Time had proven that when it came to money, his greed was stronger than his faith, and he liked it that way.

His head began to throb, but it wasn't his conscience that bothered him. It was the overriding feeling that they were going to get caught. He rubbed the engorged ridges on his bald head and reached into the credenza for a bottle of his best Scotch. He poured a shot and threw it back. As the liquor burned its comfort into his soul, he told himself repeatedly that all was well.

* * *

The house was dark and the curtains drawn, but both vehicles sat inside the garage. Jack walked around the back of the house and found the screen door standing open—not a good sign.

"Christine?" he called as he walked into the kitchen. The screen door squeaked when he pulled it shut. "Christine? Are you all right?" Setting the food on the kitchen table, he turned on the lights and ventured into the living room. "Christine?" He was about to go upstairs when he saw her sitting on the couch, wrapped in a crocheted blanket, tissue box at her side. Her lips were pouting, and her hair hung in tangles around her shoulders.

She looked heartbreakingly miserable.

He turned on a lamp and sat beside her, opening his arms in invitation. She went willingly, sobbing as soon as her head touched his shoulder. As tears racked her slender body, Jack's commitment to the investigation intensified. He would find out what had happened to Daniel, and he'd use Cedric to get some money into Christine's household. There was no telling how long it might be before she was ready to work at selling real estate again.

Heedless of her appearance, she blew her nose and threw the dirty tissues on the floor with the others. She yanked the afghan back around her shoulders and lifted her chin, daring him to say something.

She was angry again. Good, Jack thought, anger was better than pain. "Christine, I've done some work on our case, but I'd like you to eat something before we talk about it. Okay?"

"Help yourself. The fridge is packed," she said in a stuffy voice.

Jack contained the smile she'd have drawn from any man. Here she was, an absolute mess, and yet completely adorable. Trying to cheer her up, he said, "I forgot that everyone left food here. I brought a party sub and some potato chips."

"You eat it. I'm not hungry."

"I don't care if you're hungry, Christine; you're going to eat. I'll bring it in here. You don't even have to move." He went into the kitchen. "Is there beer in the fridge?" His hand stopped an inch from the door. Christine didn't drink beer. If there was beer in the fridge, it was there for Daniel. He looked around the corner and winced as his words reflected on her face.

She didn't answer.

He grabbed a Diet Coke for her and a beer for himself. "Where are the kids?"

"With my mom," Christine sniffed. "I needed some time alone."

He nodded. She did need time alone. She'd never let herself grieve in front of the children.

—68—

"Well, then, do you mind if I stay awhile?"

She shrugged and reached for a slice of the tuna salad sub. It sat on her plate for nearly ten minutes before she finally took a bite. He knew she didn't want it, but she needed to eat. He poured some potato chips onto her plate, which she nibbled most likely because of the salt.

"What did you do today?" he said.

She brushed fresh tears from her face. "Nothing. I didn't do one damn thing, and that's probably what I'll do tomorrow, too."

It was upsetting to see her like this, but since he couldn't make it better, he ate in silence. Christine picked at her sandwich, but she swallowed very little. He made a mental note to shop for things she might be more willing to eat. After eating his sandwich, he carried their plates into the kitchen and set them on the counter. Glancing out the kitchen window, he saw that the sun was beginning to set. He went back into the living room and grabbed hold of her hand. "Come on, sweetheart. We're going outside to watch the sun set. The fresh air will do you good."

She snapped her hand out of his. "I don't want the fresh air to do me good. Don't you understand? There *is* no good. Nothing is good. I'm going back to bed."

He swung her up into his arms, afghan and all, and carried her through the kitchen and onto the porch. He deposited her into a wicker chair and said, "Sit."

She sighed. "Okay. I know you're trying to help. I'll try to cooperate."

They sat quietly until the last traces of daylight faded into darkness.

"I'm going to get another beer," Jack said. "Want anything?"

She glared at him. "Yes. I want a beer, too."

He didn't argue.

When he returned with the beer, she raised her bottle. "I want to make a toast."

"Okay, shoot," he said.

"Here's to you, Daniel, wherever you are. To all our happy

memories and to a love deep and satisfying. I will always love you."

"Hear, hear," Jack said, watching as Christine upended the bottle and proceeded to drain its entire contents. "Christine, do you really think that's wise? You don't drink beer, remember? You're likely to have a major headache tomorrow."

She kept swallowing. When it was empty, she said, "Good. A headache tomorrow is better than the heartache I'm dealing with tonight." She reached out for Jack's beer. "You may as well get another one because I'm drinking yours, too."

He let her have it though he didn't think it was a good idea. She had eaten next to nothing. He was pretty sure their little party would adjourn to the toilet room soon, but he decided not to interfere. How many times had he, or Daniel for that matter, purposely pushed their alcoholic tolerance to temporarily banish an unpleasant situation? It was her right. She'd pay for that right, but he'd be here to help her. He went to get another beer. Thankfully, it was the last one.

Christine's second bottle was nearly empty when he returned.

"Damn, girl. I didn't know you had it in you."

It took a few minutes, but she finished it off and took what was left of the one he had in his hands, too. When it was empty, she said, "You know what, Jack?" She swayed slightly to the right.

"What Christine?" he said, trying to gauge her condition.

"Beer isn't so bad. Why don't I drink—" She hiccupped. "Drink it?"

"I don't know," he teased, "but it always meant more for Daniel and me."

"I see that." Her expression turned serious. "Jack, do you remember last summer when Danny and I went camping?"

He nodded, but it always made him uncomfortable when she started calling him Danny.

"There we were, all on our own. Danny built a big fire, and we grilled some fish he had caught in the lake." She cocked her head to the side. "Did you know Danny liked to fish?"

"We've only been fishing together a thousand times since we were eight."

"Oh, yeah. I forgot. Well, we laughed a lot that night, especially when he chased me through the woods because I threatened to pour his last beer into the lake." She released a quiet burp. "Oops. Sorry."

"Why on earth would you pour a perfectly good beer into the lake?"

"So the fish who didn't get caught could celebrate, but Danny didn't like that idea."

"I can understand him feeling that way. Besides, one beer isn't enough to celebrate with."

Christine looked at him with a funny expression on her face. "You mean I should've given 'em the whole sex pack?" Catching her mistake, she covered her mouth and giggled.

He shook his head. She was so darn cute.

"Speaking of sex," she said. "Danny and I had a wonderful sex life. We really did. I miss making love, and it's only been a week."

"Are you ready to go back in now?" he said coming to his feet.

She swayed. "Come on, Jack, loosen up. Tell me the truth. Did Daniel ever tell you how great our sex life was?"

He felt his face flush. "Only to say that he was very happy with you. He loved you very much."

She flashed an incredible smile. "He loved me very, very much!" When she stood, she tripped over the afghan and reached out for the handrail to steady herself. Her face went pale. "Jack? I'm not feeling so good."

He was at her side in an instant. "I'll bet not. Are you going to be sick?"

She drew both hands over her mouth and nodded.

He pulled the afghan free, swept her up into his arms, and carried her off the porch. After setting her gently on the grass, he said, "Go ahead, you'll feel better."

She waited on all fours for the inevitable. "Oh, no. This is *not* good."

He gently stroked her head. "It's okay, sweetie. I'm right here. I'll take care of you."

It didn't take long. Her stomach emptied itself again and again. When the worst was over, he pulled her to a clean spot on the grass.

She rolled over onto her back. "Oh, my goodness. I feel terrible."

"I'm sure you do. Beer isn't meant to be gulped like iced tea, ya know."

"It's not just the beer. I drank some of Daniel's whiskey before you came."

"How much whiskey?"

"Three shots."

"No wonder you feel sick," he chuckled.

"Oh, no." She got back on her knees and was sick again, leaving her weak and trembling.

"Okay, you. I'm taking you up to bed. You'll fall sleep soon."

Christine moaned as he carried her up the stairs and into her bedroom.

"Do you need to get sick again?" he asked.

"No."

"Okay, where is your nightgown?"

She crawled onto her unmade bed, gripping the sheets in an apparent attempt to anchor herself. "Middle drawer, right side."

"Is the aspirin in the bathroom?"

"Uh, huh."

He tossed a nightgown onto the bed. After finding the aspirin, he wet a washcloth and took it to her. She was lying on the bed with her pants halfway off. Trying not to look at her little black panties, he tugged her jeans the rest of the way off and helped her slide her legs beneath the sheets.

"Sit up, Christine. Put your nightgown on while I go downstairs to get you a glass of water. It's right here."

When he returned, she was safely covered.

"I'm sorry, Jack. I didn't mean to do this," she said.

"Yes, you did, but that's okay. We all do this from time to time—when things are bad, and we want to escape. I completely understand. Besides, you've helped me lots of times. Do you need to go to the bathroom before you go to sleep?"

"I already did. I'm never drinking beer or whiskey again."

He chuckled. "We all say *that*, too. Only for me, it's usually restricted to whiskey." After she had taken the aspirin, he settled the cool washcloth on her forehead. "I'm going to stay right here until you fall asleep, okay?"

"Okay. Will you bring the trash can from the bathroom, just in case I feel sick again?"

"Yep. I'll set it right beside the bed."

After retrieving the trash can, he watched her for several minutes, thinking how wrong it was that she should find herself alone in the world with two young children to raise. When he knew she was asleep, he turned on the bathroom light and cracked the door open, in case she needed to find the toilet in the middle of the night. He closed the bedroom door and let himself out through the kitchen.

During the drive home, he focused his thoughts on Daniel's anesthesiologist, Ryan Solver. He wanted to make sure he wasn't free to do this to another unsuspecting family. He thought about his friend Dr. Sassi and decided to pay him a visit. Against his will, his thoughts drifted back to Christine. He hated to admit it, but her little black underwear reminded him that he missed having a girlfriend. He closed his eyes against the memory of her bare legs against the sheets. Then another pretty face came to mind.

Elyse Dawson used to work for Dr. Sassi. Maybe contacting his physician friend could kill two birds with one stone, though it was much more likely that Elyse would stone *him*, he admitted with a grimace. If she hadn't begun pressuring him to let her and her fourteen-year-old daughter move in, they might still be together, but commitment wasn't his thing. He had tried that once, and it blew up in his face.

Perhaps working as a private investigator added to his cynicism, but it certainly seemed that commitment in words didn't equate to commitment in deeds. While there were exceptions— Daniel and Christine for one—very few relationships withstood the tests of time. He believed being single was the best option, but then again, until Daniel died, he had never thought about the possibility of being alone at the end. Who would've thought that death would come as soon as it had for Daniel?

It would be nice to see Elyse again. Maybe it would be different this time, now that he realized how empty his world was without a wife and family. He indulged himself for several minutes, remembering the intimate moments they had shared. He certainly had no complaints about her in that department. She was an aggressive little tiger. "Yep," he said aloud, "tomorrow will be an interesting day."

CHAPTER EIGHT

An experienced tongue licked potent white power from the tip of a black, ringed finger. "I ain't never tasted it this pure."

Ever aware, Anthony saw the shadows of two men move into position at the entrance of the short alleyway. He expected no less at the opposite end, but it was darker in that direction, and he couldn't be sure. "That's because I don't cut it with any crap."

"Who's yer source?"

"Like I'm really gonna tell you? Not everything has a price, Jermaine."

Jermaine, a tall, strong Jamaican man with better than average English, dreadlocked hair, and a fierce dragon tattoo on his right bicep laughed with contempt. "You think he deal only with you? My distribution channel covers five states. I kin make 'em rich. Kin you do dat?"

Anthony stuffed one hand into the pocket of his worn leather jacket and fingered the lever on his switchblade as if it were the trigger on a gun. "He's already rich. You want the powder? Give me the cash."

Jermaine's muscular frame tensed; his men were watching. "Tell me why I don't shoot you right now?"

Anthony kept his back towards the wooden fence and glanced towards the street. "You could, but then you and your boys would only have one party. That's a bit shortsighted, don't you think?"

Jermaine eyed him with criminal respect and handed him a wad of bills. "When do I get more?"

"You know how to reach me."

Anthony walked past Jermaine and ventured into the darker side of the alley, launching his switchblade as the gravel crunched beneath his boots. He wanted to know if Jermaine had guards stationed at both ends. Streetlights semi-lit the entrance, which was approximately a hundred yards ahead.

A sudden weight struck from the side, bearing him to the ground. Rolling with the attacker, Anthony managed to hang onto his knife, but he suffered several vicious blows to the ribs and face as they scuffled in the dirt. Then, suddenly, the weight of the attacker disappeared, and Jermaine stood above him, pinning his arm to the ground beneath his boot.

"Let go the knife," Jermaine said.

The shapes of four men became clear in the darkness. Two held the attacker between them.

"I like my chances better if I don't," Anthony said.

Jermaine pulled a gun and pointed it in his face. "How you like yer chances now?"

Anthony opened his fingers and let the knife clatter from his grip. One of Jermaine's men grabbed it.

Jermaine turned the gun on the attacker and extended his hand to Anthony.

Anthony grabbed it, but he was a bit unclear about where he stood. "Who's your friend?" he said as he dusted off his jacket.

Jermaine laughed. "He's not *my* frien."

The attacker, a tall, thin black man, reeked of wine and dirty clothes.

"Please, don't shoot me," he pleaded. "I was jus lookin' for some money ta feed my family. I means no harm."

Jermaine turned to Anthony. "What you say ta dat?"

Anthony wiped his bloody lip with the back of his hand. He knew what was expected of him. Street justice was as quick as it was cruel. "I think you should've stayed home."

Jermaine grinned. "Give da man his knife."

"Jus lemme go, and I'll be gone," the man said, his eyes glazed and bloodshot in the moonlight.

"Too late for that," Anthony said. With one quick swipe, he slashed the man's throat and watched as he sank to the ground with a stunned expression on his face.

Jermaine's men dropped his arms and moved away.

"He ain't nobody's frien now," Jermaine chuckled. "Go on. We'll clean up here. We been itchin' ta torch us a house anyways."

Anthony wiped his knife on the dead man's shirt. "Enjoy your party," he said and sauntered out of the alley without looking back. After returning to his Harley, a sardonic smile twitched at his swollen lip. It had been a long time since he'd killed anybody. It felt kinda good knowing he still had it in him.

He replayed the dramatic scene in his mind. For a moment, there, he had thought his time was up. He might not have cared before, but he did care now. He cared about Trina. He felt for the wad of bills in his pocket. By selling the drugs his uncle paid him in exchange for his services, he planned to build a new life for himself and Trina—a life different from the way he lived now—provided, of course, she'd have him.

CHAPTER NINE

After a brisk shower, Jack dressed nicer than he usually did, choosing a pair of casual grey slacks and a black Tommy Bahama shirt. As he tugged a comb through his wet curls, he knew there was no point in trying to get them to do anything special. Unless he greased them down—which he did only when he dressed in disguise—they did their own thing, no matter what he wanted. It was funny, but what had always been an annoyance to him was a plus when it came to attracting women. They loved his curls.

He laid down the comb and splashed on some aftershave.

Leaning forward, he examined his face in the mirror. He was almost forty. He had a few more wrinkles, a bit more grey, but he was still reasonably good-looking. He touched the small Z-shaped scar near the corner of his right eye, a scar he had gotten the summer he turned ten. It could have been much worse.

He and Daniel had trespassed onto a neighbor's farm looking for eggs. As they crossed the field towards the chicken coup, they had stumbled upon a bull and his harem. The bull charged, sending them scurrying in opposite directions. The bull pursued Daniel, who easily scrambled over the south fence to safety. When Jack turned to see where the bull was, he ran headlong into a barbed-wire fence, which ran along the south and east boundaries of the property. He was lucky; another quarter-inch and it would have caught his eye. He winked at himself with silly good humor. "Here's to Elyse still thinking I'm hot."

A few minutes later, he stopped by the diner for a cup of his favorite Brazilian coffee. The familiar bell, the wafting aromas, and the bustling crowd, all felt welcoming. He glanced around for Edna, the counter clerk, but he didn't see her. Being inside the coffee shop wasn't nearly as difficult as it had been the last time he was here. He ordered his coffee to go.

It wasn't long before his mind was awhirl with the many topics that had kept him awake during the night. One of the people on his mind was his new client, Teresa Lindsay. Over the years, he had heard dozens of reasons why men were unfaithful to their women—and vice versa—but dang! Teresa was attractive and intelligent. A man should be shot for neglecting a woman like her—or like Elyse, his conscience accused him. Would she welcome him back? Would he feel differently this time around? A man could do a lot worse than a woman like Elyse. She was smoking hot. What man wouldn't want her? But he hadn't—not beyond the bedroom anyway. When he was honest with himself, he knew there was something about her that kept him at bay. He hoped it would be different this time.

He was so preoccupied with the possibility of seeing Elyse again that he nearly passed Cedric Johnson's office complex. Pulling into the parking lot, he parked well away from Cedric's Mercedes.

Josh left him waiting in the conference room for nearly twenty minutes before he joined him—ample time to rekindle the envy he felt the first time he saw this room. An image of the dead cat he found in his office flashed through his mind, making him grimace. That would never happen within these perfect walls.

"Jack," Josh said as he burst through the door. "Sorry to keep you waiting. We didn't have an appointment, did we?"

The two men shook hands.

"No, but I need to ask you an important question."

Josh pulled up a chair. "I only have a few minutes, so let's get to it. Did Mrs. Steinberg sign the contract?"

"No, and I'm not sure I'm going to recommend it."

"What is it, Jack?"

"How many times has Cedric sued Ryan Solver?"

Josh looked stunned. "Why would you ask me that?"

"Solver was the key defendant in both files your assistant gave me to review. Are you out to get this guy or something?"

"My assistant gave you client files?"

"She did."

"Look, Jack, Cedric makes his living holding negligent parties accountable. Both cases against Solver were successful."

"Like hell they were! If those cases had been successful, my friend would be alive right now. How can he still practice medicine?"

Josh sighed, and his face fell. "To be honest, I asked Cedric the same question. Cedric feels that by negotiating settlements against Dr. Solver, we'll force an end to his practice by rendering him uninsurable."

"Will he face jail time?"

"It's not a criminal case. Aside from ending his practice, the most you can hope for is a decent settlement for your friend's family."

"Forget the money. I want that SOB behind bars!"

Josh rose. "Look, I know how you feel, but delays won't help anyone but Dr. Solver. We'll do everything we possibly can, but we can't do anything until Mrs. Steinberg signs that contract. What other option do you have?"

Unfortunately, he was right. They could find another attorney, but because Cedric *had* prosecuted Solver twice before, there was a good chance he had valuable information. "I'll talk to Christine, but I demand to stay in the loop. Keep me posted every step of the way. Agreed?"

"Agreed," Josh said. "Oh, and would you mind not mentioning to Cedric that Stacy gave you client files to review? I'd hate for her to lose her job, and that's exactly what would happen."

"I understand."

The two men shook hands again, and then Josh held the door for Jack.

"Uh, one last thing," Jack said. "I didn't really mean forget the money. They need it."

"Don't worry, Jack. We're gonna get this guy. You'll see."

* * *

"Have you lost your mind?" Josh thundered.

"I've been telling you there's something fishy going on around here," Stacy said. "If you won't help me figure it out, maybe that detective will."

"I've worked extremely hard to get where I am. I won't stand by and watch you ruin this firm's reputation with your petty suspicions."

"Fine, then. Help me get to the bottom of it. Doesn't it strike you as odd that Cedric has handled all three Solver cases?"

"Do you know something you're not telling me?" He wasn't about to admit it, but he had wondered why Cedric didn't tell Jack about the previous Solver cases. He also wondered why Cedric hadn't told *him* that the Steinberg case was another Solver death.

Stacy sighed and shook her head. "I haven't figured it out yet, but I've been studying those files. There's another common denominator. I feel it in my bones."

"You get a paycheck. Why do you care?"

Stacy shut the door to Josh's office. "Because I'm tired of seeing the women who come in here seeking justice become a pawn for making Cedric Johnson wealthy. That's why."

"Then you're in the wrong profession, aren't you?"

"I'm an assistant, Josh, not an attorney. The reason I'm here is because I work for you, an attorney who hasn't yet sold his soul for the sake of making money. If that day ever comes, I won't be assisting you any longer."

"Have you forgotten that the innocent victims who come in here gain someone knowledgeable to fight for them, so that the guilty party can't take advantage of them, which they would surely do if it weren't for us? Instead, our clients walk away with verdicts and settlements they would otherwise not have received."

"Money doesn't fix everything, Josh."

"What's with you, Stacy?"

"I grew up without a father because of an irresponsible, incompetent doctor like Ryan Solver. Life was so hard after

Daddy died that Mama started drinking and going on spending sprees to make herself feel better. After a few years of that, we lost our house, the car, everything we owned. When faced with bankruptcy—an unforgivable sin according to my grandparents—Mama hung herself. I found her one day when I came home from school, swinging from the back porch. After that, I got dumped with an aunt who liked her obnoxious little yappy dogs better than she liked me—not that I didn't like her yappy dogs. I did."

Josh frowned. "Stacy . . ."

"Don't you even think about feeling sorry for me, Joshua Royce. I'm a survivor. I worked my way through school, and I've made a decent life for myself."

"I didn't mean—"

"According to the Steinberg file, that woman has two kids. I don't want them going through what Mama and me did. Is that so hard to understand?"

"We're trying to get them some money."

"Yeah, so you can make money. No one cares what happens to the Steinberg family months or years from now. It's all about the quick buck. And since that's true, why hasn't it occurred to you that if I'm right, and Cedric is guilty of doing something illegal, you could end up with the majority of his clients for yourself?"

"Look, I'm sorry you had a terrible childhood, but that doesn't give you the right to take matters into your own hands. If Jack tells Cedric about those files, we'll both be looking for another job." Noting the stubborn tilt of her chin, he said, "All right. If you find something that deserves my attention, let me know. Otherwise, do your job and stop interfering. You got that?"

"Yeah, Josh, I got it. And you can forget about coming by my place for dinner tonight. I'm suddenly quite sick of you."

Josh watched the bounce of her short little dress as she grabbed her purse and stormed out the door. As an afterthought, he wondered if she meant what she said about dinner.

* * *

Jack was uncharacteristically apprehensive as he walked down the hallway looking for Suite F on the sixth floor of Dixie Medical Center's Physician's Tower. He knew Fred Sassi would see him if he had time, but getting past a miffed Elyse might be difficult. It had been several years since he'd seen his college buddy, and he'd never been to his office. When he stepped inside the medical suite, it became immediately apparent that his friend was doing quite well for himself. He wondered what kind of car he was driving—certainly not a ten-year-old Camry. Banishing the thought, he flashed his most charming smile and approached the attractive, young receptionist.

"Good morning," she said as a pleasant blush stained her cheeks. "May I help you?"

"I'm Jack Kendall. I need to see Dr. Sassi about an urgent matter. He isn't expecting me."

"I'm sorry, but the Doctor is extremely busy this morning. Would you care to make an appointment? His next opening is about eight weeks out."

So much for irresistible charm, Jack thought. He pulled out a business card, which he had remembered to put into his pocket this morning, and presented it like a badge. "Show this to Dr. Sassi. He'll see me." He bit back a smile as her eyes widened. The words Private Investigator had gotten him through many doors during his career.

"Yes, sir. I'll be right back."

Moments later, the door leading to the inner offices opened, and a familiar voice called his name. He walked through the door and came face-to-face with Elyse.

"Good morning, Jack."

"Good morning, Elyse. Long time, no see." She was even prettier than he remembered. Her thick brown hair had grown halfway down her back.

"Hum," she said, her green eyes flashing with disdain. "Follow me." She led him past the examination rooms and into Dr. Sassi's private office. "You can wait here," she said waving him towards the sofa, which sat beneath the only window in the small office space. She closed the door abruptly, dashing his hopes of rekindling anything other than resentment.

He spent the next half-hour perusing the titles on the bookshelf, many of which were obscure and boring titles about body parts and disease. Finally, he settled onto the sofa with a *Sports Illustrated* magazine, which he was glad to find buried beneath some medical journals on the coffee table. Sassi might have money, but his office wasn't much nicer than his—although it was cleaner.

His stomach growled. He knew he should have grabbed a bagel at the diner.

The door opened without warning. "Jack!" Dr. Sassi said, stretching out his hand, but the handshake quickly turned into a hug with mutual pats on the back.

The two of them had roomed together for three semesters in college. Although they ran in entirely different circles, they had remained friends—even after Jack had backed his rusty old pickup truck into Sassi's brand new Corvette at a friend's graduation party.

"You look like hell," Sassi said with a grin. "But since you aren't in an exam room, it must be something other than your health that brings you here in the middle of my busy day."

Jack chuckled. "I'll only take a minute of your time, Sass. Thanks for seeing me."

Dr. Sassi motioned for Jack to sit down as he dropped into the chair behind his desk.

"What can I do for you, and how can I bill it to your insurance company?"

Jack chuckled again, but then his mood turned somber. "Do you remember Daniel Steinberg? You met him at Kevin's graduation party."

"Brave of you to mention that party, but yes, I remember. Wasn't he the fellow who twisted his knee water-skiing a few years back?"

"Oh, yeah. I forgot about that." He swallowed a lump in his throat. "Daniel died recently, during elective surgery."

"I'm sorry to hear that," Dr. Sassi said.

"Our attorney has sued the anesthesiologist twice before, but he's still practicing medicine."

"And you're here for what, Jack?" Dr. Sassi said, looking irritated and uncomfortable all at once.

"Do you know Ryan Solver?"

"I know of him," Dr. Sassi said.

"Is there anything you can tell me about him?"

Dr. Sassi rose to his feet. "I don't appreciate being put in this position, Jack."

"I wouldn't ask, but I'm out of my league on this one. I promised Daniel's wife I'd find out what happened, but I don't even know where to start."

"Ryan Solver's research is highly regarded. Has it occurred to you that you may be barking up the wrong tree?"

"Not with three patient-deaths to his credit."

"I've heard the rumors," Dr. Sassi said. "Still, it could be a coincidence. What does the autopsy report show?"

"I don't know. I didn't think to ask."

"Get a copy and I'll look at it for you, but be warned. I'll deny ever having had this conversation. Agreed?"

"Thanks, Sass. I really appreciate it."

Jack stood, and Dr. Sassi squeezed his shoulder. "I'm sorry about Daniel. Death is the worst kind of thief."

"Daniel has a wife and two small children. If malpractice is responsible, then someone should answer for it."

"Proving malpractice will be difficult if not impossible."

"You might be right, but I saw some pretty big checks on our attorney's wall. Whatever the cause, I won't rest until I get some answers. I'll call you when I get the autopsy report."

"You do that."

He followed Dr. Sassi into the hallway, wondering how to go about getting a copy of the autopsy report. Surely, Christine had one, but he didn't want to ask her about it. Doctor Sassi turned into an exam room just as Elyse stepped out of one.

"Were you going to leave without saying goodbye again?"

she said.

"I didn't think you wanted to talk to me," he said.

She waited for a nurse to walk by. "We were good together, Jack. What happened?"

"We were better than good—if my memory serves correctly."

"Then why didn't you return my calls?"

He reached out to stroke her cheek, but she stepped back. "You know me. When it gets too serious, I run."

Her vulnerability vanished. "Yeah, I remember. You're only interested in mindless sex. Right, Jack? You should tell a girl that *before* she falls in love with you."

"If I did that, they wouldn't—"

"Precisely."

Knowing he wasn't helping himself, he handed her a business card. "Call me sometime. You never know when a man might change."

* * *

Cedric stepped out of the breakroom with a steaming cup of coffee and almost bumped into Josh, who looked to be heading out the door for lunch. "Was that Jack Kendall I saw earlier?"

"Uh, yeah," Josh said. "He's decided to recommend that Mrs. Steinberg sign the contract. How is your day going?"

"Is anything wrong?" Cedric asked, noting the way Josh avoided his eyes.

"No, I'm just stressed about getting my car fixed. I had no idea how much it costs to work on a BMW. That and the wedding. Elizabeth is pestering me about all sorts of details I care nothing about."

Cedric chuckled. "Play along, Joshie boy. A happy wife means a happy Joshie in the bedroom. Remember that."

Josh blushed and cleared his throat. "The Bennett depositions went well, don't you think?"

"They did. You're making excellent progress."

"Oh, I've been meaning to tell you, the Butler case has

huge potential. I'd like to discuss it with you this afternoon." The elevator opened, and Josh stepped in. "Lunch with Elizabeth. See you later."

Cedric studied him until the doors closed and then chastised himself for being paranoid.

* * *

Jack was glad to see Jon and Alexa playing in the backyard together when he rounded the house. "Hey, guys. Where's your mom?"

"Hi, Uncle Jack! Wanna play catch?" Jon said, running up for his hug.

Jack squeezed him the best he could with two bags of groceries swinging from each hand. "I do, but let me say hello to your mom first. I'll be right back."

"Mama's still in bed," Alexa said as she leaned in for a sideways hug. "Nanna says she's sick, but I think she just misses Daddy."

Jack lifted her drooping chin and looked into her woeful blue eyes. "We're all still sad, aren't we?"

Alexa nodded.

"Hey, Jon, where's your other mitt? There aren't any rules against girls playing catch."

"Ah, no," Jon said, making a fist and striking his thigh.

"Go get your other mitt, Jon," Alexa said.

"You go get it," Jon said.

"Okay, guys," Jack said. "Whoever finds the mitt, and has it here when I get back from talking to your mom, wins ten dollars. Ready, set, go!"

Alexa squealed and raced towards the house with Jon on her heels.

"Hey, wait for me," he called after her. "It's my mitt."

Jack followed them into the kitchen and smiled as he heard them bounding up the stairs. He set the bags down and began putting the groceries away. He opened the fridge and was pleased to see that little remained of the party sub.

"Hello, Jack," a familiar voice said.

He turned to see Christine's mother standing by the staircase. "Hello, Nora. I didn't realize you were here. How are you?" He stepped forward, and they embraced.

Nora was like a second mother to him. After his own mother died, she had made it a point to be there for all the important events of his young life. He would never forget, nor could he repay, the great kindness she had shown him.

"I'm fine. Thanks for asking," she said. "Christine hasn't been up all day. I think she has the flu or something. She was quite sick to her stomach last night."

"I'm sorry to hear that. Can I go up and see her?"

"Of course," she said, moving out of the way. "She's a mess, though. She'll be embarrassed for you to see her."

"What's a little mess between friends?"

Nora reached out and touched his arm. "I appreciate what you're doing for her and the children. They adore you, you know."

He kissed her cheek. "I can promise you one thing, Nora. I'll always do my best."

"I know you will," she said. "Go on up. I'll put the groceries away."

He went upstairs and tapped lightly on Christine's door. When she didn't answer, he turned the knob and stuck his head inside.

She sat propped against her pillows, holding a washcloth over her forehead. "Go away, Jack."

"Feeling that good, are we?"

"Ummm. Why did you let me drink beer last night? I hate beer!"

"I know it. I should've wrestled you for the three bottles you grabbed out of my hands. It's all my fault."

She wrinkled her nose. "What got into me?"

"Oh, I can't imagine. It's not like you're under any stress or anything." He reached for the washcloth and headed for the bathroom. "Have you taken any aspirin lately?"

She nodded but grimaced immediately. "I could probably

take two more."

He returned with the washcloth and sat on the foot of the bed, careful not to jar it.

Christine swallowed the aspirin and sighed as she situated the cool cloth back over her eyes and forehead. "Jack?"

"Yeah?"

"How did I get undressed last night?"

"Not to worry. You pulled your pants most of the way off by yourself, and you took your shirt off while I went downstairs to get you a glass of water. You were completely covered when I came back upstairs, so your virtue and your dignity are very much intact on this fine sunny day."

"I'm sorry you had to see me like this."

"Are you kidding? You've helped me dozens of times. I still owe you. Okay?"

She let out a sigh. "Okay."

"Christine, you know I'd never do anything to hurt you or the kids, drunk or sober. You know that, don't you?"

"I know."

"I brought you some of that disgusting cherry yogurt you like, so make sure you eat it. Okay?"

He saw a hit of a smile on her lips. "Okay."

"Good. Now, I owe one of your little urchins a ten-dollar bill. I'm on my way outside to see which one it is. Oh, I have surveillance tonight, but I'll check on you first thing in the morning. We need to talk about signing with the attorney who was here the other day."

"Okay," she said again.

She sounded so cute; it made him smile. "Get some sleep. Your headache should go away soon."

"I hope so."

"And Christine, one last word of advice. No alcohol today."

"You mean, ever!" she said, but then groaned in renewed misery.

He closed the door and chuckled.

* * *

It was mid-afternoon when Jack returned home to read through the Lindsay file. The suspect, Dr. Alan Lindsay, practiced medicine in the Physician's Tower at Dixie Medical Center. His wife, Teresa, suspected the pool of professional women in and around the hospital as the likely source of his extramarital affair. The strategy was simple. He would tail the suspect until a rendez-vous occurred.

He had made the greater part of his living dealing with scenarios like this. Normally, he found satisfaction in helping an innocent mate find the proof they needed to make important deci-sions, but with Daniel's case needing attention, he found it diffi-cult to pursue anything else with his usual zeal. He had accepted this case for one reason—to pay the bills. He yawned and refo-cused on the file before him. According to Teresa, if tonight were typical, Dr. Alan Lindsay would leave the house around seven o'clock and return home shortly before midnight.

He flipped through the photographs a second time and paused when he came to the sage green Lincoln with *Cool Doc* plates. He frowned and shook his head. Why did everyone around him enjoy a superior quality of life? He worked hard, too. Like most people, he had made his share of mistakes in his twenties and early thirties, but he'd done better lately. Now, here he was, about to turn forty, and life was still a struggle. He wasn't sure why it suddenly bothered him, but it did.

Having familiarized himself with Dr. Lindsay's particu-lars, he retrieved his spy box from the back seat of his car and reorganized its contents. Experience had taught him that situa-tions can shift rapidly, and it paid to be prepared. He glanced at his watch; he had time for a quick nap before heading out.

Stripping down, he slipped between the sheets and set the alarm for six o'clock. When he closed his eyes, a lazy smile played upon his lips. It might take a few days, but Elyse would call. She may have acted offish, but she wanted him. She was uninhibited and confident in a way that made him absolutely crazy. She'd call.

His thoughts of Elyse were making it difficult to fall asleep.

He drew a second pillow into his arms and flopped onto his side. Much better. A few minutes later, his lips fluttered softly in his sleep. When the alarm buzzed, it sent him lurching upward. "I'm on it," he sputtered, and then realized where he was. He hit the snooze button and fell back onto the bed. "I hate that thing," he muttered, his heart still thumping.

Less than a minute later, he opened one eye and scowled at the offending timepiece. Had he hit the snooze button or had he hit off? Deciding not to risk it, he hit the off button and got out of bed.

After a leisurely shower, he was feeling much more himself and excited about the opportunity to play detective. With a smirk on his face, he put on his sunshades and swaggered out the door.

CHAPTER TEN

Two dark-haired women whispered together beside a hospital bed at Union General Hospital, struggling with the decision to end their mother's suffering. A loaded syringe lay inside an open drawer within reach.

"I can't do it," said Carolyn, the eldest. "I thought I could, but I can't."

They glanced at their mother, a wrinkled and bruised eighty-year-old woman, but there was no movement, only slow, shallow breathing. Each breath seemed like the last, so far were they in between.

"She made us promise," Donna said. "This is what she wants."

"You do it, then," Carolyn urged.

"I knew you were going to do this," Donna grumbled, turning from the bed. "I'll do it, but I'm not making this decision by myself. Are you sure that you agree?"

A tortured moan turned their attention back to their mother.

"If they could just keep her comfortable, that would be one thing, but this horrible cycle of agony and morphine," Carolyn said, shaking her head. "I can't stand to see her in such pain."

"The doctor says it's just a matter of time," Donna said.

Carolyn sighed. "I know. She has suffered so much already. I agree we should do it, but I don't want to watch."

Their mother moaned again, bringing them back to her side.

"Mama," Carolyn said, "we're here. Can you hear us?

What do you want us to do?"

They waited, but there was no indication that their mother even knew they were there.

"Mama?" Donna said. She looked to her sister. "I can't stand this! Do you agree?"

Carolyn nodded, but when her sister reached into the drawer, the color drained from her face. "Wait," she said anxiously. "I want to say good-bye." She picked up her mother's hand and kissed it tenderly. "Don't worry, Mama. You'll be with God soon." Tears began to fall down her cheeks. "We'll miss you every single day."

Donna tugged on her sleeve. "You better go before I lose my nerve."

Carolyn gently laid her mother's hand on the bed and kissed her forehead. "I love you, Mama," she said and fled the room.

"Hey, Mama, it's almost over," Donna whispered as she lightly stroked her non-responsive cheek. "We love you so much. We're only doing this because you were adamant about what you wanted when it got to this stage. If you've changed your mind, please forgive us."

Donna brushed tears from her eyes as she inserted the needle into the IV, just as the nurse had shown her. Once she had it positioned, she whispered, "Tell Daddy we miss him."

Trina Oliver stood behind the curtain in discreet silence, watching as Donna pushed the liquid into her mother's bloodstream. Though mercy had prompted this killing, she felt a queer and overwhelming fascination for it, as she always did when she watched someone die. The second Donna pulled the needle free, she stepped forward. "Here, I'll take that."

Donna never took her eyes off her mother's face.

Trina slipped quickly from the room and into a supply area to dispose of the evidence. She was just about to drop the needle in the sharps-waste bucket when someone snatched it from her hand.

"Well, well, well," Doctor Thad Winchester said, blocking her exit. "Isn't this interesting?"

Trina took two steps back. "What are you doing here? I thought they were keeping you locked in a basement across town."

"I'm filling in for the coroner this week. Why are you here? You're a surgical nurse; that woman isn't your patient."

"What do you want?" Trina said.

"A friend of mine just died on this floor." He held up the empty syringe. "Isn't that a coincidence? I'll bet there's another death on this floor any minute now." As Trina's gaze fell to her feet, he pressed another syringe into her hand. "Stick the old lady with this within five minutes of her death. You got that?"

"I can't go back in there! Are you crazy?"

"You'd better. I'd hate to have to mention what I just discovered. Now get in there, before she codes."

"What good is a dead guinea pig?" she said, dropping the syringe into the pocket of her scrubs.

"Let's just call it research. She's got nothing to lose, thanks to you."

"I didn't give her cancer, you know."

"No, you saved her hours, if not days, of unspeakable misery. I'm sure she'd thank you if she could."

Trina didn't trust this side of Thurston Oliver Winchester III. "Anything else?"

"Yes, now that you mention it. Does the word incest mean anything to you?"

Trina was so surprised; she laughed. "Well, you know what they say about forbidden fruit."

Thad glanced over his shoulder as an orderly walked by. "You're playing a dangerous game, Katrina."

"And you're not? I got my transfer papers today. I don't appreciate being reassigned for the sake of your selfish ambitions. If you want my help, then you'd better start paying for it."

"I paid for your entire education, Miss Oliver, and I expect a few favors from you in return. If I'm not mistaken, your new position includes a sizable raise. Who do you think arranged for that? You might try being grateful for a change."

"Grateful? You owe me, old man."

"You overvalue yourself. I could easily replace you."

"Yeah? You just try it. I've got a lot of dirt on you, you know."

Two nurses paused near the doorway. Once they had moved on, Thad held up the empty syringe. "What happens if the autopsy reveals murder?"

"There won't be an autopsy, *Daddy*. Why would her daughters want to prove murder when they killed her themselves?"

"Oh, there'll be an autopsy, all right, because you'll tell them they need one in order to throw off suspicion."

"And if I refuse?" she said.

"One word from me... and your job is history."

"You wouldn't dare!"

"What will it be?" he said. "The window of opportunity is closing."

"Oh, all right! I don't know why I help you."

"I like you with short hair, by the way. Very sheik. Black suits you better than blonde."

"I don't care what you think." She shoved past him so he wouldn't see the tears that stung her eyes.

"Five minutes, Katrina."

She nodded and kept walking.

* * *

The fact that the Lindsays lived in a gated community didn't bother Jack. He got into these neighborhoods the same way every other non-invited resident did—on the coattails of whichever vehicle entered through the gate first. He checked his watch repeatedly and occupied his mind with thoughts of Elyse. Growing impatient, he considered trying random codes on the keypad, but fate was conveniently kind. A small Toyota pickup truck with a Domino's Pizza sign attached to the roof approached the gate.

The driver paid no attention to Jack as he pulled his Camry up behind him. He rolled down his window in hopes of seeing the code the boy entered, and was rewarded when a voice over the intercom said, "Punch the pound key, and hit 4949."

"Thanks," the young man answered back.

The pizza guy was in, and Jack was right behind him, armed with the gate code for future reference. He loved it when things like that happened. It made him feel like the universe was smiling down on him with pleasure. He drove past the Lindsay residence, which was located about halfway down the block on the right side of the street. The sage green Lincoln with Cool Doc plates sat parked outside the open garage.

Continuing past the elegant two-story charmer, he found a place to turn around and parked beneath a magnolia tree where he could watch the house. Sure enough, at 7:02 p.m. the suspect pulled out of the driveway. The upper-class neighborhood was situated near the main freeway, so he wasn't surprised when the Lincoln merged onto the interstate and headed south. Following at a distance, he fully expected the doctor to take the Lakeland exit, which he did. A few minutes later, instead of taking a left towards the hospital, he continued straight through the traffic light just as it turned yellow.

"Dang it!" Jack swore. He'd been so sure of his destination that he had followed two cars back. Now, he was stuck at the light! When the light finally changed, he proceeded five or six blocks into a trendy section of town called the Fondren district. This popular, revitalized section of Jackson was an area he rarely frequented. After cruising down several side streets, he caught a glimpse of the suspect's car, two vehicles ahead of him. "Clean living and self-denial," he muttered with a grin.

The Lincoln turned into a small private parking lot and parked facing the fence. Jack drove past the lot, did a U-turn, and parked along the street where he could clearly see the car. To his surprise, a teenage boy emerged. After the Lincoln had beeped twice, the boy broke into a casual run and jogged back up the street in the direction they had come.

So, where was Lindsay? Jack followed the young man around the short block to a fine restaurant called La Bells, which was tucked away amidst the pines that bordered an upper-class residential neighborhood. The runner handed Lindsay's keys to another young man, and then he jumped into a black sedan and drove off. Jack chuckled. The boy was a valet. The unexpected laughter left a smile on his face. At least he knew where Lindsay was—which wasn't at his office where he told his wife, Teresa, he was going.

He drove past the valet stand and parked behind the restaurant, among the lower-class cars that likely belonged to the employees. Deciding what to do next, he checked his wallet. He only had ten dollars—barely enough for coffee in a place like this. He also had a Master Card, which was currently over the limit. Rather than stress over his finances, he decided upon another strategy—one that was much more interesting.

After checking the perimeter, he reached into the back for his spy kit and set it on the front seat. He selected a stiff, salt and pepper mustache, the type typically worn by someone on a very strict schedule, and affixed it into place. Next, he used hair gel to slick down his stubborn curls, primping in the mirror until he was satisfied. After donning a pair of thick, black-rimmed eyeglasses, he took the phonebook out of the glove box and looked up the number for La Bells.

"La Bells," a man said against a backdrop of noisy clatter.

"Is the manager in?"

"He's here somewhere, but it's rush time. Can he call you back later?"

"I'm about to show up on your doorstep to investigate a complaint. If the manager is too busy to talk to me, then I'll conduct my visit without him. Makes no difference to me." Jack snapped his phone shut and grinned. "That should stir things up." By the time he reached the kitchen, the red carpet would be out, and the royal treatment would begin. He chuckled at the thought. He may not make much money, but he certainly enjoyed his work.

He reached beneath the passenger seat for a large, flat box, which contained several rolled up garments. Selecting the white one, he shoved the box back under the seat and closed the spy kit. After making sure the coast was clear, he stepped out of the car and shook out his lab coat. Pleased to see minimal wrinkles, he reminded himself to thank Christine for the helpful packing tip. Patting his authentic-looking ID badge, he stalked around the building to the kitchen entrance and rapped sharply on the door.

Within seconds, the slide bolt moved, and the door swung open. He flashed his I.D. badge. "Inspector Wallace from the Health Department. I have a few questions. May I come in?" He just loved doing that. It was such a rush to see people react to what they perceived as an authority.

"Yes, sir. Come on in," said a dark-haired, gangly young man as he stepped to the side.

Jack looked down his nose at him. "Are you the manager?"

"Yes, sir. I'm Timothy Jones, sir." He glanced nervously over his shoulder. The kitchen employees were clearly listening. "What kind of complaint did you get?"

Jack brushed by him and began looking around. Chefs, waiters, dishwashers, and everyone standing around, immediately found reasons to turn their backs or leave the area altogether.

"It's fairly routine," he said, pretending to be too preoccupied to answer the question. After examining the surprisingly clean floor and stainless steel sinks, he lit upon an idea. He turned abruptly and bumped into Timothy, who was following too closely.

"Sorry," Timothy said, backing out of the way.

"Have you been serving salad this evening?"

"Yes, sir. We serve several types of salads. Which are you referring to?"

Jack felt a moment of panic. It should've occurred to him that a fancy place like this would serve multiple salads. "I want to see the lettuce."

"Which lettuce, sir?"

He looked down his nose again, this time through his

glasses. "All the lettuce. Do we have a problem here?"

Timothy shook his head. "No, sir. Not at all. Right this way."

Jack followed him into the walk-in refrigerator where Timothy pointed out several salad bins. Accepting a clean pair of gloves, Jack pretended to examine the contents, turning individual leaves as if anticipating bugs. Normally, he'd have fun doing this sort of thing, but Timothy, whom he guessed to be in his early twenties, was pacing anxiously. He felt a bit guilty. "Is there a reason you're so nervous, Timothy?"

"Yes, sir. I just bought a new truck. I can't afford to lose my job."

After digging around in three bins of lettuce, he snapped off his gloves and handed them to Timothy. "Seems like your job's secure, son. Everything looks fine here. I'm going to take a stroll through the dining area, but don't worry. I'll wait to take notes until after I leave. No need to alarm anyone, right?"

"No, sir," Timothy quickly agreed.

Jack pushed open the swinging door and looked out upon the maze-like dining area. Half-walls and room dividers partitioned the dimly lit room, and a sequence of cozy booths circled the perimeter. As he wandered through, searching for Dr. Lindsay, he realized he didn't recognize anyone, which made him wonder if he wasn't traveling in the wrong circles. Why was everything pointing, lately, to his lack of financial standing in the world? Scowling, he continued to scan faces as he walked by. An ornate, Italian-style fountain decorated a wall near the front entrance. Pausing to admire it, he considered building something similar in his backyard—after he bought a new car, of course, which was first on his list. He glanced into the adjacent section and saw Dr. Lindsay sitting at a cozy table with a lovely young woman. He hovered as close as he dared, but the fountain muted the conversations of those around it. Content with having spotted his suspect, he headed back to the kitchen.

Young Timothy was waiting. "I called the day-manager," he said with more confidence than he'd shown thus far. "He wants you to call him."

Jack headed for the back door. "No need. Everything checks out here. Have a nice evening, son," he said and slid the deadbolt so he could leave.

Back inside his car, he shed the lab coat and pulled off his glasses and mustache. After cranking the engine, he parked as close to the entrance as he could, which was still some distance away because of the spaces reserved for valet parking. Nevertheless, he had a decent view of the valet stand and hoped to capture a few shots as his suspects waited for their cars.

He spent the next several minutes adjusting his camera equipment. When everything was ready, he slouched in his seat to wait. It was nearly nine-thirty by the time Dr. Lindsay and his date exited the restaurant. They stood talking together beneath the lamp-lit awning while two valets jogged off to retrieve their vehicles.

Jack opened his car door and slipped out. Positioning himself between two bushes, he snapped several quick shots. "Good, good. That's good," he mumbled. "Now kiss her, you lousy, cheating . . ."

The young woman laughed at something Doctor Lindsay said and hugged him. Jack captured the quick embrace and waited for the kiss, the one that would persuade his client to keep him on the case until he could get more evidence.

Lindsay's Lincoln, followed by a silver BMW, pulled up to the curb. Jack focused tighter on Lindsay's date and captured several good shots. Just then, the curvaceous body of another woman suddenly blocked his view. Annoyed, he glanced up. He was so surprised to see Elyse he almost dropped the camera. He hadn't noticed *her* inside the dining room. She was talking with an impeccably dressed older man.

At that moment, Lindsay kissed his date on the cheek and left her in the care of the young valet, who opened the door of her BMW.

"Dang it! I missed it!" There was no time to waste if he was going to follow his suspects, and yet he paused to watch Elyse climb into the sleek, black Jaguar that had pulled up behind the silver BMW. He clicked several shots of Elyse and her date. "Are you serious?" he grumbled. "He's old enough to be your father."

A Porsche pulled in immediately after the Jag, so he couldn't make out the Jaguar's license plate. Frustrated, he got back in his car and sped off to catch the BMW. Forcing himself to focus on Doctor Lindsay, he wondered why just a kiss on the cheek. Either the affair was just beginning, or they were publicly discreet. Whatever the reason, it was inconvenient.

As he approached the interstate, he realized he had delayed too long; the BMW was nowhere in sight. Normally, he'd be upset with himself for blowing an opportunity, but instead, his thoughts turned back to Elyse. How could he compete with that? What woman would climb into a ten-year-old Camry when she could ride in Jag?

"She's not gonna call," he said with a shake of his head. He was disgusted with her, sorry for himself, and too keyed up to go home. He drove by Christine's house, which was dark and quiet. He hoped that meant she was getting some sleep tonight. Though she didn't talk about it, the dark circles beneath her eyes revealed how difficult her nights were. He wished he could relieve her burdens, but she had to adjust to life without Daniel by herself. No one could do it for her. The same was true for him. There were times when he wanted to talk to Daniel more than he wanted anything else, but that didn't matter. Daniel was out of reach. It was difficult to accept.

When he finally got home, he popped a beer and kicked back in his recliner. After jotting some notes on the Lindsay case, he made a to-do list. His number one priority was persuading Christine to hire that attorney—Cedric Johnson.

* * *

Elyse felt like a naughty teenager as she followed Doctor Thad Winchester down the dimly lit hallway, past the morgue and into the lab. The basement floor of the hospital was creepy enough in the daytime, but at night, with their footsteps echoing in the empty hallway, it felt like she was entering a horror chamber. She hated slasher movies and hurried to keep up.

"Here we are, my dear." Thad switched on a bank of bright fluorescents, which illuminated an extensive inventory of gadgets and equipment.

"Wow," she said, truly impressed. She swiped a finger along the base of a large stethoscope and saw that it was clean. "It would be challenging, I admit, but as I explained over dinner, I majored in chemistry. It would be nice to use my formal education." She moved around the room, examining her prospective environment.

"It's a small lab," he said, "but busy enough, especially since I oversee several coroners in town. As you know, my assistant left suddenly, so I could use your help immediately—particularly with the paperwork."

"But you'll teach me lab work, too, right?" she said, confirming what he had said at dinner.

He chuckled. "Indeed. Is it settled then?"

"I'd like to think about it over the weekend. Can I let you know on Monday?"

"Certainly. It's your decision, of course, but there's a high demand for lab assistants. It's a more progressive career path than the one you're on."

"I would need to give Dr. Sassi two weeks' notice, of course, but I'm willing to come in on the weekends to help you catch up."

"While you're considering it, think about what you would do with an extra fifteen thousand dollars in your pocket every year." He leaned towards her with an amused smile. "They say money is addictive."

She laughed. "So they do." She listened with interest as he pointed out several pieces of equipment.

After the brief tour, he said, "Come now, Miss Dawson, let me walk you out. I still have work to do this evening. We'll talk again on Monday, yes?"

"Yes. Thank you for considering me, and for dinner, too."

"My pleasure on both counts. You come highly recommended." He held the door as she walked through.

As her heels clicked down the hallway, she calculated that it would take five more years in her current position to work up to the beginning salary Thad offered, plus she would have earned an extra seventy-five thousand dollars during those same five years—not counting any raises she might earn in her new position. With a daughter headed off to college soon, and her own student loans to repay, how could she refuse?

* * *

Well after midnight, Trina clocked out of work and tried to reach Anthony for the tenth time in a row. The winds were stronger than normal, and lightning flashed in the distance. She shivered violently and hurried towards her car. Aiding in the death of the old woman had created a dichotomy of emotions for her to sort through. In her mind, it seemed far more criminal to require people to agonize to the very end rather than help them finish life peacefully.

Buckets of rain suddenly dumped from the sky giving credence to the southern expression 'It has come a flood.' She made a run for the parking garage. Instead of waiting for the elevator, she yanked the stairwell door open and climbed to the third floor where she had parked near the back wall.

Thad was wrong about the old woman not being her patient. She had assisted the surgeon, who had removed the lower portion of her right lung some nine months earlier. In spite of their efforts, the cancer had returned. She reminded herself that the old woman's decline had weighed heavily upon her two daughters, who had stayed faithfully by her side, placing their own lives on hold to ensure that their mother's every need was met. Had there been any hope, she wouldn't have interfered, but with only agony ahead, it had seemed in everyone's best interest to offer an alternative. It was also the perfect opportunity to test her father's latest formula. She frowned. He never appreciated the risks she took for him. He expected it.

Her lips pursed as she remembered his threatening words, 'What happens if the autopsy reveals murder?' It was a stupid threat. She had much more dirt on him than he could ever produce on her. It was to her advantage that he underestimate her, but it still hurt. Reaching her car, she peeled off her dripping jacket and threw it in the back seat. She was shivering, so she cranked the engine and turned up the heat. Here, out of the wind, it wasn't nearly as cold, but the erratic temperature changes between winter and spring were playing havoc with her immune system.

As she began to warm, the dramatic tensions of the day pulsed throughout her body and throbbed between her legs. Images of her and Anthony on his living room floor came to mind unbidden. She glanced at her phone again to see if he had returned her calls or sent a text. She didn't like being ignored. The longer she didn't hear from him, the more possibilities she imagined.

She could, of course, pick up any guy she wanted, but sex with anyone other than Anthony was out of the question right now, especially with Thad breathing down her neck every time she turned around. Besides, she was determined to get pregnant with Anthony's child and, thereby, produce an *acceptable* Winchester heir. She scoffed at the thought. God knew her father saw her as anything but. She was illegitimate—a fact he never let her forget. According to him, she was a tainted, dirty secret that could ruin his good name. Over the years, he had paid for her silence in various ways, one of which had been her education, as he had so pointedly thrown in her face this afternoon. As a child, she had hungered for every second of his rare attention. She had foolishly thought if he would only get to know her, he would love her and want to be part of her life. As she grew older, she began to realize that he might never accept her. To this day, he still refused to acknowledge her as his daughter.

Warm now, she leaned back against the seat and tried to relax her shoulders. She could see the rain falling on the outer side of the half-wall that wrapped around the perimeter of the parking structure. She was in no hurry to leave. She rubbed her eyes and continued to brood about her father.

As if classifying her as a worthless bastard wasn't enough, her father kept her estranged from his entire family. Her grandfather, Thurston Oliver Winchester II, had apparently been scant in his interactions with *his* only son—until Thad's wife, Susan, had finally borne him a son, a beloved grandchild upon which the older Winchester showered the best of everything. Her half-brother, Thurston Oliver Winchester IV, received everything she so desperately longed for. He was the pride of the family. She knew this because she was in the habit of breaking into her father's home, specifically into his private study, to keep herself abreast of his private affairs—both business and personal. She had read her grandfather's letters over the years and had come to understand the insufferable Winchester proclivity for control, which explained but didn't excuse the deplorable way her father treated her.

When her half-brother died five years ago, she had hoped Thad would remember that he had another child, but his attitude towards her only worsened. She had continued to receive money for nursing school, as well as a modest income to get by on, but they rarely spoke in person. In truth, he only contacted her when he needed her help—the reason he provided her with an education in the first place. Even though she knew his motives, she cooperated because any resemblance of approval felt better than his rejection—a truth about herself she didn't like.

Her phone vibrated, bringing her back to the present. It wasn't Anthony, so she ignored it. Deciding to go to his apartment, she backed out of her parking spot.

When her cousin, Anthony, had suddenly reappeared two years ago, she had thought her father would name him as his heir, but that didn't happen. Thad's interest in his nephew wasn't the least bit philanthropic. Had she thought it through, she would have known that and saved herself months of needless worry. Thad didn't value Anthony, which was evident by the way he had treated him after his parents died. Instead of adopting his brother's only son, Thad had allowed him to become a ward of the state. He had his heir. What need did he have for Anthony? She didn't know what their current arrangement was, or how they had reunited, but she was determined to find out. The more dirt she collected on her father, the more leverage she'd have.

The main freeway through town was nearly devoid of traffic, but she guarded her speed anyway, knowing the police often stationed themselves in strategic spots along the typically busy thoroughfare. The rain had finally stopped, allowing her to settle into the twenty-minute drive.

She was looking forward to lying next to Anthony tonight. The warmth she felt in his arms was a comfort she hadn't known before. He made her feel *wanted.* Would he reject her once he learned they were cousins? She pushed the thought out of her mind.

Producing a child together was the only way either of them would ever get their hands on Thad's money, and even then, only if it were a boy. For their child to qualify, Thad would require the child to be legitimate, which would mean marrying Anthony, which would give her the added satisfaction of gaining the Winchester name—a name that was hers by right, but had always been denied. A smug little smile tugged at her lips. As the mother of the Winchester heir, she'd have access to the entire Winchester fortune. The trick was to make Anthony marry her, and that meant securing a relationship and keeping him faithful.

Her stomach tightened as she punched the numbers at the main security gate. Once it had opened, she counted twelve driveways, turned left, and then parked beneath one of the river birch trees that grew beside the fence surrounding her father's estate. She was quite good at sneaking onto her father's property. Nevertheless, if Thad caught her here, there'd be hell to pay.

Her thoughts kept returning to their encounter that afternoon. She wondered about the injection he had instructed her to give her dead patient. It made no sense. The woman had passed. She decided to check his journal notes—if he still kept them locked in his safe. It had been several months since she had last risked a look at them.

Grabbing her backpack from the back seat, she pulled out a pair of blue jeans and a black T-shirt. She stepped out of the car and waited for a few sets of headlights to pass, then stripped off her medical scrubs and wiggled into her jeans. Once she was dressed, she dodged a few more headlights, and then climbed onto the roof of her car and over the fence. She landed on the other side with a crunch of gravel. A shiver crept up her back as she made her way towards the house. If Anthony was home, would he be alone?

Until today, she had thought her relationship with Anthony had been a secret, but the 'incest' word had completely shot that notion. So much for cutting and dying her hair. She should have known he'd find out, but it was too late to worry about that now. For all she knew, she might already be pregnant.

The lights were on in Anthony's apartment. She glanced towards the main house and saw that Thad's office was also ablaze. She knew he'd be pacing. Sure enough, about fifteen seconds later, his glowering face appeared and then retreated. She dashed across the courtyard and up the stairs to Anthony's apartment. She tried the door, stepped inside, and locked the door behind her. "Anthony?" she said in a loud whisper. "It's me, Trina." Concerned that her silhouette might be visible through the blinds, she switched off the overheads and reached for the lamp, gasping when she saw Anthony sprawled across the couch. A hand-mirror sat on the coffee table with a thick, powdery line drawn across it.

"So, that's why you didn't call." She picked up the hundred-dollar bill and snorted the powder. The rush was immediate. With a contented sigh, she reclined next to Anthony and lightly stroked his chest. "Come on, Anthony, wake up. You wanna make love, don't ya?"

Stirring from his stupor, a lazy smile spread across his ruggedly handsome face. "Sure, I do. I'm so glad you're here."

"What happened to your lip?" she said, gently touching his swollen mouth.

"Just a little fight. Come here, baby."

Trina pulled back as he tried to take her in his arms. "Let's do a line together first."

Anthony forced himself into a sitting position and dumped the remainder of the vial onto the mirror. Using a razor blade, he divided the powder into two lines. Trina snorted hers first, and then Anthony did the same. They looked at each other and smiled, and then their clothes began coming off between passionate kisses and desperate groping. Trina tripped as she stepped out of her jeans and fell to the floor laughing. Anthony scooped her up, carried her into the bedroom, and laid her gently on the bed. He undressed and joined her.

"I've been trying to reach you," she said.

"You found me."

"There is so much to tell you about my day."

"Later," he said as he kissed her into silence.

As their kisses deepened, she began to give herself to the moment. She never felt about someone the way she did about Anthony. With each thrust of his body, it became easier to ignore the truth that Thad had so callously thrown in her face today. Anthony may be her cousin, but he was kind and considerate in ways no one else ever had been. That had to count for something, didn't it?

* * *

After checking on her children for the third time, Christine wandered back into her bedroom and shut the door. It was late, but she still couldn't sleep. She pulled a photo album out from the bookshelf and set it on the bed. Flipping through the familiar pages, she came to the photograph she sought—a picture of Daniel at last year's family reunion. She loved this photograph because it captured Daniel's intelligence and fun-loving nature. A sad little smile tugged at her lips as she stroked his cheek with the tip of her finger. She closed her eyes and shook her head. It had never occurred to her that something like this would happen. Leaving the album open, she laid it on Daniel's pillow and got out of bed. Chill bumps rose on her arms. Looking for something warmer to wear, she opened the closet and froze when she saw Daniel's shirts hanging neatly on his side. Without thinking, she wrapped her arms around the entire bunch of them and took a deep, soulful whiff. His scent lingered in the fabric, transporting her, for one brief moment, into his arms. She held her breath lest the moment fade. Her shoulders began to tremble as wave after wave of grief washed over her. Clinging to his clothes, she collapsed to the floor, pulling several of Daniel's shirts down with her.

CHAPTER ELEVEN

It was a beautiful sunny morning. Jack arrived at Christine's house expecting a noisy repeat of the day before, but both cars were in the garage, and the house was still dark. He went around to the back of the house, reached for the outside key, and let himself into the kitchen. The house was quiet. Someone could have picked them up, he supposed. He flipped open his phone and dialed Christine's number. He was about to leave when he heard it ringing upstairs. Taking the stairs two at a time, he found her bedroom door closed and locked. "Christine? Are you all right?" He knocked loud enough to wake her, but there was no response. Reaching for his wallet, he took out his favorite gadget. Within seconds, he was in.

Christine was lying still on the bed.

"Christine," he said a bit louder as he stepped into the room. "Christine?" He saw a pill bottle and a glass of water sitting on the nightstand and his heart stopped. "Oh, God, no!" He rushed over and plucked up the bottle. It was full. He was so relieved his knees weakened. It was Ambien. She might be out, but she wasn't completely out.

As he turned to leave, something red next to Christine's skin caught his eye. Looking closer, he realized she was wearing one of Daniel's favorite shirts, a red polo shirt, which was easily twice her size. Then he saw piles of Daniel's shirts, dozens of them, surrounding her. As he looked down into her peaceful face, he wondered what it would be like to have a woman love him like that. He picked up a T-shirt that he had given to Daniel a few years back. "She loves you, buddy. You're a lucky man." He laid the shirt back down on the bed and quietly closed the door behind him.

* * *

Anthony groaned as he awoke on the floor of his apartment, stiff and naked. He tried to recall how this had happened, but yesterday's OxyContin binge had left his brain foggy. His day hadn't even started yet and, already, he was in a foul mood. His mind began to wander down pathways that only made him feel worse.

He didn't like to admit that he was depressed, but who wouldn't be after losing both parents in a horrendous car accident? His life could've been so different if his uncle would have cared about what happened to him after the accident. He closed his eyes against the pain. It was a betrayal, plain and simple. Thad had betrayed his father, and Thad had betrayed him—his one and only nephew. He shouldn't have had to endure abusive foster homes, or live on the streets in the under-maze of New Orleans's darkest sector where he'd had to kill and steal in order to survive. If Thad had done what he ought to have done, he'd be a promising young golfer right now instead of a high school dropout with no future. His fists clenched with rage. He would have died out there if it hadn't been for Angel.

A mixture of grief and gratitude filled him whenever he thought about Angel. Since neither emotion was welcome, he pushed her memory aside, reached for his jeans, and put them on. As he turned, he saw a silver envelope lying on the floor where it had fallen through the mail slot in the front door. Scooping it up, he tossed it on the coffee table and shuffled to the kitchen to make some coffee. A full and steaming pot and a handwritten note waited on the counter.

Good morning, sleepy head. Thanks for a great night. I'm out of here before your landlord sees my car parked outside the gate. Call me.

"So that's why I was naked," he said with an amused

twitch of his lip. As the memories of their lovemaking resurfaced in his brain, they also stirred his blood. "Damn, that girl is hot." He looked out the kitchen window at the beautifully manicured courtyard and saw smoke wafting from two of the chimneys in the main house. "Slimeball," he said as his smile faded.

Granted, his life had improved since Thad's detective found him that day he was searching the shelters for Angel, but he wasn't fooled by his uncle's sudden interest in his welfare. No, Thad had wanted something, and they had struck a deal.

He sipped the coffee and sighed as the steam warmed his face. It was cool to have a woman do something nice for him for a change. Other than Angel, the only women he'd ever known were drug-whores—girls who'd steal you blind the second you looked the other way. Trust didn't come easily for him, but with Trina, he felt the hard edges around his heart softening, and he was glad.

He settled onto the couch and picked up the silver envelope. He didn't know what Thad did with the information he provided, but he had his suspicions—not that he cared. Whatever his uncle was up to, he'd certainly seen worse and had probably done worse himself. Little shocked him when it came to human misbehavior. No, he didn't care what his uncle was doing. He intended to use him until he had enough money to do what he wanted, and then he'd set matters straight between them, and it wouldn't be pretty.

He was tempted to turn on the TV, but he opened the envelope instead. To his surprise, it didn't contain a new assignment, only drugs. Though his uncle didn't know it, he sold most of the OxyContin he received. He may have spent his adolescence on the streets, but he remembered the privileged life he had led prior to his parents' deaths, and he wanted it back.

Dark clouds threatened as they usually did when he thought about his father. They had been extremely close. They had played golf together nearly every weekend of his childhood. It had been his childhood dream to become a professional golfer, or perhaps even a firefighter. How ironic that instead of saving lives, he'd been guilty of ending them. Angel had tried to convince him that he could recover, even after his years on the street, and he could, he thought, as long as he had enough money. He wanted a normal life somewhere—far from Mississippi. Another year, he figured, and he'd have enough.

His thoughts returned to Trina. She was the true addict, but she was also very smart. She managed to carry on what appeared to be a highly respectable life, while at the same time, indulging in nearly every drug she could get her hands on. No one would guess that after a long day of conscientious nursing, her demons came out to play, especially if she had lost a patient that day. His body responded to a sudden vision of her from the night before—until the memory of Angel's laughter made him feel guilty. Rubbing his eyes, he banished Angel from his mind again and weighed the bottle in his hand. Though gifted with tremendous will power, there were days when the lure of cash just wasn't as strong as the call of oblivion. Today was one of those days.

Despite his better judgment, he opened the bottle and dropped several pills into the grinder. When the powder was ready, he snorted a thick line through his trusty Benjamin Franklin. As the drug changed his perspective, he leaned back against the couch and let his mind travel at will.

"Thanks, Uncle. You lousy SOB."

* * *

"Hello?" Christine mumbled into the phone.

Jack smiled. "Hey, you. Been up long?"

Christine yawned in his ear. "Call me later, Jack. I don't want to get up yet."

The line went dead, but Jack's smile got bigger. Forty-five minutes later, he found Christine just as he had left her.

She sat up slowly and stretched. "Hi, Jack. You can leave the pizza, which smells heavenly, by the way, but I'm not up for having company."

Undeterred, he gathered a section of Daniel's shirts and laid them beside her pillow. After setting the pizza box on the bed, he handed her a plate. "I think it would be criminal for me to leave this entire pizza without even eating one piece, don't you?"

"That would be cruel. Dig in."

In between bites of pizza, he filled her in on the previous night's visit to La Bells. "You should have seen it, Christine. That poor kid acted as if I had the power to cart him off to jail. I hate to admit it, but I actually felt sorry for him."

"What were you wearing?" she said, popping a piece of pineapple into her mouth.

"My salt and pepper mustache, thick eyeglasses, and my white lab coat. Thanks for the packing tip, by the way. The coat wasn't even wrinkled. Remind me to show you my identification badge sometime. It looks very authentic. Just like that," he said, snapping his fingers, "Mr. Wallace from the Health Department had free run of the entire restaurant." Christine chuckled, which was just what he was aiming for. "Now remember, Christine, the whole reason I'm even at this place is to document the activities of a cheating husband. Here I am, waiting between two bushes . . . The light is right. The camera is ready. I'm about to get the goodbye kiss when Elyse, of all people, steps in front of the camera. I was so surprised; I missed my shot!"

Christine laughed. "I can *so* see that happening to you! Whatever happened between you two anyway? I thought you were going to marry that girl."

He frowned at the mere mention of the 'M' word. "What can I say? It didn't feel right."

"Okay, I'll drop it. Are you working tonight?" she said, licking the sauce from her fingertips.

"Yes, and I need to get going. I'm glad you like the pizza."

Christine reached for his hand. "Really, Jack, thanks for everything. I don't know what we'd do without you." Her big blue eyes suddenly filled with tears.

"He'd do the same for me if I left someone behind."

"How about *you*? Are you okay? I know this has to be difficult for you."

In a flash, he was on his feet. "I have to be okay. I have to look out for you guys, don't I?"

"Daniel would be proud of you, you know. I'm sure he's watching us this very moment." She ran her hand along the stack of Daniel's shirts. "I'd trade every single tomorrow for one more night in his arms."

He sat back down on the edge of the bed. "I'd trade places with him if I could. I'm so sorry, Christine."

She nodded and swallowed back tears.

"By the way," he said, rising again. "On the way over here, I set an appointment for nine o'clock tomorrow morning to discuss your case with Cedric Johnson and possibly sign papers. Can you be ready by eight-thirty?"

She had just taken another bite, so she nodded.

He was glad to see her eat. "I'll come by early to see the kids before we go."

"Jack," she called as he headed out the door.

"Yeah?" He was struggling with his emotions. Thus far, he'd managed to hold everything in, but he understood the difficulty she was having in being strong in front of her children. That's how he felt about her. He had to be strong so she'd have someone to lean on.

"Jon seems to be doing fairly well, except at prayer time, but Alexa has me worried. She refuses to wear anything but black. I've tried to talk to her about it, but she ignores me. I'm not sure what to do."

"I noticed her wearing black the other day, but I was hoping it was a coincidence. I'll give it some thought. Call me if you need me."

"Shut the door, will you?"

Jack shut the door and headed down the stairs, eager to escape his intense feelings. He was fine until she showed tenderness towards him, and then he felt like falling apart. What was wrong with him?

He made the mistake of looking into the living room when he hit the bottom floor. Things were so different a few weeks ago. He walked towards Daniel's recliner and stared down at it. Tears stung his eyes. Finally allowing himself to express his grief, he dropped to his knees, braced his head on the soft brown seat, and let his emotions run their course.

* * *

Teresa had just put the last of the dirty dishes into the dishwasher when she heard the garage door open. She hurried through the kitchen and past the laundry room, but her husband had already backed out onto the street by the time she reached the garage. Gripping her hands into fists, she closed her eyes and tried to get control of her emotions.

"He's off in a hurry again, I see. Such is the life of a busy doctor, I guess."

Teresa opened her eyes to see the neighbor trimming the waist-high hedge that separated their properties.

"Good evening, Mr. Blackwell," she said, smiling through clenched teeth. "How are you tonight?"

"Good, good. Just thinkin' on how frustrating it must be to have other women dictating your husband's schedule all the time."

"Then I wouldn't recommend marrying an obstetrician. Babies don't consult appointment calendars when they're born."

He chuckled. "True, that. Nevertheless, if you're ever hankering for company, just let me know. Now that my wife's passed, I could use some intelligent female company—if you know what I mean."

This wasn't the first time he'd expressed interest. Hoping to discourage him permanently, she said, "Be careful with your clippers, Mr. Blackwell. It's dangerous to flirt with another man's wife." Satisfied with his surprised expression, she went inside to call Jack.

* * *

Jack was still on his knees when his cell phone rang. Wiping his eyes with the back of his hand, he said, "Jack here."

"This is Teresa. Alan just left the house."

Glancing at his watch, he said, "Any ideas where he's going?"

"Is that supposed to be funny?"

"Sorry, Teresa. Can you hold on a second?" Laying the phone down, he grabbed a handful of tissues from one of the many tissue boxes Christine had scattered around the house and blew his nose. "Sorry about that. I'm back."

"Are you all right?"

Too drained to be embarrassed, he said, "Yeah, I'm fine. I lost my best friend recently. I guess I couldn't hold it in any longer."

"Oh, yes, you mentioned that. If this isn't a good time—"

Jack cast a quick glance up the stairs, and then hurried out to his car. "No, it's the perfect time. When did he leave?"

"Five minutes."

"I'll see what I can do."

"Thanks, Jack."

Grateful for something to focus on, he jumped into his car and worked his way through a maze of streets and into a parking lot along the frontage road of I-55. Because there was only one main corridor through this part of town, there was a good chance he'd see Alan Lindsay drive by. Five minutes later, he caught sight of Lindsay's car.

Jack merged onto the freeway, congratulating himself on his strategic thinking. He weaved his way through traffic until he was two cars behind the Lincoln. A few minutes later, the doctor took the exit towards Dixie Medical Center. Jack wasn't taking any chances; he stayed one car behind him. When Lindsay turned into the hospital entrance, Jack pulled over and watched his suspect drive into the parking garage. Several minutes later, Dr. Lindsay emerged on foot, strode quickly along the sidewalk and through the sliding glass doors of the Physician's Tower entrance.

Jack cruised through the parking lot until someone vacated a strategic spot where he could monitor the tower and the hospital entrance. Once the sun had dipped below the golden horizon, he reached for his spy kit and set it on the front seat. He told himself that on the off-chance Lindsay had noticed him, he would alter his appearance, but in truth, he was getting antsy, and this would give him something to do.

He attached an ordinary brown mustache, put on a pair of gold-rimmed glasses, and settled down to wait. An hour went by. When a shift-change occurred, he found himself pleasantly entertained by the throng of people coming and going—especially the ladies. Two young nurses currently held his attention as they chatted together at a round, concrete table. One, a brunette with shoulder-length, curly hair, seemed intent upon studying the book in front of her, yet she half-participated in her friend's animated conversation. He marveled at how easily she seemed to bounce between the two subjects. He could never do that. He was trying to identify what it was about her that had caught his eye when an attractive blonde came into view. One thing was certain; a physician would have ample opportunity to meet attractive women. Too bad he hadn't thought of that when he selected his career.

Glancing back towards the hospital entrance, he did a double take as Lindsay's Lincoln pulled out of the parking garage. Chastising himself for getting distracted, he backed out of his spot and hurried into position. Instead of turning towards the freeway, Lindsay ventured into the Fondren district again. Jack followed for several blocks and was surprised to see him turn into a dark alley. He immediately glanced about for a place to park, but he saw nothing open for at least a block. Suddenly, the tail lights of a Volkswagen Rabbit flashed red as it pulled out in front of him, causing him to slam on his brakes. Recovering from the close call, he smiled with cocky satisfaction and pulled into the empty spot.

Grabbing a brown wool cap from his garment box, he tugged it over his head and got out of the car. Fortunately, the sky was clear, and the half-moon helped him avoid the smelly rubbish piles that cluttered the alleyway as he went in search of Lindsay's Lincoln. When he was approximately fifty yards in, an engine started and headlights blinded him. Shielding his eyes, he dodged to the left, accidentally bumping a six-foot-high wooden fence. Seconds later, a ferocious-sounding dog charged against it with such force Jack wondered if it would hold. Whirling back into the light, he saw headlights coming straight for him!

He sprinted for the entrance, straining to hear the engine as the gravel crunched beneath his feet. Just as he made it out of the alley, the sage green Lincoln screeched to a stop. Jack couldn't make it back to the car, so he stood his ground and faced Lindsay, who then sped off with a screech of rubber, leaving him to deal the repercussions, which were already racing through his mind.

"Dang it! Dang it! Dang it!" Jack cursed as he turned around in a frustrated circle. There was no denying the anger in Lindsay's eyes. He definitely didn't like being followed. The cap and disguise might have protected his identity, but he couldn't use his Camry again. Disgusted with the entire situation, he climbed back into his car and shoved his keys into the ignition. "You've got to be kidding me." He rolled down the window and ripped a pink piece of paper from beneath his windshield. Fuming, he turned on his dome light and scanned the ticket.

"What fire hydrant?" He burst from the car and glanced around, certain there had been a mistake. It was there, though, half-covered by an overgrown bush. Clenching his jaw, he got back inside and dialed Teresa.

"Hello, Jack," she said.

He rolled his eyes. Why did she always answer when he'd rather leave a message? "I have some interesting news to report."

"Yes, I'm sure you do."

"I beg your pardon?" he said, hoping she'd say something to let him off the hook.

"Carry on, Jack. What have you got to tell me?"

Keeping his voice positive, he said, "I have some pictures of your husband embracing a woman he met at La Bells last night. Let's meet tomorrow to see if you recognize her."

A moment ticked by. "Two o'clock, my office. What else?"

He heaved a heavy sigh. "He spotted me. Your husband knows he's being followed."

"Yes, he does. He just called, and he's madder than a wet hen. It's rather funny, actually, but I didn't mean to hire an amateur. Perhaps tomorrow's meeting should be our last."

"He kissed her, though only on the cheek. When you see the pictures, I think you'll want me to continue my investigation." Her silence told him he'd hit home, but he wasn't proud of it.

"Don't be late," she said and hung up.

He struck the steering wheel. He couldn't afford to lose this case!

* * *

"I don't see why I have to go to bed so early," Alexa grumbled.

Christine sat on the edge of the bed watching her daughter take her slow, sweet time arranging her pillows. "Come on, Lexie, get settled. I need to say goodnight to Jon, too."

"I am settled," Alexa snapped as she slid beneath the sheets. "I don't need you to tuck me in."

Stung, Christine rose to her feet. "Fine, but you better watch your tone with me. You're getting dangerously close to getting grounded."

"Grounded from what? The only place you've let me go since Daddy died is school and Nanna's house. Go ahead; ground me. See if I care!"

"I don't appreciate your attitude, young lady. Say your prayers, and ask God to help us both be in a better mood tomorrow. Good night."

"If you prayed about your own attitude, maybe Daddy would still be here," Alexa shot back.

Christine gasped. "Why would you say such a horrible thing?"

Alexa flopped onto her side and faced the wall.

"Alexa, tell me why you said that?"

"Go say goodnight to Jon."

Not knowing what else to do, Christine left the room, but she paused outside the door. Before Daniel's death, she and Alexa had been very close—not that there weren't times when they butted heads, but this was different. She didn't know how to deal with her daughter's anger. She wished she could talk to Daniel. He had such wonderful insight when it came to her relationship with Alexa. She heaved a heavy sigh. How many ways would Daniel's death affect their family? It seemed endless.

She tapped on Jon's door and went inside. "Hey, son, are you already in bed?"

"Yes, Mama."

She crossed the room and sat beside him. "Did you say your prayers?"

"Nah. I'm not gonna pray anymore."

"Why not? I'm sure God likes it when you talk to Him."

A hopeful expression lit his youthful face, which shone angelically in the moonlight. "Do you think God could give Daddy a message for me?"

"I'm thinking He could, don't you?" she said as she softly stroked his cheek.

"Maybe, but I'm not talking to God anymore. Will you ask Him to tell Daddy he forgot to build my fort? I need to know what to do."

"Yes, I'll ask Him."

"Will you ask Him right now?"

"You know what, Jon? I'm not ready to talk to God yet, either. I'll let you know when I am, though. How's that?"

"Okay, Mama. Good night."

Christine stepped into the hallway and closed the door. She felt guilty for not handling either situation as well as Daniel would have done.

* * *

Jack was still brooding over the night's events when he got home. The house was dark, and he left it that way as he moved through the kitchen. He grabbed a beer out of the fridge and wandered into the den. He settled at his computer to do some research on Daniel's anesthesiologist, Dr. Ryan Solver. Two hours passed with little progress. Several magazine and newspaper articles detailed Solver's accomplishments, but he found nothing about his previous lawsuits, which made him wonder at the reliability of using the Internet for research. Perhaps he wasn't looking in the right places. He jotted a note to ask Cedric Johnson's junior attorney, Joshua Royce, where to look.

Next, he read several articles about the procedures for prosecuting a medical-malpractice case, which apparently was no easy task. In fact, the more he learned, the better he felt about signing the contract with Cedric Johnson. Since Cedric had sued Dr. Solver twice before, it seemed likely that the information he had gathered would help to strengthen their case. Having concluded his research, he checked his email. Afterward, he plopped into his recliner to catch the late-evening news, but he was having difficulty concentrating. He was irritated over getting caught following Alan Lindsay.

After half-listening to the daily ration of mayhem and murder, he went back to the computer to print out the pictures he had taken at La Bells the night before. Some of them had turned out surprisingly well, especially the close-up of Dr. Lindsay's attractive young date—*young* being the operative word. He shook his head. That Alan Lindsay would risk losing a beautiful, intelligent woman like Teresa over a fling with someone half his age was heartbreaking. He glanced through the other photos and stopped when he got to the ones of Elyse and her date. Her curvaceous silhouette was enough to get him thinking about dating her again, at least until he thought about the possibility of her sleeping with her date—another example of an older man seeking the companionship of a far younger female. He obviously had money, but he had to be at least twenty-five years older than she was and not in any way her type. *He* was her type.

Jack pushed on his belly. While there was a soft outer layer, the muscles beneath were hard and strong. He had inherited good genes, which made it easier for him to stay in shape than it was for most people, and Elyse loved his hair. She would wind his curls around her fingertips and say he had the most wonderful hair she'd ever seen. Not that he agreed, of course, but it was still nice to hear. He sighed. How could she be attracted to someone so much older than she was? "It has to be the money," he mumbled. If the guy drove a ten-year-old Camry, would she go out with him? He had his doubts.

After arranging the photographs and writing a brief summary for his meeting with Teresa the following afternoon, he turned the computer off and went to bed. As he lie thinking about Elyse, he made a mental note to start charging more for his work.

* * *

Teresa threw her wine glass, causing shards of crystal to rain upon the grey granite hearth in her living room. "You could've just told me."

"If you had suspicions, Teresa, you should've asked," Alan shot back with uncharacteristic venom. "But no, you had to hire some two-bit detective to follow me around like I'm some sleazy criminal. Damn right, I'm angry."

"Well, that makes two of us. If you think I'm going to stand quietly by while you break our marriage vows again, you've got another thing coming. You want me to ask? Fine, I'm asking. Who are you seeing?"

Alan rose from the sofa and paced some distance between them. "I'm not having an affair, Teresa."

"Yeah? Then who did you have dinner with last night?"

Alan's eyes shifted away. "It's not what you think."

Pain shot through Teresa's heart as she saw he couldn't deny it. "That's what you said about Claire, too. And for the record, *Alan*, I didn't believe you then, and I don't believe you now." The memory of his betrayal surged through her so powerfully she turned her back to keep him from seeing her face.

"I can't change what you believe," he said in a lower voice.

Summonsing the bravado that had gotten her through a multitude of difficult situations, she shot him a dazzling smile over her shoulder. "What did he do to get himself noticed, huh? You know, for future reference?"

"I don't want anyone but you. I never have."

She faced him, now, challenging him with the slightest elevation of her chin. "Then give her up."

Alan heaved a heavy sigh.

"I want a divorce," she said.

He squared his shoulders and looked her in the eye. "If you want to end our marriage, Teresa, you'll have to end it yourself." He stalked through the living room and out the front door.

She stared after him for a moment, her heart pounding with emotion. In a silent huff, she poured herself another glass of wine and went upstairs to move her things out of the master bedroom.

CHAPTER TWELVE

Morning dawned amidst overcast skies, but Jack's spirits had sufficiently recovered. He may have been caught spying, but he had gotten some pretty damning photographs for his trouble. Though it hadn't been true lately, he was generally a happy person. He tried to see each new day as an opportunity to improve his life, or so he was telling himself when he reached Christine's house, just after eight o'clock, and saw a red Mustang convertible parked in the driveway. He knew who owned it, and all his pleasant thoughts abruptly disappeared. Instead of going around to the back of the house, as he usually did, he rang the front bell. The most beautiful blonde *anybody* had ever seen opened the door and flashed her gorgeous amber-colored eyes in his direction.

"Well, if it isn't Dick Tracy," she said with a sneer on her cherry-colored lips.

"Crystal Washington. Aren't you all perky in your little tennis outfit? Please, tell me you are just leaving." He walked past her into the living room.

"Now, why would I be leaving, when I've only just arrived?" she said with her honey-sweet Southern drawl.

"It took you long enough to get here. Christine could have used your support days ago."

"I've been in Italy on a photo shoot; thank you very much. I didn't hear about Daniel until yesterday. I came right away."

"And was your current love interest in Italy with you?" he said as he poured himself a cup of coffee.

Crystal laughed. "Taking a lover to Italy is like taking sand to the beach. Romans don't bother themselves with silly notions like fidelity. Perhaps that's why I like it there so much."

"I sincerely doubt the Romans would appreciate your summation of their moral code. Does your lover *here* know that you're unfaithful?"

"She's more conventional than I am, so I don't mention it. We're playing tennis while you and Christine are out this morning. Would you like to meet her, Jack? I know how much you drool over things you can't have."

"No thanks. Where's Christine?"

"I'm here, Jack," Christine called from the top of the stairs. When she came into the kitchen, she glanced knowingly between them. "I see you've gotten reacquainted."

"Unfortunately," Crystal said, casting a dirty look in Jack's direction.

Jack sipped his coffee.

"I wish you two would play nicely together," Christine said as she grabbed a yogurt from the fridge and a spoon from the drawer.

"It's not likely," Crystal said. "Jack isn't one of my many adoring fans."

"Cheating is selfish and deceitful. That's all I'm saying."

"Well, since I know you're equally stubborn, I guess we'll go," Christine said. "Make yourself at home, Crystal. I'll be back in time for lunch."

"I shall," she said as she kissed Christine on the cheek. "Good-bye, Jack."

Jack felt silly for withholding a response, but he assured himself that he'd get over it.

When he opened the passenger-side door for Christine, several pieces of paper slid out onto the driveway. "Sorry. I forgot to clean my car out last night," he said as if this were the first time she'd seen his car like this. Basically, it was always like this. He closed his spy case and set it on the back seat.

Christine smiled and waited patiently. "How did it go last night? Did you get anything helpful?"

"Yeah, really helpful. I got caught."

"Oh, no! What happened?"

Having cleared the seat, he stepped out of the way. He went around the front of the car and climbed into the driver's seat. "How long is what's-her-name staying?"

"She's my cousin, Jack. She flew all the way from Italy just to see me. I can't ask her to leave."

He started the car. "The only reason I dislike Crystal is because of the way she treats people. I've seen how she operates. She doesn't care who she hurts as long as she gets what she wants."

"I know she comes off that way, but she has a soft side, too. Besides," Christine said, "Crystal makes me laugh. I need to laugh, Jack. I really do."

He took a long sideways look at her. "Yeah, ya do. For that one reason, I'll try to be nice. Okay?"

"Thanks, but don't let her run all over you, either. I'd hate to give her an unfair advantage in your little war."

They traveled together in amicable silence. When they arrived at Cedric's office, they were shown immediately to the conference room.

Jack gently elbowed Christine. "Isn't this room fantastic?"

Jannette Augustine, Cedric's assistant, returned with a coffee tray and assured them that Mr. Johnson would be joining them directly. Jack used the time to glance through the notes he'd taken the other day when he snapped pictures of the Solver-patient client files. He hadn't studied them in detail yet, but one thing was certain; Josh's assistant had wanted him to know that Cedric had sued Dr. Solver twice before. He wanted to know why.

A few minutes later, Cedric Johnson entered the conference room, followed by Joshua Royce. "Good morning Mrs. Steinberg, Mr. Kendall," he said, shaking their hands. He took his place at the head of the table.

"Jack, Mrs. Steinberg," Josh said as he also shook their hands. He sat on the opposite side of the table, to Cedric's right.

"Let's get straight to the point," Cedric said. "Time is of

the essence. Josh has begun gathering data and preparing correspondence. Though they're expecting it, it's time we let Solver's
insurance company know we're filing suit." He looked to Josh,
who then pulled the contract from a neatly arranged folder and
slid it across the table towards Jack.

Jack looked at Christine, but she was clearly leaving
the negotiations up to him. "You were confident we'd proceed,
weren't you?"

"Let's just say I felt sure you'd make the wise decision,"
Cedric said.

"The decision is not yet made. I have a few questions."

"Shoot."

"How many wrongful-death cases have you prosecuted
involving patients who have died under Dr. Solver's care?"

Cedric flashed inquisitive eyes towards Josh, who had
his gaze fixed on the table. "Why would you ask that?" he said,
glancing back to Jack.

Remembering his promise not to expose Josh's assistant,
he said, "I'm conducting my own investigation, remember?"

Cedric eyed him with what Jack interpreted as more
respect. "This case will be the third, and if I have anything to say
about it, it will be the last. What else have you learned?"

Christine glared at Jack. "Are you saying he's sued Daniel's
surgeon before?"

"Not his surgeon," Jack said, regretting that he'd failed to
update her on the facts. "His anesthesiologist."

"Mrs. Steinberg," Cedric said, "your husband died at the
hands of a physician who doesn't always perform at peak ability.
Believe me, when word of your husband's death gets out, what's
left of Ryan Solver's reputation will be ruined along with his practice. You can rest assured that your family will be the last to suffer
injustice at the hands of Ryan Solver."

"If he's killed two other people, why didn't anyone warn
us?" Christine said, her voice rising with her outrage.

"It's up to each patient to do his own research," Josh said.
"He's still licensed to practice medicine."

"That's unconscionable! How can he get away with that?"

Cedric shrugged. "Doctors are virtually immune, and juries are notoriously unpredictable. Solver settled the previous two cases out of court, without admitting guilt. Considering that this is his third wrongful-death suit, his insurance rates—if he can find insurance—should shoot so unreachably high he'll be forced to close his practice."

Christine glanced from Jack to Cedric. "I want that man in jail!"

"I understand how you feel, but the best we can hope for, here, beyond what I've described, is reasonable monetary compensation."

"Money won't replace my husband, Mr. Johnson. I want justice!"

"Christine . . ." Jack said.

Cedric stood and pressed all ten fingertips on the table. "Look, folks, though my motivations are different from yours, I am equally outraged. Since jail time is out of the question, we need to concentrate on what we can accomplish—namely, putting an end to Dr. Solver's medical practice, and getting some insurance money into your household." Cedric made eye contact with Jack, and then Christine. "Are you prepared to move forward?"

"Jack?" Christine said with pleading eyes.

His insides screamed that something wasn't right, but he hadn't had time yet to get to the bottom of it. She was waiting for him to make the decision. "Sign it, Christine."

The briefest smile touched Cedric's lips. "Josh will brief you on what to expect. We'll need a complete statement including names, numbers, dates, and appointments. There are forms to sign requesting medical records, the autopsy report, and other pieces of information. Work with Josh. I'll be in contact with you as needed." He extended his hand to Christine, which she reluctantly shook. "Mrs. Steinberg, thank you for the privilege of representing you."

Shaking Jack's hand, he said, "Keep me posted on how your investigation progresses."

Jack watched as he strode from the room, envious of his confidence—not to mention his Rolex.

"Jack, Mrs. Steinberg," Josh said, calling their attention back to the table. "Let's get the paperwork out of the way before we discuss our strategy."

* * *

Back in his office, Cedric poured himself a double Scotch. He didn't like surprises. Jack's knowledge of his involvement with the previous Solver cases made him extremely nervous. He wiped his brow with an initialed handkerchief and began pacing. They couldn't risk having anyone dig too deeply. He had worked far too hard to have his reputation ruined by a two-bit, amateur detective.

The intercom buzzed. "Josh would like to see you, sir. Is this a good time?"

Cedric slammed down the Scotch and settled at his desk. "Send him in."

A moment later, Josh breezed into the office with a triumphant smile. "They signed it. It seemed touch-and-go there for a minute, but like always, you reeled them in."

Cedric produced a fake smile. "Child's play. I was rather surprised, though, that Jack had uncovered our involvement in the Jackson and Hernandez cases. He doesn't seem exceptionally bright to me."

Josh dropped into a chair and brushed something from his suit pants. "I'm not sure I agree with your assessment."

"Oh? And why is that?"

"I don't know. He comes off a bit scattered, I guess, but I think there's more going on there than he lets on."

"Are you basing your opinion on anything in particular?"

"No, you're probably right. Maybe he's got good sources."

Cedric scratched his chin and decided that his initial impression was accurate. "Any news on the Butler case?"

Josh's face brightened. "The depositions are scheduled for early next week. I've been practicing."

Cedric reached for his glasses. "Good. Anything else?"

"Yeah. I was wondering why you didn't tell me the Steinberg case was another Solver death. I was surprised to learn that myself."

"It must have slipped my mind, but you didn't look surprised in the meeting. Maybe you're getting better at hiding your feelings than I thought."

"That's encouraging," Josh said.

Cedric opened a file and gave him an impatient look.

Taking the hint, Josh headed for the door. "About Jack Kendall," he said, turning back.

"Yes?"

"I just wondered if we shouldn't give him some footwork to do. You know, make him feel like he's helping."

"I'll give that some thought though it sounds like he's doing a good job of keeping himself busy."

"You know best," Josh said and closed the door behind him.

Cedric leaned back in his chair and considered how best to deal with the inconvenient Jack Kendall.

* * *

It had taken some doing, but by the time Jack pulled into the driveway behind Crystal's red Mustang, Christine seemed more settled about their decision to sign with Cedric.

"I'll just drop you off. I've got an appointment to prepare for anyway."

Christine opened the passenger-side door. "Who are you meeting?"

Jack wondered why he mentioned it. "My client."

Amusement colored her cheeks. "You mean the woman whose husband caught you following him last night?"

He had the presence of mind to realize she was teasing, but he gave her a dirty look anyway. "Yeah, that one. Now get in the house, or I'll take you with me."

She laughed. "Want to come by for dinner tonight? The

kids will be back from Mom's. I know they'd love to see you. Say, six thirty?"

Jack watched her flip the hair from her face as she got out of the car. "Sure," he said. "I'll bring Chinese."

"Cool. See you then."

He waited until she was inside the house before backing down the driveway. Hearing a thud, he glanced in the rear view mirror and saw that he'd tagged the neighbor's trash dumpster, which was sitting on the sidewalk. It teetered, but remained standing. He hit the gas and continued down the street. He wasn't concerned about the damage. There were, after all, some benefits to driving an old car.

* * *

Stacy jumped up from her desk and followed Josh into his office. "How did it go?"

"We got them to sign," Josh said. "You should've seen Cedric. They were hesitant, but he reeled them in—just like child's play."

"The future of the Steinberg family isn't child's play, Josh. It matters. The wellbeing of an entire family is at stake."

Josh reached for his calendar and began flipping through the pages. "Don't go off on that again. I'm quite aware of your feelings."

"Elizabeth is dropping by so you can take her to lunch at twelve thirty. She wants to go to Broad Street Bakery, which she just *knows* you love, so she can pick up a book at Lemuria. Other than that, you've set aside your entire afternoon to prepare for the Butler depositions."

He tossed his calendar onto the desk without checking for himself. "Since when are you and Elizabeth all buddy-buddy?"

"We aren't, and I'm not finished with our other conversation. What about justice, Josh? Isn't that the reason you got into law in the first place? Or has working for the great Cedric Johnson changed your focus?"

"Cedric signs your paycheck, Stacy. You would be wise to

show more respect."

"I get paid to do good work, not to kiss Cedric's butt. You do that well enough for both of us." The astonished look on Josh's face made her laugh.

"If you're not happy here . . ." he said.

"Oh, don't go getting your panties in a wad. I'm just askin'. Why can't you get that guy off the street?"

"You've been here long enough to know wrongful-death suits don't work like that. If we don't go to trial, we negotiate a settlement. The family gets compensated, we get compensated, and life goes on."

Stacy rolled her eyes. "I'm taking a long lunch. Do you need anything before I go?"

His gaze dropped to her chest, and he gave her a sly smile.

"Is sex and money all you think about?"

"You didn't seem to mind the other night. In fact, you rather seemed to enjoy my preoccupation."

"Yeah, well, that's because I was drinking wine and feeling frisky. Today, I have PMS and I'm annoyed. Don't worry, though. I'll get over it in a day or two—unless you say something else to piss me off."

When she reached the door, she threw a spiteful look over her shoulder. "Kiss Elizabeth for me."

* * *

Jack was dreading this meeting. It wasn't so much that he feared Teresa would fire him, he just hated for her to see him in a bad light. He'd never been caught spying before, and he wasn't sure how to overcome it, except by shifting the focus to the photographs. Hurting her in order to stay employed didn't sit well either. Suspecting your mate of cheating is one thing, seeing photographic evidence of it is quite another. Nevertheless, that was why she hired him. That was his job.

He pulled into the parking lot and parked in the shade of a row of Bradford pear trees, which were abloom with white flowers. Turning off the engine, he paused to watch a flurry of petals swirling in the wind. Unable to delay any longer, he stepped from the car, shook out his best sportcoat, and put it on. He took a deep breath as he looked up the glass face of one of the tallest buildings in the city. Teresa's office was in the penthouse suite. After checking his file to be sure he had everything together—a concept he had gleaned from observing Josh—he locked his car and headed for the lobby.

The elevator rose quickly and opened onto a beautiful hardwood foyer, which was on the inside of an elegant office suite, much like Cedric's, only larger. Straightening his shoulders, he approached the cherry wood reception desk and pretended to clear his throat. "I have a two o'clock appointment with Teresa Lindsay."

The elderly receptionist looked up at him through thick trifocals. "Do you have ID?"

He pulled out his business card and driver's license.

After checking them carefully, she handed them back. "Have a seat, Mr. Kendall."

About ten minutes later, Jack nearly jumped out of his skin when someone approached from behind and tapped him on the shoulder.

Realizing what he'd done, the young man rifled a glance towards the receptionist, but the woman was on the phone and hadn't witnessed his mistake. "Sorry about that, Mr. Kendall. I'm Michael Thompson. Mrs. Lindsay will see you now."

"What's with her?" Jack said, nodding towards the reception desk.

Michael's cheeks flushed with embarrassment. "That's *Mr.* Lindsay's aunt. She's worked here forever. They've suggested she retire but, well, she's still here."

"Ah," Jack said and followed him down the hallway to a private elevator.

The inside of the elevator was constructed entirely of cherry wood and adorned with beveled mirrors and a Venetian chandelier, the value of which easily exceeding everything Jack owned. He straightened his suddenly inadequate jacket and reminded himself to raise his professional rates. Though he generally thought well of himself, he wondered why a woman of this caliber had come to him in the first place. There were plenty of high-powered detectives. Why choose him? It was surprising that she hadn't taken one look at his office and canceled their appointment.

When they arrived on the executive floor, Jack felt his heart skip a beat as he glanced around. The décor was top-notch, even nicer than Cedric's office. It reminded him of something he'd see in a designer magazine—not that he looked at those. He followed Michael through a set of two-leaved doors and into the executive suite. "Nice digs," he muttered under his breath.

"Tell me about it," Michael said. "You should see the conference room, and wait till you meet Mia."

"Mia?"

Michael gave him a knowing smile and turned to take his leave. "Have an excellent day, Mr. Kendall."

A professionally dressed Asian woman with long black hair and dark almond eyes rose from behind an elegant reception desk and walked towards him.

Jack felt his face brighten.

"Welcome, Mr. Kendall," she said, extending her hand for him to shake. "I'm Mia. Teresa will be right with you. May I bring you something to drink? I just brewed a fresh pot of coffee."

"Coffee sounds great," he said, trying his best to appear confident and relaxed. He had never felt more out of place in his entire life.

"How do you like it?"

"Excuse me?"

"Your coffee?" she said politely, but Jack saw amusement on her lips.

He couldn't even imagine what it must be like to be this attractive to the opposite sex. "Sweet," he said, anticipating the opportunity to see the back of her fitted black skirt as she walked away.

"My pleasure," Mia said.

Jack's lopsided grin appeared as his eyes traveled the curves of her back and rested on her tiny waist where her hair bounced with each measured step. Mia was petite, graceful, and completely captivating. No wonder Michael was smitten.

The double doors to his right opened, and Teresa stepped forward wearing a tailored suit. Her loose blonde hair shone like summer wheat against her jacket of Carolina blue. She looked every bit as elegant as he remembered.

"Jack, thanks for coming by."

He smiled and shook her hand. "My pleasure, Mrs. Lindsay. This is quite a place you have here."

"Please, call me Teresa." She nodded towards the kitchen. "Lovely, isn't she?"

"I'll say," Jack said a bit too quickly.

Teresa laughed. "I recognized the look on your face when I came out. Mia affects men that way, but let me assure you, she's extremely competent at what she does. She has two MBA's to her credit."

"I'd expect nothing less," he said.

When Mia returned with his coffee, Teresa gracefully motioned for him to enter her office. "Thank you, Mia. Please, hold my calls."

"Of course," Mia said and closed the doors behind them.

The focal point of Teresa's office was an amazing salt-water aquarium, which captured Jack's attention the moment he stepped into the room. The tank, a living stream of color, ran the entire width of the twenty-foot-wide space. The solid cherry base formed the lower half of the structure, which was clearly designed to preserve the phenomenal view of the city that remained visible through the vaulted windows above it. Plants, photographs, shells, and other interesting items decorated the bookshelves on either end.

"Wow," Jack said. "This is incredible. I've never seen anything like it."

Teresa beamed. "It's a natural reef aquarium."

He pointed to an undulating formation with wafer-thin

spirals rising from a thick, royal blue base. "What is that?"

She joined him at the tank. "That's a stony coral known as a Chalice. There are several varieties." She pointed to a round blue coral, rimmed in dark green and dotted with bright orange spots. "That's my favorite. It's called the My Miami Chalice."

"It looks like a painted mushroom."

She smiled. "It does, doesn't it? This teal and burgundy section is made up of Acan colonies. The largest one has over two hundred heads. Those on the left are neon Candy Cane colonies."

Everywhere he looked, he saw animated-looking creatures. He was fascinated. "What are these orange and white striped fish?" he asked as two zoomed by.

"Clownfish. I like them because the females are larger than the males, who are responsible for guarding the young."

"Now why doesn't that surprise me?" he teased. "What about these cool yellow fish with pointed noses?"

"Those are Tangs. They're quite common, but I like them anyway." She pointed to the bottom of the tank, near a rocky ledge. "That little guy is an emerald crab."

"You'll probably laugh at me for saying this, but I feel richer for having seen this. I could stare at it for hours."

"Thank you. If you come again, I'll point out more of my favorite residents." She took her place behind her desk and invited him to sit in one of the leather armchairs in front of it. "Okay, Jack, tell me what happened last night."

"I'm not exactly sure," he said, noting the change in her tone. "After your husband left the hospital, he wound his way through an older neighborhood in the Fondren district and into a dark alleyway. I figured he was heading for a back entrance, so I parked my car and followed him in on foot. He obviously turned around somewhere because he came out the same way he went in."

"And?"

He cleared his throat. "We made eye contact. I was in disguise, so he won't recognize me, but I'll need to use a different vehicle in the future."

Teresa shrugged in a surprisingly human way. "It would've been nice to have had more time before he found out, but it doesn't matter. In a way, it's satisfying to know he'll be looking over his shoulder every time he turns around. Show me the pictures."

He saw her tense and clench her jaw. "You're sure?" he said.

Her eyes hardened. "Give me the pictures."

He opened the folder and pushed the photographs across the desk.

She studied each one carefully. "My God, Jack. She's so young."

He knew to remain silent. Seeing the object of a cheating spouse's affection was an extremely difficult moment.

Teresa closed her eyes for several seconds. When she opened them, she was strong and resolved. "Find out everything you can. I want to know who she is and where she works. It'll be more difficult now that they know they're being watched."

He heaved an inward sigh; he was still on the case! Taking a chance, he pulled out one of the pictures of Elyse and her date. "Do you recognize either of these people?"

"That's Dr. Winchester. I don't know him personally, but I've seen him at several parties around town. My husband says he's third-generation Harvard stock, well respected in the medical community. Why do you ask?"

Jack choked on his coffee. "Sorry," he gasped. "Went down wrong."

Teresa handed him a tissue and waited for him to stop coughing. "Were the four of them together?" she said.

"No. I just wondered if you might know them. What can you tell me about Winchester?"

"Not much, other than he works at Dixie Medical Center, and the woman he's with isn't his wife."

Jack looked down to hide his disappointment. Elyse was seeing a married man. He wouldn't have thought she'd do that.

"I'd ask Alan for you, but as you can imagine, we had quite a tiff last night."

"Do you know the woman?"

"It's common knowledge that Thad and Susan have their problems, but I wouldn't have expected this—especially not in public. Susan is a wonderful woman. She deserves better than this. I suppose it's horrible to take comfort in knowing I'm not the only one whose husband is an idiot."

"Rest assured, Teresa, the world is full of idiots."

She awarded him with a half-smile. "Actually, Alan is a good man. He's been a wonderful husband—except for this—and his affair with Claire," she added. "Which, of course, I could never prove."

Jack gave her time to compose herself.

"Okay, what's next?" she said.

"I get more creative and keep digging."

Teresa took a white envelope from a drawer and tossed it across the desk. "There's two thousand dollars in there. Come back with everything I need to nail his ass to the wall, and I'll give you five thousand more."

He smiled. That was well over the amount they had agreed upon. "I'll get to the bottom of this. You have my word on it."

She stared at the photo of Alan's mistress. "No matter what I say, no matter what I do, I can't compete with youth."

Jack tucked the envelope into his pocket and headed for the door. "For the record, Teresa, if your husband can't see what an amazing woman you are, he's an absolute fool."

"Finish this quickly. I want to be divorced by the end of summer."

* * *

"Stop! You can't go in there!" Jannette yelled as she pushed from her chair.

Doctor Ryan Solver slammed the door in her outraged face, locked it, and then turned a menacing glare on a surprised Cedric Johnson.

"Have you lost your mind?" Cedric said as he rose to his feet. The intercom buzzed repeatedly until Cedric pushed the button. "It's all right, Jannette. I'll take this meeting."

The distraught doctor's face was red with anger. "You're suing me again?"

Cedric stayed behind his desk, near his revolver. "This is highly inappropriate, and you know it."

"I'm a revolving target, and I demand to know why!"

"Perhaps your technique isn't what it once was."

"That's BS, and you know it. I've had a perfect record for thirty-five years and now, suddenly, I'm incompetent? I've lost three patients in two years, Johnson. Three. I stand to lose my entire practice!"

"What do you want from me?" Cedric said, moving his hand closer to the drawer.

Solver slammed his fist on Cedric's desk. "Tell me who I'm up against!"

"You aren't making things better for yourself. Get the hell out of my office before I call security."

"I've examined the records a thousand times, Cedric. I did nothing wrong. I don't know why those patients died, but I'm innocent."

"Of course, you are," Cedric said. "That's why you settled the previous cases out of court."

"I settled because I can't risk a guilty verdict."

"Well, since you can't risk a guilty verdict, I'll have the Steinberg papers drawn up by the end of the week. Anything else I can help you with?"

"Aren't you listening to me? I'm innocent! Or don't you care about that?"

"Then leave it to a jury."

Solver dropped into a chair like a defeated man. "And if I win, and *if* I can still afford it, I can find a new insurer and continue practicing medicine. Is that it?"

"If you're lucky."

"But you'll just prosecute me again, won't you?"

"If circumstances dictate." Cedric wondered if he'd been drinking. No other explanation seemed likely.

"Who's paying you to ruin my life?" Solver demanded, appearing mere moments from a breakdown.

In his early days, Cedric wouldn't have hesitated to deliver the final blow, but now, seeing Solver face to face, he could almost feel sorry for him—almost. "Your dead patient's widow, I expect, after you settle out of court again."

Solver nodded as if accepting a fatal diagnosis. "Okay, I fold. Name your price. What will it cost to get this monkey off my back?"

"I'll speak with my client immediately."

Solver pinned him with a resentful glare. "I'm not talking about the Steinberg case, although you can give me a number for that, too. I want this thing behind me, Cedric. Permanently. You get me?"

"Get out of my office. If you ever come back here, I'll file harassment charges." He pushed the intercom button. "Jannette, call security to escort Dr. Solver out of the building."

"Don't bother. I'll see myself out!" He threw the door open and charged out of Cedric's office with the same intensity with which he had arrived.

* * *

By the end of the day, Cedric was so deep in thought that Jannette startled him when she stepped into the doorway.

"I'm about to head out. Need anything before I go?"

"No thanks. Have a nice evening."

"You, too, sir."

Cedric waited a few more minutes before retrieving the key from the center drawer, which unlocked the bottom right-hand drawer. He took out the cigar box and set it on the desk. He stared at its contents for several seconds, wondering if he was making the right decision. The good news was he was representing the third Solver case. The bad news was Jack had known that. What else might he dig up? Ryan Solver's suspicions didn't help matters either. His accusations of conspiracy meant he was piecing things together. Might someone else do the same? To top it off, he wasn't in control of the situation, which wasn't easy to accept even under the best of circumstances. He never knew what was coming until after it was in motion.

He sighed and shook his head. Control was one issue; Jack Kendall was another. There was too much at risk to keep silent. Taking a silver note card from the box, he jotted a quick note.

There's a fox in the hen house.

Satisfied, he slid the note into a matching envelope and placed it on the top left corner of his desk. After locking the cigar box inside the bottom drawer, he returned the key to its place and dialed the messenger. After the beep, he entered their secret code and headed for home.

* * *

Once the elevator closed behind Cedric, Stacy emerged from the breakroom and made her way down the shadowy hallway to the executive suite. With one last glance over her shoulder, she slipped into Jannette's office. The entrance to Cedric's office was on the right. She felt for it along the wall and let herself inside. Cedric's office was also dark, as he habitually kept his blinds closed to avoid the afternoon sun.

"Hell Fire!" burst out before she could stop it.

She had banged her leg on the corner of Cedric's desk. Furrowing her brow, she rubbed the throbbing spot, knowing she'd have an ugly bruise there for her trouble. Reaching the credenza, she slid her fingers along the top of the cabinet until she located the lamp. Her heart raced wildly as light flooded the room. She quickly shuffled through the tidy stacks of paper on Cedric's desk. Finding nothing suspicious, she started with the credenza and worked her way back to the desk, checking drawers and compartments for anything that might substantiate her suspicions. She saw Cedric's revolver in the top right drawer, but she didn't touch it. There was nothing of interest in the middle drawer, but the bottom drawer was locked. She checked the pencil drawer for the key. Finding it lying in plain sight, she mumbled, "Men," and unlocked the bottom drawer. "Stationery? Why would he lock up stationery?" She locked it back inside the drawer and returned the key to its place.

Plopping down in Cedric's chair, which was considerably larger than Josh's chair, she flipped through his appointment calendar. Stumbling upon Jack and Christine's appointment, she took one of Cedric's business cards, copied down Jack's phone number, and stuffed it into her bra. She may not have found anything incriminating, but she knew that Cedric was up to something. She could feel it. Her mother always said she had the sixth sense, but it sure didn't seem to be working tonight.

She switched off the lamp. As she felt her way around the desk, she heard something fall to the floor. "Dang it!" She dropped to her knees and felt around for it, but she couldn't find anything. Returning to the lamp, she switched it on. A silver envelope lay beneath the desk, the same stationery as had she found locked away in the drawer. She picked it up and flipped it over. It was completely blank, which gave her an idea. Using the letter opener, she sliced the envelope and read the note.

"There's a fox in the hen house. What does that mean?"

Without thinking, she dropped the ruined envelope into the shredder, gasping as the motor shattered the silence. She switched off the light and stood trembling in the dark, praying no one heard it.

When no one came, she switched the lamp on once again and returned to Cedric's chair. Going through the same routine, she took a new envelope from the cigar box, sealed the note inside, and placed it on the corner of the desk where she thought the other one would've been. Thinking to remove the evidence, she opened the shredder. To her surprise, other silver scraps were visible through the layers. She had definitely hit upon something.

Extracting the most recent scraps, she wrapped them in a tissue and stuffed it into the other side of her bra. She couldn't wait to see Josh's face when she told him what she'd found. Turning out the light, she carefully felt her way out of Cedric's office and out to the hall. About halfway to the elevator, chill bumps rose on her skin. She spun around and stared into the shadows, her heart thumping wildly in her chest. She held her breath, listening for anything that would tell her she wasn't alone. Nothing moved, but she would swear someone was watching her. She jogged to the elevator, pushed the button, and stepped inside.

* * *

Anthony had just reached for Cedric's door when the shredder warned him of an intruder. Then, to his surprise, the ribbon of light beneath the threshold went dark. He had back-tracked into the breakroom to see who it was before deciding what to do. For all he knew, it could be Cedric, though Cedric never closed his door when signaling for pickup—unless he was leaving for the day.

A few minutes later, the office door had opened, and a woman stepped out into the hallway and hurried past him towards the elevator. He hadn't expected a woman. She stopped suddenly and looked back. He pressed against the wall, but he didn't think she saw him.

When the elevator doors opened, the light revealed her curvaceous shape and shoulder-length hair. She was young, probably in her mid-twenties. Once the elevator closed, he hurried into Cedric's office to retrieve the envelope. Relieved to find it undisturbed, he stuffed it into his pocket. Instead of taking the elevator, he turned left out of Cedric's office and opened the door to the stairwell. His boot steps echoed as he flew down the stairs, hoping to catch up with the young woman before she left the parking lot. He spotted her just as she climbed into a cherry-red Volkswagen Beetle.

Mounting his Harley, he followed her for eight or nine miles to a newer apartment complex. She stopped at the communal mail station where she quickly sorted through a stack of enve-lopes and tossed the junk mail into the trash. When she pulled away, Anthony checked the trash. Her name was Stacy Young, and she lived in apartment 3C. He cruised through the parking lot until he located her car, which sat beneath a carport across from building C. Satisfied, he headed home with the silver envelope and interesting news for his uncle.

When he pulled up to the gate on his uncle's property, a security company work van pulled out of the driveway. He thought it odd, but he blew it off. He was much more interested in hearing what Thad would say about the intruder in Cedric's office. When he approached the house, he saw his uncle standing beside the open garage. He parked in his designated spot, well away from Thad's expensive Jag.

"Mind if we go upstairs?" Thad said without bothering to greet him.

Anthony followed him up the stairs, but scowled when Thad turned the doorknob and walked inside; Anthony always locked his door. "Seems you've already been in," he said coldly.

"Upgrading security," Thad said as he made himself comfortable on the couch. "Learn anything useful?"

"And then some." He handed him the silver envelope and hung his jacket on the back of the door.

"What do you mean?"

Pleased to have the one-up for a change, Anthony sat on the opposite end of the couch and kicked his feet onto the coffee table. "I caught a girl snooping around in Cedric's office tonight."

"Did she see you?"

Anthony gave him a disgusted snort.

"Tell me everything."

He related the entire incident, including how he followed her home.

"Any idea who she is?" Thad pressed.

"Her name is Stacy Young. That's all I've got, so far."

"I'll have her particulars by tomorrow afternoon. She left empty handed, you say. Are you certain?"

"She carried nothing out to the car, not even a purse."

Thad rose and walked to the door. "Good work, Anthony. You'll be well compensated, of course. Seems you'll do credit to your lineage yet."

Anthony made a face behind his back and pushed the door

closed behind him. He went straight to the fridge and popped a beer. Draining it half way down, he wiped his mouth with the back of his hand and checked his watch. Trina wouldn't be off work for three more hours yet. He took a joint from the wooden box on the coffee table, lit it, and took a long, slow drag.

* * *

"Go to your room, Alexa. I'm sick of you talking to me like this," Christine said. "And take off that black nail polish. I mean it!"

"Or what? You'll wish me away like you did Daddy?" Alexa said.

Christine turned from the pile of laundry she was folding on the living room sofa. "I would never wish you or your daddy away. What would make you think such a horrible thing?"

Alexa's pout turned into a snarl. "I heard you fighting with Daddy before he had surgery. You said you were sick of him, too! I hate you!"

Christine stood stunned as Alexa stormed up the stairs and slammed her bedroom door. She recalled the morning of Daniel's surgery. She *had* been annoyed with him for leaving his clothes all over the bedroom floor, the bathroom counter, the dresser, and every other place except the laundry basket. They'd had spats over this often, but for the most part, she had long resigned herself to his messy habits. There wasn't any heat in their argument. In fact, they had kissed and made up quite nicely before he left the house that morning. That was the last time they made love, but she couldn't explain that to Alexa. How could she make her understand? How dare Daniel leave her to raise their children without him! She fell to her knees and cried.

* * *

Jack stood in line, looking over the menu for Chinese take-out. Unable to remember what the kids liked, he took out his cell phone and called Christine.

"Jack, I can't do dinner tonight," she said, sniffing back

tears. "Can we reschedule for tomorrow?"

Jack handed the menu back to the hostess and stepped out of line. "What happened?"

"It's Alexa. She heard us arguing the morning of Daniel's surgery. She blames me for his death. I can't do this, Jack. It's too hard!"

"I'm coming over," he said.

"Not tonight. I need to think this through. Can you come by tomorrow night instead?"

"Are you sure? I could just—"

"Not tonight, Jack. Tomorrow." She hung up.

He had to respect her wishes. He had no right to go charging to the rescue. He pushed through the ornate red doors and headed for his car. Since his night was now free, he decided to drive by the Lindsay residence, but then he remembered that his car was a problem. Happy to have an excuse to call, he dialed Christine again.

"What?" she said into the phone.

"Can I borrow Daniel's truck tonight? I want to check on my suspect, but he knows my car."

"Yes, of course. You know where the keys are. I'm going to bed, Jack. Good night." She hung up again.

The house was dark when he parked his Camry in Christine's driveway. He entered the garage through the side door and switched on the light. Alexa, dressed in solid black, was standing beside Daniel's Silver Toyota Tacoma dangling the keys in her hand. "Hey, what are you doing out here? Aren't you supposed to be in bed?"

"I'm going with you," she said, pulling the keys away when he reached for them.

"Oh, no you're not. Your mom would kill me."

"Like she did Daddy?" she said, her bottom lip rising to a pout.

"Okay, unlock the truck. I'll take you with me."

She smiled for the first time in weeks. "Really, Uncle Jack?"

"Yeah. Get in."

Alexa pressed the remote and climbed into the passenger side. "Who's the suspect?" she said, her melancholy melting in the face of adventure.

"A doctor. We want to see where he goes when he leaves the house at night." He looked over his shoulder as he backed down the driveway and onto the street.

"Why? Is he cheating?"

"What do you know about cheating?" he said, surprised by her question.

"It's on TV all the time. Men get tired of their wives and find somebody else to sleep with. Was Daddy cheating on Mama? Is that why they were fighting?"

That was it; Jack pulled over. "Listen to me, Lexie. Your parents loved each other way too much to ever do anything like that."

Alexa scrutinized him through her long lashes. "If cheating is a secret, how do you know?"

He stroked her soft cheek. "Because your daddy was absolutely crazy in love with your mama. He thought she was the most beautiful woman in the whole world, and he was very happy to have her. He told me that all the time."

"Promise?"

"Cross my heart. And you *know* how much he loved you and Jon, don't you?"

"Yes."

"Cheating hurts everybody, not just mommies and daddies. Your dad loved his family more than anything else in the world."

"Besides God, you mean," she said with a tinge of resentment.

"Yes, but because he loved God, he would never do anything to hurt any of you because that would hurt God also. See what I mean?"

"I never thought about it like that."

"I want to ask you something, Lexie. How do you think your mama is doing without your dad?"

She looked down. "She cries every night after Jon and I go to bed, and she's sad all the time. She thinks we don't know, but we do."

"She misses your dad?"

"A lot."

He gently lifted her chin. "Then why are you making it harder for her by blaming her for something you know she didn't do?"

Tears filled her eyes.

"Come here, sweetie. Unbuckle your seatbelt."

Jack wrapped his sobbing Godchild in his arms and let her cry. Tears fell from his eyes, too. He loved this little girl, and it broke his heart to see her hurting. As much as he wanted to make it better, he couldn't. Daniel was gone, and nothing could bring him back.

Alexa cried for a long while before she finally pulled away, sniffling, and wiping her face on her sleeve.

Jack opened the glove box and handed her some tissue. He waited quietly for her to collect herself.

After a minute or so, she said, "Okay. You can drive now."

He pulled back onto the road, but he glanced at her several times. She no longer looked upset, just quiet in her thoughts. When they pulled up to Lindsay's neighborhood, he punched in the gate code and waited for it to open. "Now we see if his car is home. They live in the house just after that black car," he said, pointing to the right. "We're looking for a green Lincoln."

Alexa craned her neck to look up the driveway as they drove by. "A light just came on inside the garage!"

"I'm going to turn around. Tell me if a car pulls out of that driveway."

She twisted in her seat to watch behind them.

Once he had turned around, Jack pulled to the curb and shut off the engine.

"What happens if he comes out?" Alexa said, her voice changing from sorrow to interest.

"We follow him." A few minutes later, Lindsay's Lincoln

turned left out of the driveway.

"Hurry, Uncle Jack, he's leaving."

"Good work. Now we've got to keep him in sight." He followed at a safe distance, hoping it would turn out to be a quick trip to the grocery store, but the doctor merged onto the freeway, heading south. "Oh, boy. Here we go. Was your mom up when you snuck out?"

"She was crying in her room. She'll never even know I'm gone."

"I hope you're right."

Several minutes later, Lindsay took the hospital exit.

To Jack's relief, the Lincoln pulled into the parking garage of Dixie Medical Center. "Guess we can go home now. He's just going to work."

"Rats! Can we check on somebody else?"

"Can't think of anyone, but I could drive through Baskin Robbins on the way home."

"Chocolate sundae!"

"Me, too."

After picking up their ice cream, they wound their way back to Christine's house. "What's with the black clothes?" he said, hoping the ice cream had bought him some license.

Alexa's tongue stretched out to lick chocolate ice cream from around her mouth. "I'm mourning."

"Aren't you doing it a bit too long?"

"I don't think so. Scarlet O'Hara wore black dresses for weeks."

"But that was in the olden days. People don't do that anymore."

"There are girls in my class who wear black all the time."

He wasn't sure what to say to that. "What colors make you happy?"

"Blue. Daddy said it matches my eyes."

"I know. Your daddy thought you had the prettiest eyes ever."

"That's because they look like Mama's." She bit her lip as

she dug chocolate clumps from the bottom of the cup.

"You're right about that. You look a lot like your mama." While they drove in silence for a few minutes, Jack thought of ways to get her to wear colors again. "Got a question for you. Do you think your daddy would want you to keep mourning, or do you think he would want you to be happy?"

Alexa stuffed the empty ice cream cup into the to-go bag and wiped her mouth with the last napkin. "He wouldn't want me to be sad, but I can't help it."

"I've heard that colors can make people happy. Do you think there's any truth to that?" She shrugged. "Wanna make a deal?" he said, knowing that Daniel had often made deals with the kids when he wanted them to do something.

"How much?"

"How much would it take to get you to stop wearing black for a whole week?"

"A week would cost you a lot," she said. "How about a day?"

"How much for a week?"

"Hmm. How about two movies—without Jon—and ice cream after each movie?"

"We can't leave Jon behind. He's sad, too."

"How about you make your own deal with Jon?"

He chuckled. "Okay. One whole week, starting tomorrow. Deal?"

"Deal." She held up her little finger, and they performed a pinky swear.

Jack had no sooner turned onto Daniel's street than a police car passed him with flashing lights, startling him. A few moments later, another drove by. "Uh-oh," he muttered.

Both police cars parked in Daniel's driveway. Christine stood on the porch gripping her stomach as she talked with two more officers.

Alexa's eyes shimmered with tears. "Will they take me away, Uncle Jack?"

"Not you, sweetie. Me, maybe. I knew this was a bad idea."

He pulled into the driveway. "Come on. Let's get out."

Christine saw Alexa and came running. "Thank God! Where have you been?"

"I, we..." Jack stammered, struggling to come up with a good explanation.

"I heard you and Uncle Jack talking on the phone," Alexa piped in. "So I climbed into the back of Daddy's truck, and I didn't tell Uncle Jack I was there until a little while ago. He said we had to come straight home, or you'd be worried. Right, Uncle Jack?" she said, turning an innocent face towards him.

"Right," he said, but he was shocked by her lie, and at the same time, grateful. He turned to Christine. "I should've called you as soon as I knew, but I thought you might be asleep. I didn't want to wake you." He glanced over at one of the officers. "Hey, Charlie."

Charlie, a hefty blue-eyed country boy with a boyish face and heavy fists, nodded in his direction. Jack and Charlie went way back, but their relationship, by its very nature, was uncomfortable at best. For all his innocent looks, Charlie was as tough as they come. Jack definitely wanted to stay on his good side.

Officers from the other police cars joined the group.

"Yes, you should've called me," Christine said as she pulled Alexa close. "You scared me half to death!" Still holding onto Alexa, she added, "I'm sorry to have troubled you, officers. Everything is fine now."

"Glad she's home safe, ma'am," Charlie said. "Good night, folks."

The three of them watched the police officers get back into their vehicles and drive away.

Alexa wiggled free. "Don't be mad, Mama. If you forgive us, I'll stop wearing black for a whole week."

Christine looked at her with surprise. "A whole week?"

"Yep. Goodnight," she said and escaped into the house.

"Good idea. I'm headed home, too," Jack said as he made a beeline for the car.

"Jack?"

He turned back.

"Did she tell me the truth?"

"Close enough. I'm sorry I didn't call you."

"Don't ever do that again. Okay?"

"Never. Sleep well. I'll call you tomorrow."

"Don't forget about dinner tomorrow night," she called after him a moment later.

Back inside his Camry, Jack was struck by the drastic difference between his car and Daniel's new truck. He was beginning to comprehend that his shabby living conditions were the direct result of his tendency to delay making decisions that would change his environment. Daniel had driven a ten-year-old Dodge before buying that truck, six months back. Daniel believed that people live the lives they do simply because that's the life they choose. While that philosophy didn't apply to everyone, there was clearly some truth to it. As Americans, we are free to decide where we live and what kind of work we do. We decide what type of housing we prefer, and what we do on our time off. That being true, he didn't have to drive his ten-year-old Camry. He had a choice. He could stop procrastinating. If he didn't start making some profound changes in his life, his time on Earth could end without him ever experiencing the lifestyle he wanted. Was it really that simple?

He decided to sleep on it.

* * *

Anthony revved his Harley the second Trina walked through the sliding glass doors of Union General Hospital. It was Thursday, her last day of work before starting her new position at Dixie Medical Center the following Monday morning—a rare three-day weekend.

Trina trotted towards him with a smile.

Anthony smiled back. If he had his way, they'd be in bed before midnight.

"Hey, handsome. Wanna take me home?" She threw her leg over the seat and snuggled up close.

"I'll take you anywhere you want," he said. "Let's go to your place."

"Can't. My roommate's parents are visiting. Let's go to your place instead."

His breath caught as her hands slid beneath his shirt and part way down his pants. "Okay, but we can't get caught."

"We seriously need to talk about your landlord," she snorted.

Anthony released the clutch as Trina's hands dipped lower into his jeans. Concentrate on the road, he told himself, concentrate on the road. By the time they approached the property gate, he was ready to take her then and there.

She swung herself off the bike and then clung to him for a desperate kiss. "Call me when the coast is clear."

He rolled down the winding driveway missing her warmth at his back. As fate would have it, Thad was standing at his study window when he entered the garage. Pretending he hadn't noticed, he climbed the stairs and went inside. His cell phone rang immediately.

"Got an assignment for you," Thad said.

"Good," Anthony replied. "I could use another payment about now."

"I've paid you a bloody fortune in that stuff. Better watch yourself, or you'll snort up your entire future."

"As if you'd care."

"You're such a bright boy."

"In case you haven't noticed, I'm a man, now," Anthony scoffed, tired of his uncle's disdain.

"You'll have an envelope in the morning. Make it your number one priority."

Thad hung up, so Anthony popped a cold one and turned on the lamp in the bedroom. He wanted his uncle to think he was going straight to bed, which he sincerely hoped he was. Fifteen minutes later, after verifying that Thad was back to pacing, he called Trina. "The coast is clear, but check the third-story window before you come up. My landlord's in his office."

"Yeah, I see him," she said. "I'm in the shadows beneath the stairs. See you in a minute."

Anthony took off his clothes, wrapped a towel around his waist, and dabbed some cheap cologne around his neck. He heard the front door squeak and then shut.

Trina walked into the bedroom already topless. "Come here, you," she said. They came together in a fierce kiss and fell onto the bed.

"I've thought about this all day," he said, his voice thick with desire. As he rolled on top of her, everything but Trina ceased to exist.

CHAPTER THIRTEEN

Stacy drummed her fingers impatiently on the desk. Josh was twenty minutes late, and she was having a hard time sitting still. She had thought a lot about the note she found in Cedric's office. It seemed to imply that someone *inside* was getting close to information Cedric didn't want them to have. She had no proof, but she thought it had to do with the Solver cases. The telephone rang, making her jump, but the receptionist at the front desk picked it up. She checked her e-mail again, but there was nothing new.

Each of the three Solver deaths had occurred with different surgeons. Dr. Solver appeared to be the only common link, except for the fact that Cedric had managed to secure representation for all three families, which had earned him a small fortune. She had to be missing something. Who was the mysterious messenger? She had checked Cedric's office first thing this morning. The silver envelope was gone. The messenger had to have picked it up sometime after she left. She shuddered. Thank goodness, he hadn't caught her snooping.

Josh finally strolled in, yawning as he walked by her desk.

"Morning, boss. You're late."

"Hum," Josh mumbled and laid his briefcase on his desk.

Stacy went to get him a cup of coffee. A few minutes later, she lingered at his doorway. "I brought you some coffee."

"Thanks."

"What's with you today? I can count on one hand the number of times you've been late. Are you sick or somethin'?"

"Hungover."

"That's a first. I didn't think you drank much." She handed him the mug and settled into her usual chair.

"I had an argument with Elizabeth."

She grimaced. She wanted to believe he'd leave Elizabeth to be with her, but Elizabeth's family was wealthy and traveled in social circles that would benefit his career. That was important to Josh. He was very ambitious.

"Sorry," he said, realizing his faux pas.

"Forget Elizabeth and listen to me. I'm definitely onto somethin'." She laid the tissue holding the silver confetti scraps on his desk. "I found this in Cedric's shredder last night. It matches the silver stationery he keeps locked in his bottom desk drawer."

"What were you doing in Cedric's office, let alone his desk drawer and shredder?"

"Ryan Solver came bustin' up into Cedric's office yesterday afternoon. Everyone heard them arguing."

"Where was I?"

"At the library preparing for the Butler depositions. Solver is convinced that someone has it out for him. I heard him ask Cedric how much it would cost to get the monkey off his back."

Josh frowned. "That could mean several things. What did Cedric say?"

"We couldn't hear everything, but Cedric didn't deny it. He wants to meet with Mrs. Steinberg to discuss an early settlement."

"That's interesting." He sipped his coffee and rubbed his temples. "But that doesn't explain what you were doing in Cedric's office. You're getting dangerously close to breaking the law, Stacy. I can't condone that. I am a lawyer, after all."

Her eyes gleamed with intrigue. "I also found a note Cedric left on the corner of his desk. It said, *'There's a fox in the hen house.'*"

"Now that sounds odd. Maybe you *are* onto something."

"Told you so."

"Don't do anything foolish. I want to give this some thought—once I can think clearly, that is," he added with a grimace.

"Well, don't think too long. If we're right about this, it's a big damn deal."

"That's a very big if."

Satisfied with his reaction, she emptied his out-box and returned to her desk.

* * *

Jack was in the middle of a steamy dream about Elyse when his cell phone rang. Though reluctant to let the dream go, he picked up the phone to stop it from making noise.

"Did I wake you?" Christine said.

"No," he lied, opening one eye to look at the clock. It was a quarter to eight.

"Good. I just wanted to remind you about dinner tonight."

"Dinner," he mumbled. "Six o'clock. Chinese."

"You got it. See you then."

A lazy smile spread across his face as he dropped the phone and attempted to settle back into the dream.

"Okay, Elyse. Where were we?" About thirty seconds later, his alarm clock went off. Elyse's face dissolved, and he was forced to acknowledge that his day had started, whether he liked it or not. Sometime during the night, before the dream about Elyse, he had decided to make an appointment to see Dr. Lindsay. Aware that romance often begins in the workplace, he thought there was a chance that the woman Lindsay was seeing worked for him directly. After pondering which ailment to fake—a difficult task because he was reliably healthy—he settled upon insomnia.

He rambled into the kitchen to zap a cup of yesterday's coffee in the microwave. While he waited for it to heat, he called Dr. Lindsay's office to make an appointment. Due to a last minute cancelation, they had an immediate opening. Though he wasn't happy about going so soon, he grabbed his coffee, got dressed, and headed out the door.

* * *

Two silver envelopes lay on the living room floor in front of Anthony's door. As he bent to pick them up, he saw a yellow sticky note attached to one of them. It read, *Open First.* Inside he found his new assignment.

> *Follow and report on Stacy Young. Deliver the second envelope tonight.*

Anthony dropped the first note into the shredder, which sat beneath the end table at the far end of the couch. Obviously, Thad was worried that Stacy might learn something he didn't want her to know. After drinking the rest of his coffee, he put on his leather jacket, grabbed the remaining silver envelope, and set out to find his new target—the curvaceous Stacy Young.

* * *

Halfway through the new patient paperwork, Jack noticed—first with appreciation, and then with concern—that all the patients around him were women. Taking in his environment, he saw the maternal magazines, photos of newborn babies, pamphlets on breastfeeding, and that several of the women present were pregnant. How had it escaped him that Dr. Lindsay was an obstetrician? He laid his clipboard down and bolted.

Determined to salvage the wasted morning, he pulled out his phone and called Cedric Johnson's office. He wanted to see if Josh had obtained an autopsy report so he could take a copy to Dr. Sassi. He knew Christine probably had one, but he couldn't bring himself to ask her for it.

"Law offices of Cedric K. Johnson," the receptionist said into the phone.

"Is Joshua Royce available?"

"One moment, please."

"Joshua Royce's office," a female said with a slight southern drawl.

"Is Josh in?"

"He's in a meeting. Can I help you?"

"Is this Stacy?"

"Yeah. Who's this?"

"Jack Kendall. Are you Josh's secretary?"

"No, I'm his *assistant*."

"Point taken. I was wondering if you might have lunch with me today. I feel like we should talk."

Silence.

He glanced at his phone to see if the call had dropped. "Stacy?"

"Yeah, I'm here. Give me a second, will ya?"

"Take your time."

Jack couldn't help smiling at the audacity with which she conducted herself. Few had the courage to speak up for themselves. Even fewer, the willingness to pay the consequences for having done so. He admired her spirit.

Several more seconds passed.

"How about Hal and Mal's at eleven thirty?" she said.

Of all the places she could pick, why did it have to be one of his and Daniel's favorite hangouts? "Perfect," he said. "See you at eleven thirty."

Irrespective of location, he was glad that she agreed.

* * *

After spotting Stacy's car in the parking lot outside the building that housed Cedric's law firm, Anthony enjoyed watching dozens of women wearing tight-fitting skirts and high-heeled shoes leaving in groups for lunch. Among them, though she walked by herself, was Stacy Young. Anthony followed as she drove the short distance to Hal and Mal's Pub.

* * *

Entering Hal and Mal's didn't bother Jack nearly as much as he thought it would. It was hard not to like the place, with its New Orleans, French Quarter ambiance and excellent Cajun and Southern-style food. He immediately spotted Stacy, who waved to him from a table near the wall. As he settled in, he was surprised to see how stressed she seemed, especially when she put on a pair of sunglasses and a baseball cap.

"Hiding out, are we?" he teased.

"I don't want to be seen with you."

"Thanks a lot," he said.

"Don't take it personal. You never know who's around."

"Are we avoiding someone in particular?"

"I've got suspicions. How much do you charge?"

Thinking she was about to hire him to track down an unfaithful boyfriend, he said, "I'm not taking any new cases right now. I'm trying to investigate Daniel Steinberg's death. I thought, maybe, you could help *me*."

"We're talking about the same case. You interested in what I got to say or not?"

Another smile twitched at his lips. "Lay it on me, sister."

* * *

Anthony, who had frequented Hal and Mal's Pub several times over the past weeks, ducked into the bar to place a to-go order for their famous chicken mozzarella sandwich. Knowing he'd be able to see the entire restaurant from the foyer, he went to see if Stacy was sitting alone.

He recognized Jack Kendall immediately. He was one of Daniel Steinberg's cronies—a private detective. He recalled overhearing the account of Jack and Daniel conducting surveillance, and how Daniel had dropped out of a tree in front of an old woman and her dog. He had thought it funny at the time. He wondered for the first time what his uncle was doing. If Jack Kendall was involved, did that mean things were getting out of hand, or were Jack and Stacy an item?

When the waitress handed him his to-go order, he went outside to wait for them to leave. Forget following Stacy Young; he was reassigning himself to Jack Kendall.

* * *

Stacy leaned forward. "There's this ganglord, biker dude that comes by Cedric's office at night to pick up and deliver silver envelopes. It's really weird because when Cedric's there, he leaves as soon as the envelope exchange takes place. Like, the only reason he stayed was to wait for this dude."

"And this makes you suspicious?" Jack said.

"Enough to sneak into Cedric's office and snoop around. He keeps silver stationery locked in his bottom desk drawer."

"And how do you know that?"

She lowered her sunglasses and raised a brow.

"Could this biker dude be a needy relative?"

"You sound just like Josh," she snorted.

"Josh knows about this?" he said with surprise.

"Yeah, but until I found the note in Cedric's office last night, he didn't take me seriously either. Now, he thinks I'm on to somethin'."

"What did the note say?"

"There's a fox in the hen house."

When a harried waitress stopped suddenly to take their order, Stacy nearly jumped out of her seat.

Jack considered her carefully. She hadn't seen the waitress coming, but still. Something had this girl spooked. "Any idea what the note means?"

"Whatever it is, it can't be good."

"I don't see why you're making that leap," Jack said. "How do you know it isn't some piece of information relating to a case?"

"Because, if it were a regular message, he would've had his assistant wait for it. It's not like Cedric to do anything for himself he doesn't have to do."

"What makes you think it has something to do with Daniel Steinberg's death?"

"It might not be about your friend, per se, but I think it has something to do with that piece-of-crap doctor, Ryan Solver."

"The anesthesiologist. So, that's why you gave me those files. I still don't see what this has to do with silver envelopes."

Stacy took off her glasses and met his gaze. "Think about it. Cedric's communicating with *somebody*." He must have looked doubtful, because she added, "Mama always said I have the sixth sense about things. When I feel like this, I'm usually right."

Jack didn't necessarily believe in that, but it certainly seemed that she had uncovered something nefarious. "How many times have you seen this . . . biker dude?"

The waitress delivered their drinks and hurried on.

"I only saw him once, but he's been there twice just this week. There's no telling how many times he came before that."

Though she was adamant, it seemed to him that she was connecting dots that didn't belong on the same page. "Okay, if Cedric is messaging someone, then presumably, the messenger should return with a reply. Right?"

Her eyes brightened. "Maybe even tonight."

"You're not thinking of approaching the guy, are you?"

"Not in this lifetime," she snickered. "But I am hoping to get a look at the note he delivers. Unless, of course, they exchange in person. Sometimes Cedric waits for him; sometimes he doesn't."

Lunch arrived.

"How can I help?" he said before taking a bite of his heavenly-smelling, double-decker sandwich.

She made a face. "You're the detective. I thought you'd know."

He chuckled. "Maybe I should start by researching the Solver files."

"Now, you're talking. I'll make copies and get them to you in the next day or two, but you can't tell anyone. I can't afford to lose my job over this."

"Yet it certainly seems that you're willing to risk it. Why is that?"

"Mrs. Steinberg has two kids. I lost my daddy because of a lousy doctor like Ryan Solver. Only, Mama couldn't afford a real attorney, so we lost our case. We lost our house, our car, and everything else we owned, too. Mama hung herself a few months later."

"I'm sorry to hear about your parents, Stacy. Mine are gone, too. Tends to make you feel alone in the world, doesn't it?"

She wiped a tear before it could fall. "I am alone in the

world."

He laid his hand on the table for her to take. "Not completely. Friends?"

She stared at his hand for a few seconds and then laid her hand in his. "Does this mean you won't charge me?"

He chuckled again. "Researching those files will help my investigation. Let's start with that, shall we? My dime."

"That's cool. I'll call you when the copies are ready. I'm hoping to copy them tonight." She wrapped her sandwich in a napkin and left him to finish lunch by himself.

* * *

Jack left Hal and Mal's several minutes after Stacy. When he climbed into his Camry, Anthony scoffed. Private detective work must not pay much. Having long since finished his sandwich, he put on his sunshades, tied a blue bandanna over his head, and kicked his bike into gear. An hour later, Jack turned into his third new car dealership. He had test-driven three Toyota pickup trucks at the last place, so when he got behind the wheel of a black Dodge Ram, Anthony figured he had some time to kill. Using his cell phone, he looked up Jack's address. Once he found it, he decided to pay a house call.

Jack's neighborhood was of a higher caliber than his car, Anthony decided as he glanced around to see if any of his neighbors were outside. Believing himself to be unobserved, he walked around the side of Jack's house and approached the gate. It wasn't locked, but neither would it open. He leaned a powerful shoulder into it, but it still wouldn't open. "Piece-of-crap gate." He took a few steps back and rammed his entire body against it, wincing as it fell flat on the ground. "Great. Nothing like announcing that someone's been in your backyard."

After glancing over his shoulder, he walked on top of the gate and around to the back porch. The kitchen door, which was constructed half of glass and half with wood, was locked, but the sliding glass doors along the patio were open. After a cursory look around, he headed for the back part of the house. Finding nothing of interest, he worked his way back to the kitchen, which—like the rest of the house—was a complete disaster. His nose twitched at the stench of rotting food wafting from the trash can. Dishes towered in the sink, and mail and miscellaneous junk buried the counters. Passing through the informal dining room, he entered the den and scoffed at the disorganized jumble. Having spent several years homeless, he appreciated having a roof over his head and was motivated to keep it clean. Jack, apparently, didn't share that appreciation.

After rifling through multiple piles of paperwork, he picked up a photograph of an attractive young woman embracing an older man in front of La Bells restaurant. He glanced through the file beneath it and realized they were subjects of an extramarital affair. He flipped through the additional photos and was surprised to find one of his uncle laughing with a beautiful woman. He laid the picture on the copier and pushed the button. His uncle would definitely want to know that Jack had *this*.

Beneath another folder, he found one of Jack's business cards. Though it was badly coffee-stained, he stuffed it and the copy of the photograph into his pocket. Next, he uncovered a file on Daniel Steinberg. He quickly scanned the notes, but there was nothing in it to suggest that Jack had any suspicions about Cedric, or more specifically, about his uncle. He searched the desk drawers but found nothing relevant.

Entering the kitchen for a second time, he opened the fridge, which was basically empty except for a six-pack of beer. Grabbing a bottle of beer, he exited through the kitchen door, leaving it unlocked behind him.

* * *

After meeting Stacy for lunch, Jack had exhausted the rest of his afternoon test-driving new trucks. It was a toss-up between a silver Tacoma like Daniel's and a black Dodge Ram. It was exciting to think about actually owning one. He felt like a teenager anticipating his first set of wheels.

Realizing he'd passed one of his favorite watering holes,

he made an impromptu U-turn and pulled into the parking lot of O'Malley's Tavern. Like usual, the bar was packed. Classic ACDC rocked through the sound gear and out the speakers. Just like home, he thought with a smile. He allowed his shoulders to relax for the first time in days and waved down the waitress to order a draft. Happy to see an available pool table, he picked up a cue stick and gauged its condition with a frown. After checking the others, he chose the best available and began taking random shots. He'd spent the better part of his college weekends in pubs like this, earning most of his rent money. After sinking the eight ball, he set up his second rack. A solid, as well as a stripe, fell on the break.

"I'll take solids," a deep voice said.

He turned to see a strapping young man, wearing a cool leather jacket, approach the table. "Why not? Maybe I'll teach you a trick or two." He gestured towards the table. "After you." The kid sank two in a row. Jack chuckled to himself. He had learned long ago not to judge people by their age; this was the reason. "Nice shooting," he said.

After motioning for a beer, the kid turned towards Jack and said, "Thanks."

Jack extended his hand. "I'm Jack."

"Well, Jack," the kid said as he shook his hand, "let's see what you can make out of that mess."

Jack assessed the table; all of his options were bad. He finally tried a sharp left angle into the center pocket. "In there," he said, pumping his fist as the eleven ball dropped, but he missed his next shot.

In the time it took for *Junior*—as Jack dubbed him—to sink his next two balls, Jack had pretty well sized him up: worn leather boots, blue jeans, flat wallet, tight T-shirt—the kind guys wore to impress girls—and dark sunshades perched on top of his closely-shaven head. He wasn't the preppie type, but not a redneck either. He was like a street kid with manners. Jack casually felt for his wallet.

"So, Jack, what do you do when you aren't teaching pool?"

Junior said with unexpected humor.

"I solve mysteries, mostly, and chase women." It was his turn. He sank the ten ball but missed the twelve on a tough bank shot. "You?"

"Motorcycles and women."

Jack hoisted his beer. "To women." He took a big drink while Junior sank a powerful bank shot in the right corner pocket, but in doing so, he nudged one of Jack's balls, which parked itself right behind the eight. Junior attempted his last shot but missed. He smiled and hoisted his beer. "To women."

Jack watched him for a moment and tilted his head. "Have we met before?"

"Don't think so."

Jack's thirteen ball rolled to the edge of the center pocket, but it didn't fall.

Junior leaned in and sank his last ball.

Scratching his chin, Jack said, "Seriously, I think I know you from somewhere. What's your name?"

"What's it matter?"

"Just askin'," Jack said.

He murdered the eight ball and then laid his cue stick on the table. "My name's Anthony. See you around, Jack."

"Anytime," Jack muttered as Anthony strutted for the door. Making a face, he picked up Anthony's cue stick and dropped it into the rack.

* * *

Stacy ducked into the copy room just minutes before the daily exodus of firm employees. She kept her eyes on the door and drummed her nails on the counter as pages zoomed through the state-of-the-art copy equipment and emerged into two perfect stacks.

A good while later, she stuffed the copies into her backpack and set it on the floor. Next, she gathered the original files and opened the copy room door. The hallway was quiet, and all the offices on this side of the building were dark. Josh's office, which was two doors down from the copy room, was also dark. After returning the original files to the corner of Josh's desk—where they'd been for the past few weeks—she returned to the copy room for her backpack. Rather than strapping it on, she shoved it beneath her desk to grab on the way out. It was almost seven-thirty. If tonight were typical, the messenger should've come and gone by now. Feeling delightfully stealth-like, she crept past the reception area, made the ninety-degree turn, and continued towards Cedric's office. Jannette's door was closed, which meant that Cedric had gone home for the day. She pressed a hand to her stomach and slipped inside.

* * *

No longer in the mood for pool, Jack paid his tab and headed for the door.

"Hey, Jack!" someone called from across the room.

He turned to see one of his college buddies, Kevin Thomas, waving to him from a table near the window. And Kevin wasn't alone. Had he gotten a divorce?

"What are you drinking?" Kevin said as he reached for a chair from an adjacent table.

"Whatever's on draft. How are you doing, Kevin? It's been forever since I've seen you." They grasped hands in a street-style handshake that ended in a hug.

Kevin, a good looking, solidly built black man, grinned. "I'm still bustin' the bad guys. Made Captain last year, remember?"

"Don't remind me," Jack teased. "I still get a headache every time I think about that party. And who's this?" he said, turning a smile on Kevin's attractive companion. "Hello. I'm Jack."

Deep dimples emerged beside her full and pretty mouth. "So I gathered. I'm Suzaun."

"Suzaun is my cousin," Kevin said, making Jack's day. "We were just catchin' up on some family gossip. You'd be amazed at what goes on in our family."

"You've always got interesting stories. I'll give you that," Jack said. He and Kevin had made some interesting stories of their own, but, thankfully, Kevin didn't mention that in front of Suzaun.

"Check this out," Kevin said. "Remember when Auntie Doris freaked out because my cousin Robert and his boyfriend said their vows last summer?"

"Yeah…" Jack said, immediately uncomfortable.

"Now they want to adopt a baby, but Auntie Doris ain't havin' none of it. She's threatening to bounce Robert completely out of her will if they adopt, and he's her only child."

"I see," Jack said.

"Well, what do you think?" Kevin pressed. "Do you think two men should be allowed to adopt a child?"

Jack glanced at Suzaun, but her expression made it clear that she wasn't getting in on this one. Clearing his throat, he said, "What do you think, Kevin?"

Kevin took off on a diatribe about how people are entirely too preoccupied with other people's business.

Suzaun leaned forward, her dimples flashing with her smile. "Good luck stopping him now."

Suzaun's cleavage was difficult to ignore, but Jack forced himself to focus on her face. "Yeah, I've heard him do this once or twice," he said under his breath. As he listened to Kevin, he exchanged glances with Suzaun and wondered if there might be interest. Her long black hair was coarse but flowing, and her skin was the prettiest shade of mocha he'd ever seen. He thought her beautiful, and he wanted to make her smile. Her dimples were adorable.

A few minutes later, Kevin had exhausted his topic and his beer. "Y'all order another round. I'll be right back."

"Sure thing, Kev." Turning to Suzaun, he said, "Think we should cut him off?"

"You and whose army?"

Jack chuckled and signaled the waitress for another round. "Are you visiting?"

"I've lived here since I was two."

"You're kidding me? You've lived in Mississippi all this

time, and we've never met?"

"I doubt we run in the same circles."

"Perhaps we should rectify that." He gave her his lopsided smile, the one that usually charmed the ladies.

* * *

Stacy crept forward in the dark, her heart pounding with excitement. She hadn't told Josh about her plans tonight because she knew he wouldn't approve. Though she was nervous, she wasn't afraid. Whatever Cedric was doing, she knew him well enough to know it didn't involve violence. Insurance fraud, maybe, but not violence. She reached out for his desk. Despite being careful, several papers rustled to the floor.

"Hell fire! Not this again." She found the credenza and turned on the lamp. Scowling at the papers, she dropped to the floor to gather them up.

"If you're searching for trouble, you've found it," a deep voice said from the doorway.

Stacy gasped as she pushed Cedric's chair back and crawled under the desk. Because of the privacy panel, she couldn't see anything until two black boots stepped forward. Her heart was thumping so wildly that she thought she might faint. She remembered Cedric's gun but was afraid to take her eyes off the boots. "I didn't find anything. I swear it!"

"Seeing as you're innocent and all, I'll make you a deal. It's my only offer, so listen up. You've got until midnight tonight to pack your trash and get out of town. *If* you do as I say, Miss Stacy Young, age twenty-six, living at 112 Forest Maple Drive, unit 3C, I'll forget about this little spying incident." He took two steps closer to the desk. "Wanna see what happens if you fail to keep your end of the deal?"

"No! I'll do whatever you say," Stacy said, her eyes locked on the boots.

"You'd better. Otherwise . . ."

A switchblade snapped open in front of the boots, sending her recoiling so fast she caught her temple on the side of the desk.

"Ouch!" she said automatically, though she was far too scared to feel any pain. She watched in horror as the messenger cut a shallow line across the palm of his hand, raising a trail of blood.

"Do we have a deal?" he said.

"Yes! I'll leave town tonight. I swear it!"

The injured hand gripped itself into a fist and squeezed until blood appeared at either side, and then his other hand wrapped a blue bandanna around it. "I was hoping you'd be reasonable. Now take out your cell phone and leave a message for Cedric Johnson. Tell him a family member has taken deathly ill, and you're leaving town immediately. Tell him you won't be back." He banged on the desk. "Do it now!"

"Okay!" she shrieked. Her hands were trembling so badly that she had trouble punching the numbers. The office was so quit, they could hear the office phone ringing in the lobby. Once she reached the proper extension, she cleared her throat, took a deep breath, and waited for the beep. "Mr. Johnson, this is Stacy Young. I just got a call from Montana. My Mama's had a stroke, and I'm leaving tonight to be with her. Sorry for the short notice, but I quit. I'm sure you'll replace me soon." She snapped it shut and wiped tears from her eyes.

"You're a good liar, Stacy girl. Now pass your cell phone under the desk." She rolled it towards the boots. "Good. Now I have a list of those nearest and dearest, don't I? If I find that you've called anyone other than Cedric Johnson, you're dead by morning. If you tell a soul about this—"

"I won't. I won't! I'm leavin' town, just like you said."

"You're lucky you didn't see my face. Otherwise, you'd be dead already."

"All I saw was your boots! And your knife!"

He scoffed. "That's more than Cedric's ever seen. Now keep your head down, or you'll find out real quick what I can do with this knife."

The boots retreated.

Stacy kept her eyes glued to the floor for several minutes. When she finally crawled out from beneath Cedric's desk, her legs were so shaky she had to grasp the credenza for support. So much for Cedric and nonviolence!

* * *

Jack stole an appreciative glance down Suzaun's blouse as she averted her attention to speak to the waiter.

"So," Kevin said to Jack when he returned, "have you decided on the issue of gay couples and children?"

Jack grinned. "After hearing everything you said about people being entirely too preoccupied with other people's business, it is my firm opinion that since my thoughts on the matter will have no bearing on what your aunt decides to do with her will or her money, I am staying out of your family affairs."

Suzaun laughed. "You catch on quickly."

Kevin settled into his chair and reached for his beer. "You always were smarter than you look."

"I ought to be. You trained me."

"You're a cop?" Suzaun said, looking surprised.

"No, but he was," Kevin said. "A damn good one, too."

"That was a long time ago," Jack said. "Now I'm just a private detective."

"Really? What kinds of cases do you work on?" Suzaun said.

Jack tugged at the collar of his shirt. "Most of my clients come to me seeking proof of marital infidelity."

"I see," Suzaun said. "In other words, you provide them with the information they need to make important decisions about their lives."

Jack, who hadn't realized he was focusing on the table, looked into her eyes—the most amazing eyes he'd ever seen. They reminded him of shimmering amethyst. What she said was true, but in his mind, he had disappointed his father's memory by quitting the police force. He used to say it kept him humble, but in truth, that kind of thinking had held him back. He was beginning to see that. "Thanks, Suzaun."

"You're welcome."

"Come on, now. We've got gossip to catch up on." Their small talk continued until the alarm on Kevin's cell phone beeped a few minutes later. "Sorry to leave you, Suz, but Al Fannin is hosting poker at his place tonight. I said I'd drop by." He elbowed Jack in the side as he put on his jacket. "See that she gets home safely, Jack. And I do mean safely."

"Smarter than I look, remember?"

They shook hands again.

"Watch out, Suz. He's a true ladies man."

"I'll be calling you, Kev. I'm working on an important case, and I could really use your help," Jack said.

"You know where to find me. I'm at the office more often than I'm home."

The cousins hugged each other, and Kevin tossed a fifty on the table. "See ya."

"Hey, what about your change?" Jack said.

"You don't go to a poker game plannin' to lose, do ya? Give it to Suzaun."

When Jack sat back down, he realized that Suzaun was studying him, so he pretended to study her in return.

"What?" she said.

"I was just thinking that you look nothing like your brawny cousin."

"Our fathers are half-brothers. I have twelve cousins, but Kevin and I are the closest."

As the evening wore on, they ventured only fleetingly into the realm of questions Jack really wanted to explore. Suzaun remained somewhat guarded, which only increased his interest, yet she was vivacious in a way few women managed with sincerity.

It was still early when they left O'Malley's. As they approached Suzaun's car, he said, "Could I interest you in dinner? There's a great Asian place up ahead."

"Sure. Why not?"

Suzaun snuggled close as they walked towards a complex of shops and restaurants, seeking his warmth in the face of a cold and gusty breeze. "You said you are working on an important case. Care to share?" she said, sweeping her long black hair out of her face.

Jack thought of Daniel and looked away. "I'm investigating my best friend's death."

"Oh, I'm sorry to hear that."

"Thanks. Me, too."

After a casual dinner, he walked her back to her car for the second time that evening. "I'd like to see you again," he said, realizing it had been ages since he had asked anyone out.

She smiled. "You don't know anything about me. I'll bet I'm nothing like you imagine."

He tilted his head. "Is that a yes?"

Dimples flashed, and she laughed. "It's a maybe. It's a definite maybe." She pulled a business card from her purse and pressed it into his hand. "Thanks for a fun evening. I haven't laughed this much in a long time."

Jack debated the wisdom of attempting a kiss but decided against it. Women seemed to like it better when men were patient. "You're welcome," he said. "I'll call you soon."

His breath caught at the sight of a long, shapely leg through the slit in her blue jean skirt as she slipped into the driver's seat of her red Mustang convertible. After she had driven away, Crystal Washington came to mind. Did all gorgeous women drive little red sports cars? It certainly seemed like it. He headed for his car, which reminded him that he was in no position to ask anyone out on a date. How would Suzaun feel about riding around in his ten-year-old Camry when she had a shiny new sports car of her own to drive? On the way home, he thought about the new pickup trucks he'd driven that afternoon. As much as he might want to, he knew he couldn't afford a new truck right now. He could barely make his mortgage payments. Even if he raised his rates, he rarely had more than one client at a time. He exhaled in frustration. Making changes was a lot harder than simply talking about it. That was for sure.

When he got home, he dropped his keys on the counter

and hit the *play* button on his answering machine, half-hoping Suzaun had called to leave him a message.

Beep. "Hey Jack, it's Christine. Where are you?"

He groaned as his stomach clenched into knots. "I knew there was someplace else I was supposed to be." He checked his watch; it was half-past ten. He closed his eyes and shook his head. How could he explain to Daniel's new widow that he had gotten hot on some babe and had forgotten about dinner? The euphoria of the evening drained away. How could he have forgotten Daniel's family?

* * *

The slightest sounds echoed off taut nerves as Stacy threw her clothes into the trunk of her car, trip after trip, an armful at a time. Towels, sheets, makeup, shoes—everything she owned—she stuffed into garbage bags and in to every nook and cranny of her extremely small car.

* * *

From a distance, Anthony watched Stacy pack her car. There was no question that she had taken his threats seriously. He glanced at his watch and chuckled. It was a quarter to midnight.

His pocket vibrated as someone named Josh left yet another message on her cell phone. Moments later, a light blue BMW sped into the parking lot and parked a few spaces from Stacy's car. When a preppy-looking young man emerged and jogged towards Stacy's door, Anthony stiffened and felt for his knife. He suspected that whoever Josh was, he had just arrived. Following behind him, Anthony positioned himself close to Stacy's apartment where he could hear their conversation through the open door. One wrong word from Stacy and it would be her last.

* * *

Still in shock, Stacy took one last look around her apartment and wondered where she should go. She didn't have a mother in Montana. In fact, since her mother's death, she didn't have anyone—except Josh. As if summonsed, Josh appeared in the open doorway.

"Why haven't you answered your phone? I've been trying to reach you all evening."

Stacy shrieked and then dissolved into tears.

Josh glanced around the apartment. "Where's your stuff?"

Stacy looked at her watch; it was eleven forty-five. "Listen, Josh, Mama's had a stroke. I'm moving to Montana to be with her."

"You were going to leave without telling me goodbye?"

"I'm telling you now, so hug me bye cuz I gotta go."

Josh gripped her by the shoulders and forced her to look at him. "What's going on, Stacy?"

Stacy felt the minutes of her life ticking away like sand in an hourglass. Afraid that the messenger might walk in on them at any moment, she twisted free and headed for the door. "I already told you. It's over between us; marry Elizabeth. She seems like a real nice girl."

"But this is so sudden," he said, raking a hand through his hair.

"Yeah, well, strokes are like that." She guided him out the door, but her hands were shaking so badly she couldn't get the key into the deadbolt.

Josh took the keys and locked the door. "You're coming back, aren't you?"

She grabbed the keys out of his hand. "No. Are you gonna hug me bye, or not?"

Josh pulled her into his arms, but she remained rigid and pulled back quickly.

"You've got me worried, Stace. Are you sure you're all right?"

She didn't have time to deal with Josh and his feelings! "I'll be fine, but Mama needs me." Turning away, she ran to her jam-packed car and climbed in.

Florida, she told herself. She'd settle somewhere in Florida.

* * *

Anthony took note of Josh's license plate before revving up his Harley, running it through his mind repeatedly until he was sure he wouldn't forget it. He stayed close behind Stacy as she merged onto the freeway heading south. Depending on which freeway she took at the interchange, he'd have a pretty good idea of her destination. He chuckled as he recalled the dazed look on Josh's face when Stacy pulled away and ran to her car. Men were such dolts when it came to women.

A sudden thought came to him. If Josh was Stacy's boyfriend, what did that make Jack? Was Stacy seeing both men, or were she and Jack working together? Why had Jack taken a picture of his uncle? How much did he know? How much did Stacy know? Considering what he had just witnessed, it seemed clear that Josh was the boyfriend. That being the case, he was beginning to see why Jack was a threat.

Fifteen minutes later, when Stacy headed south towards New Orleans, Anthony took the next exit and circled back. Because of Stacy, he hadn't delivered his uncle's message for Cedric, and he wasn't returning home without doing so. While waiting for a traffic light, he unwrapped his injured hand. The slash was a good three inches long. He squeezed it into a fist and chuckled. Girls were so damn easy to scare.

* * *

Anthony had no sooner placed the silver envelope on the corner of Cedric's desk than his cell phone rang. Seeing that it was Trina, he turned left out of Cedric's office and took the stairwell exit, his youthful legs descending the stairs at a trot.

"Hey, baby girl, what's up?"

"I'm up," she said into the phone. "My roommate's gone for the weekend. Wanna tuck me in?"

"Hell, yeah. I'll be right over." When he hit the bottom of the stairs, he remembered that he had important information for his uncle. It was a short debate. Trina was the one thing in his life that made him happy. As far as he was concerned, she came first. He thought about that and smiled.

CHAPTER FOURTEEN

Slamming doors woke Stacy, who had spent a fitful night sleeping in her car. Stiff, cramped muscles made themselves known as she sat up and looked around. A young black couple, who had parked next to her, entered a Victorian style building, which served as a welcome station for visitors entering the State of Louisiana. She got out of her car, stretched her legs, and then followed them into the building. While they talked with the attendant, she made a beeline for the ladies room. As she washed her hands, she looked into the mirror and wondered what would happen now that she had been banished from Jackson. She tried to smooth her hair, but her bangs refused to cooperate. Giving up, she rinsed her mouth and called it good. Now that the panic had begun to wear off, it was time to focus on a plan. With only ten dollars in her purse and less than a quarter tank of gas, she needed to find a bank.

Back inside the lobby, she helped herself to a complimentary cup of coffee and waited for the attendant to finish helping a short line of travelers. She reached for her cell phone but remembered that it was in the hands of the messenger. The sick feeling she'd had the night before returned. She couldn't contact anyone without it. Like everybody else, she knew she should have backed up the numbers, but she never got around to it. What was she going to do?

At last, the welcome attendant—a proper-looking young miss in her twenties—looked her way. "Can I help you?" she said, her accent ten times as thick and southern as Stacy's.

Though self-conscious about her appearance, Stacy faced

her with the same boldness with which she faced life. "How far are we from the nearest gas station?"

"About twenty-five miles."

"That's the closest?"

The attendant, whose nametag identified as Trudy, pulled out a map and highlighted their location. "Is there anything else I can help you with?"

"Is there a phone I could use?"

Trudy smiled sweetly. "There might be one at the gas station."

Stacy spotted her cell phone sitting on the counter next to her keyboard. Their eyes met.

Trudy picked it up and dropped it into her purse. "I'm sorry, but that's my personal phone."

Stacy gave her a dirty look and went back out to the car. Once inside, she cranked the engine and turned on the heat. It took a few minutes, but she finally felt warm for the first time in hours.

* * *

Cedric stepped off the elevator and was pleased to see that although his law firm stayed closed to the public on Saturdays, several offices were abuzz with activity. He went straight to the breakroom, poured himself a cup of coffee, and retreated to his office. He was expecting an envelope from the messenger. Signaling his desire for privacy, he closed the door and settled at his desk. A silver envelope lay on the corner. He grabbed it and sliced it open.

> To quote my favorite author... The fox is
> Young, but the dogs are on her tail.

Cedric leaned back in his chair. He had to be referring to Stacy Young and the message she left about quitting her job, but how could Thad know about that? Was he tapping his phone lines? Swallowing his outrage, he focused on the issue at hand. He had thought Jack was the fox. What had Stacy done to make herself a target? Clearly, Thad had threatened her.

This whole damn thing was getting completely out of control. If they weren't careful . . . He dropped the note into the shredder. The more he thought about it, the more he thought Thad was mistaken. Should he tell him he was chasing the wrong fox? Did Thad know something he didn't? Pursing his lips, he decided to bide his time.

* * *

Jack slept late, despite his resolve to apologize and reschedule with Christine. As fate would have it, she called him first.

"Hey, are you awake?"

Jack held the receiver close to his ear and waited for the world to drop into place. "Hey, Christine," he mumbled, his tongue thick and dry from sleep, "I was just about to call you. I'm really sorry about dinner."

"Do you know how worried I was? It's not like you to miss dinner, of all things. I was afraid something horrible had happened."

Adjusting to the fact that another day had started without him, he sat up. "I ran into an old friend, and one thing led to another. How about tonight instead? I'll bring Chinese."

"All right, but I might be a few minutes late. I have to meet with Alexa's school teacher at five."

"On a Saturday? That doesn't sound good."

"No, it doesn't. This hasn't been easy on any of us."

Jack pushed to his feet and headed for the coffee maker. "You can fill me in tonight. Want me to come by at six-thirty instead?"

"How about I fill you in over breakfast? I'm about to make pancakes."

He shoved the coffee filter back in the box. "I'm on my way." After quickly checking his e-mail, he stepped into a steamy shower and propped his arms against the shower wall. He closed his eyes and let the hot water pound his back. He had a lot on his mind. He wanted to work on Daniel's investigation, but so far, he hadn't accomplished much. Without access to the evidence, what could he do? He hoped the Solver files would reveal something useful.

He still felt guilty about missing dinner. Of all the rotten timing! He had promised to be there for Christine and the kids, but how could he regret meeting Suzaun? Grief struck him suddenly and took his breath away. What he really wanted was to talk to Daniel. They had virtually known all there was to know about each other's lives, and his insight would be especially helpful right now. If it was difficult for him to accept that Daniel was gone, how must it be for Christine?

Turning towards the showerhead, he let the water strike his face and chest. Next subject: Doctor and Mrs. Lindsay. Getting proof of her husband's affair would be more difficult now that everyone was on notice. Teresa believed that the young woman was likely employed by the hospital or one of its many associate facilities.

Since coming up with a plan would require more thought than he was ready to give it, he picked up his razor and let his thoughts drift back to Suzaun. Pleasant visions of the previous evening flooded his mind: the touch of her hand, the sparkle in her eyes, the challenge in her voice. What had she said? *'I'll bet I'm nothing like you imagine.'* Well, he was imaging quite a bit just now. He nicked his chin and winced. Yeah, he wanted to see Suzaun again, and he wanted to see her soon.

* * *

Elyse's rhythmic footsteps echoed down the long basement hallway. She was having serious reservations about leaving her position with Dr. Sassi. She passed the morgue and shuddered. Was the extra money worth it? Did she really want to work with dead people? She tentatively entered the lab and glanced around.

"You're five minutes early," Thad said, his voice warm and soothing to her frayed nerves. "That's a good sign."

Elyse set her purse on the edge of an empty desk—presumably hers. "I wouldn't celebrate just yet. I'm not sure this is the right move for me. How can you stand cutting into dead bodies?"

Thad leaned on the edge of his desk. "Believe it or not, you get used to it, but that's only a small part of what we do. Our main responsibility is to diagnose and study disease. Surgical samples from living patients will keep you plenty busy, believe me. You need not enter the morgue if you don't want to."

"But you do perform autopsies."

"Of course. Autopsies reveal the cause of death and are required by law in certain circumstances."

"Yes. Your work is very important."

"Indeed. By the way, I ran into Dr. Sassi last night at a medical conference. He said he'd be sorry to see you go, but he wishes you all the best, of course."

"Oh, my God. You told him?"

Thad chuckled. "We discussed the possibility, but not to worry. Everyone understands making a move that involves professional growth and more money."

Elyse turned her back, which was stiff with dread.

"Elyse, let's go get some coffee and talk about this. You're not committed to anything."

Feeling childish, she turned around and smiled. "Thanks. It's an important decision. I don't want to make a mistake."

"Understood." He held the door and waited for her to walk through.

Elyse didn't drink coffee, but she appreciated the time to consider her options.

* * *

Jack heard Jon and Alexa arguing as soon as he stepped onto the deck. He opened the screen door and entered the kitchen. "Hey, guys."

"Uncle Jack!" they cried and ran to him for hugs. He patted Jon's head and stroked Alexa's cheek, which was flushed with annoyance. Daniel had often commented on his daughter's independent spirit. She clearly had a mind of her own, which was evident by her entirely black outfit.

Jon grabbed his hand and tugged him towards the back door. "Come and see my new fort, Uncle Jack. It needs a lot of work; maybe you can help me."

Allowing himself to be pulled outside, Jack followed Jon, who took off at a trot towards the back fence, rattling off plans as he went. "I've got a hammer and some nails," Jon said, "but we need some big boards. Do you know how to build a window?"

"I do," Jack said, thinking it had been a long time since he had jogged anywhere. A huge oak tree with massive branches stood in the back, right corner of the yard. He and Daniel had climbed this tree as children, when the house had belonged to Daniel's parents. He hadn't paid any attention to it in years and was surprised to see how much it had grown.

After listening to Jon's entire wish list, they walked back to the house. The smell of sizzling turkey bacon caught his attention. He grabbed a piece from the pile, which sat cooling on a plate.

Christine saw him and popped his leg with a hand towel. "Get out of there! Breakfast is almost ready. Where's Jon?"

"I'm hungry," Jon said as the screen door squeaked and then slammed behind him.

Jack smiled and licked the grease from his fingers.

Christine set a bottle of orange juice on the table, along with four plastic cups. "Okay, everybody, grab a plate. We're serving from the stove today."

Jon, of course, went first, then Alexa.

Jack got in line behind Alexa and whispered, "I thought we had a deal?"

Alexa scooped a petite portion of eggs onto her plate and two pancakes. "There aren't any movies I want to see right now. Like my nail polish?"

"Where on Earth did you find black nail polish?"

"I'm sure that's one of the first questions her teacher will ask when we meet with her this afternoon. Right, Lexie? I've asked her repeatedly to take it off."

Alexa settled into her place at the table. "That's probably not the first question she'll ask."

"Your grades were good on your last report card. Have they slipped?" Christine said.

Jack dished up his food.

Alexa bit down on a piece of bacon. "She's upset because I punched a boy in the face yesterday."

Christine's mouth fell open, and Jack had to cough to keep from laughing. It *was* surprising. Alexa had always been a petite little thing, but apparently, she was quite capable of standing up for herself. Jack set his plate on the table and turned to dish one up for Christine.

"Alexa, are you saying you hit somebody?" Christine said, sinking into her chair.

Jack set a plate in front of her.

"I couldn't help it," she said. "He made me mad."

"What happened, Alexa?" Jack said, his tone calmer than Christine's.

"He said Daddy went to hell, so I punched him."

"What?" Christine exclaimed.

Jack stepped behind Christine and put a hand on her shoulder. "Why would he say that, Alexa?"

Tears pooled in Alexa's eyes. "He said Daddy must have done something bad, so God killed him."

Despite Jack's hand, Christine rose to her feet. "That's not true! God doesn't kill people. It was an accident."

Just as quickly as they'd come, Alexa's tears dried up. "I'm not stupid, Mama. That's why I punched him."

Jack bit back a smile and joined them at the table. "Orange juice, anyone?"

* * *

Elyse settled into a comfortable booth in the hospital cafeteria.

"How do you like your coffee?" Thad said.

"Tea, actually, and a bit of sugar."

Elyse noted Thad's broad shoulders as he walked away and thought him quite attractive for an older man. He seemed steady and wise. She was intrigued by what she might learn in the lab, but making big decisions had always frightened her. That's why she had remained in the same job since college; it was predictable and familiar. She yearned for change, but she wasn't sure this was the right direction.

Returning with two steaming cups, Thad sat across from her with a pleasant smile. "I must admit, it's nice to have an excuse to come up for air now and then."

"You work long hours?"

"I do, but that's because there isn't anyone special to tempt me otherwise. What about you? Are you seeing anyone?"

"I go out now and then, but there's no one special."

"Tell me about your family," he said. "Didn't you say the other night that you have children?"

"One," she said with a wry smile. "A fifteen-year-old daughter who's going on thirty. They grow so quickly these days. I need to start saving for college."

"All the more reason to accept my offer," he said with a wink.

"What about you? Do you have children?"

He stiffened. "I lost my only child, a son, five years ago. A drag racing incident, of all blasted things. He died in the Emergency Room—before they could do surgery," he added with tight lips.

The pain in his eyes touched her deeply. She took hold of his hand but almost dropped it. Had he felt the electricity between them? "I'm sorry," she said, trying to cover her surprise. "I can't even imagine what that must be like for you."

"There aren't words," he said, lifting his hand from hers. "Tell me why you're having second thoughts about advancing your career. You're the perfect candidate for what I have in mind."

She looked away. There was something unsettling about him, and yet it wasn't unpleasant. "I don't know, exactly."

"I thought you were interested in sharpening your clinical

skills and earning more money. Have your desires changed?"

She was beginning to feel that they were having a double conversation.

"What did Dr. Sassi say when you told him?"

"He was a bit surprised, of course, but losing valuable people comes with the territory. He certainly wasn't upset."

Elyse let that sink in. "I'm not sure I'd be happy working in the lab. It feels creepy down there."

Thad chuckled. "As I said, you get used to it. Would you prefer to back out?"

Elyse sighed. "I'm sorry. I'm just not sure."

"Work is backing up. I need to hire someone soon."

"I know. It's probably just anxiety about leaving something I know, for something I don't." Her eyes met his again, but her answer wasn't there. "I could use the extra money."

"And here I thought you were looking forward to working with me."

Elyse smiled. "Can I let you know after I talk with Dr. Sassi? I plan to call him at home this afternoon."

"Elyse," Thad said, "keep in mind that I need someone who can completely dedicate themselves to their work. People's lives are gravely affected by our research."

"Once I make a decision, I'm dedicated."

"That's good to hear." He held her gaze. "Do what's best for you and your daughter. Happiness can't be purchased with dollar bills, even those with lots of zeros."

"True, but they sure would come in handy."

"All right then, here's the plan. Instead of doing paperwork today, you go home and decide what you want to do. There's no point in training you for a position you may not want."

"Thanks for understanding."

Thad rose first. "Would you care to give me your answer over dinner tomorrow evening?"

Elyse smiled in a decidedly feminine way. She was flattered and certain there was more going on than just an interview. "I'll look forward to it."

* * *

Stacy sat in her cramped car staring at the colorful entrance of the New Orleans Audubon Zoo—the only place she'd ever visited in this diverse cultural hub of Louisiana. Her gas tank was full, but after withdrawing all of her savings from the bank, she was forced to acknowledge that only two hundred dollars stood between her and destitution. She glowered as she considered the gravity of her situation.

Going back to Jackson was impossible; the messenger knew who she was, where she lived, and all of her personal details. Following that train of thought, she gasped. What would happen when he went through her cell phone data and found out about her and Josh? Chances were, he already knew, but she had to find a way to warn him, even if it meant borrowing someone's cell phone to do it. Without money and a cell phone, her options were extremely limited. It galled her to run away, but what choice did she have?

Exhausted from the intense stress of the past twelve hours, she reclined as best she could and eventually faded off to sleep.

* * *

After breakfast, Jack went home to make some phone calls. There was no use denying it; he was thinking about Suzaun again. Focus on anything else seemed futile. Was it too soon to call? Reaching into his back pocket, he withdrew her business card and dialed the number.

"Hello?" Suzaun said into the phone.

His pulse quickened. "Hello yourself, Suzaun."

"Hey, Jack."

A silly smile crept across his face as he imagined her dimples.

"Jack?"

"I'm here. I just wanted to thank you for last night. I had a great time with you."

"Thanks. So did I."

"Would you like to go out for drinks tomorrow night?" he said and held his breath.

"Sure, I'll go to dinner with you."

He indulged in a silent fist pump.

"I have something in the early evening," she said, "but I can meet you at eight o'clock. How about Bravo!?"

"Bravo! is one of my favorite places. Eight o'clock it is then." After the call, he was ready to concentrate on business. He had already looked up everything he could think of regarding Dr. Solver, anesthesiology, and rhinoplasty. It was frustrating to admit, but this case was out of his league. He had no choice but to rely on the expertise of others, which brought Kevin Thomas to mind. He dialed the police department.

"Captain Thomas, here."

"Hey, Kevin. Great to see you yesterday."

"You're not calling about Suzaun, are you? I stay out of her personal business."

Jack *had* wanted to discuss Suzaun. Switching topics, he said, "I didn't mention this yesterday, but you remember Daniel Steinberg, don't you?"

"Yeah, man. Real sorry to hear about him passin'."

Jack stepped out onto his back patio to pace. "Christine has hired an attorney who believes his anesthesiologist, Dr. Ryan Solver, is at fault. As it turns out, the attorney has sued the guy twice before. I want to run a background check on both those guys. You know, the stuff I can't get off the Internet. Trust anyone?" The horizontal gate caught his eye. He frowned and walked over to take a look.

"There's a guy I use from outside the department. His name's Gloster. Tell him I gave you his number."

Jack rushed back to his desk to jot down the information. "Thanks, Kevin." He heard someone in the background say, "Sorry, Captain, it's urgent."

"Jack..."

"Later, buddy, have a good day." He shoved his phone into his back pocket and went in to the garage to retrieve his spy kit from the back seat of his car. After dusting the gate and the exterior doors, he was surprised to discover fresh fingerprints. Had someone been inside his house? He conducted a general inventory, but nothing seemed to be missing. What was the motive, if not robbery? A pro wouldn't leave prints, let alone a busted gate. It was disturbing, but he doubted they'd be back.

Turning his attention to the matters at hand, he wondered if Stacy had managed to copy the Solver files. He dialed her number, but it went straight to voicemail. "Stacy, it's Jack. Give me a call at this number. Chow."

"Chow?" he repeated with disgust. He shook his head and glanced at the clock. He had a lot to do before heading over to Daniel's—to Christine's house for dinner.

* * *

Anthony straggled out of bed just before noon. He and Trina had spent a full night of it, and he hadn't come home until five o'clock this morning. The silver envelope lying in front of the door caught his attention as soon as he walked into the living room. Yawning, he scooped it up and headed for the kitchen to start the coffee. Taking a knife from the drawer, he opened the envelope and withdrew a pill bottle containing ninety OxyContin tablets. He weighed it in his non-bandaged hand and considered indulging, but decided against it. His future plans were becoming more important than getting high. He could see himself living with Trina.

A bittersweet ache throbbed in his chest as Angel's face came to mind. He had sworn he'd never leave her, but he had, in the end, but only because she tricked him. He clenched his fists, which abruptly reminded him of the cut on his left hand. He peeled off the bandage that Trina had wrapped around it the night before.

The winter two years ago was brutally cold. He'd gone out to get more medicine though they both knew that Angel's illness had progressed far beyond anything he could steal. When he returned with something to ease her cough, he only found a note.

Angel had left their cozy shelter to keep him from witnessing the end—damn her! She wanted him to remember her alive. He had searched the hospitals and public shelters, which was how his uncle's detective found him. Thurston Oliver Winchester III had finally sent someone in search of his nephew. He scoffed. As far as he was concerned, his uncle's window for concern had shut the day he allowed the State to take him into foster care. The only reason he had come looking was because he wanted something.

His eyes hardened as he poured himself a cup of coffee and sank onto the sofa. He fingered the pill bottle for a long while, absently listening to it click as he turned it end to end, considering the arrangement he had with Thad. He reminded himself that he was here by choice. He knew what he was doing. He was free to leave anytime he chose, and he would, too, as soon as he had enough money.

His mind shifted back to Trina. He had never imagined that sex could be like this, so unpredictable and exciting, but it was more than that. Trina *wanted* to be with him. It was intoxicating. His cell phone vibrated in his pocket. He chuckled at the timing.

"Yeah?"

"Hello, my frien. I'm lookin' for mo' candy."

Recognizing Jermaine's voice, he said, "Just came into some. I'll meet you tonight. Same, same, ten o'clock."

"We'll be at da burned out house. Don't give it ta no one else now. I'm countin' on it."

"Bring the cash times two, and it's all yours." Anthony ended the call and dropped the pill bottle into the box on the coffee table. "Now, where was I? Ah, yes. Trina." A slow smile spread across his face.

* * *

After a morning spent doing emergency laundry, Jack headed for the police station with the fingerprints he'd lifted from the sliding glass door. Pushing through the chaotic activity, he spotted an officer with his feet propped on a messy desk, holding a phone to his ear. The bored look on his face made it clear that he was waiting for his party to return to the line.

"Is Captain Thomas in?" Jack said, dodging the shoulder of a harried assistant, who rushed by with a mountain of files.

"Haven't seen him all day."

Jack nodded his thanks and waded back through the maze of bodies. Once outside, he walked down the crowded sidewalk towards his car, annoyed with himself for not calling ahead.

"Watch yourself," an officer barked as he passed on Jack's left.

"Hey, Jack! What are you doing here?"

Jack was surprised to see Joshua Royce striding towards him with his hand extended.

"I owe you for covering my backside the other day," Josh said with a relaxed smile.

Jack grasped his hand. "No problem. I'd like to believe we're on the same team. Are you here about the Steinberg case?"

"No. I'm checking on another client."

Jack made a quick, calculated decision. "You know, Josh, I've been thinking. It seems that there's more going on with Dr. Solver than unfortunate coincidence. Either he's on some kind of bizarre killing rampage or someone has it out for him. I'm beginning to wonder if it's not the latter."

"That's exactly what I suggested to Cedric, but he won't hear of it. He says Solver's like every other doctor who's plagued with malpractice suits; he's under tremendous stress and more likely to be careless."

"Maybe," Jack said, "but I've read dozens of articles on Solver. He was highly regarded until this sudden string of deaths."

Josh shrugged. "Things change."

"Tell me about it."

"Why are you here?" Josh asked.

"Someone broke into my place yesterday. Funny thing is nothing's missing. I know the captain. I came to drop off fingerprints, but he's out. I don't want to leave them with anybody else."

"Jack, there's something I should . . ." He paused and

looked away.

"What is it?"

"You really want to be on my team?" Josh said.

"What've you got?"

Josh gestured to a bench, out of the way of foot traffic. Once they were seated, he said, "There's been some strange things going on in our office lately, and I intend to get to the bottom of it—with or without Cedric's blessing."

"Go on."

"You remember Stacy, my assistant?"

He smiled. "You mean the one with serious curves and attitude to burn?"

"Look," Josh interrupted, "we have a thing going on the side, so watch your thoughts there, okay?"

"Not the same girl whose parents you met for dinner the other night, I take it?"

Josh blushed and shook his head.

Jack didn't say anything, but he didn't like the idea of Stacy setting herself up to get hurt. Nor did he approve of Josh cheating on his fiancé. If he was already cheating, why get married?

"Here's the thing," Josh said. "Stacy left a voicemail for Cedric last night saying she quit her job. She said she was going to Montana to be with her mother, who has supposedly suffered a stroke. The weird thing is Stacy's mom died several years ago. I didn't remember that until after she left."

"I'm not following you," Jack said. "Has something happened to Stacy?"

"We had plans to meet last night. When she didn't show up, and wouldn't return my calls, I went by her apartment. It was completely cleaned out. She had taken all her belongings and thrown them into her tiny little car. It was so jammed packed; I'm surprised she could even drive it. If you knew Stacy, you'd know that's not how she does anything. She's an organization freak. And she was shaking and scared. I think somebody threatened her."

The hair on the back of Jack's neck bristled. "Do you have

any idea who would do that?"

Sudden bursts of profanity near the police station entrance draw their attention. Josh grinned as a young male officer struggled with a rather large and belligerent prostitute, who was clearly under the influence, bedecked in feather boas, and non-too-willing to be led anywhere. A second officer rushed forward to flank her on the right, and together they forced her into the station.

"You were saying?" Jack said.

"Stacy tried to tell me that Cedric was up to something illegal, but I wouldn't listen. It's hard to imagine the great Cedric Johnson as anything other than the superb attorney he is, but what if she was right?"

"What did she tell you?" he prompted, knitting his brow as he thought back to Stacy's version of the story.

"On several occasions, Stacy witnessed a messenger exchanging envelopes with Cedric after hours. She describes him as the ganglord, biker dude type with a dark leather jacket, blue jeans, and black leather boots." He gave Jack a pointed look. "She's right about one thing. Cedric doesn't often stay after-hours, and he certainly doesn't wait for messengers."

That was the same story Stacy had told him. Though tempted, he refrained from divulging that he and Stacy had met for lunch. "It sounds like something's up. Any ideas about where she might have gone?"

"No," Josh said, "and she's not answering her phone."

Jack was kicking himself for not backing her up when he *knew* she was going to copy the Solver files. Now she was missing.

Josh's brows also creased. "Stacy said she wasn't coming back. Isn't that odd for a girl who's never lived anywhere besides Mississippi?"

"What do you suggest?" he said, growing angrier with himself by the moment.

Josh gave him a dirty look. "How should I know? You're the detective."

* * *

Anthony made quick work of the locks on Jack's office door. Once inside, he closed the door and began searching. "Whew," he groaned. The thick, pungent air reminded him of his years on the street. Back then, he would've considered himself lucky to find shelter in a place like this, even with the musty smell. Thankfully, those days were behind him. Shaking it off, he searched Jack's cluttered desk, and then the trash cans and file cabinets. He found nothing related to his uncle or Cedric Johnson. Stepping into the bathroom, he snickered at the stack of *National Geographic* and *Time* magazines, which towered in the corner next to the toilet. "It must suck to get old." While he relieved himself, he heard something crawling around in the ceiling. Reflecting on the shabby conditions of Jack's existence, he considered torching the place but decided against it. He'd wait to see what his uncle had to say.

He concluded his search and went back outside, leaving the door unlocked. He wanted Jack to know that he was being watched. Straddling his Harley, he popped the clutch and sped down the street. For him, at least, the day was far from over.

* * *

Doctor Ryan Solver sat behind his desk in his home study, three sheets to the wind, and none too happy to be disturbed. In a fury, he backhanded a stack of unpaid bills off his desk, sending them fluttering to the floor. "Stay out of my business," he yelled, glowering at his wife of forty-three years.

Anita Solver, timid by nature, stood her ground. "Ryan, I'm just saying . . ."

Ryan rose from his desk and stumbled to the wet bar to pour himself another drink. This room, decorated with safari colors and tribal artwork, was supposed to be his safe haven. By agreement, Anita rarely entered. "Didn't you hear me, woman? It's my bloody problem, and I'll fix it myself."

Anita usually backed down, but today, she placed both hands on her narrow hips and raised her prominent chin. "You listen to me, Ryan Solver. You're losing everything we've worked for, bit by bit. Instead of drinking yourself to death, why don't you—"

Ryan hurled his shot glass, well wide of his wife, shattering it against the antique beveled mirror that hung on the wall near the doorway.

Anita gasped and covered her mouth with a shaky hand.

Ryan staggered forward and pointed to the door. "Get out! I want to be alone."

"If you'd stay sober long enough, we could fight this thing together!"

A dumbfounded look crossed his face, and then he clutched his chest and grabbed onto the bookcase to steady himself.

"Ryan!" Anita cried as she rushed to his side. She wrapped her arm around his waist and guided him towards an armchair.

When his bad knee buckled, he worried that the weight of his upper body might crush her, but she managed to get him into the chair. Leaving him, she rounded the desk, yanked open the center drawer, and snatched up an aspirin bottle. As she rushed for a glass of water, he wondered if this would be the end of all his troubles. He glanced at the broken glass, which lay shimmering on the rust-colored carpet. That mirror was a third-generation heirloom on his wife's side. He'd had no right to break it. What was worse, he knew Anita would lie to her family and confess to having broken it herself. For the first time in many years, he felt ashamed. Despite his stormy raging through the years, Anita had remained unshakably loyal. He didn't want her to see him die, especially not in their home.

She handed him the glass and aspirin. He swallowed the pills, took a few slow breaths, and then sighed as the tension eased. "It's all right," he said. "I feel a little better now."

She picked up the desk phone. "I'm calling 911. They need to check you out."

"I said I'm all right!" he snapped. "If you really want to help me, bring me something to eat."

"Yes, this is an emergency," she said into the phone.

Wresting the receiver from her, he slammed it down and pushed her away from the desk, sending her tripping over her feet as she sprawled to the floor.

"You brought that on yourself, Anita. You know how I get when you ignore me." When she didn't move, he knelt beside her. "Nita?" He gently turned her over. She was alarmingly pale. "Christ." He picked up her wrist and checked her pulse. "Nita, can you hear me?"

She tried to say something, but it came out slurred. Her pale blue eyes fluttered and then closed.

He shoved to his feet and dialed 911. "I need to report an emergency," he said without taking his eyes off his wife's face.

"They're already on their way, sir. Would you like to stay on the line?"

"No." He returned to his wife, picked up her hand and kissed it repeatedly. "Hang on, Nita. They're coming. You're going to be all right." He checked her pulse again, but it was weaker than before. An intense wave of fear exploded inside his head and drained through his body, shaking him to the core. "Don't you leave me, dammit!"

Moments later, he heard sirens screaming up the street, and then someone called to him from downstairs.

"Up here!" he yelled. "Hurry." The shock of the situation sobered him considerably, and in the rush to follow, time seemed to shift into an eerie slow motion.

A team of paramedics rushed up the stairs and into his study. Someone helped him into a chair, clearing space so that the technicians could work on his wife. Two police officers arrived.

"Is she all right?" he said, craning his neck to see around the broad shoulders of one of the paramedics. He and Anita had been together since high school. Though they argued often, he absolutely adored her. She was his rock, and he was hers. He couldn't bear it if she . . ." Her sister," he mumbled. "I should call her sister."

A burly police officer patted his shoulder. "Stay calm, Mr. Solver. They'll be plenty of time for phone calls later."

A second officer gestured towards the scattered papers and broken glass on the floor. "What happened here? Were you two arguing?"

Ryan rubbed his eyes. "Yes, and she fell. It happened so fast."

"You reek of alcohol," the other officer said. "Do you always drink so early in the day?"

"That's none of your damn business," Ryan snapped, feeling both annoyed and threatened by the question.

The officers looked at each other.

Another team of paramedics brought in a stretcher, and soon they were heading downstairs with his unresponsive wife.

Ryan got up to follow. "Wait, is she all right?"

The first officer laid a hand on his shoulder. "Hold it there, Mr. Solver. We need to ask you a few questions."

Shaking free, he lurched towards the door. "That's my wife. I need to be with her."

Instead of arguing, they each took a side and escorted him down the steps and into the back of a squad car.

* * *

It was nearly five o'clock, time for the daily shift-change at Dixie Medical Center. Jack parked his car where he could monitor both the hospital and the physician's tower. Though it was a long shot, he hoped to spot Lindsay's mistress.

As before, there was a surprising amount of activity. Dozens of people came and went during the next forty-five minutes. Twice Jack thought he saw her, but when he compared the women with the photographs from the evening at La Bells, each one proved wrong. Finally, though, the mystery woman appeared. She was talking on her cell phone, gesturing vividly, and paying little attention to her surroundings. He watched her for a few moments, but then his heart sank. The light of day revealed something that the shadows of the night had concealed; she was pregnant.

He snapped several quick shots and then got out of the car and followed her into the parking garage where he watched her climb into the same BMW he had seen at La Bells. Taking note of the license plate this time, he hurried back to his Camry and wrote it down. Within a few seconds of leaving the hospital grounds, he was right behind her.

He gradually increased the distance between them, though he doubted she would have noticed even had he rode her bumper. Different scenarios ran through his mind. Few single nurses could afford a car like that. Was she a doctor? That might make more sense. And the baby? That wasn't news he wanted to give Teresa Lindsay.

Twenty minutes later, Miss BMW—as he now dubbed her—pulled up to the gate of an expensive condominium complex. He decided not to follow directly in behind her. Instead, he drove past the complex and turned around. By the time he pulled up to the gate again, she was nowhere in sight.

About ten minutes later, he followed a pickup truck through the gate. As he cruised slowly down the main street, he realized that the homes didn't have their driveways out in front. At the ends of each block ran an alleyway, which ran behind the townhomes and provided access to their private garages. Not knowing which direction to take, he drove down the right side, and then the left. He saw her car in an open garage, the third house from the end. Noting the unit number, he drove past her unit and turned onto the connecting street. Enough progress for now, he decided. He was already fifteen minutes late for dinner with Daniel's family, and he wasn't about to stand them up again.

* * *

After throwing up, Trina wiped her mouth and flushed the toilet in the ladies room on the fifth floor of Dixie Medical Center. As she washed her trembling hands, a smile spread across her face. She was finally pregnant with the Winchester heir.

* * *

"Mama will be down in a minute, Uncle Jack," Alexa said. "She's getting her keys."

"Keys for what?"

"Jon, Alexa, let's go! I want to get back before Jack gets here," Christine said as she thudded down the stairs and rounded the corner where the object of her concern stood grinning at her. "Oh, you're here."

"I am," Jack said, reaching out for a hug. She was wearing a pink frilly skirt and a sheer white blouse. "Did I misunderstand our plans? You look like you're going out."

"Did you bring Chinese?" she said, clearly expecting him to say no.

Jack was mortified.

"I figured," she said. "I'm cooking a roast."

"Is that what I smell?" he said, but the fact that she had assumed he'd forget didn't set well with him, nor that she was right. He wanted to be dependable. What was wrong with him?

"Jon, did you remember your toothbrush?" Christine said.

"Yes."

"Alexa?"

Ignoring her, Alexa said, "Bye, Uncle Jack," and went outside.

Having rounded up her children, Christine glanced over her shoulder on her way out the door. "Make yourself comfortable. I'll be back in fifteen minutes."

From the living room window, Jack watched them back down the driveway. He was alone in the house for the first time since Daniel's death, and it felt strange. He'd been alone here dozens of times over the years, but only when Daniel was on his way home from somewhere. On those occasions, he'd grab a beer and watch TV, but this time he wasn't waiting for Daniel. He was waiting for Daniel's wife, she was dressed up, and a heavenly-smelling roast was cooking in the oven. How the hell did that happen?

Not one to dwell on uncomfortable topics, he sank into the recliner next to Daniel's chair and turned on the news. He sat for a minute or two and then got up to look out the window. He sat back down again, but he couldn't stay put. Finally, he wandered outside to evaluate what needed to be done in the yard. He could easily spend an entire weekend here, so overgrown was everything.

The sun had dipped behind the trees, and a soft yellow hue settled over the yard. He looked towards the big tree where Jon wanted to build his fort. They needed to buy some lumber, but he had the necessary tools. Carpentry was one of his favorite hobbies.

A few minutes later, Christine pulled into the driveway. She handed him two bottles of wine, which he carried into the kitchen. "Why are the kids at your mom's house tonight? I was hoping to spend some time with them."

She reached for the wine glasses. "I know, but I desperately need to relax. You know I don't drink when the kids are home. Do you mind?" she said, giving him the look that always worked with Daniel.

"Wine sounds good," he said. They moved easily around the kitchen together. He knew where most things were. Within a few minutes, they went back out onto the deck.

Christine settled into her chair. "Alexa's teacher decided to give her another chance, but if she hits anybody else, she'll be suspended."

"That seems reasonable. What about the black nail polish?"

"Her teacher says lots of kids wear black. It's the *in* thing right now."

Jack shook his head. "I don't get it, but I guess we all did things our parents didn't understand."

A breeze fluttered through, and Christine closed her eyes. "I can talk to him out here, you know."

"I'm glad."

She lifted her glass. "To you, Daniel, my love. No matter what happens, I will always love you."

"Hear, hear," he said, lifting his glass.

When darkness had chased away the last traces of light, Christine said, "Why don't you stay out here while I put dinner on the table? I'll come and get you in a few minutes."

The moon was full enough for Jack to wander towards the

back fence to make some quick calculations. After looking things over, he decided that Jon would have a mighty-fine treehouse, the kind Daniel would have built for his son if he could.

"Dinner's ready," Christine called from the house.

The lights in the kitchen were out, and two candles flickered in the dining room. He was surprised, but he knew better than to think she meant anything by it.

"Come in, Jack," she said when he hesitated in the doorway.

Steam from the roast rose from the table and lingered like a rain cloud in the soft light. "Dinner smells wonderful," he said, taking his usual seat. He glanced at the head of the table where Daniel's chair stood guard, and then back to Christine. He could see that she'd gone to considerable trouble to look attractive tonight, although natural beauty radiated from her like the rays of the sun. "You look great. Are you sleeping through the night now?"

"Most nights, but I dream about Daniel a lot. How about you?"

"I miss talking to him. He's the one who kept me straight when I might otherwise have gotten off track."

"Me, too," she said. "Daniel was always steady and stable. Since this happened, I feel just the opposite. When I lay in bed thinking about my children, and how they depend on me, I feel so overwhelmed. How can I keep them safe and secure when I feel like I'm drowning? I need to find them a father."

Jack choked on his food and barely managed to swallow it.

Christine jumped to her feet and rushed to his side. "Are you all right?"

He coughed and waved her back. This seemed to be happening a lot lately.

"I'll get some water," she said and rushed to the kitchen.

When she returned, Jack took several gulps and gradually caught his breath. "Christine, listen to me. Things will get easier, and you'll begin to feel more sure of yourself again. The last thing you need is another man right now. You need time to heal."

She glared at him. "How do you know what I need?"

"Because, sweetheart, it's written all over your face. You're in love with Daniel. As you should be."

"But what about the kids? I feel so inadequate."

"They need time to heal, too," he said gently. "Everyone is adjusting."

She sat quietly for several seconds. "You're right, of course. I could never marry somebody just for the kids. It would never work."

"No, it wouldn't. Be patient. It's fresh yet."

She wrinkled her nose. "To be honest, I can't imagine anyone other than Daniel."

"You see? You did the exact right thing by inviting me over. Whenever you're feeling desperate for a man, I'll set you straight. Deal?"

She gave him a half-smile. "Deal. Thanks for being such a good friend. Having you around makes all the difference in the world. I couldn't do this without you, Jack. I mean it."

"I'll be here whenever you need me."

"So what's the next step in finding out what happened to Daniel?"

He reached for a piece of garlic bread. "There are several things we need to do. For one thing, I need to talk with my friend at the police department about some fingerprints I found on my back door."

"What fingerprints? Did someone break into your house?"

"I think so, but something must have scared them off before they could take anything. The only reason I knew they were there is because they busted my gate." He took a sip of wine. "As far as Daniel's case goes, I got the name of a guy who's supposedly some kind of super sleuth. I'm gonna have him run background checks on Dr. Solver and Cedric Johnson—the kind that covers what I can't get myself."

"You don't trust our attorney?"

He dished out a second portion of mashed potatoes. "Hell no, I don't trust him, but that's not to say he isn't our best option.

I'll let you know if he digs up anything interesting."

"You'll figure it out. You always do."

A sudden wave of grief struck the pit of his stomach. He looked down at his plate and chose his next words carefully. "Christine, as much as I like to tell everyone that I'm a brilliant detective, I know I'm not. I'm behind on technology, I forget half the things I need to do, and I usually take note of the wrong details."

"That's not true! You've solved every case you've ever taken on. Haven't you?"

"Yeah, but look at the car I drive."

"What's wrong with your car?"

"It's old and messy, like my office and my house. What I'm trying to say is the research I've done on Daniel's case doesn't lead anywhere. I can't do this on my own. Murder is . . ."

Christine's hand froze with a bite halfway to her mouth.

"Malpractice is out of my league. I don't even know where to begin." That wasn't easy to admit, nor was it exactly true. His conversation with Josh had left him thinking otherwise, but he didn't want to burden her with their suspicions just yet.

Christine stood up and came around the table. "Push your chair back."

"Why?" he said, but he did as she asked.

She sat on his knee and took his face in both hands. "You listen to me, Jack Kendall. Don't you dare take the responsibility for this investigation upon yourself. Whatever you can do will help, but remember, no matter what happens, Daniel is still gone." Her cloudy blue eyes locked with his cloudy brown ones, but there was no romance in their gaze, only the simple strength friends impart in times of need. She wrapped her arms around his neck and laid her head on his shoulder.

He held her and closed his eyes. A heavy sigh escaped him as the weight of his friend's death lifted from his shoulders. He might not be able to solve the case, but he could be here for her and the children while they adjusted to their lives without Daniel. That much he could do. Without their father, the kids—especially

Alexa—were becoming a challenge for Christine.

"Jack?" she said as if reading his mind. "Did I overhear you say something about helping Jon build a fort?"

Reluctant to break the comforting contact, he held on. "Yeah, and it looks like the yard could use some attention, too." He wondered why women always smelled so good. It was so soothing. "What if I come by in the morning and spend the whole day here? I really want to see the kids. I've got plans tomorrow evening, but I can come back Monday morning to finish whatever else needs to be done."

Christine pulled away and went back to her chair. "Jack, I know I shouldn't ask this. I know it doesn't matter, but do you think I'm still . . . I mean, am I still . . ."

He grinned. "Are you trying to say something there, little Missy?"

Blushing, she said, "Never mind, I'm just blabbering. The kids and I will help with the yard work. They won't like it, but if Daniel were here, he'd have them out there helping."

* * *

Stacy was only halfway through her first hurricane from Pat O'Brien's, and she was feeling it. As she strolled down Bourbon Street, she found herself enthralled by the sights and sounds of Louisiana's French Quarter. Street musicians played quality jazz, and people painted themselves from head to toe like metallic-looking statues and stood frozen in awkward positions to amaze the passersby who dropped money into their tip jars. On another block, a group of talented black children tap-danced on the sidewalk in such perfect unison that Stacy stayed to watch two complete routines before moving on.

She stopped at several interesting shops along the way and saw everything from funny T-shirts with obscene wording, to leather whips and feather boas. Most stores rocked with Cajun carnival music and featured dozens of racks, if not entire walls, of tacky beaded necklaces, which came in every imaginable shape, size and color—some outrageously obscene. Unable to fathom that anyone would actually wear such offensive items, she turned to leave but had to wait as two drunk women wearing necklaces comprised of blinking male body parts stumbled by on the sidewalk. She shook her head and wondered how they'd feel in the morning when they realized what they'd done the night before.

Trying not to trip on the uneven sidewalk, she paused to take another sip of her drink but thought better of it. She was feeling dizzy. She had never had a hurricane before, but she suspected it was the type of drink that snuck up on you. She started paying attention to the thick and tempting aromas floating on the air. There were as many eateries in the French Quarter as there were shops. She saw signs for hot dogs, jambalaya, seafood, lasagna, steaks, burgers, and even pizza. Cutting through the crowd, she paused to look at one of the many menus posted along the street. As she glanced into the restaurant, she saw a bleached-blonde waitress carrying a plate piled high with crawfish, complete with eyes and pinchers. She set the tray in front of a heavyset man wearing a plastic bib. He immediately plucked one up, broke it in half, and to Stacy's horror, sucked out the head.

"That's disgusting," she muttered under her breath, and someone laughed.

"You ain't from around here, are you?" the hostess sneered as she returned from seating guests.

"Yes, I am," Stacy said, "but I've never seen anybody do that before. That's got to be the most disgusting thing I've ever seen."

The hostess, a young Cajun with coarse black hair and beautiful brown skin, picked up a menu. "Don't knock it till you try it. Them crawfish is good eatin'. Now, you want a table or don't ya? We got lots of people waitin'."

The man, who had just finished ravaging the other half of the crawfish, tossed the empty shells into a bucket and grabbed another. Stacy's mouth twisted. "No, thanks."

Continuing down the street, she was surprised to see X-rated posters plastered on the windows of several buildings. Distracted by the shocking images, she bumped into a scantily clad woman wearing stilettos, nearly upsetting the tray of shot glasses she was carrying.

"Watch it, honey, or you'll be buying every last one of these drinks," the tall Spanish-looking woman said with a snarl.

"Sorry," Stacy said, stepping out of her way. Only then did she see that there were several women wearing stilettos and carrying shot glasses. It took a moment to figure out what they were doing. These nearly naked women ignored the couples and single females in the crowd, but offered free shots of alcohol to the men passing by. Once they accepted, they were invited to peek behind the velvet curtains where X-rated shows were in progress. Stacy felt her eyebrows rise. Before tonight, she had considered herself a modern and liberated woman. Now, she realized she had lived a sheltered life. If the South was the Bible Belt, this was most certainly Sodom and Gomorrah.

On the next block, on the sidewalk, along an ornate wrought iron fence, a variety of artists displayed their works. Amid the artists were the tents of the fortune tellers and palm readers. Stacy was tempted to see what they would say about her future, but she decided she'd rather not know. The crowd, which had grown considerably larger during the hour, included people from multiple countries and every level of society. Everyone seemed to revel in the unique freedoms granted within this small section of the city. Alcohol was legal on the street. Drug deals happened in the shadows. Marijuana drifted from the joints people smoked while walking down the street. No wonder her mother had forbidden her to come here with her high school friends! As she craned her neck for a second look at a man with wicked-looking spikes protruding from his chin, she tripped over the curb. She caught herself but spilled half her drink down the front of her shirt in the process. Laughing at herself, she swallowed the rest of it and threw the cup in the trash.

She loved the narrow streets and the unique, historical architecture, especially the three-and-four-story buildings with balconies and wrought iron railings, where colorful hanging flowerpots swung in the soft southern breeze. Knowing she needed to eat, she took a deep breath and tried to sort out the competing aromas. Food, alcohol, uncollected trash, and what she suspected might be urine, all added to the atmosphere of the place made famous for its decadence. Up ahead, a huge crowd gathered in an intersection and on the upper balconies lining the streets. People were chanting something in unison, but the music blasting from the nearby bars and restaurants made it difficult to understand. She wanted to check it out but realized that she had circled around to Pat O'Brien's again—a second entrance—and wandered in to use the bathroom and get something to eat.

The hostess seated her in the outer courtyard, near the fountain, where she watched plate after plate of mouth-watering dish go by. Her head was swimming with alcohol, and she was afraid she might get sick. When the waitress brought water, she drank the whole glass. A few minutes later, when the guests at a neighboring table got up to leave, she snagged their basket of crackers, which quickly helped to settle her stomach.

After eating some of Pat O'Brien's famous red beans and rice, she felt ready for more adventure. She even ordered another hurricane to-go. While waiting for her change, her eyes popped wide as a huge rat scurried along the thick, crumbling wall of the courtyard. She pointed it out to the waitress when she returned, but the woman looked at her as if she were crazy.

"It's only a rat," she said and walked away.

"Right," Stacy mumbled. "How silly of me."

Back on the street, the crowd in the intersection had grown. Curious, she waded through the pressing throng to see what was going on. From the balconies above, men were chanting for the women to lift their shirts. When they did, they would throw beaded necklaces down to them as a reward. Glancing around, Stacy saw dozens of women, in various stages of drunk, wearing multiple strands of colored beads.

At that moment, in response to the male clamor, several women lifted their shirts at the same time and then collected the beaded necklaces as they rained down on them from above. Women were flashing on the balconies as well, she saw, to the great delight of the men on the street, who threw their beads up for them to catch. Stacy could scarcely believe what she was seeing. It was a wonder they all weren't arrested!

A swarm of men suddenly surrounded her, pointing their cameras in her direction and chanting for her to lift her shirt. "Hell, no!" she said as she crossed her arms over her chest. "I'm not doin' it." Her heart thundered in her ears as she pushed through the men, who were still circling and calling for her to show herself. Finally, she broke through the edges of the crowd and continued down the street, away from the intersection. "These people are crazy!" she exclaimed, but no one paid any attention. It was a frightening thing to be in the center of a mob, and it had happened so quickly!

She had seen quite enough of the French Quarter!

* * *

Jack backed down the driveway, wondering if Christine might be genuinely interested in him. If so, he had a lot of thinking to do. There was no doubt that she was a great catch, but to him, she had always been Daniel's wife. "And Daniel's wife wears tiny black underwear," he heard himself say aloud.

He shook his head to banish the thought and decided to drive by *Miss BMW's* place to see what he might learn. Stopping at the bottom of Christine's driveway, he pulled the emergency brake. After checking the perimeter, he grabbed his spy kit from the back seat. Using the rear view mirror and a black eyeliner pencil, he darkened his two-day beard and mustache.

"Christine had a weak moment," he told himself in the mirror. "There was no more to it than that."

He spiked his curls with hair gel and put on a pair of wire-rimmed glasses.

"She sure felt wonderful in my arms, though."

He took care to cover the Z-shaped scar near the corner of his eye.

"If Christine were the woman for me, I wouldn't be hot on Suzaun, would I?"

Yes, he thought to himself. What guy wouldn't be hot on Suzaun?

While Jack talked to himself in the mirror, an idea occurred to him. He got out of the car and plucked a yellow rose from the neighbor's bush, which was more or less on the border between the two houses. He walked back up the driveway and rang the bell.

"Who is it?" Christine said through the door.

"It's me, Jack."

Christine turned the deadbolt and opened the door. "Why on earth didn't you—Oh!" she said and took a step back.

He grinned and turned his cheek in either direction for her to admire. "Great, right?"

She laughed. "You're so crazy."

"I brought you a flower," he said, presenting the rose for her to take.

She smiled. "Thanks. I hope the neighbor didn't see you take it. Where are you going?"

"To see if a certain married doctor makes house calls."

"I'm sorry I asked."

"In this case, my client is an amazingly cultured and attractive woman. If her husband doesn't see that, he's not only blind, he's an idiot."

Christine hoisted the rose. "Go get 'em, Jack."

"And so I shall. Good night, dear lady." A grin spread across his face as he walked back to his car. He just loved dressing incognito.

* * *

Christine closed the door and smiled. Jack was always good for a laugh. When she turned around, her breath caught as her eyes rested on her husband's recliner. "Did you see that, Danny? He'll never change." In her mind, she could see Daniel sitting there, smiling up at her with his beautiful brown eyes. "He's right, you know. I could never be with someone just for the kids."

Moving closer to the chair, she said, "I know you didn't mean to, Daniel, but you left me in a really tough spot. Have you seen the way Alexa treats me now? She heard us arguing that morning. She blames me for your death. I've tried to tell her we made up, but she won't listen. It's not like I can tell her we made love afterwards." In her mind, she heard him chuckle—as clearly as if he actually did. Wanting to believe, she said, "Daniel, are you here?"

She sat on the edge of his recliner and turned as though she were sitting upon his lap, looking into his face. She gently touched the back of the chair, imagining that she were touching his chest. One of the cloth buttons was missing.

"Do you have any idea how much I miss you?"

She slowly unbuttoned her blouse and tossed it on the floor. Closing her eyes, she allowed her mind to drift. She imagined the silky feel of his soft brown hair between her fingers and the warmth of his hands, feather-light against her skin.

"I'd trade every single tomorrow for one more kiss," she whispered.

When she opened her eyes, they shimmered with tears. She could taste them on her lips. She reached for Daniel's light blue lap blanket and leaned back in the recliner. Taking a deep whiff, she sighed and covered herself, content to surround herself with his scent, which still lingered in the soft cotton blend. *This* was as close to Daniel as she could get.

Closing her eyes again, she said, "You probably already know this, but Jon is mad at God. He doesn't say his prayers anymore, and I don't blame him. You were the religious one. Why didn't God take me instead of you? If it wasn't for the kids, I swear I'd follow you." She gasped and fell silent. It was true, but to hear herself say it was shocking even to her.

Though she knew she shouldn't, she allowed herself to contemplate taking her own life. She was tired of pretending to be strong in front of her children. She wasn't strong; she was weak, and she wanted Daniel to wrap his arms around her and make everything all right, but that was the problem. The very person she longed to turn to was gone. How could she possibly go on without him?

As her tears began to flow, she thought she heard Daniel say, "Promise me you won't leave them, Christine. Promise me."

She was so surprised, she said, "What?"

"Promise me you won't leave them."

Clinging to his voice, whether real or imagined, she whispered, "All right. I promise, but I don't like it! I want to be with you."

"The time will come for us to be together, but you have to raise our children first."

"And then we can be together?" she whispered.

"Then we can be together."

Peace settled over her then and floated around her like a comforting cloud. She allowed herself to hear more of his words, tender and sweet, words she needed and wanted to hear, whether real or imagined.

As she drifted towards sleep, wrapped in the warmth of Daniel's favorite blanket, a contented smile remained on her lips. "I love you, Daniel. I always will."

* * *

Jack turned down a side street just before reaching the entrance to Miss BMW's condominium complex. He parked halfway down the block, in the moonlit shadows of a huge oak tree. A howling wind blew through, causing the lower branches to scratch against the roof of his car—not that he cared. He put on his hat and jacket, and got out of the car.

Lights shone from nearly every house, but the street was surprisingly quiet. It was an older, well-cared-for neighborhood, with mature trees and manicured yards. Tilting his head upward, he located the moon, which was hiding behind dark, fast-moving clouds—a fit night for stalking shadows. A shiver crept up his spine, making him shudder. He pulled the collar of his jacket higher around his neck as he headed down the sidewalk, towards the main road. For the fun of it, he added a limp to his gait. He didn't need it tonight, but it was a good opportunity to practice. Forgetting to limp once effected in someone's presence was the kiss of death in his business. He chuckled to himself. Even after all these years, it amazed him how the doors to alternative worlds opened simply because he changed his appearance.

For self-entertainment, he cast a furtive glance over his shoulder, tugged his hat lower on his forehead, and turned the corner. Maintaining his limp, he strolled down the main street and up to the apartment complex gate. Stepping out of the light, he ducked beneath a tree to wait for the next resident to open the gate. While he waited, his thoughts centered upon Suzaun and their date the following evening. And *that*, by necessity, made him think about money. He reflected on how nice it would be to take a woman out to an expensive restaurant without hoping that she'd be happy with drinks and appetizers, and not expect a full meal.

Why having money mattered all of a sudden, he wasn't quite sure, but after spending time in Cedric's office and Teresa's penthouse suite, and seeing the expensive cars everyone seemed to be driving, he was more aware of the things he didn't have, and much less content with the things he did. Being happy-go-lucky was all well and good, he decided, but having money and living well was infinitely more appealing.

Impatient after only five minutes, he considered scaling the fence. The barrier was eight feet tall, not counting the decorative spires at the top of each spindle, and constructed with two horizontal bars, neither conveniently placed for climbing. He identified the best location, which was approximately fifteen feet to the right of the gate, where a mid-sized boulder shortened the distance to the top. The landing space on the other side, however, looked iffy. It was too dark to see how the ground sloped beneath the vegetation.

He looked back at the gate and then to the top of the fence. He knew he should wait, but he decided to climb it anyway. Stripping off his jacket, he flung it over the fence. Next, he climbed onto the boulder, grabbed hold of two spindles, and hoisted himself into a precarious balance on the upper horizontal bar. From there it was a long drop, but he landed easily enough, thanks to a bush that padded his fall. He was feeling pretty darn pleased with himself until a mud-splashed Jeep rolled up to the gate. Scowling at it, he dusted the leaves from his pants. "If I had waited just a few more minutes, but *nooooo,* I couldn't wait. All right, where's my jacket?"

It was so dark by this section of fence that it took several seconds to find it. Careful not to snag it, he pulled it from the bush and put it on. It was still warm. Once the taillights of the offending jeep disappeared down a side street, he stepped onto the sidewalk. After taking a few steps, he began to limp in earnest. Hoisting his pant leg, he saw that he had gouged his ankle in the fall. It was bleeding, but not enough to worry about. Switching his limp to the injured side, he ambled along the sidewalk and kept his head down. As he considered the vehicles that passed by, he assigned the neighborhood an upper-middle-class demographic. The young woman clearly had money, but there was a world of difference between this neighborhood and Dr. Lindsay's.

He went the long way around the block and entered the alley from the opposite end, which was closer to Miss BMW's garage, thereby reducing the possibility of disturbing any dogs. To his surprise, her garage door stood open, and Dr. Lindsay's car sat parked next to her BMW.

"Bingo."

He ducked between the two cars and cupped his hands against the window of Lindsay's Lincoln. The interior was immaculate. The inside of the BMW, however, was a different story. Wadded up fast-food bags, empty cups, crumpled receipts, and several pieces of clothing littered the back seat and floorboards. It reminded him of his car. He tried the doors, but they were locked.

After snapping a few pictures—including one that showed both license plates—he limped his way back out to the street. The air had turned colder in the last few minutes, making the walk back to the gate less pleasant. He hated the thought of giving these pictures to Teresa Lindsay. While photographs of the vehicles parked inside her private garage weren't what he'd call irrefutable evidence, it did indicate an intimate connection. If there was nothing to hide, why not park on the street?

"Just one more affair in one nation under God," he muttered with disgust. He absolutely loathed cheating.

The moon had finally emerged from behind the clouds, and despite the chill, it was a beautiful night. When he reached the gate, he ducked into the shadows. He needed proof that Lindsay was the driver of the Lincoln tonight.

An hour had passed before Lindsay rolled up to the gate. Jack could see him through the window and snapped some quick shots, including one of the license plate as the car rolled through the gate. He stepped back to await the next car to exit, which, thankfully, wasn't long.

On his way home, his mind whirled with all the many tasks that needed attention. He needed to set an appointment with Teresa Lindsay, drop off fingerprints, meet with Kevin Thomas, order the background checks on Dr. Solver and Cedric Johnson, obtain a copy of the autopsy report, meet with Dr. Sassi, call for the results on Miss BMW's license plate, pick up fort supplies, check on Christine and the kids, set aside time to do yard work and build Jon's fort, and he desperately needed to go grocery shopping and do laundry. He was also worried about Stacy. It bothered him that he hadn't been there when she needed him. He hadn't been there for Christine, either, all because he'd been besotted with Suzaun.

Suzaun . . . A lazy smile lit his face. They had a date planned for tomorrow night.

And what about Christine? Was there a possibility that something might develop with her in the future? Women were blowing his mind lately. Feeling tired and overwhelmed, he turned down the heat and concentrated on the traffic.

* * *

The moon was out from behind the clouds, illuminating more than Anthony would have liked. He tugged his black knitted cap over his ears and looked both ways before entering the alley. His quick eyes searched the shadows, but Jermaine's guards were suspiciously absent. He knew the crunching gravel announced his presence long before he reached the sixth gate on the right, which opened into the back yard of the burned-out house.

He hesitated. That this meeting was taking place within the confines of the yard meant one of two things. Either Jermaine trusted him now, or he was planning something unpleasant. With one hand on his knife, Anthony reached over the fence and unlatched the gate. He pushed it open with his boot and saw the footpath, which led through the overgrown grass to the precarious remains of the covered porch where a small group of men gathered.

Jermaine, who was wearing a silver earring and a red bandanna over his head, looked up and waved him over. His three companions stood in a circle passing a joint between them.

Anthony approached the men, cautious but unafraid.

"You rememba my friens," Jermaine said.

"I do. I was wondering where your guards are."

Jermaine grinned. "No need for guards among friens. Right, bro?"

A scrawny skeleton of a man handed the joint to Jermaine. After taking two hits, Jermaine offered it to Anthony.

"Business before pleasure," Anthony said.

Jermaine handed the joint back to the man. "Let me see it."

Anthony produced two vials of powder. "Let's see the cash."

Jermaine reached for the powder. "Gimme a taste, first."

Anthony closed his fist. "Same as last time. Give me the dough."

One of the men, an unkempt white man in his early twenties, broke from the circle to stand at Jermaine's side. "Give it to him, Jermaine. Let's get this show on the road."

Jermaine grumbled, but he dug into his pocket and handed the cash to Anthony.

After flipping through it, Anthony gave him the vials. "I'll take that joint now."

Jermaine nodded, and the man gave it to Anthony.

Anthony hit it hard. As the smoke wafted around his face, the men dropped into a circle to divvy up the powder on a make-shift table. "I'll just take this with me," he said and headed for the gate. No one even looked up.

* * *

Stacy's head was spinning as she stumbled her way back towards the parking lot on Decatur Street. It was late, but you'd never know it by looking at the crowds. Outside one of the bars, a man dressed in a grenade suit jumped up and down as if he were going to explode. As everyone laughed, pretty women handed out free drink samples and shuffled people inside. Stacy watched from the shadows, but managed to avoid being swept along with the crowd. When the path cleared, she continued to make her way towards the river. Many of the retail shops had closed, but the bars and restaurants would remain open until the wee morning hours. She giggled as she stepped onto a curb and fell back again. It had been ages since she'd allowed herself to get drunk.

She wasn't entirely sure where she was, but the parking lot had to be somewhere along the riverbank. As she approached the blurry traffic lights, a horse-drawn carriage crossed in front of her. The painted lettering on the side of the coach read, *"Ghost and Vampire Tours."* As she stared after it, she realized that New Orleans was everything she'd heard about and more.

When the light changed to green, a riotous group of twenty or so crossed together and then splintered into different directions. She tripped over the curb again and went down on her knees. Several hands helped her to her feet. Too drunk to be embarrassed, she mumbled her appreciation and entered the parking lot to find her car. Twenty minutes later, she began to worry. Had she returned to the right lot? Her search eventually took her down the street to another parking area. They looked very similar, situated below the levee as they were. Finally, she spotted her car and reached into her pocket for her keys. Once inside, she locked herself in and laid her head against the steering wheel to see if she could stop the world from spinning. She typically handled her liquor well, but there was something ruthless about those hurricanes. No wonder they were famous. She closed her eyes as her head continued to spin.

She knew she shouldn't be driving, but parking in the French Quarter wasn't cheap, and her tab increased with each passing hour. Determined to find a safe place to recover, she backed out of her spot and pulled up to the exit booth.

"Sixteen dollars," said a punked-out girl with multiple face piercings.

Stacy reached into her back pocket but came up empty. Puzzled, she checked her other pockets. "My money's gone. That's weird. I just had it a few minutes ago."

"Happens that way down here. Stay or pay. That's the deal."

Glancing to see if anyone was behind her, Stacy said, "I guess I'll back up."

"Whatever," the girl said.

Backing up was more difficult than she expected. It took several frustrating tries, but she finally managed to return to her parking spot without hitting anything. She laid back against her seat and wondered what to do. If her money was gone, she was in serious trouble. Unable to concentrate, she decided that a few more minutes wouldn't make much difference, so she reclined as much as possible and dozed off. A few minutes later, the people who had parked next to her returned. Stacy heard them and rolled down her window. "Excuse me."

A young woman, the female half of the couple, turned and said something in a foreign language.

Realizing that conversation was impossible, Stacy mimed using a cell phone. "Please, just for a minute."

The woman nodded and handed over her cell phone.

Stacy dialed Josh, but he didn't answer. "That's annoying," she grumbled. He was probably with Elizabeth again. "Just one more minute, okay?"

The woman nodded. Her husband, boyfriend, or whoever he was, said something, but he seemed patient enough.

Stacy dug in her purse until she found Jack Kendall's number. Suddenly, he was her only hope.

* * *

Thad was waiting inside Anthony's apartment, which irritated him more than normal because Trina wasn't feeling well today and had to cancel their evening plans. "You planned on waiting up for me, Uncle?"

"Yes, as a matter of fact, I did. How considerate of you to come home at a decent hour for a change," Thad said. "What information have you gathered?"

Anthony poured himself a Jack and Coke. "Can I get you anything?"

"Just information," Thad said.

Joining his uncle on the couch, he said, "I learned enough to earn a huge bonus."

"Let's hear it."

"You've got a far bigger problem than Stacy Young. She had lunch with one of Daniel Steinberg's buddies yesterday—a private detective named Jack Kendall. Whatever Stacy knows, Jack knows." Seeing he had his uncle's attention, he took a swallow of his drink before continuing. "Since I know where Stacy lives and works, I decided to follow Jack instead. Over the course of the afternoon, while he occupied himself truck shopping, I broke into his house." He pulled a folded sheet of paper from his pocket and handed it to Thad. "I found a picture of you and this woman on his desk."

Thad flinched and tucked the paper into his pocket. "Anything else?"

Anthony kicked his feet onto the coffee table and smiled. "Plenty. I caught up with Jack after I searched his house. Since I had some time to kill before delivering your message, I beat him at a game of pool, just for the hell of it. Afterwards, when I went to Cedric's office, I caught Stacy Young snooping around again, so I threated to kill her if she wasn't out of town by midnight. She went, too. I followed her home and watched her pack, just to make sure." He chuckled. "I doubt she'll ever come back."

Thad grunted in what Anthony interpreted as approval. "What else?"

"I took Stacy's cell phone. Jack's number is on her call log, but he's not listed by name, and she apparently calls someone named Josh several times a day. *He* showed up at her apartment just before she left town last night."

"Is he a problem?"

"Nah, I heard their conversation. She didn't tell him anything. From their text messages, I gather she's an extra piece he has on the side. She told him it was over between them and to marry somebody named Elizabeth. Well, did I earn my bonus?"

Thad set a vial on the coffee table. "Indeed. I'll have it for you tomorrow, along with another message for Cedric. See if you can find out who Josh is. If he's a threat, deal with it. As far as Jack Kendall is concerned, I don't want him interfering in my affairs again. Capiche?"

"Yeah, Uncle. I capiche."

CHAPTER FIFTEEN

Jack was sleeping with a smile on his face when the phone rang. He felt for it on the nightstand, trying not to wake up all the way. "Hello," he mumbled.

"Jack, this is Stacy. I need help."

Hearing her desperation, he sat up. "Stacy?"

"Yeah, from Cedric Johnson's office. I'm stuck in the French Quarter. Someone stole my money, and I can't get out of the parking lot. I'm sorry to bother you, but Josh won't answer his phone. I'm really in a bind. Can you help me?"

Jack reached for the lamp and turned it on. "Where are you?"

"In some stupid parking lot on Decatur Street. That's all I know."

He rubbed his eyes and thought through the options. "Can you get to a hotel? I can give them my credit card number."

"It's worse than that. I don't have anywhere to go once I check out. I spent last night at a rest stop."

"Has someone threatened you, Stacy? Is that why you left Jackson?" Her silence raised the hair on the back of his neck. "Are you all right?"

"It's hard to be all right after someone threatens to kill you with a switchblade. Pat O'Brien's hurricanes are effective at making you care less, but my head sure is spinning."

"Who threatened you?"

More silence.

Jack swung his legs out of bed and began getting dressed. "Look, I'm on my way. It'll take me about three hours to get there.

Are you safe where you are?"

"As far as I know. I really hate to bother you, Jack, but I don't have any other options."

"Can I call you back at this number when I get close?"

"No, I'm borrowing this phone. The messenger took mine."

"The messenger? Holy crap!" Jack stuffed his wallet into his back pocket and headed out. "It's 3:00 a.m. I should be there by six. Stand out on the street, so I can find you, or borrow another phone and call me at six o'clock. Okay?"

"Thanks, Jack. I owe you one."

* * *

Christine sat up in the bed, trying to determine what had awakened her. She glanced over at Daniel's side of the bed and frowned. It was his job to check out noises. Stepping into her slippers, she wrapped a robe around herself and ventured into the hallway. She checked on Alexa first; she was fast asleep. Next, she checked Jon's room. His bed was empty. Alarmed, she hurried down the stairs. "Jon?"

After checking the living room and kitchen, she went back upstairs to look again. Panicking, she grabbed her phone and called Jack. She got voicemail. "Jack, it's Christine. I can't find Jon. You don't have him, do you? Call me back." She checked the garage and then went out to check the yard. The sun was just beginning to rise. Jon wasn't on the deck, and it wasn't like him to leave the house in the dark. She was about to go inside when a flashlight caught her attention. Jon was at the fort, no doubt too excited to wait for Jack. She sighed with relief and dialed Jack again. "False alarm. I found him. Call me when you get this message." She quickly changed her shoes and headed out to recover her son.

* * *

Three hours and three cups of coffee after her phone call, Jack cruised down Decatur Street searching for Stacy. The French

—224—

Quarter looked like a ghost town in the early morning hours. It would be noon before people began to roam the streets again. He spotted Stacy leaning against a three-foot-high wall, gripping her stomach and shifting her weight back and forth to stay warm. He pulled along the curb and rolled down the window. "Jump in. Let's go get some breakfast and then come back for your car."

Stacy got in and immediately cranked up the heater. "Thanks, Jack. I really appreciate this."

She looked as if she'd been run over by a steam engine, but he knew better than to say so. "I know where an Ihop is. How does that sound?"

"Perfect." She closed her eyes and was asleep before he turned onto Canal Street.

* * *

"I really think if I weren't already on the floor where I could crawl under the desk, he would've killed me," Stacy said as they climbed back into the car after breakfast.

"I shouldn't have let you copy those files without back up," Jack said. "This has become a complete nightmare. Do you have somewhere to stay? Do you know anyone outside of Jackson?"

"Not without my cell phone."

"You're welcome to stay in my guest room until we can work something else out. Are you okay with that?"

"I rather stay in my own bedroom, but things being as they are, I accept and appreciate your offer."

"Good. Let's go back for your car. Once we get to my place, you can rest up a bit, and then we'll go to the police station. My buddy is a Captain."

When he didn't get a response, he glanced over. She was nodding off again. He smiled and let his thoughts turn to Suzaun. A few minutes later, he checked his watch. It was just after seven o'clock. There was no avoiding it; he'd be late for fort building. He dialed Christine.

"Hey, Jack. False alarm."

"What alarm?"

"Didn't you get my messages? Never mind. I found Jon in his fort before dawn. He's so cute when he gets excited."

"Yeah, well, tell him I'm running late. I ran into a bit of an emergency, but I'll do my best to be there by noon. I'll be headed back to Jackson as soon as I can."

"Is everything all right?"

"It will be. See you soon."

"Over and out," she said, surprising him and making him smile. Women were such wonderful creatures. Just then, Stacy let out an unladylike snort and dropped deeper into sleep.

* * *

Trina leaned against the doorjamb, watching as Thad examined something grisly beneath the microscope. With her stomach being unpredictable lately, she thought it best not to look too closely. As a child, she'd been afraid of the cold, depressing laboratories where her absentee father spent most of his time. Funny, she thought, how feelings stay with you. It was still a creepy place.

"Anyone I know?" she asked.

"Shouldn't you be working somewhere?" he said without looking up.

"I'm on break, thank you very much. And how are you, Daddy dearest? Or would you prefer I start calling you grandpa?"

Thad's shoulders stiffened. "Is Anthony the father?"

"Seems you'll finally have an acceptable heir. Your own blood," she said with more acid than she intended. "A grandchild. Should I begin making preparations to move in? I'll need a full-time nanny, of course."

Thad sat on a rolling stool. "So it's like that, is it? You finally found a way to get your hands on my money?"

Trina wasn't as confident as she pretended. No matter how many times she told herself his that rejection didn't matter, it did. "Why not? It's not going to happen any other way. I'm not good enough, remember?" His withering glare made her stomach churn.

"How does Anthony feel about this?"

"I haven't told him."

"Does he know he's been screwing his cousin?"

She flinched and looked away. "No."

"When you tell him about the baby, leave that part out. After all, we want him to marry you, don't we?"

She nodded.

He squinted as he considered her. "An heir, you say?"

"A potentially legitimate heir," she added.

"You're more like me than I gave you credit for."

For a split second, she felt like running to him for the hug she'd never gotten—a childhood dream she was reluctant to give up even now. But he wouldn't hug her; she was a bastard child. How many times had he reminded her of that? Her stomach turned, and her knees went weak. Glancing around, she dropped before a trash can and vomited. When she felt his hands on her shoulders, it took a moment to realize that he was actually trying to steady her.

He pushed a tissue into her face and guided her to a chair. "I've been thinking about this little scenario since you dropped the incest bomb the other day," he said.

She eyed him with thinly veiled vulnerability.

"I must admit; I rather welcome the idea. I'm not too old to instruct a grandson, to prepare him for his proper place in the family. That's why I haven't interfered with your midnight trysts, which you've been so careful not to throw in my face." He gave her a stern glare, but then a smile spread across his face. "I've begun interviewing nannies."

"You'll let me move in?" she said tentatively.

"Not into the main house, of course, but with Anthony—if he'll have you."

"Wow. I should've done this a long time ago."

"Tell Anthony I'll be by to discuss this change in affairs."

Still trembling, and unable to trust his good will, she got to her feet and headed for the door. Then a smile like his appeared upon her similar features. "It seems my work here is finished."

As she pushed through the door, he said, "That's what you think."

* * *

Little Jon, dressed in denim overalls and his hammer swinging from his belt loop, started whooping and hollering as soon as Jack pulled into the driveway. "Uncle Jack! Mama says we have to eat lunch first. Come on, it's on the table."

Jack's stomach growled as he followed Jon into the kitchen.

"Good morning," Christine said as she handed him a quarter of a peanut butter and jelly sandwich. "That's your appetizer." She laid a square down for Jon and Alexa as they took their seats at the table.

After wolfing it down, Jack said, "Good morning, yourself, Christine. I didn't realize I was hungry." He poured a cup of coffee and sat in his regular chair.

"Are you kidding?" she said. "When aren't you hungry?"

"I can't deny it, I guess."

"Did everything work out this morning?"

Deciding not to worry her with the truth, he said, "Yeah, everything's great." He saw she didn't buy it, but she let it pass. "So, Jon, about your fort, do you think it should have a trap door?"

"You mean it? A real trap door?" He looked at his sister. "Will I be able to lock it, so no one can come up unless I let 'em?"

Alexa wrinkled her brow. "That's not fair, Uncle Jack. If he can lock me out, I'll never be allowed up there."

"That's because you're a dumb girl," Jon accused.

"I can't help it if I'm a girl. That doesn't mean I don't want to be in the fort."

"Okay, children," Christine said impatiently. "The fort's not even built yet, and you're already having skirmishes." She set more sandwiches on the table and turned back to grab a bag of potato chips and a carton of milk.

"Why does Jon get a fort and not me?" Alexa said.

"Because it was my idea," Jon said, scowling at her with their father's expression.

"But I'm older."

Jack started to take a bite of his sandwich but stopped. "Ah, are we saying grace around here anymore?"

"No," Alexa said. "Mom and Jon aren't talking to God anymore."

Several silent seconds went by, during which it became painfully clear that the void left by Daniel's death went far deeper than the ordinary issues of life. He took a bite of his sandwich and followed it with a big swig of milk. "Okay, guys, I have a plan. Alexa, go get me a pen and a piece of paper." Excitement lit her face as she pushed from the table. Jack glanced at Christine; she had seen it, too.

Having a natural talent for drawing, he sketched out a two-room fort that included two ladders and two separate entrances. Each side of the fort was half enclosed. One faced north; the other faced south. In the common wall, he drew a window with shutters, which were lockable from either side—one fort with two private quarters.

"Well, what do you think?" he said.

Jon looked at his sister. "I like it. Otherwise, she'll bring stupid girl stuff up there."

"What about you, Alexa?" Jack said.

"I like it."

"What about our deal?" Jack said.

Alexa bit her bottom lip as she considered an answer—she was wearing solid black again.

"What deal?" Christine said.

"Sorry, it's between me and Alexa. Right, Lexie?"

Alexa glanced at her mother, then back to Jack. "There aren't any movies I want to see right now."

"How bad do you want a fort?"

"All right, what's this about?" Christine said. "It sounds like you're talking in code."

"Sorry, it's private code," he said, winking at Alexa.

Alexa smiled. "Today only. Then we're even?"

Jack shook his head. "Not good enough."

Christine stood by.

"A whole week? That's outrageous! My friends will think I've stopped mourning already."

"How badly do you want a fort you can sneak off to and have slumber parties in?"

"Don't tell her that! No promises, Alexa," Christine said.

Alexa's eyes locked with Jack's. "If I ever decide to give up my side of the fort, can I go back?"

"Then I get both rooms. Right, Uncle Jack?" Jon piped in as he licked peanut butter off his fingers. "Maybe you should make a door instead of a window."

"Not until you're eighteen. How about that?" Jack countered.

"That's highway robbery! You're no fun to negotiate with, you know that?"

Jack chuckled. "It's your decision, Lexie."

"I'm thinking," she said.

"All right, enough of this," Christine said. "Go change your clothes, Alexa. If it's going to be half your fort, then you're going to do your share of the work."

Jon beamed as little boys do when their siblings get into trouble.

Seeing it, Christine added, "You'll both be helping with the yard work, too, so wear your dirty sneakers."

"All my sneakers are dirty," Jon said.

Alexa exhaled in resignation. "Oh, all right. I'll go change." She stomped up the stairs.

"Hurry up, Uncle Jack," Jon said as he bounded out the screen door.

"Right behind you, Jon. You can start taking supplies out of my car if you like."

"Yippee," Jon cheered as he jumped off the deck.

Christine shook her head and began washing the dishes. "I don't have the patience anymore. I'm losing it, Jack."

"No, you're not. The kids will come around." He reached into the sink to rinse his hands, and then he popped her lightly with the dishtowel. "And so will you."

She shrieked perfectly, and he barely ducked out the door in time to avoid the wet rag she threw at his head.

* * *

Nightmares of Angel tormented Anthony until late into the morning. After hitting the snooze button for the fourth time, he forced himself out of bed and into the kitchen. Coffee was the only thing that could get him moving on a day like this. He glanced at the microwave clock. It was half past noon.

After starting the coffee, he picked up the manila envelope from in front of the door. It contained a message to deliver and his bonus. He tossed the silver envelope onto the coffee table, next to his keys. He was tempted to drop a few pills in the grinder but reminded himself that selling drugs was more profitable than doing them.

Placing the bottle into his stash box, he sprawled on the couch to consider how best to neutralize an inconvenient Jack Kendall.

* * *

Doctor Ryan Solver bit his tongue to keep from cursing as he followed Peter Bradshaw, his highly accomplished, hotshot attorney down the concrete stairs of the court building and into Peter's car. Once inside, he let loose. "Why the hell didn't you get me out sooner? Do you have any idea what it's like in there?"

"Do you have any idea how hard it was to arrange your bail? Three patients and a wife dead in a two-year period tends to complicate matters. They're calling you a serial killer, you know."

Ryan felt as if he'd been punched in the stomach. "Nita didn't make it?"

"Oh, my God," Peter said. "They didn't tell you?"

"Where is she?" Ryan said, his voice cracking with emotion.

"I'm so sorry, Ryan. I thought they told you. I'll take you to the hospital. That's where they're keeping her until the autopsy is done."

"Why are they doing an autopsy? Cleary, she had a stroke."

Peter looked troubled. He started the car and pulled onto the street. "The police report states that you were intoxicated, and there were signs of a struggle. Broken glass, paperwork scattered on the floor, bruises on your wife's wrist. Were the two of you arguing?"

Ryan felt his chest tighten. "Hell yes, we were arguing. We've been arguing for forty-three years. What do they think happened?"

"They claim there was a life insurance policy on your desk, detailing the coverage you have out on your wife."

"We've had those policies for twenty-five years. Surely, they don't think—"

"Ryan . . ."

"I should have seen this coming. They're planning a witch-hunt, aren't they? What am I facing?" He wanted to talk to his wife. How could he get through this without her quiet strength? Tears stung his eyes.

The attorney pressed his lips into a straight line. "You'd better hope she died of natural causes because, pending an investigation, you could be facing murder one."

* * *

Christine was wearing a yellow blouse and her favorite pair of blue jeans, but her jeans were too big and settled lower on her hips than she was comfortable with. The full-length mirror on the back of her bedroom door confirmed what she already knew; she had lost weight since Daniel's death.

She lifted up her shirt and turned to the side. She was definitely too thin. She could buy new clothes, she supposed, but she wasn't in the mood for shopping. Having been blessed with good genes, she had always been happy with her appearance, but as she examined herself more closely, she saw dark circles beneath her eyes and frowned at her reflection. She looked exhausted— which she was. She still wasn't sleeping well. In an odd way, she took satisfaction in looking the way she felt. It wouldn't seem right to be hurting so much on the inside and have your outward appearance suggest otherwise. She turned from the mirror and went downstairs into the kitchen, but she had washed the dishes earlier and was at a loss for what to do. Keeping busy seemed the best protection against despair, which she felt more deeply than she let on, even to Jack. She looked out the window towards the treehouse and decided to check on their progress.

Seeing his mother approach, Jon dropped his hammer and ran towards her. "Mama, look! My side's almost done."

"I see," she said, admiring the quality of Jack's work. "It looks pretty sturdy."

"It's real sturdy, Mama. Come on up."

Jon grabbed her hand and led her to a newly constructed ladder that reached through a hole in one-half of the two-room treehouse, which was about eight feet off the ground.

Jack's smiling face filled the hole as she looked up. "Hey, Christine. Jon, did you find that box of nails yet?"

"Oh," Jon said and ran to their supply pile. "Here they are."

Christine waited for Jon to scurry up the ladder and then climbed up after him. She watched as Jack drove the last few nails into the window frame. The walls and floors were finished.

"One side down, one to go," Jack said.

Impressed, Christine peered through the window into a duplicate room on the other side. "Will you need two ladders?"

"Yep," Jon said. "I'm painting mine blue."

"Speaking of Lexie," Christine said glancing around, "where is she?"

Jack brushed the sawdust from his face. "She went to the bathroom—again."

"Oh," Christine mused. "I didn't see her."

"I think that was the point," Jack said. "Okay, Jon. Down we go. We've got to work on Lexie's ladder."

"Why me? It's her ladder," he complained as he descended through the hole.

"Ladies first," Jack said, gesturing for Christine to follow.

Christine turned around and started down the ladder. "I guess that makes me the First Lady, doesn't it?" She glanced up at Jack's lopsided grin and smiled.

* * *

"Hello?"

"Hello yourself, Suzaun," Jack said, unable to wait until he got home to call. "I'm looking forward to seeing you tonight. What time should I pick you up?"

"Pick me up? Oh, I don't know you well enough to— I mean, I thought we were meeting at Bravo!"

Jack swallowed hard. "We *could* go there, if you really want to, but I thought we could try an action date."

"A what?"

Jack tapped his fingertips on the steering wheel; the traffic light was taking forever to turn green. "Do you like to bowl?" There was complete silence on the other end. "Suzaun? Maybe it's a stupid idea. Bravo! is fine."

"No," she said. "I wasn't expecting it; that's all. I like to bowl, actually. I just haven't done it in a long time."

"Does that mean you like the idea? Cuz if you don't, I'm fine with Bravo!"

"No, I'm down with it. Bowling sounds like fun."

"Cool. How about the lanes across from Old Venice Pizza, say eight o'clock? We can catch some dinner afterwards."

"Eight it is. See you there."

After their conversation, Jack began a mental inventory of the aches and pains that were beginning to make themselves known. Building the fort had turned into a major project, but so far it was an awesome experience. Children were an amazing mixture of aggravation and wonder. He found it fascinating to observe them throughout the day as they bounced between excitement and boredom, sometimes within seconds. They were helpful one moment, lazy the next, but they had all worked well together despite their sibling rivalry. He thought about the many times he had called for some specific tool, only to find his helpers missing. He chuckled. Just how often did a normal child have to use the bathroom anyway? Not as often as those two did today; he was sure of that.

The fort was nowhere near finished. They'd be back at it the following weekend, and they hadn't even started on the yard yet. As much as he was looking forward to seeing Suzaun, he found himself dwelling on the materials he needed for the fort. It felt nice to be part of a family. It wasn't too late to start one—maybe with Suzaun.

When he arrived home and stepped from the garage into the kitchen, he was taken aback. The kitchen was spotless, and the aroma rising from the stove made his mouth water.

"Hey," Stacy said as she walked from the den into the kitchen. "I didn't hear you come in."

Jack, still sweaty and covered with sawdust, took a beer from the fridge and offered it to Stacy.

"Thanks," she said. "I wanted one earlier, but I didn't want to raid without permission."

"Raid away," he said and pulled another beer out for himself. He raised his bottle to clink with hers. "To new beginnings."

"Amen," she said and took a long drink.

"Wow. I don't think my kitchen has ever looked this good. You've been busy."

"Nothin' else to do, so I made spaghetti. I hope you're hungry."

"Thanks, Stace, but I forgot to tell you. I'm going out tonight."

"Oh. That's okay. I just thought . . ."

"I've always heard spaghetti is better the second day. Can I raincheck for tomorrow night?"

"Sure. What time?"

"I'll have to let you know. Sorry to miss out, but I have to hurry. Is everything okay in the guest room?"

"I washed all the bedding this afternoon. Hope you don't

mind."

"Make yourself at home. I apologize for leaving you alone tonight, but I already had plans."

"That's cool. Can I use your computer?"

"If you unbury it first." He dropped his empty bottle into the trash. "Okay, I'm headed for the showers. Anything else before I go?"

"Think I should call Josh?"

As logical as her question was, Jack didn't like being reminded that they were seeing each other. "I think it's best if I call him," he said. "We don't know how deep the problem is. For all we know, my phone might be bugged."

"Oh, no! The copies of the Solver files are under my desk! The messenger scared me so bad I forgot all about them. We've *got* to call Josh. If he finds them and doesn't know what's happened—"

"He might take them to Cedric." Jack pulled out his cell phone. "What's his number?"

Stacy rattled it off, and Jack began pacing. "Josh, Jack Kendall here. I've got some important information for you."

"Yeah? What's up?" Josh said into the phone.

Jack glanced at Stacy. "Can we meet somewhere?"

Stacy pulled on his arm, trying to get close enough to hear the other side of the conversation.

"Tomorrow afternoon is open," Josh said.

"No. It has to be tonight."

"I have plans."

"So do I," Jack said, "but this is urgent. Any chance you could meet me in the bar at Old Venice Pizza in forty-five minutes?"

"Yeah, okay. I'll be there," Josh said.

Stacy reached for a bowl, loaded it with spaghetti, and topped it with thick homemade sauce. She twirled a bite onto her fork, blew on it, and then offered it to Jack.

"The least you can do is taste what you're missing."

He happily obliged. "Dang, woman. You sure can cook."

"Well, I didn't get this big butt by starving myself to death.

That's for sure."

Jack cranked his neck to judge for himself. "It looks pretty darn good to me."

Stacy laughed. "You're as much of a tease as I am. Go get cleaned up; you stink." She tossed a smile over her shoulder and disappeared into the den with her dinner.

Jack shook his head. With women in the world, why did guys ever hang out with each other? Women were much more interesting.

"Hey, Stacy?"

"Yeah?"

He followed her into the den and glanced around as if he'd never seen the place before. "Wow."

She sucked a noodle from her fork. "You don't clean much, do you?"

"How do you feel about guns?"

"Why?" she said.

"Someone broke in here the other day. I doubt he'll come back, but you never know. Besides, it's time we catch ourselves a ganglord, right?"

"You catch him; I'll shoot him. How's that for teamwork?"

"Remind me never to tick you off."

"I wouldn't recommend it."

"Right," Jack said and headed for the shower. He was having second thoughts about arming someone as bold as Stacy.

* * *

Thad was seated at a corner table and smiled as she approached.

"Good evening, Elyse. You look lovely, as usual."

"Thank you," she said as he held her chair, but she knew her smile was half-hearted. Once they were settled, she said, "I've been thinking about this all weekend. I'm sorry to disappoint you, Dr. Winchester, but I've decided against your offer. While money is important, so is enjoying my work. I'd miss my patients, especially the children."

"If your mind was made up, why didn't you say so on the phone?"

Startled by his tone, she said, "I wanted to tell you in person. I—Would you prefer to call off dinner?"

"Not at all. In fact, it's *almost* good news."

"Excuse me?" she said, caught off guard again.

The waiter arrived with a martini for Thad. "May I get you something, miss?"

"A cosmopolitan, please." The waiter nodded and moved on.

Elyse caught Thad's gaze lingering on the plunging neckline of her silky black dress. She had worn it to entice him, but she was feeling unsettled by his annoyance and not at all sure she wanted to pursue their flirtation.

"As it happens," he said, "another position has come up—though it will be several months before it pans out."

She waited for him to continue.

He smiled. "It seems I'm about to become a grandfather. I've decided to hire a full-time nanny."

"Oh, congratulations. I love babies!" But then her smile faded. "I'm confused. You said you lost your only child."

Thad took a sip of his martini. "Forgive me; I misspoke. My nephew is the child's father. Since my brother died, my nephew and I have become quite close. I'll be a grandfather by proxy."

"I see. How exciting for you."

"Thank you. I'm quite pleased myself. My nephew and his wife live in an apartment above the garage. There's also a private guest suite attached to the main house. It has two bedrooms, a comfortable living space, and a pool and tennis court you can use. If you're interested, it might help both of us accomplish our goals. Say, seventy-five thousand dollars a year, in addition to free housing for you and your daughter?"

Elyse felt her eyebrows rise. "I'm leasing my apartment. How soon did you have in mind?"

"My grandson is due sometime in late October or early November. When does your lease expire?"

She smiled. "November first."

"How convenient. Are you interested?"

* * *

"What's up?" Josh said as he approached Jack at the bar.

"It's about Stacy. Let's grab a table." Jack led the way to a secluded booth, but in the back of his mind it registered that his attire lacked the class and style of the younger man. No wonder Stacy was interested in Josh.

"You've heard from her?" Josh said.

"She's staying at my place for now."

"What! Why?" Josh said with a scowl.

"Our mysterious ganglord caught her searching Cedric's office. He pulled a switchblade and threatened to kill her unless she agreed to leave town. She called me from New Orleans."

"Why didn't she call me?" Josh said.

"She said she tried, but you didn't answer your phone."

"I haven't had any missed calls."

"It would have been late last night."

A sheepish stain colored his face. "Now, I remember. She did call. I was staying with Elizabeth and erased her message without listening to it. Is she okay?"

Jack bristled with irritation. Fortunately, he was better than Josh at concealing his feelings. "The messenger, as Stacy calls him, took her cell phone, so there's a pretty good chance he's aware of our connections to Stacy. Which means Cedric is, or soon will be, equally informed. I'm afraid we've all been compromised."

Josh paled. "What should we do? Go to the police?"

"I'm planning to see my Captain buddy tomorrow. I'll let you know what he says. In the meantime, watch your back. There's no telling what lies at the heart of all this. Whoever's behind it won't appreciate our involvement. Did you leave any messages for Stacy that might compromise us further?"

Josh's horrified expression answered in the affirmative.

"What, exactly, did you say?" Jack said.

"Only that I miss our . . ." Josh rolled his eyes. "This is crazy. I can't believe Cedric is involved in something like this. It makes no sense. Why risk his practice, let alone his reputation?"

"Maybe Stacy's right. Maybe Cedric does have something to hide. She made copies of the Solver files for me to study, but she was so shaken by her encounter, she forgot about them until a little while ago. They're in a backpack beneath her desk. Can you get them for me tonight?"

"If what you suspect is true, and Cedric finds out I'm involved with Stacy . . ."

"There's more at stake here than your job, Josh."

"I'm not very good at hiding my feelings, I'm afraid."

"You don't say?" Jack teased.

"Not news to you, I see," he grumbled.

"Look, it's my job to read people. Cedric's, too. If you can't trust yourself, call in sick tomorrow."

"Can I talk to Stacy?"

"Our phones might be bugged. Just get those files and meet me in the alley behind Cedric's office later tonight. Say, eleven thirty?"

"Yeah, sure. I'll be there. I'm taking Elizabeth to some vampire flick she wants to see. It gets out at ten thirty."

"Perfect. I'll be waiting at eleven thirty."

They shook hands, and Josh left the bar.

Jack paid the waitress and waited for her to come back with his change. One thing was certain. He, Josh, and Stacy were on the same team now.

* * *

Jack's eyes quickly adjusted to the dim, hazy interior in the bowling alley. Concluding that he had arrived first, he went to the bar and ordered two draft beers. Suzaun was just walking in when he rounded the corner to wait for her in the lobby. Her tall, slender body looked amazing in her tight blue jeans and white fitted shirt. Almost every male in the room turned to look her way. "Way to go, Jackster," he mumbled to himself. To her, he said, "Hey, Suzaun." He kissed her cheek and handed her a frosty mug. "You look amazing."

"Thanks," she said, dimples appearing with her smile. "I don't hear that very often."

"Really? We can certainly remedy that. Let's check in."

A few minutes later, they were bowling their first round. Over the course of the next two hours, Jack developed an entirely new appreciation for bowling; he absolutely loved watching Suzaun move. The beer and laughter flowed freely, and their scores improved with each of the three games they bowled.

Later, over a delicious wood-fired pizza at Bravo!, the conversation grew more personal.

"So, Suzaun, what do you see in your future? A family of your own some day?"

She shook her head and sipped her wine. "No. Not for me."

Unaccountably disappointed, he said, "Why ever not?"

Suzaun placed both elbows on the table and leaned forward. "In case you haven't noticed, I'm black. I prefer white men—and white women, for that matter. I wouldn't do that to my kid. Besides, I like my body the way it is."

He wondered about her statement, but opted for humor. "I'll drink to your body, Suzaun—any time."

She blushed. "What about you? Any kids in your future?"

He thought about that for a moment. If he said yes, did that mean no Suzaun? "There are plusses and minuses to both scenarios. I could be happy either way."

She looked at her watch. "I should be heading home. Busy day tomorrow."

"Suzaun?" Jack said.

"Yeah?"

"Do you know me well enough to invite me back to your place?"

She laughed, and Jack felt mortified. "The answer to that question is complicated," she said. "You see, I do know you better now, and that's just it. You're a really nice guy, Jack. You're down to earth, and funny. You're genuine and caring. You are the husband type."

"That's a good thing, isn't it?"

"It is, but I'm not looking for a husband."

"That's perfect because I'm not looking for a wife. No strings attached."

"I think, Jack, we should say good night here. It was fun. It really was, but we don't belong on the same page. I'm sorry."

* * *

How Elyse got from La Bells restaurant and into Thad Winchester's bed was still a bit hazy. He had invited her to his house to see the guest suite, but somehow they ended up in his bedroom. Feeling smothered, she tried to push his shoulder away from her face. "Lift up, you're crushing me."

Thad slowed the pace and looked down into her face. "I'm sorry; it's just been so damn long."

A few moments later, he was hammering away again.

Elyse shoved harder. "You're hurting me, dammit!"

In one swift move, Thad rolled onto his back and pulled Elyse over with him. "Let's see if this is better."

Elyse's hair fell like a cascade of silk around her waist. "Good idea," she said. Closing her eyes, she began to move, smiling as she used the most effective weapon in her arsenal to secure her future.

Later, when their breathing had returned to normal, she said, "Were you serious about hiring me as a Nanny, or was that just a ploy to get me into bed?"

He wrapped his arms around her waist and stroked her hair. "No ploy, but to tell you the truth, I could get used to this. You feel absolutely wonderful."

"Yeah? You feel pretty wonderful yourself."

Within moments, they slept together peacefully.

* * *

Jack was glad that he and his ego had somewhere else to

go.

"The husband type," he scoffed as he drove towards the back of Cedric's office complex, which was the first of several buildings that formed a row along a city block. "Why didn't that feel like a compliment?"

The alley was extremely dark. Secure inside his car, Jack hoped that he was the only one using the cloud cover to his advantage tonight. He glanced at his watch. Josh was five minutes late. Finally, the grey metal door—the only back entrance—opened and then closed. When Josh approached the passenger's side door, Jack unlocked it and Josh climbed in.

"Got 'em," Josh said. "Let's get out of here."

Jack pressed the locks and made his way back out to the street.

"This is exciting," Josh said. "How often are you involved in something like this?"

Relieved to be away from Cedric's office, he said, "My work usually means the end of a bad marriage or partnership, not murder."

"Murder?"

He reached over and tapped the backpack. "If my hunch is correct, yes."

"I know I'm not the most important piece of this puzzle, but my career sure seems to be in jeopardy, and it feels like there's nothing I can do about it."

Jack turned into a nearby parking lot where they had agreed that Josh would leave his car. "Can you keep a game face tomorrow?"

"I'll do my best," Josh said. "I need to be there to hear what's going on."

"Just remember to act concerned about Stacy and her mother."

"Right," Josh said. "Tell Stacy I'm glad she's safe."

"Will do."

Jack waited until he had driven off in his gorgeous BMW before heading home. As he waited at a red light, he glanced over at the backpack. He sure hoped those files revealed something useful.

* * *

Anthony did a double take as Jack drove past him in his Camry. He scoffed; the stupid jerk had no idea his days were numbered. A few minutes later, Antony turned into the alleyway behind Cedric's office building and used his passkey to enter through the grey metal door. After dropping off the silver envelope, he trotted down the stairwell with a smile on his face. Trina would be off work in fifteen minutes.

* * *

Although he was normally oblivious to the businesses he passed, Jack began looking for a place to stop. Having Suzaun dump him after only one date pricked his ego more than he wanted to admit. Whiskey, he decided, was the best way to dull his unpleasant feelings. He pulled up to a convenience store and went inside.

Grabbing a bottle of Coke for the whiskey he had at home, he turned to peruse the snack display, which was on the end-cap of the last aisle. Wondering how much money he had, he reached into his pocket, accidentally scattering coins in the process. Annoyed, he bent to retrieve them.

A woman shrieked, which startled him so badly, he almost dropped the Coke bottle he was carrying.

"Don't shoot! Take whatever you want."

"Open the register," a female demanded. "Put the money in the bag. Now!"

Since he was already near the ground, he set the Coke bottle down and reached for his gun, which he'd had on him in the alley, but it wasn't there. He had left it beneath the front seat. "Figures," he mouthed silently, and crept towards the front of the store.

"That's all of it!" the attendant said.

"Give me the coins, too. Hurry up."

From mid-aisle, Jack could see the checkout counter in a round, corner mirror. The robber, who was small in stature, wore a knitted cap and waved a gun in the attendant's face. The attendant, a rounded young woman in her early twenties, threw handfuls of coins into a bag, and then shoved it towards the robber. Raising her hands, she said, "Please don't shoot! I got three kids."

He risked a better look through a row of paper towels, which were standing on the top shelf to his left. The bandit had a long blonde braid, which had escaped her cap. He ducked as she threw an anxious glance over her shoulder.

"You got diapers and baby food in here?"

"Yeah," the attendant said. "On the last aisle, near the front."

"Get 'em for me!" the robber demanded.

"Okay. They're right over here." The attendant came rushing around the corner and nearly tripped over Jack, who held a finger to his lips, begging for silence.

The attendant screamed.

"What is it?" Not waiting for an answer, the robber tucked the moneybag under her arm and ran out the door.

Jack and the attendant looked at each other in dazed relief. "It's okay," he said. "She's gone."

"She could have killed me!" the young woman wailed and then dissolved into tears.

Jack wrapped his arm around the distraught woman's shoulders. "It's all right. She's—" He heard his Camry fire up and his tires squeal. "My keys!" He patted his empty pockets and dashed outside, but the girl, his car, his keys, *and* his gun, had all fled the scene. He hung his head and grumbled a few choice words. Accepting the grim reality, he took out his cell phone and dialed Kevin Thomas.

"Captain Thomas, here."

"Hey, Kev, it's Jack. I need to report a robbery."

"That's what you said yesterday. I thought you were coming by to drop off the prints."

"This is another one, a convenience store robbery. The

perpetrator just drove off in my car."

"All right. Let's hear it."

Jack recounted the story, including the fact that he'd left his car unlocked.

"We'll get right on it," Kevin said. "I'll need you to look through some photographs. If it's who I think it is, this is her third robbery this month."

"Yeah, I know the drill. Think they'll find my car?" Jack said.

"Considering what you drive, you should hope not."

"Very funny."

"Gotta laugh while you can, my friend. Gotta laugh while you can. I'll send Officer Sampson to take your statement. Tell him I said to drop you off at your place afterwards."

"Thanks. I'll be in first thing tomorrow morning, and I'll bring the prints."

"Find me after they finish with you downstairs," Kevin said.

Multiple sirens screamed in the distance.

Jack gritted his teeth. "Uh, there's one more thing."

"Yeah?" Captain Thomas said.

"My revolver is under the front seat of my car. It's loaded."

Silence.

"Kevin?"

"I'll get back to you."

Jack closed his phone. This just wasn't his night.

* * *

Anthony and Trina were hard at it when a knock startled them. Trina gathered the sheets around herself while Anthony stepped into his jeans.

"Stay put," he said, and shut the bedroom door. Trying to hide his irritation, he opened the front door and said, "Uncle."

Thad brushed by him and made himself comfortable on the couch.

"Can't this wait? It's one o'clock in the morning."

"For what? For you to finish banging your girlfriend?"

Anthony tensed.

"Sit down. We need to talk."

Anthony joined him on the couch, but his guard was up. This didn't feel like a typical meeting.

"Why aren't you out after Jack Kendall tonight?" Thad said.

"How far do you want me to go, and how fast?"

"The SOB took my picture, which means he's watching me. I thought we covered this."

"You've been paying me to deliver messages, not rough people up," Anthony said a bit louder than he intended. They simultaneously glanced at the bedroom door.

"You'll be well compensated," Thad said.

"Fine, I'll take care of it," Anthony said. "Now if that's everything, I'm going back to bed." He rose and waited for Thad to do the same.

"Let's talk about you and Trina," Thad said as he patted the couch. "What are your intentions?"

"My intentions?" Anthony said, glancing at the bedroom door again. He sat back down. "What do you mean?"

"Do you love her?"

"I don't know. Why do you care?"

"I'm related to the child she carries, assuming the paternity test pans out."

Anthony blinked a few times. "Are you saying Trina's pregnant?"

Thad chuckled. "So, she still hasn't told you. How very interesting."

"I still don't see what business this is of yours."

"She's carrying my heir. That makes it very much my business. Let me know when you decide on a date. To inherit my fortune, that child must be legitimate." He tightened his robe and let himself out.

Anthony stared after him, stunned, and then outraged.

* * *

While the convenience store attendant gave her statement to the first police officers to arrive, Jack waited in the background for Officer Sampson. A few minutes later, he pulled into the parking lot with lights flashing.

"Hey, Charlie."

"Jack," Charlie said as he hoisted his weight out of the car. "What happened here tonight?"

After recounting the story for a second time, he asked the multi-million-dollar question. "Captain Thomas suggested you might be willing to drop me by my place. Would you mind?"

Apparently, he did, because Charlie frowned something fierce.

"If it's not convenient . . ." Jack said.

"No, I'll drop you off, but you better be at the station bright and early tomorrow morning, or it'll be my butt that gets kicked for it. And that wouldn't be in your best interests, if you catch my meaning."

"First thing tomorrow morning."

Charlie shook his head. "You're a pain in my backside, you know that Kendall? Standby while I finish up."

By this time, additional police cars and two news crews had arrived. The attendant, whose name Jack still didn't know, seemed to enjoy the lime light. He backed away from the crowd, but a reporter spotted him and snapped a series of photographs, blinding him with the flash. Annoyed, he raised his hand to block his face.

"Hey, I'm a private investigator. The last thing I need is my face plastered on TV. Can you delete those photos, please?"

The reporter—a young kid barely out of high school—said, "Get over yourself, dude. This is the top story of the day."

Charlie, having wrapped up his duties, caught the exchange and placed one of his beefy hands on the kid's shoulder. "Ditch the photos, son. He's on our side."

"Ah, come on. Not even one?"

"Helping criminals for the sake of a news story is bad

business. Delete them, or I'll seize your camera and do it for you."

"Oh, all right," the reporter grumbled, "but I don't have to do it, you know." With Charlie watching over his shoulder, he deleted Jack's photos and went to try his luck with the mob surrounding the attendant.

"Thanks, Charlie," Jack said.

"You owe me a cup of coffee."

"I'll even buy the doughnuts. Let's get out of here." Jack slid into the back seat of the squad car. "Home James," he said, but that was *after* Charlie had closed his door.

* * *

Anthony downed two quick shots of Tequila. When he opened the bedroom door, Trina was sitting cross-legged on the bed. "Anything you wanna tell me?" he said.

"I was waiting for the right time. I'm not askin' you ta marry me or anything."

"No," Anthony scoffed, "my landlord did that for you. How well do you two know each other, anyway?" Trina looked away. "I asked you a question," he said.

"He happened across me when I was throwing up at work."

"And?"

"He asked me if I was pregnant. How was I supposed to know he's your uncle?"

"Who said he's my uncle?"

Trina's eyes widened with guilt.

"He claims you're carrying his heir. Care to explain that?"

"You're the father, Anthony. That makes him your baby's granduncle. He can name any heir he chooses."

"You've discussed the terms of his will? What aren't you telling me, Trina?"

"Okay. I'll tell you, but let's talk about it in the living room. I don't believe in arguing in the bedroom."

Anthony stepped aside to permit her to pass. He paused for another shot of tequila, and then joined her on the sofa. "Okay,

I'm listening."

"First, if you don't want us, just say so. I'm more than capable of taking care of myself. I've been doing it my entire life."

"Answer my question. How do you know my uncle?"

"You answer my question first. Do you want me and the baby, or not?"

"I thought you were on the pill."

"I was, until recently."

"You tricked me?" Anthony hissed, shooting to his feet.

"Not on purpose. But since it happened, I may as well be happy about it. Right?"

"I don't like being trapped!"

"Then consider yourself untrapped. I already told you, I can take care of myself!"

Anthony's temples were pounding. Under different circumstances, he might have welcomed the news, but hearing it from his uncle? "Do you need money for an abortion?"

Trina's eyes flashed as she stormed into the bedroom and started pulling on her clothes. "I'll assume full custody and spare you the hardship of dealing with either one of us. How's that, you selfish son-of-a-bitch?"

"Fine by me. I hate little kids."

"Fine. Consider us gone." Trina grabbed her purse and headed for the door.

"I want a paternity test!" Anthony shouted.

Trina gasped and spun around. "You're accusing me of cheating?"

"If the shoe fits," Anthony said, but he wasn't sure why he was provoking her.

"Let me tell you something, Tony Boy," she said, jabbing a pointed finger into his chest. "I don't have to trap a man to get one. If we're done, just say so. I'll have another man in my bed so fast your head will spin."

Anthony raised his hand to strike her, but Trina didn't flinch. In fact, she raised her chin, daring him to do it. He turned his back.

After a moment, Trina wrapped her arms around his waist and laid her head against his back. "I'm sorry for not telling you sooner."

Her comforting warmth melted his anger. Turning around, he drew her against his chest and sighed into her hair. He didn't want to lose her. "Is it really a boy?"

"It's too soon to tell."

Anthony smiled for the first time since he'd heard the news. "Come on," he said. "Let's go to bed."

Trina smiled, too. "I thought you'd never ask."

CHAPTER SIXTEEN

It was nearly three in the morning before Jack's head hit the pillow and ten o'clock before he woke up. He stared at his stubbled face in the bathroom mirror without really seeing it. What kind of misery leads someone to commit armed robbery for diapers and baby formula? If the police found her, he wouldn't press charges. He wanted nothing to do with separating the young woman from her child. When he entered the kitchen a short time later, Stacy handed him a cup of coffee.

"How do you like your eggs?"

He graced her with his lopsided smile. "You're spoiling me for all other women. You know that?"

"Yeah, yeah, that's what they all say. There's a message on your recorder from a guy named Kevin. They found your car."

"Nothing like good news to start the day."

"They're dusting it for prints."

"The files!" He rushed back down the hallway in search of his cell phone. Grabbing it from the dresser, he dialed the police department and headed back to the kitchen.

"Hey, Kevin, it's Jack. I had some important files in the back seat of my car. Any chance you've seen them?"

"Got 'em right here," Kevin said. "Along with your gun. I thought we agreed you'd be in early."

"Sorry, I just got up. Can you be available in an hour?"

"Unfortunately, yes. A hotel fire turned into an all-nighter, but I plan to be outta here by noon."

"I'm on the way," Jack said.

After scarfing down breakfast, Jack sat at his newly organized desk to make a few quick calls while Stacy finished getting ready. He had to admit, sitting at a tidy desk made him feel as though he were in control and more expensive. He was definitely going to raise his professional rates. He dialed his first number.

"Cedric Johnson's office."

"Good morning. Is Mr. Johnson available?"

"No, but Joshua Royce is here. Can he help you?"

"Yes, thanks."

After waiting ten minutes, he hung up and called again.

"Cedric Johnson's office," the same voice said.

"This is Jack Kendall. Josh never picked up."

"I'm sorry, but it seems he's been called into an emergency meeting. Can I have him call you back?"

"Yes. He's got my number." He sure hoped Josh upheld his end of the deal. He didn't like trusting his fate into someone else's hands, especially when their poker face was as transparent as Josh's. Turning his attention to the next item on his list, he dialed Teresa Lindsay. He was hoping to leave her a message, but she took his call.

"I was expecting to hear from you," she said. "Have you made any progress?"

"I have. Can we meet this afternoon?"

"Tell me, now," she said.

"I'd rather talk in person."

Teresa breathed an exasperated sigh. "All right. Two o'clock."

"See you then."

He was absolutely dreading telling her that her husband's mistress was pregnant. There was no way to sugarcoat it, either. No matter which words he used, the message was going to hurt. Having completed his calls, he jotted a list of supplies for Jon's fort.

Stacy walked in wearing a short skirt and a tight top.

"Wow," escaped his mouth before he could stop it.

"May as well look cute, right?"

"I'm all about being seen in the company of cute." He held

the door for her, appreciating the swing of her skirt as he followed behind.

* * *

Doctor Ryan Solver paced the confines of his attorney's conference room knowing that both men watched his every move. Listening to them discuss the viability of his practice and the suspect quality of his work was more than he could stand. "Why won't you listen to me? I did nothing wrong! I don't know why those patients died, but it sure as hell wasn't because of me."

Peter Bradshaw, Ryan's attorney, exchanged a look with the insurance company's attorney, J.R. Kramer and cleared his throat. "We have to cover these questions, Ryan, to prepare our grounds of defense."

"Defense?" Ryan snorted. "Is that what you call it? You're not trying to defend me. You're trying to settle for the least amount possible—and my reputation be damned."

J.R. Kramer, a short, squatty fellow with thick glasses, grunted. "We've been down this nasty road before, Dr. Solver, so you may as well make it easier on everyone by answering our questions."

"And where does it end?" Ryan said, leaning on the table with his fists. "Tell me, *Mr.* Kramer, if I agree to settle out of court again, will your company insure me going forward?"

"That depends." Kramer took off his glasses and gestured with them as he spoke. "Generally speaking, rates increase per incident, but with this being your third claim, I can't guarantee what the underwriters will decide."

Ryan closed his eyes and let the bad news wash over him. He had expected it, of course, but hearing it was more difficult than he had anticipated. Without his practice, there was nothing left to live for. "What happens if I pay the settlement from my own funds?"

Kramer's eyebrows shot up, and Peter rose to his feet.

"We've discussed that, Ryan," Peter said. "It's not in your best interest, and it probably won't make a difference anyway."

"Is that true?" Ryan said, staring at Kramer.

"Well, I . . ." Kramer pulled a handkerchief from his pocket and blotted his forehead. "Are you saying you'll pay off the deceased's family and leave us out of it altogether?"

"Can I do that?" Ryan said glancing from one man to the other.

Peter looked to Kramer.

"I'll have to get back to you," Kramer said. "I can't make any promises, but if we don't have to pay a claim on this, then I might be able to arrange for your premiums to hold at the current rate. Of course, your risk ratio still rises. That will catch up with you at some point. Do you have that kind of cash?"

Ryan flinched. Not trusting himself to speak, he walked to the window and looked out.

"Mr. Solver's wife passed recently," Peter said. "She had a sizable life insurance policy."

"My condolences," Kramer said. "Look, I'm scheduled to meet with my colleagues at two o'clock this afternoon. I'll confer with them and call you with their decision. Just so I'm clear, you're willing to foot the entire bill in exchange for a waiver of premium increase for another year."

"Guaranteed in writing," Ryan said.

"Are you sure you want to do that?" Peter said again.

Ryan sank into his chair. "If I settle out of court, I'll look guilty. If I fight, I'll go through years of trial, and no matter the outcome, you'll cancel my insurance, which means the end of my practice."

"There are other insurance companies," Peter said.

"Not for me, there's not. After the Hernandez case, Kramer's company was the only one who would touch me. Any way I look at it, I'm screwed. The only way to keep my practice is to do what I'm suggesting." He turned to Kramer. "Am I reading the situation correctly?"

"That pretty much covers it," Kramer said, closing his briefcase. He rose from his seat and stretched out his hand for Ryan to shake. "If you can keep your insurance, you can keep your practice. Let's shoot for that."

"I just want this over with. Paying off Steinberg's widow seems like the fastest route."

Kramer shrugged. "It's your money."

Ryan winced at his choice of words. Never in a million years did he think Anita would go first.

Peter put his hand on Ryan's shoulder. "I understand how you must feel, Ryan, but I can't advise you to settle with your own money."

"There are no winners in a situation like this," Kramer said, "but maybe this will soften the blow."

Ryan watched the attorneys part. Afterwards, Peter turned to him and said, "If it were me, I'd take that money and live out the rest of my life in comfort. To hell with medicine; retire."

"It's not that I haven't thought about it, believe me, but I won't walk away from my career barred like a dirty criminal. It's been my life's work, my identity. Without it, I don't know who I am."

"Well," Peter said, "at least you won one battle today."

"Oh, yeah? Which one is that?"

"You'll pay for it, but I'm guessing you'll get to keep your insurance."

The impact of those words hit Ryan with such force he had to turn away. He could continue practicing medicine. Maybe.

* * *

Cedric shoved the silver card and envelope into the shredder and continued pacing back and forth across his office, unable to settle the nagging worry in the pit of his stomach. What did he mean, *'Know anyone named Jack or Josh?'* What did Winchester know about Jack? Why was he suspicious of Josh? What had he done with Stacy? The answers he came up with were unthinkable. Talking to Josh would help immensely. He couldn't keep a secret if his life depended on it. Circling back to his desk, he hit the intercom button for the fourth time in the last half hour. "Any word from Josh yet?"

"No, sir. I'll let you know as soon as I hear from him."

"Thank you."

Cedric's anxiety level was over the top. He couldn't sit, he couldn't work, and he couldn't leave. There was nothing to do but wait for Josh to turn up. His face went pale. What if Josh disappeared like Stacy did? He might never know what happened. How had he ever allowed this situation to develop?

* * *

Shortly after eleven o'clock, Jack and Stacy got out of the taxi in front of the police station. At Stacy's insistence, she had taken notes while Jack had rattled off the topics they needed to address. It was surprising how the very act of transferring the swirling list out of his head and onto paper had made him feel less stressed.

"Are we ready?" Jack said, already heading down the sidewalk.

Stacy grabbed his arm. "What happens if the messenger finds out I'm back?"

Seeing how stressed she was, he realized he'd spent zero time helping her prepare. "One step at a time, Stacy. Whatever you do, tell the truth."

She bit her bottom lip. "Will they arrest me for snooping around in Cedric's office?"

"Were you snooping, or were you simply retrieving something from your boss's in-box, like the conscientious employee I know you are?"

"Yeah, that's it. I made a mistake on a report, and I stayed late to fix it before Cedric saw it the next day. How's that for employee dedication?"

"You understand, of course, that my official advice is for you to tell the truth."

She winked at him and smiled.

It was quiet in the foyer, which was a pleasant surprise after the chaos of Jack's last visit. The same officer was on the phone again with his feet propped in the same position. He recognized Jack and pointed towards a glassed-in office, which was in the far corner of the room.

"Thanks," Jack said and stepped aside for Stacy to go first.

The closed mini blinds in Kevin's office made the fishbowl office private. Jack rapped lightly on the door.

"Yeah?" called an exasperated voice.

Jack turned the knob and stuck his head inside. "Is this a good time?"

Kevin looked up from a thick pile of paperwork. "Come on in, Jack."

Jack stepped inside Kevin's small but immaculate office, followed by Stacy. "Kevin, this is Stacy Young. There's another incident we need to report."

"Damn, Jack. How many fiascos can you manage at once?" He motioned for them to take a seat.

"I'm about at my limit. How about you?" Jack said.

"That depends on what you tell me. We have several topics to cover. How do you want to handle this?"

"Let's start with Stacy, and then she can wait outside while we finish up. Everybody good with that?"

Stacy nodded.

"What's this about, Jack?" Kevin said, resuming control.

"It's complicated, but let's just say I suspect that Daniel Steinberg was murdered as part of an insurance scheme involving Dr. Ryan Solver and an attorney named Cedric Johnson. Cedric Johnson is one of the top—"

"I know who he is, Jack. If you're making accusations against him, you've got a lot of explaining to do."

"Stacy works for Cedric Johnson, or rather, she did. Apparently, there's a courier between Cedric Johnson and Dr. Solver. Stacy has observed a ganglord, biker dude type coming in after hours to pick up and deliver silver envelopes with Cedric Johnson."

"That's her side of the story," Kevin said pointing to Stacy. "Stick to your side of the story."

Flustered, Jack had to think a second before he could

continue. "Stacy's direct boss is a young attorney named Joshua . . ." He glanced over at Stacy.

"Royce. Joshua Royce," she said. "What Jack's taking forever to tell you is that the messenger caught me in Cedric's office Friday evening and threatened to kill me if I didn't leave town. So, I did. I packed up my entire apartment, quit my job, and got the heck out of Jackson—just like he told me."

"Yet, here you are today, sitting in a Mississippi police station. Why did you come back?"

Stacy glanced at Jack.

"Well, Miss Young?" Kevin pressed.

"I got robbed in New Orleans and couldn't contact any of my friends without my cell phone."

"Which the messenger has in his possession," Jack added.

"Where's your phone, Miss Young?"

"The messenger took it, right before he sliced his hand open with the switchblade knife that he threatened to kill me with."

"What?" Jack exclaimed. "You never told me that?"

"You didn't ask," Stacy said defensively.

"Let's answer these in order. Why are you back in Mississippi?"

Jack felt that Kevin wasn't being very supportive and was surprised at how protective he felt of Stacy, who was clenching her fists in her lap.

"Look, Kev, something's very clearly going on here. First Daniel dies, and then Cedric Johnson solicits Christine to hire his firm to sue Daniel's anesthesiologist, Ryan Solver. Then, thanks to Stacy, I found out that Cedric has sued the same anesthesiologist twice before. They settled out of court both times without admitting guilt. I'm just waiting for him to ask Christine to settle, too."

"And someone broke into your house, don't forget," Stacy said.

"Yeah, here are the prints," Jack said, handing the packet across the desk to Kevin.

Kevin picked up his desk phone and dialed a three-digit

extension. "Spencer, I've got some prints in here. How soon can you process these?"

Jack glanced over at Stacy and gave her an encouraging smile.

"Thanks," Kevin said.

The door opened, and a female officer stepped in to collect the prints.

When she closed the door, Kevin said, "Now, for the third time, Miss Young, why are you back in Mississippi?"

"I didn't have anywhere else to go. Like I said, without my cell phone, I can't contact anyone. I had Jack's number in my purse, so I called him."

"Thank you. Now before you tell me why you had Jack's phone number in your purse, tell me about the knife incident."

She glanced at Jack. "I was getting something from Cedric's in-box when the messenger came in. I was already on the floor pickin' up something I dropped, so I crawled under the desk. All I could see were his boots." She brushed a tear from her eye. "He knew my name, my age, my address, everything. He told me to call and leave a message for Cedric Johnson—right then—sayin' that there was a sickness in my family, I was moving out of state, and had to quit my job immediately. Then he took my cell phone and told me to be out of town by midnight."

"What about the knife?" Jack said, ignoring the annoyed look he got from Kevin.

"He asked me if I wanted to see what would happen to me if I didn't do exactly what he said. I said no, but he bent down in front of the desk, where I could see both of his hands. He popped out a switchblade and sliced the palm of his own hand." She drew an invisible line across her hand.

"Then what did he do?" Kevin said.

"He squeezed his hand into a fist until blood appeared at each end, then he wrapped it in a blue bandanna. He said I was lucky not to have seen his face, or I'd be dead already."

Jack gave her a sympathetic pat on the back.

"So I packed up my stuff, and I left town. Just like I said."

While Kevin contemplated her story, Jack was kicking himself for not realizing sooner that Stacy was traumatized by what had happened, and that her life had turned upside down overnight. Whoever was behind all this had a lot to answer for.

"Has anyone else seen this messenger person?" Kevin said.

Jack and Stacy looked at each other. "Just me," she said. "In fact, I don't even think Cedric has seen his face."

"What do you mean?" Jack said.

"It was something he said to me when I was under the desk," Stacy said," shivering at the thought of it. "When I swore I had only seen his boots, he said that was more of him than Cedric had ever seen."

"Is it possible that someone is threatening Cedric, or that he's the victim of a blackmail scheme?" Jack said.

"Maybe," Kevin said, glancing back at Stacy. "Do you think you would recognize this character if you ever saw him again?"

"I'd recognize his boots, but I didn't get a good look at his face. All I know is that he wears biker clothes. You know... jeans and a black leather jacket. He had a blue bandanna wrapped around his head the first time I saw him go into Cedric's office."

"That's a start. Now, why did you have Jack's phone number in your purse?"

Stacy looked to Jack.

"It's complicated," Jack said. "The bottom line is that Stacy and I met regarding our suspicions that Cedric isn't what he seems."

"Tell him about the files," Stacy prompted.

"What files," Kevin asked.

Jack looked at Stacy. "Stop helping, okay?"

She drew a pretend zipper across her lips.

"Come on folks, I don't have all day," Kevin said sharply.

"Stacy's been looking through the files on Dr. Solver's victims, but nothing has turned up yet."

Stacy looked down to cover her surprise, but Kevin called

her on it.

"Is that true, Miss Young?"

"I still think there's a connection we're missing, but I haven't found it yet."

"Where are those files now? And, Jack, let her answer."

It was difficult to keep quiet; he didn't want her to tell Kevin she copied the files.

"They're at the office," Stacy said. "It's against company policy to remove them without written permission."

Jack exhaled.

"Okay, so let me get this straight. You and Jack think there's some kind of insurance scheme between Dr. Solver and Cedric Johnson—who has sued Dr. Solver twice already. Is that what you're telling me?"

Hearing it stated aloud made Jack realize how absurd it sounded. Why would a doctor participate in wrecking his own career? Nevertheless, he nodded, as did Stacy.

"Was there much blood?" Kevin asked.

"No, but it scared me so bad that I banged my head on the side of the desk."

Jack patted her hand. It was upsetting to think of her trapped beneath the desk.

"What I'm getting at, here, is the possibility of finding DNA at the crime scene. We need to send a team in there to check it out."

"You can't!" Stacy said. "If you go in there, the messenger will know I told someone. He'll come after me."

"Stacy, if there's DNA, it will help us catch the guy," Jack said.

"No, he'll find me!"

"Okay, let's talk this through," Jack said. "What if *I* collect the evidence without Cedric knowing about it?"

"Officially, you can't do that," Kevin said. "Who else knows about this?"

Jack caught Stacy's eye. Should they tell him about Josh?

"That's all we have to say for now. Maybe we'll remember something else later."

Kevin eyed them for several uncomfortable seconds. "Miss Young, is there anything you want to add?"

"Yeah. I don't want that gorilla coming after me. He needs to believe that I left town."

"We'll do everything possible to protect you," Captain Thomas said. "As you said, it's a complicated situation. Where are you staying, Miss Young?"

"With me," Jack said. "There's nowhere else for her to go."

"Would you take a seat outside the door, Miss Young? We'll need a written statement, and you'll need to look through some photographs."

Stacy nodded and let herself out.

Kevin picked up the phone. "Linda, get Charlie in here, and have Robertson escort Miss Young to an interrogation room to collect her statement. Keep her out of sight until Charlie finishes with Jack. Oh, and get Gloster on the line."

Jack glanced at his watch and frowned. He had an appointment with Teresa Lindsay at two o'clock.

Kevin picked up a pen and began jotting notes. "Give me a minute to catch up."

"Take your time," Jack said, betraying his impatience by fidgeting in his seat. He glanced around at various items, including a cot, which stood upright against the wall. "Do you sleep here now?"

"Only when I'm in the doghouse."

"That must be pretty often if you keep a cot in here."

"There's truth to the saying, '*If the wife ain't happy, then nobody's happy.*'"

Jack chuckled. "I'll remember that if I ever get married."

"Gloster on two, sir," a voice said over the intercom.

Kevin picked up the phone. "Gloster, Captain Thomas here. I need a complete workup on a Cedric K. Johnson. He's the attorney handling a case I'm looking into." He stopped writing and pushed back in his chair. "I see. What do you suggest? Right, I'll wait for his call," Kevin said. "Thanks, Richard."

"What was that about?" Jack asked.

"Conflict of interest. Seems Gloster does some work for Cedric Johnson. He's going to see if a buddy of his might be able to give us what we need."

"Will he mention it to Cedric?"

Kevin gave him a disgusted look. "It's not the first time we've been in this situation. We send a lot of work his way; he's not about to jeopardize our connection. I should have a report by tomorrow afternoon. At least, that's how it usually works."

"What's the status of my car?" Jack said.

"The store attendant has identified the suspect—a young woman, newly delivered, with a criminal record as long as your arm. We have her prints on file. They match the ones taken from your steering wheel."

"I've decided not to press charges. What will happen to her baby when you find her?"

"That depends. Are you getting soft in your old age?"

"I'm seeing firsthand how difficult it is for a family when there's no father around. As for the mother, there's no telling what has transpired in her life. Now her child will suffer, too. It's a nasty circle."

"Yes, it is," Kevin agreed. "Have Charlie walk you over to pick up your car after he takes your statement."

"I have a two o'clock appointment. Can I come back after that? It's pretty important."

"Then you should've come in earlier," Kevin said with a pointed look.

Jack could see how intimidating Kevin might be for someone who didn't know him. "What about the files you found in my car?"

Kevin reached behind him for a backpack and laid it on the corner of the desk. "If these are what I think they are, I don't want to know about it. You've got twenty-four hours to find DNA. Otherwise, I'm going in. You got that?"

"Thanks, Kev. One more question. Has Suzaun said anything to you? About me, I mean? Did she—"

Kevin held up his hand to interrupt. "No, she hasn't. But there's something you should know, Jack. Suzaun has a partner. A female partner."

Jack hid his disappointment behind a smile. "Well, that explains it. How else could she resist my charming self? You'll call me when you get the report back on Cedric Johnson?"

"I will," Kevin said. "Now, I have a question for you. Are you involved with Stacy Young?"

"If you mean sexually, no. Stacy has nowhere else to turn. Because of her, we may have uncovered a scheme that has already killed three people, including Daniel. I owe her a great deal."

Kevin stood and grabbed his keys from the top drawer. "If what you suspect is true, you better watch yourself. Men in Johnson's league play to win."

A knock sounded, and Charlie opened the door. "You wanted to see me, sir?"

"You two know each other, right?"

"Hey, Charlie," Jack said.

Charlie grunted.

"Jack and his friend Stacy have been telling me some interesting stories. There's a lot to sort through, but it seems they may have stumbled upon something rather serious. I'm headed out for a few hours. Use my office to collect his statement. And Jack, if I find you've withheld anything important . . ."

"I get it, Kev—I mean, Captain, but can we discuss strategy before moving forward? There are several people who stand to get hurt by this. I want to protect them if at all possible."

"Duly noted."

"Any chance you can run a license plate for me?" Jack said.

"Like we're not busy enough? Give it to Charlie. Now, if you boys will excuse me, I'm way overdue for a nap with my wife. Charlie, take Jack over to get his car when you're finished here."

"Yes, sir," Charlie said, but he shot Jack a dirty look behind Captain Thomas's back.

"Oh, one more thing," Jack said.

"Save it. I'm hungry, I'm cranky, and I'm out of here."

After Kevin had shut the door, Charlie settled behind the desk with a pen and notepad. "Yer more trouble than yer worth. You know that, Kendall?"

"Yeah, I've heard that before."

"Not often enough," Charlie said. "Okay, let's start at the beginning."

* * *

"And you didn't know anything about this?" Cedric asked a second time.

"Not until you told me. Apparently, it was a sudden decision," Josh said, determined not to say the wrong thing. It was difficult to hide information from Cedric, the man whose career he wanted to emulate, but until they got to the bottom of whatever was going on, he had to.

"I've heard rumors about the two of you," Cedric said.

"I'm engaged to Elizabeth."

"You're not sleeping with Stacy on the side?" Cedric said.

"I can't say I haven't thought about it," Josh said. "She's hot, but she's also a damn good assistant. Who's spreading rumors?"

"It doesn't matter," Cedric said. "I'll deal with it." He put his reading glasses on, which usually signaled the end of a meeting.

Josh headed for the door.

The intercom buzzed, and Cedrick picked up the phone. "Yes?"

Josh glanced back and saw him stiffen.

"I'll take it," Cedric said, his eyes locked on Josh. "Johnson here. What can I do for you?" He waved him back into the room. "I see. What does he have in mind?"

As he listened, Josh marveled at how calm and collected Cedric sounded when he knew the opposite was true.

"I'll get back with you by tomorrow afternoon," he said, ending the call.

"What was that about?" Josh said.

A wicked smile spread across Cedric's face, relieving

the worry lines around his eyes and mouth. "That was Solver's attorney. It seems Dr. Solver has come into some unexpected cash. He's made us an offer."

"How much?"

"One million dollars."

"You're kidding me. Why would he do that? We've barely filed suit."

"To avoid getting dropped by his insurance company. Set an appointment with Mrs. Steinberg, and tell her to invite Jack. As much as I dislike it, she won't budge without his say so." Cedric eyed him from above his reading glasses. "Think you can handle that?"

"I'll call him today," he said, resenting Cedric's tone.

As he reached for the doorknob, Cedric said, "Do you ever call Stacy at home?"

Realizing he might have Stacy's phone records, he said, "Sure. She knows where everything is. In fact, I tried to call her several times Friday night, but she didn't answer. I figured she was out on a date or something. Why?"

"It just seems strange. Who leaves town in the middle of the night?"

"I've never known her to lie," Josh said.

"Perhaps that's because she's good at it."

"Maybe, but I don't see what the problem is. Let's just replace her and get on with it." Josh let himself out of Cedric's office and stopped by the reception desk to pick up his messages. As he flipped through them, he saw one from Jack. He sure hoped Jack knew what he was doing because the spy business was stressing him out!

* * *

Jack was on his way to Teresa's office after dropping Stacy off at the house. He was already fifteen minutes late, so when Teresa called, he wasn't surprised. "Hey, Teresa."

"I have a three o'clock appointment. Should I push it back?"

"I'm right down the street. Want to postpone?" Jack said, half-hoping she would.

"No, come on up."

On days like this, Jack hated his job.

A few minutes later, as he sat in front of Teresa's desk, the stress in her eyes made him feel as though he were delivering a death sentence.

"What have you learned?" she said, pressing her lips together.

"She lives in an upper middle-class condominium complex located a few blocks from Dixie Medical Center. She drives a silver BMW. I'll know her identity no later than tomorrow." He handed her the photographs. "The first one is a shot of her private garage, which is located behind her house and accessed via private alleyway. As you can see, their cars are parked side by side. The second one is a shot of your husband exiting her complex around twelve thirty last night. Care to confirm that he was out?"

Teresa's gaze hardened as she stared at the pictures. "Lousy son-of-a-bitch. Photographs taken at a public place are one thing; pictures of him leaving her apartment are quite another." She looked at the first photo again and sighed.

"Teresa..." Jack said, swallowing the lump in his throat.

When their eyes met, he handed her the picture he'd taken of her husband's mistress in the full light of day. "She's expecting."

"What?" Teresa said, grabbing the picture from his hand.

He wanted to comfort her, but experience had taught him that silence was best.

Teresa rose to her feet and opened the door for him to leave. "Call me when you have her name."

As Jack walked by her, he said, "You're right, Teresa. He's a lousy SOB."

* * *

The sky was dark, and the rain was falling so hard Jack's windshield wipers were having difficulty clearing the glass. Traffic was at a standstill on the interstate, so he took the side streets, but even they were slow. Deciding to make the best use of his time, he called Josh.

"Royce, here," Josh said after the receptionist put him through.

"It's Jack. What's up?"

"Cedric wants to meet with you and Mrs. Steinberg at your earliest convenience. Can you come in tomorrow morning at nine o'clock?"

"What about?"

"Does nine work?"

"I'll arrange it. Josh, we need to talk."

"Can I call you later? I have someone in my office."

"ASAP."

"Will do. If you know of anyone who does assistant work, send them my way, will ya?"

Jack chuckled. "Something tells me you'll have a hard time replacing the one you had."

"I miss her already. Tell her that for me, will ya?"

"Got it," Jack said. "Over and out." He was looking forward to seeing Stacy again himself. What was up with that?

* * *

Anthony had parked his Harley beneath the thick branches of a tall pine tree, which sheltered him from most of the rain, but the wind whipping through soaked him at an angle. He'd been watching Jack's house for nearly three hours. He was cold, wet, and, at this point, ready to take it out on his new target. He gritted his teeth as his stomach cramped sharply, doubling him over. Eventually, it eased, and he straightened. He moved gingerly at first, but everything seemed back to normal—except that the wind had kicked up again. He shivered violently and pulled the collar of his jacket high around his neck.

Twenty minutes later, the garage door opened, and he was surprised to see Jack's white Camry pull in next to a red Volkswagen bug. "So, the little snoop is back," he said, scowling at the cut on his hand. Now, he'd have to deal with both of them.

His stomach cramped again. Gripping his side, he made an executive decision; he needed to find a bathroom—fast.

* * *

Jack had his hand on the kitchen door when it opened from the inside.

"Hey, Jack. Are you hungry?"

He laid Stacy's backpack on the kitchen counter. "I'm pretty much always hungry," he said with a smile. It sure was nice having someone to come home to. No wonder Daniel liked being married. Thinking of Daniel reminded him of Christine. "Give me a second. I need to make a quick call."

Stacy picked up the backpack and carried it into the den. She was still wearing her short little skirt, he saw. "Hey, you," Jack said into the phone.

"I can't do this, Jack," Christine said. "The kids were too upset to go to school today, and I'm too upset to make them feel better. I miss Daniel so much. I can't do this!" She burst into tears.

Jack's chest tightened. "It's going to be all right. Really, it is."

Stacy returned to the kitchen.

"Can you come over? We need you," Christine said.

Her voice sounded weaker than normal. This was not the Christine he knew. "Sure, sweetheart. I just got home. Give me a few minutes, and I'll be right over."

"Thanks, Jack," she said and hung up.

"I didn't know you had a girlfriend," Stacy said.

"I don't. That was Christine. I need to go over there. She and the kids are having a difficult time of it."

"But I was just about to make dinner."

"That's okay. I'll pick up something on the way. The kids always like pizza."

"I'm going stir crazy, Jack. Your entire house is clean, your laundry is done, and I'm bored out of my mind."

He felt torn because he wanted to ask about her ordeal, but his first loyalty was to Christine. "Wanna come with me?"

"What if the messenger sees me?" she said, her eyes clouding with worry.

"Yeah. Maybe we shouldn't chance it."

"How long will you be gone?" she said, her lips rising to a pout.

He hated to leave her. "I might have some hair dye. How would you feel about trading your gorgeous blondish-brown for temporary, dark brown?"

"I thought about that earlier, when I was cleaning your bathroom—which was disgusting, by the way—but it's 'Just for Men.' I don't know if I can trust it."

"I'm not sure I like you cleaning my bathroom."

Stacy reached into the fridge for a pitcher of tea. "Don't go getting into a tizzy on me. I was just cleaning. You know, with soap and water?"

"It's embarrassing to know that you've cleaned my toilet." He accepted the glass she offered and took a drink. "Dang, girl. That's the best sweet tea I've had in ages."

"Yeah, I'm good at lots of things." She returned the pitcher to the fridge. "And about your bathroom, it's no more embarrassing than knowing you've heard me snore."

He laughed. "Okay, I'd say we're even."

"Oh no, we're not. You had a mountain of hair piled against the baseboards. As for the base of your toilet—"

"Okay, already. I'll do better. I promise."

"Good. You'll never get a woman to fall in love with you if she sees how you keep house." He must have looked offended because she laughed. "So, if I dye my hair dark brown, you'll take me with you?"

"Can I help?" he said.

"No, but you can watch. How's that?"

"For real?"

"Yes, and if you're really good, I'll let you paint my toenails pink tomorrow. How's that?"

"Now, that would be cool." He didn't say it, but he had always wanted to do that for somebody. He might get to wear great disguises, but the girls got to do the really cool stuff.

"What are you doing with dark brown hair dye anyway? Men look good with a little grey."

"I'm a detective. If it's natural, I look younger. If it's dark brown, I look different. If I add grey, I look older. It's part of the art."

"I see." She set her glass in the sink. "I sure hope I look good with brown hair."

"There's only one way to find out."

His lopsided grin appeared as he followed her down the hallway.

* * *

It was still raining when Anthony settled back into position, but his stomach felt better. While he was contemplating what to do about Jack and Stacy, their garage door opened. Jack's car backed out of the driveway and headed up the street. From his position, he couldn't tell if Stacy was with him. As much for spite as to get out of the rain, he decided to wreak some havoc. If the girl happened to be home, he'd make good on his promise.

He went around the side of the house and over the gate, which was still lying flat on the ground, he saw with disgust. The sliding glass doors were locked, as was the kitchen door. Glancing around for ideas, he picked up a brick and shattered the window in the upper part of the kitchen door. When he reached in to unlock it, he ripped a hole in his jacket—the jacket Angel had stolen for him just weeks before she died. Seeing the gash, fury exploded in an agonized growl into which every past injustice merged. "You're gonna pay for this! You're gonna pay for this if it's the last thing I do!"

He kicked in the lower half of the door, sending the remaining glass flying. Once inside, he searched and destroyed the back part of the house first. After checking the den, he went into the garage and felt along the wall for a light switch. Confirming that it was Stacy's car, he released the hood and did some creative demolition with his switchblade. "That's for coming back. When I find you, we'll settle for the jacket."

Back inside the house, he continued his destruction, ransacking and slashing his way through the den, and then the kitchen, emptying the cabinets of the dishes and glasses, and shattered them against the wall. Afterwards, he helped himself to a bottle of beer, and then smashed the remainder of them, one after the other, on the floor.

As he was about to leave, an idea occurred to him. He reentered the hall bathroom and dumped out Stacy's makeup bag. As a lipstick rolled across the counter, he plucked it up and wrote across the mirror.

> *You had your chance.*
> *Now you'll pay in blood.*

A hard rain pelted him as he jogged back to his Harley. Just as he reached it, tornado sirens blasted overhead, startling him nearly out of his skin. He looked up into the dark, menacing mass of clouds and noticed the wind pitching in changing directions and the lightning flashing every few seconds.

A deafening crack of thunder exploded directly above him, making him duck with a forearm over his head. As thunder rolled through the clouds, the ground rumbled beneath his feet. He swung a leg over the seat and started his motorcycle. He needed to get out of there while he still could.

* * *

Tornado sirens competed with the raging thunder, which cracked so loudly it sounded like cannon fire. Stacy covered her hair the best she could and ran for the back door, leaving Jack to carry the pizza. The door was unlocked, so she dove inside without knocking. Jack was fast on her heels.

"Christine?" He set the pizza box on the counter and shook the droplets from his hair.

"Jack! I'm in the bathtub with the kids."

Jack took hold of Stacy's hand and practically dragged her into the living room and then pushed her towards the hallway.

"Down there. Go!"

Stacy covered her ears as more thunder exploded overhead. "Aren't you coming?"

Jack fixed his eyes on the television set where Stacy saw the tri-county map in central Mississippi flash red with warning. The rolling news bar at the bottom of the screen said tornados had been confirmed on the ground and moving east at an alarming speed.

Jack urged her down the hallway. "Go on. I'm right behind you."

She didn't want to go without him, but she went to look for Christine.

* * *

Anthony was soaked as much from passing vehicles as from the rain itself, but he toughed it out long enough to get to the parking structure at Dixie Medical Center. Retrieving a towel from the small trunk, he dried his face and head. He certainly wasn't afraid. Any Southerner worth his salt had been through hundreds of tornado warnings. It came with the territory.

He pulled his cell phone from his pocket and dried it off. He had ten missed calls—all from Trina. It rang, now, in his hand. "You miss me bad, don't ya?" he said, chuckling because it was the other way around.

"Where are you? Have you heard the sirens?"

"I'm in the parking garage." He leaned over the concrete half-wall and looked up into the swirling clouds. "I have to admit, it looks pretty nasty out here."

"Don't chance it, Anthony. The atmosphere is completely unstable. Another band of storms is heading straight for us."

"It ain't no big deal, Trina. It'll blow over. It always does."

"Are you coming up?"

A strong gust sent shivers down Anthony's spine. "Nah, I'm soakin' wet. I'm gonna wait for a break in the storm and then go home. You comin' by after work?"

"I'd love to come."

"You're such a bad little girl."

"Yeah, maybe you should spank me."

"Look, I hate to hang around the parking lot all day. Can I take your car home and pick you up later?" he said as a shiver ran up his back.

"Sure. I'll grab my keys and meet you in the lobby."

"Thanks, babe. You're the best."

"And don't you ever forget it either." She hung up before he could reply.

* * *

Stacy stopped short upon seeing Christine in the bathtub with her children. Her protective position over them touched her heart in a way that felt, well, maternal—not that she wanted those feelings. A family of her own was not on her wish list. She'd seen way too many moms left alone to raise their children.

"Who are you?" the boy asked.

"Uh, you must be Jon. I'm Stacy."

"Where's Jack?" Christine said.

"Right here," Jack said as he entered the crowded bathroom. "Hey, guys. Are we playing hide and seek again?"

"There's tornados, Uncle Jack," Jon said as he squirmed from under Christine's arm. "Big ones."

Stacy took stock of the pretty woman before her and wondered if she might be in love with Jack. Christine looked at her with seemingly equal curiosity.

"It's pretty bad out there," Jack said. "I'll take Stacy to the other bathroom."

"You're not squishing me into a bathtub," Stacy said. "Let's wait here."

Thunder boomed over the house, eliciting a shriek from Alexa.

"It's okay, everybody. It'll pass soon," Jack said.

Jon sheltered close to his mama as the rain and hail pounded the roof.

Huge magnolia trees scratched against the house, making

it sound as if the walls were coming apart. Branches snapped in the gusting wind like rifle fire in the distance. A window shattered somewhere upstairs.

Stacy saw Christine and Jack exchange glances and knew what they were thinking; would they hear a freight train soon— the ominous warning of a tornado touchdown?

Alexa's sky-blue eyes shimmered with tears.

Without thinking, Stacy dropped to her knees and took hold of Alexa's hand. "Don't worry, sweetie. It'll be over soon."

Alexa kept tight hold of her hand, creating an instant bond between them.

Jack went to check the weather report again.

"You sure are pretty," Jon said. "Are you Uncle Jack's girlfriend?"

"Jon," Christine rebuked.

"Well, is she?" Jon said.

Stacy laughed, which relieved the awkward moment. "No, we're just friends."

"Why not?" Jon said. "He's not married or anything."

"Jon," Christine said a bit sharper, "mind your own business."

Stacy whispered as if sharing a secret, "He's too old for me."

"Hey," Jack said. "I heard that."

Stacy winked at him, which made him smile.

"It sounds awful out there," Christine said. "What are they saying?"

"The worst is to the East now."

"Can I get out then?" Jon said.

"No," Jack and Christine said at the same time.

Stacy said, "Jinx," and despite being frightened, Alexa smiled.

* * *

On the way home from Christine's house, Jack swung into Dixie Medical Center's parking lot, hoping to see Dr. Lindsay's mistress again. He still didn't know her identity, but he expected a phone call at any moment. If he didn't hear from Kevin soon, he would take the information he had gathered and dig it up himself from public records.

Stacy sat quietly for once, content to dig around in his spy kit.

Fewer and fewer people poured through the doors as the shift change progressed. Jack was beginning to think he had missed her when she finally appeared.

"Bingo."

"Which one?" Stacy said.

"Just watch." He got out of the car and walked down the sidewalk, setting himself up to intercept his suspect. Her pleasant expression made it easy for him to approach. "Hey, don't I know you from somewhere?" he said, using a version of his lopsided smile.

The young woman searched his face and then tilted her head. "I don't remember you."

"I'm so disappointed," he teased.

"Sorry," she said over her shoulder as she kept walking.

"Wait," he called after her. "Didn't you have dinner at La Bells recently? I could swear I've seen you before."

She turned. "I did, actually. How do you know that?"

"It's hard not to notice a pretty woman."

She gave him a half-smile. "Thanks. I needed that today."

He kept a respectful distance. "It seems I've also met your husband. Convenient that he's an obstetrician."

Her face flushed as she lovingly stroked her belly. "He's my father, not my husband. I'm not married."

"Forgive the assumption," he said, bowing in retreat. "I wish you and your little one the greatest happiness."

"Thanks," she said and continued down the sidewalk.

Jack walked back to the car with a huge smile on his face. Teresa was wrong about her husband. He wasn't cheating. At least, not right now. Finally, some good news. He opened the car door and was surprised to see Stacy crouching in the floorboard.

"What are you doing?"

She pressed a finger to her lips and motioned him inside.

Playing it cool, Jack got in and started the car.

"He's here," she said, her eyes spooked with fear. "I saw him."

"Who?"

"The messenger. He rode right by you on a Harley. Didn't you see him?"

Jack immediately glanced around, but there was no motorcycle in sight. "How long ago?"

"Three, four minutes, maybe. I don't think he saw me."

"That's a relief. Which way was he headed?"

"He was leaving."

"Are you sure it was him?" He backed out of the parking space and headed for the main road."

"Do you think I'd cram myself into this tiny little space if I wasn't? Is it safe to come out?"

"I think so," he said, disappointed for having missed an opportunity to follow the so-called messenger. Learning his identity might connect him with Dr. Solver, but he was thinking more along the lines of settling the score for him threatening Stacy. He wondered if the messenger was the one who trashed his gate and left prints on his back door.

Stacy crawled back onto the seat and glanced around. "What?" she said in response to the amused look on his face.

"Nothing. Did you notice anything unusual about him?"

"He was wearing the same leather jacket and a blue bandanna. That's how I know it's him."

"A lot of people dress like that. Did you recognize his face?"

"I've never actually seen his face, but it was him. I know it was."

"I wonder what he's doing here," Jack said, casting a concerned look at Stacy. He wasn't convinced that she had seen the messenger, but she was clearly upset. "Let's get you home."

"You mean your home. I'm officially homeless."

"Stacy, I'd like to discuss what happened that night in Cedric's office. Do you think you can talk about it?"

"I'll try. I know it's important."

"After dinner," he said. "I went light on the pizza, so I'd be hungry for your spaghetti tonight. I can't wait to taste more of your cooking."

"Good decision. I'm one of the best cooks you'll ever meet."

"It's a good thing you're so humble," he said.

"Who said I want to be humble?"

* * *

Cedric walked down the hallway to see if anyone was working late, but the offices were dark. He stopped by the break-room and perused the company bulletin board while he heated a cup of coffee. A pink birth announcement caught his eye. "Wow," he said aloud. "I just thought she was fat." When the microwave beeped, he grabbed the mug and went back to his office.

As his thoughts drifted to the Solver case, he heaved a sigh of relief. Once the Steinberg case settled, Jack would have no reason to continue his investigation, and life would return to normal. But he knew it wasn't quite that simple. What he had thought was a onetime deal had turned into a nightmare. Worry creased his brow until he reminded himself that four hundred thousand dollars would go a long way in making him feel better. Well, two hundred thousand—once he paid the devil his due.

He opened the credenza and added some Bailey's Irish to his coffee. He wondered what had happened to Stacy Young, and more importantly, what plans there were for Jack and Josh. He couldn't bear it if something happened to Josh. He needed to make it perfectly clear that once the Steinberg case was behind them, he was done, he was out, and he was moving on with his life.

Settling at his desk with purpose, he unlocked the bottom drawer and withdrew a silver note card. After carefully considering his words, he wrote . . .

*Call off the fox hunt. Without complications,
the dispute will settle quickly, perhaps even this
week. Delivery soon, same same. Next beep.
P.S. This is it. I fold. I'm done. I'm out.*

He sealed the envelope and laid it on the corner of his desk, yet he stared at it for several seconds, making certain he'd said what he wanted to say. With a heavy sigh, he dialed the messenger, waited for the beep, and then punched in the code to request message pickup. It was a move he might regret if Jack turned out to be a serious threat, but he wanted no part in arranging his death. Surely, it was obvious that if something suspicious were to befall Jack, Josh, *and* Stacy, the public scrutiny on him and his law firm would ruin his reputation and destroy everything he had worked for. His hand froze with his cup halfway to his mouth. He, himself, had given Winchester that power. His entire future now rested on the unpredictable whims of his partner in crime. "God in heaven, what have I done?"

* * *

Trina was naked and waiting in Anthony's bed when his cell phone beeped. Anthony spit a mouthful of toothpaste into the sink and picked up his phone, which was sitting on the nightstand. He checked the caller ID—Cedric Johnson was signaling for pickup. "Talk about bad timing," he said.

"What is it?" Trina said, reaching out to unbutton his jeans while he paused beside the bed. "Surely it can wait a few minutes."

Anthony looked down at her with a lazy smile. "It can wait all night, as far as I'm concerned."

"I was hoping you'd say that."

* * *

"Oh, my God, Jack! Your house is trashed," Stacy said, stepping back into the garage.

Unable to conduct two conversations at once, Jack

motioned for her to wait while he finished his call. "Yes, I know her identity."

"Really? And which nurse whore is it?" Teresa said into the phone, managing to sound miffed and nonchalant in the same breath.

"Can we meet tomorrow?"

Teresa sighed. "Since I know there's no point trying to persuade you to tell me now, let's meet at your office. How's two o'clock tomorrow afternoon?"

"Fine. Just be sure you've got the right woman. I'd hate to ruin the life of an innocent person."

"See you at two o'clock." After he ended the call, Stacy grabbed his arm and pulled him into the house. His mouth dropped open as her words finally sank in. Glass crackled beneath their feet as they took a cursory look around. "Don't touch anything," he called after her as she headed down the hallway.

"Jack!"

He found her staring at the bathroom mirror. Her haunted eyes met his in their reflection.

"He knows I'm here," she said.

"I'll call the police," he said, but his phone rang as he reached for it, startling them both. "Jack, here."

"Jack, it's Josh."

"I'm a little busy at the moment." He took Stacy's hand and led her back to the garage.

"Solver wants to make an offer from his private funds," Josh said.

Jack opened the passenger-side door for Stacy, and she got in.

"I thought he was broke," he said and went around to the other side.

"Who is it?" Stacy whispered.

"Josh," he mouthed.

"Put it on speaker phone."

Jack frowned and shook his head.

"I did some checking after Cedric gave me the news," Josh

said. "Seems Solver's wife died over the weekend with a hefty insurance policy over her head."

Jack didn't know what to say. He couldn't be happy that Solver's wife had died, no matter how horrible he was. "What else did Cedric say?"

"He wants to meet with you and Christine tomorrow morning at nine o'clock. He thinks your case will settle quickly, maybe even this week."

Stacy pointed to herself. "Ask if Cedric said anything."

Jack nodded. "Has Cedric said anything about Stacy?"

"He asked if I ever called her at home. I threw him off, and I kept a straight face the entire time."

Jack wasn't betting on that. Josh had a lot to learn about the art of bluffing. "Look, Josh, someone has vandalized my house. I'll be tied up here for a while, but I need to get into Cedric's office again tonight. Can you meet me there later?"

Stacy pointed to herself again, indicating she wasn't about to be left behind.

"Why?" Josh said, sounding doubtful.

Jack glanced at Stacy. "I need to collect some DNA. If I don't get it myself, the police will get it for me. It has to be tonight."

"The police? God, Jack, this is getting way out of hand. Are you sure about this?"

"You should see my place. It looks like a tornado ripped through it."

"It *was* a nasty storm," Josh said.

"Tornados don't write on the bathroom mirror in red lipstick. The messenger knows Stacy is here."

"What are you going to do? Do you need a place to stay?"

While he appreciated the offer, he wasn't sure he wanted to reunite Josh and Stacy. It would be entirely too weird if Stacy wanted to sleep in Josh's bed. "I'll let you know. Ten o'clock tonight, same parking routine."

"For Stacy's sake," Josh said. "See you then."

Once they hung up, Stacy said, "I'm going with you. Just because I'm female doesn't mean—"

Jack held up his hand. "I can't leave you here, can I?" He dialed the police station.

"Hey, Dick Tracy, did you get that sample yet?" Kevin said into the phone.

"Soon. I'm calling because someone ransacked my house this afternoon. It's completely destroyed."

"Now, why doesn't that surprise me? Lots of people evacuated to shelters during the storm. It could've been anyone."

"Not with the note he wrote with Stacy's lipstick."

"What does it say?"

"*You had your chance. Now you'll pay in blood.* I think we're in serious trouble here."

"Charlie's familiar with this case. I'll send him out."

"Can't you send someone else?"

"I'm short-handed right now. What's wrong with Charlie?"

"He's probably sick of me by now. It might be best if—"

"You run your business, and I'll run mine. Is Miss Young with you?"

"She's right here."

"Do you want protective custody?"

She leaned away from Jack's shoulder and shook her head emphatically.

"She says no. Whoever's behind all this must have an awful lot to lose."

"That's usually the way of it," Kevin agreed. "Stay put."

"We'll be here. Thanks, Kev."

"Don't thank me yet. This case is getting bigger by the day. I'm riding out with Charlie."

Jack made a face, and Stacy rewarded him with a half-smile, but he could see that she was badly shaken. After the call, Jack opened the garage and moved his car so that they faced the street. "Let's open the windows," he said. "It might be awhile."

"I shouldn't have called you, Jack. I'm sorry for messing up your life."

"Hey, don't say that. Because of you, we have a lead to track down. Even if it's not related to the Solver cases, there's something nefarious going on."

"I know, it's just—"

"The Solver files!" Jack said. "Where did you put them?"

"In the laundry basket, under the printer stand."

"Lock the doors, and stay alert. I'll be right back." He heard the locks click as he reentered the house. Fortunately, the Solver files were right where she said they'd be. Relieved, he picked up the backpack and went back out to the car. "Got 'em," he said and dropped them on the back seat.

"Thank God," Stacy said.

Once he settled in, he reached over and gently lifted her chin. "I want you to know something, Stacy. I'm glad you called me. I want to help you. Are you ready to tell me what happened that night?"

"There's not much to tell. When he came into the office, I was already on the floor picking up some papers I had knocked off Cedric's desk. He said if I was looking for trouble, I had found it. I pulled Cedric's chair back and ducked beneath the desk. All I could see were his boots. I've never been that scared in my whole life."

He waited to see if she would add more, but she didn't. "What about the knife?"

"He said he was demonstrating what he'd do to me if I didn't do exactly what he said." She shivered and stared off into a memory Jack couldn't see. "I shouldn't have come back," she said.

"It's going to be all right, Stacy. We'll find him."

"I just hope you find him before he finds me."

Charlie and his quiet partner, Jeff, arrived first.

Jack and Stacy got out of the car.

"Who's this?" Charlie said, indicating Stacy.

"It's me, Stacy," she said looking confused.

"She dyed her hair," Jack said.

"Oh. Can we go inside?"

"I thought Kevin was coming," Jack said, motioning for Charlie and Jeff to go first.

"He got caught up in something else," Charlie said.

Glass crunched beneath everyone's feet as they entered

the kitchen.

"Damn, Kendall. Who'd you piss off this time?" Charlie said.

"The messenger. We know by the note he left for Stacy on the bathroom mirror," Jack said. "We'll wait for you outside."

"What are we going to do, Jack?" Stacy said when they had climbed back into the car. "Where are we going to stay?"

There weren't many options. Christine's place came to mind, but he couldn't put Daniel's family at risk. "Don't worry," he said. "I'll come up with something."

* * *

Josh drummed on his steering wheel in time with his favorite rock tune. He was beginning to enjoy the excitement and intrigue again. Of course, he felt safer knowing Jack was going in with him this time. The more he thought about the situation, the more perplexed he became. Cedric had built an amazingly successful law firm. He enjoyed a stellar reputation. Why risk it? It seemed entirely out of character.

It was a relief to see Jack pull up beside him. "Great ride, Jack," he said with a teasing grin.

Jack gave him a 'thanks a lot' look and said, "Hop in."

Josh climbed into the back seat, behind Jack. "Long time, stranger."

"It hasn't been that long," Jack said.

"I think he was talking to me," Stacy said. "Hey yourself, Josh. I told you somethin' was up." She turned in her seat to face him.

"What can I say? I was wrong," Josh said.

"Okay, guys," Jack said. "We're here for a reason. Let's get on with it."

Josh sat forward on the seat, filling the space between Jack and Stacy. "What's the plan?"

"You and I will go in while Stacy waits in the car."

"Oh no, I won't. I'd be scared to death to stay out here by myself."

"Okay. I guess that means Josh waits in the car. If we're not out in twenty minutes, call the police. Got it?"

Josh wasn't happy about being ousted. "Can't all three of us go in?"

"We can't risk someone doing something to the car, or ambushing us when we come out. We need a watchman."

Josh didn't like it, but what could he say? Jack reached under the front seat and handed him a gun. "What am I supposed to do with this?" he said.

"It ain't no big deal, Josh," Stacy said. "If the messenger appears, shoot him. Even if you miss the guy, he'll take off outta here. Got another one?"

"I'm a detective; I don't carry an arsenal, you know!" Jack said. "As for the messenger, it might be best to text us if he shows up, and then call the police. If things go wrong, then you can shoot him."

"I don't know about this. Maybe I should wait in the parking lot," Josh said.

"Okay, listen up everybody. You can both stay in the car. I know my way around."

"No, I'm going with you," Stacy said. "Sorry, Josh, but Jack needs me more than you do. Someone needs to watch his back while he gathers the sample. Besides, there might be another message."

Josh scowled. Was Jack moving in on Stacy?

"Twenty minutes, Josh. Then you call the police," Jack said.

Jack and Stacy got out of the car and approached the grey metal door. Josh watched as Jack swiped Stacy's security card several times with no success. Stacy held out her hand for the card, which worked for her on the first try. "That's my girl," he said softly. Then he remembered Elizabeth, his beautiful, cultured, educated fiancée, whose huge inheritance would set him up for life. Still, Stacy had guts—and a perfectly rounded bottom he acknowledged as it disappeared through the doorway behind Jack.

* * *

Anthony watched Jack and Stacy enter the building. Reaching into his pocket, he withdrew a loaded syringe and held it into the moonlight. He had been skeptical when Tina gave it to him, but if what she said were true, there'd be no visible signs of foul play. He tested the cap and put it back in his pocket.

Stacy, on the other hand, was an entirely different story. He had a personal score to settle with her. Gravel crunched beneath his boots as he walked past Jack's car. He launched his switchblade and followed them into the building.

* * *

Josh was beside himself. After the messenger had entered Cedric's office building behind Jack and Stacy, he reached into the front seat to lock the doors and then ducked back into the shadows. His hands were shaking so badly that he was having difficulty dialing Jack's number. It took three tries before it finally went through, but it went straight to voicemail.

"Dammit!" He pushed a few more buttons and then tapped out a text message: *Messenger behind you!*

* * *

Elyse propped herself on Thad's chest and looked into his eyes. "When do you plan to divorce your wife?"

Thad gently pushed her to the side. "Giving my wife half of everything I own isn't exactly on my priority list."

Elyse sat up on the bed and reached for her shirt. "Fine. Then maybe we should stop seeing each other until you take care of that little detail."

"What's with you women?"

Elyse got out of bed and pulled on her jeans. "Call me when I become a priority. I don't like being the other woman."

Thad caught her arm and pulled her back onto the bed. He cupped her chin and kissed her hard. "You're the only woman I care about. Isn't that enough?"

She kissed him hard in return. "Don't toy with me, Thad. I hiss when I get coiled up."

"Are you taking the nanny position? If not, I'm sure I can find lots of willing applicants."

She got off the bed and picked up her purse. "Three weeks paid vacation?"

A shrewd smile curved his lips. "Four."

He was right. If she didn't accept his offer, someone else would. "All right, then. I accept."

"But only if you stay a little longer," he said, patting the bed.

Elyse stripped off her clothes again and watched with amusement as his eyes lingered on her skin. She may as well admit it; she was tired of struggling. Thad and his money meant security—a luxury she'd never known. Whatever price she had to pay, she'd pay it.

* * *

Stacy felt her way to the lamp on Cedric's credenza and turned it on. "Look," she whispered, pointing at the corner of the desk. "A silver envelope."

"Incoming?"

"I don't know. Should I open it? I can put it in another envelope."

"Hurry." Jack pulled the evidence kit from his pocket and put on a pair of gloves while Stacy opened the envelope.

> *Call off the fox hunt. Without complications,*
> *the dispute will settle quickly, perhaps even this*
> *week. Delivery soon, same same. Next beep.*
> *PS. This is it. I fold. I'm done. I'm out.*

"That's encouraging," Jack said. "Especially if I'm the fox."

"Now who's being humble," she snorted. "They're clearly planning to meet."

"Sounds like a money exchange. Let's finish up and get out of here. Where did he cut his hand?"

Stacy pointed to the spot and then hurried through the process of replacing the ruined envelope. Meanwhile, Jack examined the carpet in front of the desk and found two small dark spots. Using a sharp pair of scissors, he cut tiny pieces of carpet from beneath the stains and brushed them into an envelope. Next, he scraped what appeared to be brown dust into a second envelope and sealed it. Taking off his gloves, he put the envelopes into his pocket. "Okay, I'm ready."

"Me, too. Did you find anything?"

"That's what I'd like to know," the messenger said as he stepped into Cedric's office brandishing his knife.

"You?" Jack said, stepping back to shield Stacy. "Anthony from O'Malley's, right?"

"And here I thought you were stupid," he sneered.

Jack felt Stacy pull his cell phone from his back pocket. "Look, I don't know who you are," he said, "but you're trespassing on private property."

"And you're not?" Anthony scoffed.

"You're making a big mistake if you think that *breaking into Cedric Johnson's office* will help you," Stacy said from behind Jack's back.

"I couldn't care less about Cedric Johnson," Anthony said. He nodded towards Jack. "What were you doing on the floor?"

"I lost an earring the last time I was here," Stacy said quickly. "It seemed likely to be under the desk, considering that's where I was when you threatened to kill me."

"I should have done more than threaten you, you nosey little snoop, but I intend to rectify that tonight. You should've stayed gone," Anthony said.

"You're the one who's in trouble," Jack said. "The police are on their way."

"Like I'm really gonna buy that one," Anthony scoffed as he pressed forward, waving his knife. "You're on my list also, Jack Kendall. How convenient that you should die here together tonight."

Stacy moved from behind Jack and grabbed Cedric's

revolver. Pointing it in his face, she said, "Care to reevaluate?"

Anthony grabbed the silver envelope, fled through the door, and down the back stairwell.

Anthony had the advantage, but Jack was fast on his heels. He yanked the door open and chased him down the stairs, but by the time he reached the bottom there was no sign of him. He pushed through the grey door and rushed out into the alley. His car was gone and Josh was nowhere in sight. As he turned to follow deeper into the alley, a cop car spun into view—kicking up rocks and dust. Headlights flooded the area, and a car door opened.

"Put your hands up! You're under arrest."

Jack raised his hands and turned slowly into the light. "Charlie? Is that you?"

"Kendall? What in tarnation are you doing here? Haven't you got enough trouble?"

Stacy burst from the stairwell gasping for breath. "Wait, you've got the wrong guy!"

"And he's getting away!" Jack said as he took off down the alley.

"Stop!" Charlie yelled. "Dammit, Jack, I can't let you do this! Stay back," he yelled at Stacy as he ran after Jack.

Jack's lungs burned as he kept to the alley, past several junctions where the messenger could have exited out onto the street. Minutes later, his side was aching and he was about to give up when he heard dogs barking up ahead. He kept running until he caught up with the messenger, who had trapped himself at a dead end. Just like the movies, he thought as he skidded to a halt several yards in front of him. "It's over, pal," he said, gasping for breath.

"For you, maybe," Anthony spat as he waved his knife to keep Jack from coming any closer.

A smile played across Jack's lips as a scene from his favorite movie came to mind. *So, this is what Indiana Jones felt like when he faced that hulking Egyptian.* "Put your hands up," he said as he reached for his gun—which, of course, wasn't there.

Anthony saw the stunned look on his face and laughed. "What now, tough guy?"

Adrenaline surged through him as he and Anthony circled each other. Anthony lunged with the knife, barely missing his stomach. "Of all the times not to have my gun," he muttered, keeping his eyes on the blade as the Anthony pressed him into the very corner he had caught him in. He thought about Christine and the kids. What if he wasn't around to help them?

The sound of people running over gravel caught Anthony's attention long enough for Jack to kick the knife out of his hand. Anthony responded with a solid fist to his right jaw. Jack blocked another punch with his forearm. Taking a chance, he grabbed Anthony's wrist and, using the only martial arts move he knew, twisted his arm behind his back.

The messenger clenched his teeth as Jack yanked higher. "Stop! You're breaking my arm!" Anthony cried.

Jack was so amazed that the move worked, he almost let go. Remembering Stacy, he said, "I'm gonna do more than that, you worthless twit! How dare you threaten a defenseless woman?"

Beads of sweat glistened on Anthony's forehead. "I'm serious, man. You're breaking my arm!"

"All right. Nobody move," Charlie said.

"Jack!" Stacy said as she stumbled forward.

"I thought I ordered you to stay back," Charlie snapped as he positioned himself directly in front of Jack and Anthony. "All right, Jack, when I say three, release him and step out of the way."

"Got it," Jack said, feeling eternally grateful. He opened his mouth and flexed his jaw. Getting punched sure seemed to hurt more than it used to.

Addressing the messenger, Charlie said, "The second he lets go, you reach for the sky, or I'll blow you away right where you stand. Do I make myself clear?"

"Screw you," Anthony said through gritted teeth.

"I warned you," Charlie said, "and I got witnesses."

"I'll cover you, Charlie," Stacy said, holding Cedric's gun like she meant it.

All three men turned to look at her.

"What?" she said, sounding annoyed. "Y'all don't know nothin' about country girls, do ya?"

"On three," Charlie said. "One..."

The messenger stomped hard on Jack's foot and shoved him towards Charlie, who stepped out of the way as Jack stumbled past him.

"On the ground," Charlie yelled. "On the ground, now!"

A dumbfounded expression came over the messenger's face as he stood frozen in the moonlight.

"Don't make me tell you again, boy," Charlie said, his finger twitching on the trigger.

Anthony fell to the ground, face first in the dirt.

Jack and Charlie glanced at each other, and then at Stacy, who looked as surprised as they did.

"Don't trust him," Jack said.

Stacy stepped forward and handed the gun to Jack.

"Cover me," Charlie said as he knelt beside him. He pulled the suspect's arms behind his back and cuffed him. When he turned him over, lifeless brown eyes stared back at him. "What the hell?"

"What?" Jack and Stacy said stepping forward.

Stacy gasped and crossed herself.

"I hate ta do this, Jack," Charlie said, "but I gotta take y'all in."

* * *

Back at the station, Kevin had made it clear that he didn't appreciate Jack advising him on what was quickly shaping up to be a complex case.

"But if you question Cedric now," Jack pressed, "he'll alert Dr. Solver and ruin our chance to catch them together."

Kevin pointed at the door. "There's a dead boy out there, and you want me to sit on it?"

"Just until we see if they arrange a meeting."

"I need to notify his next of kin. Somebody out there

knows him."

"I know him!" Jack shot back. "He's the man who threatened to kill Stacy with a switchblade knife. He ransacked my house and destroyed Stacy's car. If you expose this now, it'll keep Christine from getting a settlement that will provide for her two children, now that Cedric, Dr. Solver, and that *boy*, as you call him, have murdered her husband and two other innocent people. His kin can wait for a day or two; take care of his victims first."

"What the hell happened out there?"

Jack rubbed his eyes. "I already told you everything I know. He was fine one minute, dead the next. I'll bet his fingerprints match the ones I lifted from the first break-in at my house."

"We'll soon know about that," Kevin said.

"When will the DNA results come back from Cedric's office?"

"If it's a match, it won't take long. I've got a rush on it."

Jack clenched his fists. "When I think of Stacy trapped beneath that desk while he threatened to carve her into little pieces, it makes me crazy."

"Did you kill him, Jack?"

"No, I didn't kill him. And you know what? As furious as I am, even if I'd had my gun, I wouldn't have pulled the trigger—not unless I shot him in the leg or something. Taking a man's life . . ." He shook his head. "I wouldn't want that on my conscience."

Kevin studied him for several seconds. "You live with it, but once you kill a man, things change. The way you see the world changes, too. Thank goodness for Edna. If it weren't for her, I don't think I could take it."

"Edna," Jack said. He thought of the counter clerk at the diner. Was *that* Edna? That couldn't be Edna. "How is Edna these days?"

"She's real good, Jack. Far better than I deserve."

"I'm sure she is," he teased. Somehow, he had always thought of Kevin's wife as looking something like Suzaun, but Edna was, well . . . "Does Edna work?"

"She works at the coffee shop six days a week."

So, that *was* Edna. "It's a shame she has to work so hard just to make somebody else rich."

Kevin cocked a brow. "What do you mean?"

Realizing he'd said something objectionable, he said, "I just mean, I'm sure you'd rather she didn't have to—"

Kevin rose to his full height and pointed to the door. "You'd best get out while you still can."

"What did I say?" Jack said, rising to his feet.

"Just that you're as prejudiced as every other white, honky, bigot around here. Did it ever occur to you that my wife owns that diner? Hell, no! You figured that because she's black, she has to work there."

Jack's mouth fell open.

"That's what you thought, isn't it?" Kevin said a bit louder.

"Look, I just learned something very valuable here. I don't blame you for being angry. I'm upset with myself. I would've sworn I wasn't prejudiced. I would've sworn it, but apparently I am in ways I don't even realize." He offered his hand for Kevin to shake. "Please, Kevin, forgive me."

Kevin stared at his hand with anger in his eyes, and Jack feared he had lost his friend.

Kevin was clearly struggling, but he finally grasped Jack's hand and shook it. "I just called you a white, honky, bigot. Maybe that poison goes deeper than we realize."

Jack swallowed hard. "Thanks, man. I'll be mad at myself a good while over this one."

"That makes two of us."

Seeing all would mend, Jack allowed a sly smile to spread across his face. "How about you, me, Edna, and Suzaun all go out to dinner one night?"

Kevin chuckled. "Like I said . . . white, honky, bigot."

Jack laughed, and they shook hands again. "So what's next?"

Kevin scratched the thick stubble along his jaw. "We wait for the autopsy report. Now, tell me again. What did the silver note say?"

CHAPTER SEVENTEEN

The following morning Josh was a nervous wreck. Did Cedric know? Had the police questioned him in the night? How was he supposed to pretend that nothing had happened? He took several deep breaths to keep from hyperventilating as he stepped off the elevator. His palms were sweaty, but his pants were far too expensive to wipe them on. He headed straight to the men's room.

Leaning on the edge of the sink, he said, "Oh, really? I had no idea." He frowned at his reflection. If he didn't believe himself, he'd never fool Cedric. He wished Stacy were here. She was great at psyching him up for meetings with Cedric.

* * *

Trina put on her sunglasses, pulled the baseball cap low on her forehead, and kept her head down as she walked along the hallway towards the coroner's office, trying to keep her tennis shoes from squeaking on the clean white floor. Where the hell was Anthony? It wasn't like him to stay out all night.

She inhaled deeply as she passed the morgue—formaldehyde. It reminded her of the animals she had dissected in nursing school. Instead of feeling squeamish like the other girls had, she found it fascinating—empowering even—but she never liked the labs themselves, which of course, made no sense. Nevertheless, the apple hadn't fallen far from the tree. Too bad her father couldn't see that. She pushed through the double doors and waited for Thad to notice her.

"You shouldn't be down here," he said without looking

up. "The lobby is upstairs."

"Like, I don't know that?" she said in the same surly tone.

"What are *you* doing here?" he said, turning from his work.

She sat on the stool across from him. "It's a pleasure to see you, too, *Daddy.*"

"How many times do I have to tell you not to call me that? What if someone hears you?"

"Deny it. You're good at that, remember?" She hated herself for wondering if he would claim her after the baby was born, even if only for the child's sake.

"Why aren't you working?" he said.

"Anthony didn't come home last night. Where did you send him?"

Thad walked over to the swinging double doors and checked the hallway in both directions. "What makes you think I sent him anywhere?"

"I know about his little assignments. He won't tell me where he goes, but I know he delivers messages for you. Where did you send him?"

"I don't know where he is, but I suspect he'll turn up soon. Why don't you go home and get some rest?"

"Remind me not to count on you if I go missing."

Thad tossed his glasses on the desk. "What do you propose I do? Send out a search party?"

"He's your grandchild's father, for God's sake."

"And his work is already done," Thad said, gesturing towards her stomach.

"Like me, after I give birth?"

"If you give me a grandson, yes. If it's a girl, we might have to try again."

"Is that how you see people? For how they might benefit you?" Her voice rose with her temper. "Don't you ever wonder what it's like to be nice?"

"Nice?" he scoffed. "Are you being nice when you assist in killing people? Sure, you tell yourself it's mercy, but you get a thrill out of watching people die. Don't you, Katrina girl?"

She opened her mouth, but she found no words.

"You see? I know you better than you think. And let me tell you something else while I'm at it. Being nice only keeps you poor. You remember that."

How did he always manage to twist things? She never won when she challenged him outright. Getting control of her emotions, she said, "Yeah, I'll remember that. I'll be at Anthony's place. If you hear from him, tell him to call me." She pushed to her feet and through the swinging doors.

"That isn't Anthony's place," he called after her.

* * *

Having delayed as long as he dared, Josh smoothed his perfectly pressed shirt and knocked. When Cedric beckoned, he opened the door and went inside. "Hey, boss. An important day. Can I lead the meeting?"

Cedric looked up over his reading glasses, which made him look annoyed, even when he wasn't. "I'll handle the meeting myself."

"But why?" Josh said as he dropped into his usual chair.

"I gave you my answer. Have their paperwork on my desk before they get here."

"Fine. Anything else?"

"Have you heard from Stacy?" Cedric said, eyeing him attentively.

"No. Have you?"

Cedric gestured for him to leave.

Outside Cedric's office, Josh smiled. For once in his life, he didn't give himself away. Cedric might have his suspicions, but if he had more than that, he'd have said so.

* * *

Stacy blew a huge pink bubble and let it pop. It had been a grueling night of questioning. She climbed from the back seat of Jack's car, where she had failed to get any sleep, and into the driver's seat. When they had finally let her leave around six o'clock that morning, she'd had nowhere else to go. Jack's place was trashed, and she didn't feel like going to Josh's. In fact, she was perturbed with Josh. He'd had the gun. If he saw the messenger entering the building, why didn't he try to stop him?

She spotted Jack hurrying down the concrete stairs outside the police station. Just seeing him made her feel safer though she wasn't sure quite why. She was probably a better shot than he was. She hit the button to unlock the door, and he climbed in.

"Thanks for waiting," he said as he sank into the passenger's seat with an exhausted sigh.

"Did they torture you?" she said with a laugh. "Your hair's sticking up all over the place."

"It's a curse." He buckled his seatbelt. "Where's Josh?"

"They let him go hours ago. Lucky for him, we were the ones trespassing. Besides, he had to be at work this morning. Where to?"

"Anywhere that serves food."

"Amen," Stacy said as she hit the gas. She reached into her purse and handed him a hairbrush.

"No thanks."

"You want to get served, don't you?"

"You're way too peppy in the mornings. You know that?"

"Would you rather see my grouchy side? I haven't gotten any sleep either, you know."

Jack's cell phone rang. "Hey, Christine."

Stacy wondered again if there was more between them than friendship. It would certainly be convenient, she supposed, but somehow, she couldn't see Jack raising children. He was great with Christine's kids, but a full-time father? She didn't think so.

Jack let out a groan and closed his eyes. "Yes, I forgot. I'm on the way."

Stacy glanced over.

"No," Jack said, "but could you whip up a quick breakfast for two?" Stacy turned left and headed for Christine's house. "Yeah, Stacy and me. We'll be there in ten minutes."

"What does she need now?" Stacy said with a little more attitude than she intended.

"She reminded me of our nine o'clock appointment with Cedric. It's about settling the case—unless Cedric found out about last night."

"Why don't you call Josh? Maybe he knows."

Jack shook his head. "My brain's too tired to think right now. I sure hope she makes pancakes."

Their stomachs growled within seconds of each other, making them laugh.

* * *

An hour later, Jack and Christine sat in the conference room waiting for Cedric to join them. When he bustled in, he shook hands with Jack, and then Christine. "Jack, Mrs. Steinberg. I'll get right to the point. Dr. Solver wants to settle out of court, and he's willing to do it quickly."

Pretending to be surprised, Jack said, "I thought the idea was to bring him to justice."

Cedric cleared his throat. "The autopsy report is inconclusive. There's not much to go on."

"My husband is dead," Christine said. "Isn't that enough to *go on*?"

"Let's hear him out," Jack said softly.

Christine closed her eyes. When she opened them again, the faraway look there nearly broke his heart. Clearly, she felt betrayed.

"We can push for trial," Cedric added, "but without sufficient evidence . . ."

Jack wanted to punch him, but he had to play it cool. Cedric and the doctor might be in jail soon. It could be years before they reached another settlement, if ever.

"If we settle out of court," Cedric said, "you can tuck some money away and put the legal matters behind you. If we proceed, a trial could run into the tens of thousands of dollars, and there's no guarantee we'd win. It's your call."

Christine stood up. "Do you have any children, Mr. Johnson?"

"Yes," Jack said. "He has two sons—one in high school, the other in college."

Cedric's gaze rested on Jack for a moment. "He's right. I have two sons."

"If your life ended on Solver's table, would you want your wife to tell *your* children that she settled for a bit of money instead of fighting to put their father's killer behind bars?"

Jack tried to urge her back into her chair, but she jerked her arm free. "You said you knew how to stop him!"

Cedric laid a piece of paper on the table. "Your husband signed this consent form. He was aware of the risks."

"That doctor should be in jail, not free to do this to somebody else!" She yanked the door open and ran down the hall.

Jack rose to go after her.

"Wait," Cedric said. "Have you uncovered anything I should know about?"

Jack raked a hand through his hair, which made it stand up again. He wanted to tell him his days were numbered, but he knew it wasn't the time. Instead, he said, "Maybe."

Cedric's eyebrow rose. "Care to share?"

"When I get the details, you'll be the first to know."

Cedric eyed him for a moment. "What about the settlement?"

"I'll talk to her."

"One million dollars, Jack."

Jack's hand froze as he reached for the door.

A smile danced on Cedric's lips, the kind an opponent smiles when he thinks he's won.

Jack's pulse was racing. He was negotiating with the great Cedric Johnson for a million dollars. He would have loved to tell him to shove it, but the well-being of Daniel's family hung in the balance. Instead, he said, "I know about Solver's money. She'll take it, but only if we sign the deal tomorrow morning and the funds hit her account tomorrow afternoon."

Cedric smile disappeared. "I'll have the money deposited directly into Daniel's estate, which is already in place. Do we have a deal?"

"Yes, if you deliver."

"I need to hear it from Mrs. Steinberg."

Jack took out his cell phone.

"Before you call her, I have one more question," Cedric said.

A chill shot through him as he looked into the eyes of the powerful attorney.

"Are you dating one of my employees?"

"No," he said truthfully and dialed Christine.

"Are you coming?" Christine said with a huff.

"Do you trust me?"

"Yes, but I'm angry."

"I am, too, but I need you to tell Cedric that you'll settle Daniel's case. He's going to draw up the papers for you to sign tomorrow morning."

"I don't want to settle. I want Ryan Solver to go to jail!"

"Please, Christine, tell Cedric you'll sign the papers. I'm going to put him on the phone. Here he is." Jack handed his phone to Cedric.

"Mrs. Steinberg?"

"I don't want to speak to you, Mr. Johnson. Whatever you have worked out with Jack, I'll agree to. You have my word."

Cedric handed the phone back to Jack. "We have a deal."

* * *

After taking Christine home, Jack rushed to his office and was in the process of unlocking the door when Teresa pulled up. He walked over and dropped three quarters into her parking meter. "Good morning," he said as she stepped out of her car.

"Good morning."

He opened the office door and waited for her to enter, but felt mortified when she wrinkled her nose and stepped back.

"Good heavens, Jack. Did something die in there?"

He rushed to the bathroom and opened the door, but there were no dead animals. "Give me a second to open the windows. That usually helps."

Teresa stood in the doorway while Jack opened the windows. Fortunately, a cool breeze flowed through.

"I'm sorry about this. It gets musty when it's all closed up. I was hoping to get here before you did, to air it out."

"Remind me to give you Collette's phone number," Teresa said as she reluctantly stepped into the conference room and settled at the table. "She's very good with soap and water."

"Can I get her number now, before we forget?" he said, his face flushed red with embarrassment.

Teresa took out her iPhone and had the number within seconds.

"I need one of those," Jack said. "I'm a bit behind on technology." He joined her at the table and wrote down the number.

"Okay, Jack, who is she?" Teresa said as she tossed her sunglasses on the table.

He cleared his throat. "The woman in the picture isn't your husband's mistress, Teresa. She's his daughter."

"What? But that's impossible. We don't . . ." Her expression evolved from surprise to dawning, and then into anger. "How old is she?"

He reached for the file and handed her a clear picture of Lisa. "Twenty-five." She couldn't deny it; the evidence was there, in Lisa's blue eyes.

"Irrefutable proof at last," she said softly. "Why didn't he tell me?"

"Perhaps he didn't know."

"Tell me about her," she said, her eyes glistening with tears.

"Her name is Lisa Coleman. She's a third-year med student." He handed her a piece of paper. "That's her address."

Teresa stared at Lisa's picture. "Alan's going to be a grandfather?" She tucked the photograph into her purse and put on her sunshades. "I'll get back to you."

Jack watched through the window as she walked past her car and continued down the street. Once she was out of sight, he dialed Collette's number. "Two hundred and fifty dollars? No, thanks. I can't believe I'm saying this, but I'll clean it myself." He had just hung up when his phone rang.

"Jack, I've got some interesting news for you," Captain Thomas said. "You were right. The prints from your break-in match the ones on Stacy's lipstick—definitely the same guy. His name is Anthony Winchester. He's had several scrapes with the law in New Orleans."

Jack began closing the windows. "That's a relief. At least Stacy is safe."

"I don't think so," Kevin said. "Can you and Miss Young come by my office? There's another side to this story."

"Can't you just tell me?" he said, annoyed at having to wait.

"Come by around five this afternoon."

Now he understood how Teresa felt when he did this to her. "Yeah, yeah. See you then."

* * *

Something jostled Anthony into consciousness. He heard distant voices, but he couldn't open his eyes, and he couldn't move. The all-encompassing darkness was terrifying, like being locked inside a closet.

"Where do you want this one?" a man said.

"Stick him in the cooler. I'll get to it as fast as I can."

Anthony recognized the second voice. It belonged to his uncle.

"Want me to take him out of the body bag?"

"Thanks. The blankets are in that cabinet over there. If anyone comes looking for me, tell them I'm in the lab."

"Sure thing, Dr. Winchester."

"Wait!" Anthony screamed, but the words wouldn't form in his mouth, and no sound came out. Despite his panic, the heavy darkness tugged him back under.

* * *

Thirty minutes later, Jack pulled into Christine's driveway and parked behind Daniel's truck, which sat outside the open garage.

Jon came running. "When are we gonna finish the fort, Uncle Jack? Lexie keeps using my ladder, and I can't keep her out!"

Jack got out of the car and high-fived Jon. "Hopefully, this weekend. Where is everybody?"

"Mama's at the store and your *girlfriend* is upstairs with Lexie," Jon said.

"Stacy isn't my girlfriend, but she is pretty cool, don't you think?"

"I guess so. Wanna play catch?"

It occurred to him that Jon was acting like a normal kid. He seemed to be handling Daniel's death better than anybody. He reached out and mussed his hair. "Let me go say hello to Stacy and Alexa first."

"Yippee! My mitts are in the fort."

"I'll meet you back here in ten minutes. Okay?"

Jon took off running, and Jack let himself into the kitchen. "Hey everybody!" he called from the bottom of the stairs.

When no one answered, he went looking. Alexa's bedroom door was closed. "Anybody home?" he said. He heard Alexa giggle.

Stacy cracked the door open. "Hey, Jack, what's up?"

"Are you two having fun in there?"

"Don't let him in!" Alexa said. "I'm not ready!"

"You heard her. She's not ready," Stacy said. "We'll come out when Christine gets home."

"And when will that be?" Jack said.

"Hey, y'all, I'm home," Christine called from the kitchen.

"We'll be right down," Stacy yelled loud enough for Christine to hear.

Jack turned around and headed down the stairs.

"Hey, you," Christine said, using Jack's casual style of greeting. "How was your day?"

He felt the positive shift in her mood and held out his arms for a hug. "I'm good." He breathed in the strawberry scent of her shampoo and sighed. It was a tremendous relief to know that the messenger was dead, and he was negotiating with the great Cedric Johnson for a million dollars.

"Okay, Mama, close your eyes," Alexa said from the top of the stairs. "You, too, Uncle Jack. No peeking!" A few moments later, Alexa said, "Okay, you can look now!" She posed in the middle of the kitchen wearing a pink party dress, her hair curled into adorable ringlets, and her eyes and lips shimmering with light makeup.

"Lexie," Christine said with surprise. "You look beautiful."

Alexa turned in circles to show off her dress.

"You do," Jack said. He nodded towards Stacy, who had stepped back out of the way. She winked at him and smiled. He knew that getting Alexa to wear this dress was no small feat. Daniel had bought it for her to wear to a father-daughter dance party sponsored by her school. She had been fantastically excited about it, but at the last minute, Daniel had come down with the stomach flu and was unable to attend. Though everyone knew she was terribly disappointed, Alexa pretended it didn't matter. She had cheerfully stayed home to help take care of her father. Daniel died a month later, and she never wore the dress.

"In fact," Jack said, "you look so pretty, I think we should all go out somewhere. Is anybody hungry?"

"Let's go out for ice cream," Alexa said, her eyes sparkling with pleasure.

Christine smiled warmly at Stacy.

The screen door squeaked as Jon came in. "Yuck! You look like a stupid girl!"

"Wanna go out for ice cream?" Jack said.

"You promised to play catch," Jon said, wrinkling his brow in a way that looked so much like Daniel that he and Christine exchanged glances.

"I did, didn't I?" Jack said. "Okay, ladies, fifteen minutes."

Jon handed him a mitt and pushed back through the screen door. Jack followed, but when he heard Alexa talking to her mother, he paused.

"Do you like it, Mama?"

"Yes, I do," Christine said. "Your father would be very proud of you."

"He would, wouldn't he, Mama?"

"Yes, Alexa. I'm proud of you, too."

* * *

Trina was beside herself with worry. It was all she could do not to run down the hallway. She brushed past two interns, who were pushing a blanket-covered gurney, and shoved through the lab doors. Thad wasn't there. She went back out into the hallway.

Worrying about Anthony was making her nauseous. She had tried to take a nap after talking with her father that morning, but the same scenarios that had kept her awake during the night refused to let her rest. She was exhausted. During the long hours of apprehension, one thing had become exceedingly clear. She no longer questioned her feelings for Anthony. She loved him, and they were about to become a family.

The interns pushed the gurney through the swinging doors of the morgue, reminding her to look there for her father. She waited until they left before sticking her head inside. Thad was leaning over the body of a naked young woman, blood from the autopsy wounds dripping down her rib cage and onto the examination table. Her stomach turned. "Any news?" she said from the doorway.

Thad looked up with a tight smile. "How are you feeling?"

"Better than her," she said, gesturing towards the girl.

Thad laid the scalpel down and pulled off his gloves. "I must admit," he said as he washed his hands in the sink, "it's out of character for Anthony to go missing when payment is due. He hasn't returned my calls either."

Trina skirted the gurney with the new arrival on it and stood next to another gurney, whose occupant had, only minutes before, been removed from the cooler. She sensed the temperature difference and stepped away.

"You don't think he left, do you? I mean, maybe he changed his mind about the baby."

Thad reached out and awkwardly patted her shoulder. "He probably got drunk last night and is sleeping it off somewhere. He'll turn up."

She frowned. "Busy, huh?"

"As you can see, they're backing up." He pointed to the gurney next to her. "I was just about to start on that one when they brought *her* in here. Everybody's in a hurry. Why don't you go back to the house and take a nice Jacuzzi bath in the guest suite? Try to relax. Surely, he'll be home by evening. Then you can give him hell for making you worry."

"You're inviting me into your house?" she said, expecting him to say something now to spoil it.

"It's not too soon to take better care of yourself, you know."

Hearing him talk like this brought tears to her eyes, which she immediately blinked away.

"Thanks. I'll do that. See you later."

* * *

Anthony, who had heard every word, called to her, but nothing came out. He kicked his feet, but nothing moved. He was trapped in utter darkness. Even now, its merciless tentacles tugged on him, yet he was terrified of falling to sleep. He knew what awaited him on Thad's table.

* * *

After their outing, Alexa went upstairs with Stacy to change into regular clothing, and Jon went out to the fort.

"Thanks, Jack," Christine said as they settled at the kitchen table. "It's nice to have some fun for a change."

"We need more fun, don't we? Wanna go for a walk?"

A few minutes later, he and Christine stopped to sit on a park bench, beneath a moss draped oak tree in a park a few blocks from her house.

"Okay, what is it?" she said. "You've been waiting all day to tell me."

"Am I that obvious?" he said.

"I've only known you your entire life."

"There's been a lot going on that we haven't had a chance to discuss. First, I want to explain why I told you to sign the settlement papers for Cedric tomorrow morning."

She tensed. "I hate selling out. I thought you, of all people, understood that."

"It's a million dollars, Christine."

She rose and walked a few paces before turning back to face him. "Will Solver still practice medicine?"

"I don't know, but this is the best chance you'll ever have for getting a settlement."

"I don't care about the money. I want justice!"

"Well, I think you're about to get both. If things go as I think they will, they'll arrest Cedric Johnson and Dr. Solver any day now."

"Okay, what haven't you told me?"

He motioned for her to join him on the bench. "It all started with Stacy. When I first met with Cedric, Stacy—who was Josh's assistant at the time—gave me two client files to review. That's how I knew Daniel's case wasn't Solver's first offense, and that Cedric had sued him twice before."

"Why would she do that?"

"I'm not really sure, but I think it has something to do with her losing her father to a doctor like Solver. She knew this was Cedric's third Solver case, and she was beginning to question what was going on."

Apparently, Cedric and Dr. Solver have been exchanging messages through a courier in what appears to be an insurance fraud scheme. Unbeknownst to Cedric, Stacy had seen this messenger and gotten suspicious enough sneak into Cedric's office at night to intercept some of these messages. Unfortunately, the messenger caught her in the act and threatened to kill her if she didn't leave Cedric a phone message saying she had to quit her job and leave town immediately to take care of a sickly relative. In exchange for her life, she had to surrender her cell phone, which lists all of her contacts—including me—and leave town that very night."

"That poor girl," Christine said. "She must've been scared to death."

He chuckled. "Maybe, but put a gun in that girl's hand and she's pretty darn intimidating."

An elderly couple walked by holding hands and was clearly content to be in each other's company. Christine stared after them.

"So," Jack said to keep her focused, "Stacy packed up her apartment and went to New Orleans, where she was either robbed, or too drunk to keep track of her money. At any rate, she found herself stranded in the parking lot, with the meter going up, and no cell phone to call for help. She finally borrowed one and called me."

"That's why you were late for fort building," Christine said, piecing the puzzle together.

"I've tried to keep her hidden, but somehow, the messenger found out that she came back. He ransacked my house yesterday—well, destroyed it would be more accurate. That happened during the storm while we were here."

Christine looked horrified. "Why didn't you tell me any of this?"

"There's more. Stacy had made secret copies of the Solver files for us to study. Josh smuggled them out."

"Did you learn anything?"

"I haven't had a chance to study them yet, but if Stacy's hunch is correct, we'll be able to prove collusion between Cedric Johnson and Dr. Solver, which should get them involved in some serious legal battles of their own. *That*, if nothing else, should ruin their reputations and put an end to their respective practices." He took hold of her hands. "Justice *and* money."

"But what about the messenger? Isn't he still a threat?"

"I was afraid you'd ask that. We, meaning Stacy and I, broke into Cedric Johnson's office last night, just ahead of the messenger. Thank goodness for Josh because he saw the messenger enter the building behind us and called the police. It ended up in an alley fight between me and the messenger, who turned out to be a twenty-year-old punk with a switchblade. I chased him for nearly fifteen minutes before he backed himself into a corner." He turned his face to the side and pointed to his jaw. "You can see a bruise there if you look close enough."

Christine lightly touched the spot, which couldn't be seen beneath his two-day stubble. Tears pooled in her eyes. "Oh, Jack, what if something had happened to you?"

"Wanna hear the rest?" When she nodded, he said, "When Charlie, of all people, arrived at the fight, followed by Stacy, who had Cedric's gun, I had the kid's arm twisted high behind his back, close to the point of breaking. Charlie told me to let go on the count of three, but before I could, he stomped on my foot and twisted out of reach. Charlie yelled for him to get down on the ground, but he just stood there. Charlie warned him again, but he fell down dead. It shocked the heck out of all of us. We're hoping the autopsy reveals what happened because none of us know. He was fine one moment, dead the next. It was the strangest thing you ever saw."

Christine buried her face in her hands. "Thank goodness you're all safe. I couldn't take it if something happened to you."

"Uh, in the spirit of fairness, I should tell you that we're not entirely safe. Cedric and Solver are still at large, but hopefully unaware of what happened last night. Do you have any idea how hard it was to persuade Kevin to hold off on an official investigation until tomorrow afternoon? That's why I wanted you to sign the settlement papers in the morning—before all this happens."

"Wow. That's a lot to take in."

He nodded.

"Considering the circumstances," she said, "it's hard to say no to a million dollars."

"Yeah, that's what I'm thinking."

* * *

It was nearly five o'clock. Thad was just cleaning up when an intern ducked into the morgue.

"Hey, Dr. Winchester, I heard you were busy down here. Want me to ice these guys?"

Thad stretched his tired back and glanced at the clock. Approaching the newest arrival, he lifted the blanket and looked into the face of a strikingly handsome black man, who appeared to be in his thirties. "Yeah, stick him back in the cooler."

"What about the other one?" the intern asked.

When Thad reached for the blanket, his cell phone rang, stopping his hand in mid-motion. "Winchester," he said.

The intern rolled the first body into the cooler. "This one, too, Dr. Winchester?" he asked again.

Thad covered the receiver. "Thanks."

Skirting the gurney, he ducked next door, into his lab. "Hey, Elyse. I can talk now. What color are your panties today?"

* * *

Captain Kevin Thomas pointed to an open folder on his desk. "His cell phone is registered in the name Anthony Winchester."

"Winchester? I've heard that name recently," Stacy said, tapping her chin and squinting in concentration.

"There are several calls from a Thurston Oliver Winchester III, whose address is referenced on the cell phone contract," Kevin said, pausing to cough into a closed fist. "According to the report, Winchester's only child—a son—died five years ago in a drag racing incident. They clocked him doing one-ten in a fifty-five. They tried to save him, but he was pronounced dead an hour later in the Emergency Room."

"Winchester," Stacy muttered a second time.

Kevin coughed again and took a long swig from a water bottle. Jack and Stacy glanced at each other.

"Get this," Kevin said as he set the bottle down. "The

Jaguar you asked about belongs to the same Winchester. He's the head coroner for the State of Mississippi."

Stacy poked Jack's shoulder. "What Jaguar?"

Jack was having difficulty adjusting to the news that Elyse was dating a guy who examined dead bodies. His face morphed with disgust, and an eerie chill rose up his spine.

"Tell me," Stacy insisted.

"Give me a second," he said as he tried to regain his composure, but he shuddered.

Kevin observed them without any pretense of looking away.

Stacy bit her lip to keep from talking.

"Can I look at the report," Jack said.

Kevin handed it to Jack, but Stacy took it and began flipping through it with purpose.

"Is that my copy?" Jack said.

Kevin nodded. "The detective team found an empty syringe near Anthony's body. It's presumably unrelated, but we're checking it out anyway. Besides his phone and motorcycle keys, all he had on him was a silver envelope."

"Yeah, we know," Jack said. "Once Christine's case settles tomorrow, Cedric will signal for Solver to pick up his share of the money—the other reason for holding off the investigation. If we interfere now, that exchange won't happen."

Kevin gave him an odd look. "Jack, why would Solver use his own money to settle his case when his supposed reason for killing his patients is to scam the insurance company?"

Jack's mind began to race. This case *was* being settled differently than the other two. What was the reason? Was it just to throw them off?

"I know I've heard that name before," Stacy said, passing the report to Jack. "If I'm not mistaken, a Winchester did all three autopsies on the Solver patients."

"Even if that's true," Kevin said, "that doesn't explain why Solver's patients died in the first place. Autopsies are performed after the fact. On top of that, there's no motive. None of this makes any sense."

Jack's eyebrows rose. "Unless Dr. Solver was the anesthesiologist who worked on Winchester's dead son."

"Are you suggesting a vendetta?" Kevin said.

"Is there any way to find out who was in the Emergency Room five years ago?"

Kevin picked up the phone. "Get the Emergency Room records for one Thurston Oliver Winchester *the fourth.* Yeah. Union General, five years ago. The sixteen-year-old victim died in the Emergency Room. Right. ASAP."

"Kevin," Jack said, rising to his feet. "Where is the messenger's— I mean, where is Anthony's body?"

"It was delivered to the morgue late last night. Why?"

"Which morgue?" Jack and Stacy said simultaneously.

Kevin grabbed the phone. "Get dispatch."

"We're going to the hospital," Jack said as he grabbed Stacy's arm to set her in motion.

Kevin covered the receiver. "Like hell you are. Sit back down."

Jack and Stacy looked at each other and sat back down.

* * *

Elyse's mind wandered as she drove down Old Agency Road, enjoying the way the light filtered through the leafy canopy formed by the trees lining either side of the narrow road. She had mixed feelings about her relationship with Thad. On one hand, it was exciting to be with someone who clearly thought she was beautiful and treated her like a princess. On the other hand, she knew the likelihood of him divorcing his wife to be with her was statistically low. Despite that knowledge, she felt a genuine connection with him and wanted to see where it led.

"Okay," she said into her phone, "I just pulled up to the security gate. What's the code?" She punched in the number and waited for the gate to open. "Great, I'll be waiting." A few minutes later, she parked her tan colored SUV in the courtyard next to a black Toyota Camry. Frowning with suspicion, she looked inside the vehicle and saw various items of female apparel strewn across the back seat, including a pair of black lacy underwear, which kindled her easily fired jealousy.

She walked up the marble stairs and knocked on the door using the heavy brass knocker. When no one came to the door, she decided to see if she could get into the back yard. Visions of Thad with another woman made her feel foolish for even thinking there might be a genuine connection between them. Despite her negative thoughts, the impeccable landscaping as she rounded the house in search of a gate impressed her. Thad was quite a catch. No wonder there was other interest.

Her cell phone rang. Thinking it was Thad, she pulled it out and said, "Miss me already?"

"I do, actually," Jack said.

Wrinkling her nose, she said, "Why are you calling me?"

"I need to talk to you about something important. It has to do with the man you're seeing."

"That's none of your business, Jack. We've moved on, remember?"

"Please, Elyse, just listen to me. Do you know anything about Anthony Winchester?"

She stopped to admire a bed of white roses. "No. We haven't talked about extended family. Why do you ask?"

"Anthony is about twenty years old. He's the biker-dude type. His cell phone is registered with Thurston's address, so I thought he might live there. A son, maybe."

"I've never seen him," Elyse said, "But I can tell you he's not Thad's son. How did you know I'm seeing Thad Winchester?"

"I saw you at La Bells the other night. He drives a black Jag, right?"

"And you drive a ten-year-old Camry. So what?"

Jack chuckled. "I'd forgotten how sharp your tongue is."

"You were quite fond of my tongue once," Elyse said as she wandered back towards the front door.

"Look," Jack said, "I'm not to the bottom of it yet, but Anthony is involved in something extremely serious, and it appears that Thad may be in on it as well. Please be careful."

Elyse sat on the marble stairs and fluttered her white cotton skirt around her legs. "Fine, I'll do that. Anything else?"

"Yeah. Keep this conversation between us."

"Only if you tell me what's going on because it sounds like you're inventing things because you're jealous. Not a good strategy, by the way."

"Give me your word, Elyse. If there's anything I know about you, it's that you honor your word."

"If what you're saying is true, it'll all come out anyway."

"But until it does," he said.

"Okay, you have my word."

"Here's the deal. Anthony served as a secret courier between an attorney named Cedric Johnson and a doctor named Ryan Solver. They're running an insurance scam worth millions of dollars. After one of Dr. Solver's patients dies, the attorney— Cedric Johnson—calls on the grieving family and arranges to represent them in a lawsuit against the doctor, but it never goes to trial. The doctor settles out of court and, I assume, they split the settlement. Then it's on to the next victim."

"Wow. I'm certain Thad knows nothing about this. Are you sure I can't tell him?"

"We can't risk it. Like you said, it'll all come out at the proper time."

Elyse glanced upwards as the curtains moved in a window above the garage. She hadn't noticed that window before. "Something you said doesn't make sense. Why would a doctor kill his own patients? Someone else's patients, maybe, but not his own. He'd lose his entire practice."

"I agree, but that's what it looks like. One thing we know for sure; Thad performed all three Solver-patient autopsies. That's a pretty damning coincidence, don't you think?"

"That's all it is, Jack, a coincidence. Thad is the top pathologist in the State of Mississippi. There's no telling what all he oversees." Spotting the staircase next to the garage, she crossed the courtyard. "This isn't the average, run of the mill case for you, is it?"

"Daniel Steinberg was one of Dr. Solver's patients, Elyse. He died in Dr. Solver's care."

"Oh no! Not Daniel! I'm so sorry. I know how close you two were."

"Christine and the kids are having a difficult time of it. I'm doing all I can, but it's not nearly enough."

"Don't say that! I'm sure you're a huge comfort to them. You're like a second daddy to those kids."

"I swore on Daniel's grave that I'd find out why this happened. I won't quit until I uncover the truth."

She sighed. "Always fighting for the underdog. Right, Jack?"

"Yep, that's me, the underdog detective. There's something else, Elyse."

She started up the stairs. "Shoot."

"Anthony died last night. It was the strangest thing I ever saw. He was standing there one minute, then on the ground dead the next. The police found an empty syringe near his body. It's probably unrelated, but they're checking it out anyway. We're waiting for the autopsy report."

Elyse swallowed a lump in her throat. "Does Thad know?"

"Not yet. The police will be calling soon to notify him as next of kin."

"Thanks for filling me in."

"Just watch yourself. You know I wish you the best."

"Take care of yourself, too. I'm really sorry to hear about Daniel."

"Be happy, Elyse."

Just as she hung up, the garage door opened, and Thad drove in. She stepped back into the courtyard and went to greet him.

* * *

"If that little tramp thinks for one second she's horning in on Dad's fortune, she's got another thing coming," Trina said as she watched her father kiss the beautiful woman. Several solutions raced through her mind, all of them wicked. Turning from the window, she cranked up her favorite rap music station and settled on the couch. She knew she shouldn't, but she flipped open the wooden box on Anthony's coffee table and helped herself to a thick line of OxyContin. As the drug hit her system, she leaned back on the couch to ponder what she could do about the female threat without further alienating her father.

In all her life, he had never spoken a kind word to her until recently. She knew it was because of the baby, but still. She hoped he would finally acknowledge her as his only living child. He'd have to, if he accepted the baby as his legitimate heir—unless he claimed it only through Anthony.

Legitimate, the most hated word in her vocabulary. Unless she married Anthony, the baby would be illegitimate also. She had to marry Anthony, but that only made her smile. They had talked for hours, once Anthony had learned about the baby, promising each other sobriety and a healthy lifestyle for their family. Anthony had managed to save a nice pile of cash, so even without Thad's money, they'd make it. Her nursing position alone paid better than most two-income households. She lightly stroked her belly, which was still firm and flat. The world was a nicer place when she was high.

Her cell phone vibrated inside her pocket. She looked at the caller ID and saw that it was the hospital. "If you're calling me in to work, Estelle, I'm sick," she said to her coworker.

"Trina, you need to get down here right away. The police are here. I think it's got something to do with your boyfriend."

"Oh, my God," Trina said, jumping to her feet in a panic. "Thanks, I'm on my way." She grabbed her purse and headed for the door. "Wait! Where did I put my frickin' keys!"

* * *

Teresa looked to the mirror for courage. Would this conversation end her marriage? She took a deep breath and walked into the living room where Alan sat in his favorite recliner reading a medical journal. Lifting her chin, she said, "I had an interesting meeting with my private investigator today."

Alan tensed and laid his magazine down. "Oh?"

She sat on the edge of the sofa, next to his chair. "Care to tell me about Lisa?"

"Teresa," Alan said, reaching for her hand, but she pulled away. With a heavy sigh, he said, "What do you want to know, that you were right about Claire?"

The color drained from her face. "For starters. Was she the only one?"

"Yes. It was only once, and I have regretted it immensely—at least until I learned about Lisa."

"And when was that?" Teresa said, trying to keep her voice calm.

"About two months ago, when she came to my office. She's struggling with her pregnancy."

Teresa swallowed a lump in her throat. She wasn't ready to deal with Lisa's child. "And her mother?"

"Claire died of cancer several months ago," Alan said. "Lisa has nowhere else to turn."

"And Claire never told you?"

Alan rose to his feet. "Look, Teresa, I know I've hurt you. It was a stupid mistake, and yet now that I have a daughter, how can I be sorry? She's beautiful, smart, and kind. She's absolutely wonderful."

Tears stung her eyes, but she blinked them away. "How did she find you?"

He sat back down. "Lisa read her mother's diary."

"A diary?" she said as if he'd slapped her. "People don't record one-night stands in their diaries, Alan!"

Raising his voice in kind, he said, "Apparently, some do, especially if it results in a child." He absently rubbed the thick bristles on his chin. "Look, Teresa, it was a long time ago. Claire is gone, but Lisa . . . I can help her. Can't you just . . . forgive me?"

Teresa softened at the break in her husband's voice. Deep down, she knew he loved her. He had always loved her. Still, he could have come forward and told her about Lisa.

She picked up her purse and left the house.

* * *

It was all Elyse could do not to ask about the car in the driveway, but she held her tongue and accepted the wine glass Thad offered. He gestured for her to take a seat in the living room, so she smiled and settled onto the sofa.

"I find myself thinking about you quite a lot during the day," Thad said. "Here's to a lovely evening."

She lifted her glass and took a sip of the excellent Riesling. As she smiled up at him, she was aware of the fine quality of the glass, the rich texture of the couch, the artwork on the wall. It was a world she wanted to belong to. She had come this far; she didn't want to back out now.

Thad's phone, which was sitting on the coffee table, vibrated across the surface.

"You're not going to answer that, are you?" she said taking offense.

"Comes with the territory, I'm afraid." He reached for it. "Winchester."

Within seconds, he was scowling and on his feet. "Conflict of interest? When?" He set his wine glass on the table and grabbed his keys. "Yeah, I'm on the way." He turned to Elyse. "Please stay. I'll be back as soon as I can."

"Will you let me know when you're on the way back?"

"Of course. Make yourself at home," he said and headed out the door.

* * *

Teresa parked down the street from Lisa's condominium and considered how best to approach the young woman. The lights were on inside, so she knew that she was home. Not one to shrink from her decisions, she got out of her car and walked to the door, straightening her shoulders as she rang the bell.

When the door opened, Lisa looked up at her with pleasant

expectation. "Hello. May I help you?"

The amazing hue of her beautiful blue eyes perfectly matched those of her husband. She swallowed hard. "I'm Teresa, your father's wife. May I come in?"

Lisa's face lit with pleasure. "Yes, of course. Please, come in and have a seat," she said, gesturing towards the sofa.

Teresa sat on the couch clutching her purse.

"May I get you something to drink?"

"Water, thanks."

"Sure. I'll be right back."

Teresa admired the tastefully decorated living room. Bright, colorful artwork depicting fanciful country settings created a pleasant feel to the room—the perfect complement to Lisa's neutral furnishings. Everything was neat and perfectly in place. "Your home is lovely," she said when Lisa returned. "Especially your artwork. The style is most unique."

Lisa beamed. "Thanks. That's my *other* hobby. When I'm not cramming for exams, that is."

"Your hobby?" Teresa said with surprise. "You painted those?"

"Yeah. I hope to sell them one day, but I can't even think about that right now. Not with the ba—" Lisa cut herself off and looked worried.

"Of course," Teresa said softly. "The baby. Alan tells me you're having some difficulty. Is everything all right?"

"I'm so sorry. I didn't mean to make you feel uncomfortable. I know this must come as a terrible shock for you. It's a shock to me, too, to be honest. When my mother— I mean . . ."

"Alan told me about your mom. You've got a lot to deal with, don't you?"

She nodded and looked down at her hands, which were gripping each other in her lap. "I know you must hate me for intruding upon your life. It's just that after my mother died . . ."

Teresa covered Lisa's hands with her own. When their eyes met, the connection was genuine and instant. "Lisa, you may speak freely with me. This *has* been a shock, but that doesn't mean we can't grow to love each other. Claire will always be your mother."

"I was so afraid you wouldn't like me!" Unable to hold it back any longer, Lisa cried the tears of a multitude of hurts.

With the strongest maternal instinct she had ever experienced, Teresa held her sobbing stepchild in her arms.

Her stepchild . . .

Tears stung Teresa's eyes, as well.

* * *

Jack and Stacy could barely stand still as they waited for the elevator to arrive. He had no idea what he was going to do, but it centered on whether Winchester had already performed the autopsy on Anthony. Finally, the elevator doors opened, releasing a diverse crush of people—all of whom were in Jack's way. As soon as they stepped inside, he pushed the close-door button several times, before anyone could stick their hand inside to delay them.

They hit the basement floor running, pausing only to check the direction signs along the way. When they rounded the last corner, they slowed to a halt. At the far end of the long hallway, a huge commotion was in progress. Two police officers appeared to be questioning the medical staff, and two armed security guards seemed to be guarding a blanket-covered gurney.

Jack and Stacy looked at each other. "Anthony," they said simultaneously and continued towards the mob.

* * *

Elyse knew what she wanted to do with her time. As soon as Thad pulled out of the driveway, she headed for his bedroom. She had wondered about the spiral staircase, which stood in the far corner of his bedroom, from the first time she saw it. Energized with curiosity, she climbed it thinking that this might be her best opportunity to explore. The door at the top was ajar. When she stepped inside, she was surprised to hear rap music. A radio, she guessed, but an odd music choice for a man like Thad. She felt along the wall for a light switch and flipped it on.

The room was huge. Bookshelves lined the walls in the front half of the room on two levels, she realized when she saw the sliding ladders and the narrow walkway circling the perimeter—a semi second floor. The rugs beneath her feet were soft and exquisite. This portion of the room was divided into several seating areas, each a wonderful place to curl up with a book. As for the antiques decorating the shelves and tables, these also appeared quite costly, perhaps even museum quality, as did the artwork in the center section of the room. She took her time appreciating the wealth and character before her.

The clock on the mantel chimed, startling her and drawing her attention there. A portrait of a handsome young man hung above the fireplace. At first, she thought it was Thad, but the brown eyes in the portrait were not his. Thad's eyes were grey. This had to be a portrait of his dead son. She could almost imagine Thad gazing into the portrait on a cold, rainy night, talking to his son. She couldn't fathom the pain of losing a child.

Left of the fireplace was an aquarium filled with odd-looking fish, which didn't interest her in the least. Thad's desk sat in the back right corner of the room. Here, the music—if you could call it that—was louder and filled with f-words, completely wrong in this elegant setting. Without disturbing anything, she looked for the radio in order to turn it off. On one corner of the desk sat an intercom box from which the music seemed to come, and a small TV monitor. Curious, she pushed the power button and was surprised to see rotating pictures within a small apartment. He was clearly monitoring someone.

A chill rose up her back as the monitor brought up a clear shot of a disheveled bed. The implication turned her stomach. Was this the apartment above the garage? Was Thad monitoring the *Anthony* Jack had asked about? The rap music had to be his. She turned off the monitor and pressed the intercom button, which silenced the room.

She glanced towards the door to make sure she was still alone. Noticing a window, she walked over and saw that it overlooked the courtyard. The black Camry was gone. She remembered seeing the curtains move in the window above the garage. Perhaps the car belonged to Anthony's girlfriend. Perhaps it had nothing to do with Thad at all. It was surprising how much that pleased her.

Across from the desk, in the back left corner of the room, stood a polished mahogany wet bar with an elegant array of crystal glassware hanging from suspended racks. Reaching for a wine glass, she ducked behind the bar and opened the small refrigerator, which was tastefully encased within the woodwork. She had hoped to find an open bottle of wine, but was disappointed. She returned the glass to the rack. As she turned to leave, a slim, vertical light in the corner caught her eye. There appeared to be a room behind the paneling. She glanced over her shoulder again, and then slid the secret panel open.

* * *

A young woman with dark, spiky hair struggled to get free from one of the hospital security guards. "No, I don't believe it!" she cried. "Let me see him! He's the father of my baby!"

"I'm sorry miss, but we have our orders," a police officer said.

"Please! I have to see him!" she wailed with tears streaming down her face.

The officer motioned for the guards to take the body away.

"I'm a surgical nurse, dammit! I work here. Let me see him!"

The sound of running footsteps sent Jack and Stacy closer against the wall to let a man pass—a distinguished-looking man in a white lab coat.

"What is the meaning of this," the man demanded, still some distance from the group.

"Daddy," the girl yelled, "it's Anthony!"

The guard released her immediately.

She rushed towards the gurney, getting there about the same time as the man, whom Jack—based on his knowledge that Winchester only had one son—deduced was one of Anthony's relatives.

A police officer blocked her from touching the body. "I've warned you, miss. Stay back or I'll have to restrain you."

Barely sparing the girl a sideways glance, the man said, "I'm Thad Winchester, the coroner here. What the hell is going on?"

Jack and Stacy exchanged surprised glances. So much for deduction.

* * *

Elyse gasped as she stepped into a full-fledged laboratory filled with expensive equipment. The lab, like the rest of Thad's house, was impressively large. This room also had a desk, but it was the bulletin board above the desk that drew her attention. She walked over to take a closer look.

Pinned to the center of the bulletin board was a photograph of a man with a huge X drawn across his face. Surrounding it were several newspaper clippings, each reporting the death of one of Ryan Solver's patients—the man in the photograph. She quickly scanned the articles until she found what she was searching for—Daniel Steinberg's name. Her heart dropped into her stomach, and she stumbled back. "Thad wouldn't want me here."

Turning to leave, she caught sight of a cage sitting on the counter and saw that it held a cat, but there was something odd about it. "Hey, kitty, kitty," she said. When it didn't respond, she thought it might be deaf. Sticking her index finger between the bars, she poked it lightly, but it didn't move. Recoiling, she realized it was dead. Glancing down the counter, she saw the sink and went to wash her hands, but inside the sink lay a dissected fish on a cutting board—the same type of fish he kept in the aquarium not twenty feet away.

"What the hell is he doing?"

To the left of the sink sat a small Igloo cooler, which she opened with shaking hands. It contained several vials of yellowish liquid. Against her better judgment, she took one and hurried out of the lab. When she stepped back into Thad's study, she was careful to leave the hidden panel exactly as she found it. She rushed to the window; the garage door was closed. She couldn't tell if he had returned home. She turned the music back on and ran for the door, her heart thumping in her chest. As much as she hated to admit it, Thad was every bit as involved as Anthony in whatever was going on. He was collecting those news articles for a reason!

When she reached the landing, she decided to close the door. If it were locked, he'd have no reason to think she'd ever been inside. "Damn it!" she muttered as she rushed down the spiral staircase. All of her plans: the nanny position, the raise, a secure future for her and her daughter, all of it was out the window. While she frantically gathered her belongings, she thought about having lain with someone capable of murder.

Her heart was pounding as she made her way from the bedroom towards the living room. "Thad, darling, are you home?"

* * *

"Is this your daughter, sir?" one of the police officers said as he gestured towards the distraught woman, now stone still and focused on the coroner.

Thad glowered at the girl though her pleading face should have softened the heart of any father.

"Is this your daughter?" the officer said again.

Thad's lips pressed into a tight, thin line. "Yes. Now where are you taking this body?"

"Is Anthony Robert Winchester your nephew, sir?"

Thad flinched. "He is."

"We regret to inform you that your nephew has passed away."

"No! Not Anthony!" the girl cried, sobbing as she collapsed to the floor.

"We've been ordered to remove his body to avoid a conflict of interests. The autopsy will be performed at an alternate location tomorrow morning."

"Has anyone identified the body?" Thad said.

The two police officers glanced at each other. "Be my guest," said the one who was doing the talking.

Thad lifted the blanket without a hint of emotion.

The girl's cries immediately reduced to sniffles. She kept her face buried in her arms and waited to hear what her father would say.

"I don't see any knife or bullet wounds. What do they list as probable cause?"

Everyone looked around, but nobody seemed to know.

* * *

Anthony could hear Trina crying—Trina, the mother of his child. His thoughts were jumbled. If Trina was Thad's daughter, didn't that make her his cousin? That didn't make sense. Thad didn't have a daughter.

"All right, take him away," someone said.

"Wait!" he screamed in terrified silence. "I'm not dead!"

* * *

Off a nod from one of the police officers, two interns rolled Anthony's gurney towards the exit. Trina started after them, but one of the security guards stopped her.

"I'm sorry, miss, but you can't go with him."

"Anthony!" she cried, doubling over with grief. She looked towards her father with mascara streaming down her face, but he ignored her.

Jack's heart went out to her. No matter what Anthony had done, he hated to see her suffer.

The second police officer approached them. "Move along, folks. You have no business here."

"I'm a private detective," Jack said, presenting his ID, though he felt none of his usual pleasure at doing so. "I'm investigating this case."

"Who is she?" the officer said, nodding towards Stacy.

"Uh, this is Stacy Young. She's my assistant." There was

a lot to take in, but he was aware that Thad Winchester had suddenly focused his attention on them. "Did I hear you say Anthony's body is being transferred?"

"I'm not at liberty to say," the officer said.

"I'll be sure to tell Captain Thomas how very unhelpful you are. We left his office not thirty minutes ago. What is your badge number?"

The officer glanced at his partner, but he got no help there. "We're transferring him to Union General."

"Thank you," Jack said. "Come on, Stacy. We're finished here." When Stacy didn't respond, he glanced down and saw that her eyes were locked with Winchester's. "Are you all right?" he said, breaking their contact. He was concerned that the stress might be too much for her. Anthony had threatened her life, after all, and turned her world upside down. Seeing him dead had to be emotional on all sorts of levels.

"Yeah. Let's go," she said as she grabbed his sleeve and tried to hurry him along.

Now that the body was gone, the group broke up. Jack watched as Winchester helped his daughter to her feet.

"Go home, Katrina," he said.

His daughter sniffed and wiped her face with the back of her arm. "Home?" she repeated bitterly. "Where the hell would that be?"

Keeping his voice low, Thad said, "Go back to Anthony's apartment and get some sleep. We'll talk about this tomorrow."

Trina trudged slowly towards the elevators as Thad turned his attention back to them. "Excuse me," he said. "I heard you say that you're investigating this case. May I ask what you've learned?"

Stacy tugged on Jack's sleeve. "I'm not feeling well, Jack. I need to go home."

"Surely, you can spare a moment. That was, after all, my nephew," Thad said with condescending arrogance.

"Now, Jack. Please?" Stacy insisted.

Jack, who had never been good at multi-tasking, was

further taxed when his cell phone rang. He took it out and was about to ignore it when he saw that it was Elyse. "Excuse me," he said and took a step back.

Stacy stepped back, too.

"I'm tied up at the moment. Can I call you back?" Jack said into the phone. He didn't want Thad Winchester to know he was talking to Elyse.

"Listen, Jack, it's important. You were right about what you said earlier, only it's Thad who's heading it up."

Jack's eyes automatically shifted back to Winchester, who was watching them closely.

"Jack, are you there?" Elyse said.

"Yeah, I'm here," he said, wishing he were free to ask questions.

"Don't tell him I said this, but there's a secret lab behind the back wall of his study, near the wet bar. You can only access it from the master bedroom. He's got a photo of Dr. Solver and clippings of all three victims tacked to a bulletin board in the lab. I think he may have killed them."

It was everything Jack could do to cover his surprise as Elyse related what she had seen, including the dead cat, the dissected fish, and the vial she had taken from the cooler. She ended by telling him about the movement of curtains in the window above the garage.

"Thanks for telling me," Jack said, rolling his eyes to downplay the seriousness of the conversation. "How about you? Are you okay?"

"No," Elyse shot back. "I'm scared, and I'm angry. How could I have been so blind?"

"You just never know about people, do you? I'll be in touch soon," he said, closing the phone.

"Is everything all right?" Thad said.

"Everybody's got drama, don't they?" He took hold of Stacy's arm to give support. "As you can see, this isn't a good time for us to talk. If you'll give me your number, I'll call you later. Maybe we can meet for drinks."

Winchester handed him a business card from his wallet. "You name it; I'll be there."

"Come *on*, Jack," Stacy said, pulling him away.

They walked down the hallway in silence, but once they stepped into the elevator, Jack said, "We've been chasing the wrong rabbit."

* * *

"Alexa doesn't mind, do you Lexie?"

"No, Mama. Stacy can sleep in my bed. I'll sleep in my sleeping bag, like I do when I have a slumber party."

"Go on, Stacy," Jack said. "Get some rest. We'll have to go to the police station again soon, so take a quick nap if you can."

"Come on, Miss Stacy. I'll be really quiet; I promise."

Stacy looked shell shocked as Alexa herded her up the stairs.

Christine's patience came to an end the second Alexa and Stacy were out of sight. "We're going for another walk," she said, pushing him towards the back door. "Let's go out to the fort."

"Where's Jon?"

"He's at my mother's."

"Good for him."

The moon was full, and it lit the way as they walked through the yard towards the back fence. Once they had climbed into Jon's side of the fort, Jack filled her in on what they knew. When he had finished, Christine looked a lot like Stacy did—shell shocked.

"My God, Jack, it's all so hideous. If Thad's son died, that's tragic enough, but to murder three innocent people? It makes no sense. Daniel had no ties to Thad Winchester."

"To Thurston Oliver Winchester III, you mean," Jack said sarcastically.

"I, of all people, understand grief, but to carry out a vendetta? The pain that leads to that kind of evil is frightening."

"It's about the money, too, don't forget. It's likely all about greed for Cedric."

"If it hadn't been for you, they would have gotten away with it."

"It feels strange to have played a role in bringing it all to light, but Stacy deserves her share of the credit, too. Without her, I wouldn't have been able to do much."

Christine tossed him a weak smile. "Perhaps you make a good team."

"Well, whatever happens, I think I'll stick to infidelity cases from now on and leave the murder mysteries for the big boys."

"Good idea," she said, standing up to stretch her legs. "Oh, I almost forgot to tell you, Cedric wants to meet with us at eight o'clock to sign the settlement papers."

"Eight o'clock? Doesn't he ever sleep in?"

"Probably not, and tomorrow's payday for him, too, right?"

"Indeed," Jack said in a lighter tone. "Have you thought about what you'll do with all that money?"

"Not beyond paying off the house and setting aside money for college. It's still hard to believe all of this has happened."

Jack bumped his head on the low ceiling as he stood and moved towards the ladder. "Ouch!"

"Are you okay?" Christine said with a laugh.

"Aren't I always? Oh, did I tell you the latest on the Teresa and Alan Lindsay saga?"

"If it's more bad news, why don't you save it?"

Jack motioned for her to climb down the ladder first. "It's good news, actually. It turns out that Teresa's husband isn't cheating. Well, he did cheat—once—but according to Teresa, that was twenty something years ago. As it turns out, that affair resulted in Lisa—a smart, beautiful girl, who's in her third year of medical school and expecting a baby."

"Wow," Christine said, stepping out of the way so Jack could climb down. "That must be a shock. What happens now?"

Jack wrapped his arm around her shoulders as they walked towards the house. "I'm hoping they live happily ever after."

"Ummm, that would be nice," she said. "What about us, Jack? What happens to us?"

They stopped walking and faced each other in the soft moonlight. He tenderly brushed the hair from her cheek. "We'll live happily ever after, too. It just might take us a little longer."

* * *

Thad paced his study like a caged tiger.

Elyse was gone, and she wasn't answering her phone. It was unlike him to feel insecure, but he felt as if his entire life was spinning out of control. As he approached the window for the fifth time, he glanced out at the apartment above the garage. It had finally registered that Anthony wasn't coming back, and it was damn inconvenient.

He turned from his path and poured himself a double Scotch.

There were a number of unanswered questions, but the one that troubled him most was what had shaken Stacy Young? There was fear in her eyes when she looked at him. He'd been over the scene a dozen times. It wasn't anything he said or did in the hallway. It had to be something else. Did she know something Jack did not? She was supposed to be out of town!

Anthony's death meant that he had no way to contact Cedric Johnson without compromising their security. He suspected a drug overdose had killed Anthony, but without being able to perform the autopsy himself, he'd have to wait to be sure. He groaned in frustration. Anthony's death also meant that his grandchild would be illegitimate unless he could arrange for Katrina to marry someone else, and that was unlikely. And what about Elyse? Was she simply miffed because he'd been gone so long? He snickered at the thought. Maybe it was time to buy her a present. Women liked sparkly jewelry.

Back at his desk, he sank into his chair and uncovered the divorce papers he had received from his wife's attorney several weeks back. Maybe he should just sign the damn things and be done with it. Then, maybe, he and Elyse could marry and have children of their own. No, it was a bit too soon to be counting on that.

Speaking of children . . . He switched on the video cameras in Anthony's apartment. Katrina lay passed out on the couch with the contents of the wooden box scattered on the coffee table.

"Damn her!" If he didn't do something about her drugging, she was going to harm his grandson. Maybe he should place her in rehab until the baby was born; then she could join Anthony in hell for all he cared. He'd have his heir. He could legally adopt the boy, he supposed, but that didn't address the legitimacy issue. For that, there needed to be a marriage.

A crazy thought came to him, one he shouldn't have had at all, but after watching Anthony with Katrina . . . It wasn't that disgusting, was it? Katrina was only ten years younger than Elyse. If they married secretly, not only would the child be legitimate, it would be unencumbered with a stepfather who would likely interfere with his plans for the child anyway. There'd be no need to consummate the marriage, and they could divorce as soon as the child was born. There'd have to be a prenup, of course. He swirled his Scotch and threw it back. The idea had merit. For the right price, Katrina would come around. After all, she'd finally be a Winchester, but he'd have to divorce his wife in order to do it. Maybe he should just buy the baby from Katrina. No, that didn't solve the legitimacy issue. Damn Anthony for his bad timing!

Well, there was plenty of time to figure it out. He had bigger problems on his hands. With Anthony out of the picture, the only one who knew about his involvement with Ryan Solver was Cedric Johnson. Maybe it was time to end that relationship, too. He certainly didn't need the money. The settlements were pocket change. In fact, his financial empire was much larger than anyone knew. With the passing of his father, who had inherited an immense fortune from Thurston Oliver Winchester I, he had acquired more property and Swiss bank accounts than he could ever possibly spend.

He tapped his chin. "What to do?"

CHAPTER EIGHTEEN

Despite the hours Stacy and Alexa had stayed up talking like schoolgirls, they got up before Jack or Christine did. After surprising them with a tasty omelet, they shooed them out the door for their meeting with Cedric. If things went according to plan, the police might arrest Cedric later that afternoon.

Alexa helped Stacy clean up the dishes, and then the two of them headed outside to finish Alexa's side of the fort. It had been a long time since Stacy had built anything, but she was more than capable. In fact, she was looking forward to spending the day outdoors. It was warmer than it had been in days, and the yard was abloom with azaleas, dogwoods, and jasmine. Alexa was out the door first, chatting away, excited about the prospect of painting her ladder pink. Stacy, having lost both of her parents, was in a unique position to comfort her, and had made considerable headway in helping her work through her grief. She was happy to see her wearing a yellow shirt this morning and believed she would soon be about the business of being a carefree child again.

Too bad that couldn't be her future, too, she thought with a sigh. "Okay, Lexie, take the hammer and nails up the ladder. I'll grab the boards."

"I need to go to the bathroom," Alexa said, attempting to hand the box of nails to Stacy.

"If you've gotta pee," Stacy said, "do it nature style. Go on, go behind that tree." Seeing Alexa's surprise, she added, "I'm serious. If we're gonna finish your fort today, you can't be running back and forth to the bathroom."

Alexa's bottom lip rose to a pout, but she headed up the ladder with the hammer and nails.

Stacy smiled as she grabbed a board and followed Alexa up the ladder.

* * *

Jack and Christine waited for Josh and Cedric to join them in the conference room. Josh looked ragged, and his typically perfect hair stood askew on top. Jack thought about his own hair and grimaced. Even on a great day, he never looked as good as Josh did today.

Clearing his throat, Cedric nodded to Josh, who then pushed a short stack of papers in their direction. "Everything is in order. Take a few minutes to look it over. By signing this document, you waive all rights to collect future damages from Ryan Solver. Josh will answer any questions you may have."

"When does she get the money?" Jack said without looking up.

"As agreed, one million dollars, minus my fees, will be transferred into the estate account early this afternoon." Cedric leaned forward to shake Christine's hand. "Congratulations, Mrs. Steinberg. This may be the fastest suit to settle in recent history. You've made a wise decision." He stepped from the room, leaving the three of them alone.

Josh scribbled something on a piece of paper and slid it over to Jack.

Don't say anything. The room is bugged.

* * *

Trina took a few deep breaths and stepped into the morgue. She used to come here quite a bit during her internship, but that was before her father relocated to Dixie Medical. Ian, the broad-shouldered, bearded coroner, who had taken over Thad's position at Union General, saw her and smiled. "Hey, girl, where have you been? It's been forever since I've seen you."

Trina stuck her hands into her pockets, so he couldn't see them tremble. "I'm working at Dixie now."

"Traitor," he teased and turned to wash his hands in the sink. "What's up?"

"Did they transfer someone here from Dixie last night?" She averted her eyes to keep from making contact.

Ian grabbed a paper towel and dried his hands. "Yeah. Do you know him?"

Trina's stomach cramped, and her hand immediately moved to soothe it. "He's my fiancé, my baby's father."

"Wow, I'm sorry. What happened?"

She shrugged. "All they will tell us is that it's under investigation. Can I see him? I didn't get to say goodbye."

"I guess so. Are you sure you want to?"

She nodded.

Ian pointed to a gurney, which stood against the brick wall. "I was just about to start."

Trina's eyes locked on the gurney as she walked over. After pausing a few seconds, she pulled the blanket back and gasped.

Ian was beside her in an instant. "Are you sure you're okay?"

She nodded, but it wasn't true. She couldn't accept that Anthony was dead. All her plans included him, and now he was gone. It was surreal, horrible, and unfair. Until now, she had never understood the sorrow of losing someone you love. She thought back on the two women who had agonized over ending their mother's suffering. It made her sick to think that she had gotten a thrill out of it. For her, it had been about testing her father's formula, about winning his approval—like *that* would ever happen. Why couldn't she get that through her head? "Can I have a few minutes alone with him?" she said without taking her eyes from Anthony's face.

"I'll be right outside. Take your time."

After the door closed behind Ian, Trina lightly touched Anthony's cheek. She knew it was her imagination, but he didn't feel as cold and stiff as she expected. "I've never told you this, Anthony, but I love you. I really do." Tears fell down her cheeks and onto his skin as she leaned forward to kiss his lips. "I'm not sure I can do this baby thing without you."

Spotting a stool, she rolled it next to the gurney. "I have something to tell you, and there's no easy way to say it. Thad is my biological father. He doesn't acknowledge me because I'm illegitimate. My mother was his housekeeper. When your aunt Susan found out, she threatened to divorce him if he didn't send us away. I wanted to tell you, but I was afraid you'd freak out because we're cousins. At first, I wanted to get pregnant with your child so I could inherit some of Dad's money, but then I got to know you. You made me feel wanted. I've never felt wanted before." Tears racked her body for several seconds, and then a strained laugh escaped her. "Pretty sad, huh? I was afraid if you knew the truth, you wouldn't want me anymore."

She walked over to the sink, picked up a paper towel and blew her nose.

"I was afraid you'd figure it out when I told you my last name," she said in a stuffy voice. "But you didn't. Think about it, Anthony. My last name is Oliver, as in Thurston *Oliver* Winchester III. He wouldn't let my mother put Winchester on my birth certificate, so she gave me the next best thing." Another weak laugh escaped her. "If you had married me, and I had taken your last name, Thad couldn't deny our child. He'd be a legitimate Winchester, and so would I. I know it was awful of me. I'm sorry for not telling you.

"Those were my reasons for pursuing you, but then I fell in love with you. Now, I'd marry you, no matter who you were." She lowered the side rail, closed her eyes, and laid her head on Anthony's chest. Several seconds later, she raised her head and wrinkled her brow. Though she told herself it was impossible, she laid her head back down and held her breath. Seconds went by, but she didn't hear it again—that distinctive thump of the human heart, which she thought she'd heard moments before. Deciding she had imagined it, she lightly stroked Anthony's cheek. "Your baby and I love you, Anthony. Don't you ever forget that. Sleep well."

* * *

Anthony had heard every word. If only he could tell her, none of it mattered. He loved her, too. He wanted to take her into his arms and walk away, but he couldn't. He was bound by chains he didn't understand, and he couldn't break free. Time and again, he called out to her, but his mouth wouldn't open, and nothing came out.

When she pulled the blanket back over his face and said goodbye, he panicked. If someone didn't intervene, his life would end beneath the coroner's knife! He grasped the irony, but he was powerless to change it. The knowledge of his imminent autopsy was more terrifying than anything he had ever encountered, including the knife fights that had ended in his favor. It wasn't death he feared; it was knowing what was happening to his body before he died. He couldn't bear the terror.

Was it justice?

He heard the doors swish as Trina walked through them, leaving him to his fate.

* * *

Dr. Ryan Solver sat at his desk without seeing the untended stacks of paperwork that covered it. For the most part, he had avoided this room since Anita's death. Today, he had a reason for being here. The very thought of Anita brought tears to his eyes. He hadn't realized how much he depended upon her meek and quiet strength. He sighed heavily. Life without Anita wasn't much of a life. Their golf course estate, with all its vain prestige, had lost its appeal—like the rest of his material possessions. He had moved into the spare bedroom, but even that didn't help him sleep. There was nothing he wanted more than to feel Anita beside him in their bed once more.

But it was too late for that.

He wondered if Anita's sister blamed him for her death.

—339—

Did she think he killed her for the insurance money? He shuddered. In his mind, that money was tainted. It was blood money. Was that why he had so quickly signed it over to Mrs. Steinberg, or had it been a last-ditched effort to hold onto his practice? If he was honest, it was likely the latter.

His self-opinion dropped lower with each thought that ran through his mind. How could he deny it? Without the insurance money, his life's work would fade into memory, like his once stellar reputation. He pulled a Ruger .44 Redhawk from his desk drawer and checked the cylinder. It was loaded, but he already knew that. He laid it on his desk and threw back another shot of whiskey. Though he had tried, he couldn't seem to drink enough to drown his sorrow, calm his rage, or soothe his grief.

He swayed in his chair and closed his bloodshot eyes.

To arrive at this stage of life, when he should be enjoying the fruit of his labor, without Anita, on the verge of losing his practice, and viewed by the masses as a serial killer, was more than he could take. It was beyond unfair, but there was nothing he could do to change any of it. Nothing except . . .

He picked up the gun and put the barrel into in his mouth.

* * *

Jack and Christine had spent the morning shopping and running errands. They were on their way home when Kevin called.

"You better get down here right away," Kevin said. "And bring Miss Young with you. How soon can you get here?"

Jack glanced over at Christine. "We'll be there in thirty minutes."

* * *

The metal was cold against Solver's lips, and the smell of gun oil filled his nostrils. All of his problems could disappear in one split second: no more nights without Anita, no more meetings with his attorney, no more worries about his practice or reputation. Every problem could vanish. Just a little more pressure on the trigger and it would all be over.

Ryan swayed and was barely able to right himself again. The amount of alcohol in his system would have killed a lesser man. His finger toyed with the trigger, squeezing it a little tighter each time. He was just about to fire when a thought occurred to him. What if the investigation proved his innocence? Did it matter? Adrenaline shot through him so violently he almost pulled the trigger by accident.

Damn right, it mattered! It was the difference between dying in honor and dying in shame. He laid the gun on the desk. If he didn't fight for his reputation, how could he ever face Anita in heaven?

* * *

Jack and Stacy sat in front of Kevin's desk, waiting for him to finish a call.

When Kevin hung up, he leaned back and clasped his hands behind his head. "Elyse Dawson dropped off a vial she claims to have found in Winchester's secret laboratory. It matches the compound in the syringe we picked up near Anthony's body."

"You're kidding," Jack said. "What is it?"

"Wait. Who's Elyse?" Stacy said.

"Though it's been biologically altered, it's neurotoxin. If Anthony would've jabbed you with that needle, it'd be you in the morgue right now."

Jack shuddered.

"Hello?" Stacy said. "Who's Elyse?"

"Elyse is one of Jack's old girlfriends," Kevin said.

Why that embarrassed him, Jack didn't know, but he wanted to shift the topic. Turning to Stacy, he said, "Elyse is dating Thad Winchester now. She found a secret lab behind a wall in his study." He related to Kevin and Stacy what Elyse had told him about the lab.

"What are we going to do?" Stacy said.

"*I* am arranging for search warrants. You and Jack are staying out of it," Kevin said as his gaze shifted to Jack. "Have I made myself clear?"

"But what about Cedric?" Stacy said. "He's guilty, too."

"That one's harder. We'll question him, of course, but it's doubtful we'll learn anything. There's nothing illegal about representing multiple victims."

Jack and Stacy looked at each other. What more could they do?

Kevin scratched his head and added, "If we could link a payment from Cedric to Winchester, that would open the door, but I doubt that's going to happen. Cedric's too smart for that."

"What about the notes and the scraps of silver I found in his shredder?" Stacy said. "Aren't they damaging?"

"If we knew where Anthony delivered the notes, and could find matching stationery, maybe. But as it stands . . ."

"Tell him our other news," Jack said.

"Not that it matters," Stacy said, crossing her legs.

Jack chuckled to himself as Kevin's eyes rested on the bare under-skin of Stacy's left thigh. No doubt about it, Stacy had curves in all the right places.

"Winchester has a daughter who claims to be pregnant with Anthony's child," Stacy said.

Kevin furrowed his brow and reached for the file. "I thought his only child died in an auto accident."

"We heard him admit it," Jack said. "So did the officers you sent to oversee the relocation of Anthony's body."

"Doesn't that make them cousins?" Kevin said.

"Sounds like it to me," Jack said. "Don't forget to include the apartment above Winchester's garage in your search warrant."

Kevin looked confused. "What apartment?"

* * *

Cedric was worried and in a foul mood when he came back from lunch. He didn't like being kept in the dark. In fact, he didn't like anything about his arrangement with Winchester. Jannette held up a handful of messages, but Cedric ignored them as he brushed by her desk without even saying hello.

"Your three o'clock meeting is running late and—"

Cedric slammed his office door and sat behind his desk. Reaching for the Scotch, he threw back a shot and leaned back in his chair. Why hadn't he heard from Winchester? If they weren't careful, this whole damn thing was going to blow up in their faces. He could lose everything! And for what, two hundred thousand dollars? What good was money when you're rotting away in a jail cell? He pounded his forehead with the palm of his hand. There had to be a way out of this. He reached for the phone but stopped himself. There could be no phone calls between him and Winchester.

The intercom buzzed. When it buzzed a second time, he pushed the button. "Reschedule the remainder of my afternoon. I don't want to be disturbed."

"But sir, the—"

"Need I repeat myself?"

"No, sir," Jannette said and dropped off.

Cedric wiped his brow with a clean handkerchief. His imagination was driving him crazy. Feeding his need to do *something*, he took out a silver note card. He stared at it for several seconds, trying to decide what to write. One thing was sure; once the money hit his account this afternoon, he was finished with Winchester. To hell with him and his obsession. For all he knew, Solver might be innocent. Maybe he did all he could. Maybe nobody could've saved that boy. Finally, he wrote:

> *Funds tomorrow 9:00 a.m. Old Byram Bridge.*
> *Same, same.*

He wasn't satisfied but thought it best to wait until they were face-to-face to press the issue of dropping out of this mess. He sealed the envelope and paged the messenger. Though it would be hours before pick up, he wanted to believe there was light at the end of the tunnel. He knew Winchester wouldn't be happy about the settlement because it wouldn't affect Solver's insurance rates, but Steinberg had been a stupid risk, coming as it did on the heels of the Hernandez case. They'd be lucky not to get challenged.

A deep yawn washed over him. He was tempted to leave for the day, but he half-expected a note from Winchester explaining his silence. It had been ages since he had slept well, and it was taking a toll on his nerves. Though he tried to deny it, he felt doomed.

Two and a half years ago, after losing a landmark case that should have stabilized his career, he had found himself on the edge of bankruptcy. After confessing as much to Winchester over drinks at the Country Club, Thad had offered to bail him out in exchange for some legal favors. If only he had waited, the Preston case—a triple-car accident involving a prominent shipping company—would've bailed him out, and then some. But Winchester didn't want his money back; he wanted more favors. When Cedric refused, Winchester produced a video of him accepting a bribe from a local official—a sting operation that had kept him over a barrel ever since.

He glanced at his watch for the third time in the last ten minutes. It was barely mid-afternoon. Unable to concentrate on anything else, he logged into his bank account and was pleased to see that a four-hundred-thousand-dollar wire transfer had posted. A relieved sigh escaped him. Maybe it *would* all blow over. He closed his eyes and tried to imagine his future yacht rocking in the turquoise waters of the Caribbean—but the image disappeared. It was no use; he couldn't relax until he heard from Winchester.

* * *

Jack had his hand on the doorknob when a cell phone rang.

"That's interesting," Kevin said. "Cedric Johnson just paged Anthony Winchester. I had his calls transferred to my phone."

"He's signaling for pickup," Stacy said, her face brightening with speculation.

"A lot of good that'll do him," Kevin scoffed.

Stacy gave Jack a pointed look and tilted her head.

"It's worth a shot," Jack said.

Kevin's eyes narrowed. "Did I miss something?"

* * *

Teresa hummed to herself as she washed lettuce in the sink.

"You're home early," Alan said, startling her as he walked into the kitchen.

She turned off the water and grabbed a hand towel. "So are you."

Alan laid his jacket over the barstool. "How can I make things right between us? I hate knowing how much I've hurt you."

Teresa saw the worry in his eyes, but she was still angry. Keeping her voice light, she said, "You could start by setting the table. We're having company for dinner tonight."

"You know better than to make plans without consulting me. I'm hardly in the mood to entertain."

Teresa took a deep breath. They hadn't even discussed anything yet, and already there was tension. "Shall we have a drink?"

"You don't have to ask me twice," Alan said, turning towards the living room.

Teresa saw that his wonderfully broad shoulders looked heavy and weighed down. She knew he was feeling guilty. If she was honest with herself—to her knowledge—he had never lied to her about anything other than Claire the entire time they had been married. He was a good man, but she couldn't make light of his deceit, or the damage it had caused.

Alan stepped behind the wet bar and took a nice bottle of Chardonnay out of the refrigerator. He poured a full glass and handed it to her.

"Thank you," she said.

After mixing a martini for himself, he drank half of it and gestured for them to take a seat on the couch.

"Listen, Teresa, I've been a stupid idiot for not admitting

the truth about Claire. I told myself I was protecting you, but I was wrong. I was protecting myself."

A familiar surge of anger shot through her. Unable to sit, she walked a few steps and turned to face him. "You have no idea how much hell you've put me through. Lying damages trust, Alan! Every time you worked late, every time you changed your plans, every time you didn't call . . ."

Alan hung his head.

"Tell me the truth. Have there been others?"

"No," he said softly. "It was one night, one time."

Teresa had longed to hear those exact words, but how could she believe him?

"I have felt so incredibly guilty about that one stupid night; I can hardly stand it."

"Well, that makes two of us," she said bitterly. She had wanted to have this discussion years ago, but now that they were having it, it was more difficult than she expected.

Alan came to his feet. "There's nothing I can do to change that now, but I want us to work it out."

She knew this was as close to an apology as Alan ever got, but she'd been angry for so long, she wasn't sure how to make peace with it. "Why?" she said. "Why do you want to work it out?"

"Because I can't sleep without you next to me."

Teresa was stunned and suddenly uncertain. She turned her back to keep him from seeing her waver.

"I have tried to make it up to you a thousand different ways, but I never could," he said. "You are so damn capable; you don't need me for anything."

Knowing how difficult it was for him to discuss his feelings, she reached out and took his hand. When his eyes met hers, she saw that he was vulnerable. "You're a good man, Alan. You have always been there for me, but—"

"Please, Tessa," he said, using his pet name for her. "Forgive me."

She gazed into his troubled eyes and thought of Claire. All this pain for one selfish lapse of judgment. He had been unfaithful, and yet he had finally asked for forgiveness. Was it time for them all to heal? In the beautiful blue of his eyes, Claire's face faded, and she saw Lisa. He had a daughter. She had a stepdaughter. They might become a family—if only she would forgive.

She closed her eyes and whispered, "Thank you for finally being honest. I forgive you, Alan. I forgive you."

He took her into his arms, and they wept together.

* * *

Cedric tapped his fingers on the desk and played another game of solitaire on the computer. It was nearly seven o'clock. Where the hell was the messenger?

* * *

Kevin, after confirming that his men were in position, wondered where Jack and Stacy were. He had banned them from getting anywhere near Cedric's office building tonight, but if he knew Jack, they were out there somewhere.

If Stacy was right about Cedric not knowing what the messenger looks like, then the sting operation had a chance of success. Foster Bryant, a third-year cop whose nervous chatter had driven Kevin crazy for the past half hour, waited in the passenger's seat. He was wearing Anthony's leather jacket, a blue bandanna over his head, black boots, and dark blue jeans. Kevin turned to him. "You're on, kid."

Bryant got out of the unmarked car and swaggered the short distance down the block and into the alley behind the row of office buildings.

"Bryant?" Kevin said into his mouthpiece a few seconds later.

"Loud and clear, sir, but I'm having trouble making the passkey work."

"Keep trying," Kevin said. Several seconds passed. "Bryant?"

"Maybe the card has been deactivated, sir."

"Stacy says there's a trick to it. Do you want her to open

the door for you?" Jack said over the radio.

"What the hell are you doing on this frequency?"

"Investigation 101, sir," Jack said.

"Unbelievable," Kevin muttered. "Bryant? Are you in yet?"

"Negative, sir. I still can't make it work."

Kevin shook his head and accepted the inevitable.

* * *

After their emotional discussion, Alan retreated into his private study, and Teresa busied herself in the kitchen. She was setting the table when the doorbell rang. She glanced into the hallway mirror and straightened her shoulders. Her stepdaughter was joining them for dinner this evening. The very thought made her smile. One day soon, there would be a grandchild to love—so many blessings for one selfish lapse of judgment. Forgiveness had made that possible.

She opened the door. "Hello, Lisa. Welcome."

Lisa smiled but shyly averted her eyes. "Thank you. Our visit meant so much to me. I can hardly believe this is happening."

"Me, too," Teresa said. She led the way into the family room and pointed to a closed door near the back corner of the room. "I haven't told him you were coming. I had planned to, but something came up."

A smile lit Lisa's face. She walked over and tapped lightly on the door.

"Come in," Alan called from the other side.

When Lisa glanced back, Teresa gave her an encouraging nod. Once she went in, Teresa returned to the kitchen to check on dinner.

* * *

"You're a royal pain in my backside, you know that, Kendall?" Kevin said into the radio. "What's your ETA?"

Jack winked at Stacy. "About sixty seconds."

Stacy, who was sitting in the passenger's seat of Daniel's

truck, put both hands over her mouth to smother a giggle.

"Well then, get down there and open that blasted door."

Stacy leaned into the headset. "Why, thank you, Captain, I thought you'd never ask. Over and out."

* * *

"Teresa?" Lisa said as she stepped into the kitchen. "I told Daddy about your visit yesterday. I think he's happy that we've made friends, don't you?"

"Of course, he is, but you know how men are. They want to be the ones to think of everything."

"Is there anything I can do to help?"

Teresa took in the sight of her lovely stepdaughter standing in her kitchen and smiled. "I have everything I need. Go tell your father that dinner is ready."

"Gosh, that sounds nice," Lisa said with a sigh.

Teresa crinkled her nose. "It does, doesn't it?"

* * *

With one swipe, Stacy unlocked the door.

"Thanks," Officer Bryant said with an embarrassed nod.

Jack sent Stacy back to the truck in no uncertain terms. When she turned the corner, he drew his gun. "I'll cover you."

"Oh, no, he won't," Kevin said so loudly Jack heard it through Bryant's earpiece.

Jack waited for Bryant to make the call. After a moment's hesitation, Bryant gestured towards the staircase and took off towards the elevators. Jack pushed through the stairwell door and hauled it up the stairs. He was winded, but he managed to get there before the elevator arrived. When Bryant moved towards Cedric's office, Jack waved to him from the stairwell and ducked out of sight.

"Have you got anything for me?" Cedric said, his voice booming through the quiet office space.

Jack heard Bryant grunt out a no, and then a moment later he was walking down the hallway holding a silver envelope by its edges. Once Bryant was back inside the elevator, Jack flew down the stairs and met him at the bottom, pleased with himself for being in on stinging the great Cedric K. Johnson. He followed Bryant back to Kevin's unmarked car where he found Stacy sitting in the back seat. Bryant handed the envelope to Kevin through the open window.

"I knew it!" Stacy said. "What does it say?"

Kevin glared at Jack and Bryant. "What possessed you two to ignore my orders?"

Figuring that he was the target of Kevin's displeasure, Jack said, "I was only trying to help. If Cedric knew about what happened last night, someone needed to be there to back up Bryant."

"I'm not kidding, Jack. If you ever do anything like this again, I'll throw you in jail so fast your head will spin. Lucky for you two, nothing went wrong."

"Aren't you going to open the envelope?" Stacy said.

Kevin gave her a dirty look but carefully opened the envelope.

Funds tomorrow 9:00 a.m. Old Byram Bridge.
Same, same.

Stacy's eyes sparkled as Kevin picked up the radio. "Jackson, you out there?"

"Here, sir."

"You and Ramirez keep an eye on Cedric Johnson. Don't let him out of your sight. I'll get back to you once I make other arrangements. Over and out."

"I sure hope Christine's money transferred today," Jack mumbled.

"If everything goes according to plan," Kevin said, "when we pick up Cedric at the bridge tomorrow, he'll be in possession of a large amount of cash."

"My guess is he'll be willing to make a deal," Stacy said. "He's not the type to take the fall for this by himself."

"That's what we're counting on," Kevin said. "Nice work

everyone."

Jack high-fived Bryant, which, unfortunately, Kevin saw.

"Bryant, since you and Jack are bosom buddies now, follow him home and make sure he stays put tonight."

Bryant's smile faded. "But my shift ended thirty minutes ago."

"You should've thought about that before you disobeyed my orders. I want a complete report, first thing tomorrow morning."

Dropping his shoulders, Bryant said, "Do I have to include that bit about the passkey?"

"No, and leave Jack's participation out of it, too. Now get out of here before I change my mind."

"Yes, sir. Thank you, sir," Bryant said, retreating as he spoke.

"Thanks, Kev," Jack said. "We're staying with Christine until—"

"I know where you're staying, Kendall."

Jack gestured for Stacy to get out of the car.

"Thanks for your assistance, Miss Young. Because of your sharp thinking, we have reason to question Cedric Johnson."

She smiled. "It's nice to be appreciated."

"Nevertheless," Kevin added, "I'm placing you both under house arrest until further notice."

"Oh, come on, Kevin. That's not necessary," Jack said.

"Apparently it is. You gave up your badge a long time ago, remember? Now, you're just an average Joe. Start acting like it."

Stacy grabbed Jack's arm and pulled him away from the car.

"What does he mean, average?"

Stacy laughed. "If he thinks you're average, he doesn't know you like I do. Come on, I can't wait to tell Josh what's going on."

That comment didn't help, but he kept his thoughts to himself.

* * *

Cedric's mind was spinning as he packed his briefcase for the night. Why hadn't Winchester responded to his note? Would he hold him to their agreement against his will? It was blackmail, pure and simple, and he didn't like it one little bit. He had wanted to question the messenger, but he wasn't sure how much he knew.

Slamming his briefcase shut, he turned out the lights, closed his door, and walked to the elevator. Once he delivered two hundred thousand dollars in gold coins tomorrow, this would all be behind him—whether Winchester liked it or not.

* * *

Ian uncovered Anthony's body and dragged him onto the autopsy table where he performed a physical examination. He notated multiple scars, various tattoos, and a small bruise on his right hip. Next, he weighed and measured the body. Using his scalpel, he cut a shallow outline of the upper portion of the "Y" incision, which extended from the front of each shoulder to the bottom of the breastbone. He smiled as a thin line of blood bubbled along the cut—his favorite part of the procedure. The next cut would go deeper and extend past the navel to the pubic bone. He was about to draw the bottom part of the incision when his cell phone rang. Normally, he'd ignore it, but that specific ring tone told him the call was urgent.

Laying down the scalpel, he snapped off his gloves and answered his phone. "Coroner's office." After several seconds, his head snapped around to look at Anthony. "Neurotoxin? Are you sure?" He hung up the phone and put on a fresh pair of gloves. Returning to the body, he picked up a stethoscope and listened to several spots on Anthony's chest and frowned. He couldn't hear anything. He sat on the stool in front of his computer and typed in the word *neurotoxin*. Several articles came up. After refreshing his memory, he went back to the examination table and placed a stethoscope over Anthony's heart. He listened in one spot for nearly a minute before he heard it—a faint, nearly imperceptible heartbeat. He staggered backwards, and his face went white. "Holy Christ!"

* * *

Winchester paced the usual path in his study. It galled him to have Anthony's body taken for someone else to analyze. He was the premier forensic expert in Mississippi. Ian was a good kid, but nowhere near the same league. He had trained the boy, for God's sake.

When he approached the window for the twentieth time, he was surprised to see several sets of headlights winding their way up the driveway. It was the police! He rushed to lock the study door and returned to the window. He turned on the surveillance system and watched on video as four men split up and went around the sides of the house. Two more climbed the steps and knocked on the front door. Thad figured they had come to question him about Anthony, but he wasn't taking any chances. On the monitor, he saw an officer pounding on the front door with his fist. He finally tried the doorknob and discovered that it was unlocked.

Thad grumbled with alarm as he realized that Elyse must have left it unlocked. He watched as the men searched his house with weapons drawn. When they entered his bedroom, Thad turned off the monitoring system, stepped into his lab, and closed the hidden door. Beyond the lab, there was another room—a panic room. He wasn't too concerned at this point. No one knew about the lab except Trina, and that was only because she had made a game of breaking into his house since she was a child. He snickered. Trina wanted his money, but she couldn't betray him without incriminating herself in the process. He was safe in the lab.

Moments later, he heard noises on the other side of the wall. Deciding not to risk it, he ripped the news articles from the bulletin board, grabbed his medical journals, and entered the panic room, sealing it behind him. He was definitely safe in here.

* * *

Luckily, when Trina had come back from the store, she saw

the police cars turning into the driveway. She drove past the gate, her mind spinning with speculation. She wasn't worried about being implicated. She was way too smart for that. Her biggest concern was what it meant for her inheritance plans.

She parked along the road, well past the house. Pulling on her baseball cap, she hiked through a grassy field and into the woods surrounding her father's estate. She was searching for a tree she had climbed as a child, a tree where she had spent countless hours waiting for her father to come home from work, just so she could watch him walk from the garage into his big, beautiful house. The memories of those days defined their relationship. She had spent her entire lifetime outside his day-to-day world, waiting for him to lay down his stupid Winchester pride and welcome her into his life. Still, he had helped her in some ways. He had bought her a car when she graduated from high school, and paid for her to attend nursing school, which enabled her to make a decent living in the world, but he had always kept her at a distance.

Trina's mood darkened as she neared the tree. Nothing she did ever met with his approval. She had told herself years ago that she had stopped trying to please him, but it wasn't true. All she ever wanted was for him to love her, but Thad's love had always been centered on her half-brother, Thad the fourth. Why the world put so much value on being a male she had no idea.

Remembering her father's cruel neglect, she slapped at the waist-tall grass as she made her way towards the tree. Would things be different now? Now that Anthony was dead, would he still allow her to move into his apartment? Her breath caught in her throat. She missed Anthony more than she would have ever imagined. She'd been so concerned about making her inheritance scheme work that she had missed the simple joy of falling in love. Tears filled her eyes, causing her to trip over a root. She didn't fall, but she snagged her sleeve on a bush. Jerking it free, she kept moving.

There was a part of her that wanted Thad to suffer. When she looked back on the hundreds of times she had cried over his refusal to acknowledge her, it made her bitterly angry. True, he had finally admitted the truth last night, but that was only because he'd had no choice.

When she finally reached the tree, she was surprised to see how much it had grown. She climbed it easily and could see the entire courtyard. Half a dozen police officers carried armfuls of Thad's belongings out of the house and placed them in the back of a van.

* * *

Thad turned on the satellite monitoring system and was horrified to see that the police had discovered the lab. He shook with rage as he watched them search his sacred space. Thank God he'd thought to grab the news articles. They were the only items in the entire house that linked him with either Cedric Johnson or Ryan Solver. He'd been extremely careful.

Ryan Solver, the vile wretch. To remember that they had once been friends turned his stomach. If it hadn't been for Dr. Solver, his son might be alive today, and he wouldn't be in this predicament. Turning from the monitor, he dropped onto the built-in cot. His son . . . He'd trade everything he had for one more moment with his boy.

He bowed his head and covered his face with his hands. They had parted in anger that last night because Thad the fourth had refused to consider Harvard, which, in his mind, had amounted to disrespect for the previous three generations of Winchesters. He shook his head. If only he had let the boy choose for himself.

He glanced at the monitor and grimaced as the police confiscated the neurotoxin samples, along with his Bolivian supply of OxyContin.

"What should I do with this?" one of the detectives said, poking at the cat inside the cage.

"What's he doing with a dead cat?"

"I don't know," the first detective said, "but if the puffer skeletons are any indication, I'd say he was going to dissect it."

A tall, fierce looking man—presumably the lead detective—walked over. "At least, it doesn't stink yet. Take it out last. No need to expose it to the sun until absolutely necessary." He clapped his hands. "Alright, everybody, let's move it! I promised my wife I'd pick up dinner on the way home, and there's a lot to do here."

Was Thad the only one who saw the tip of the cat's tail twitch? Who knew how long it might be before he could duplicate this level success? It was time to give the cat another injection, but here he stood, a captive in his own house. Someone would pay dearly for this injustice. He'd see to that!

He watched helplessly as two men emptied the contents of his desk and placed it into boxes. He worried they might discover the safe, but they left his bookshelf undisturbed. For the first time in his life, he was unsure what to do. His blue-blooded arrogance had kept him from planning what to do under this set of circumstances. His medical career was over, that much was certain, and he'd have to leave the country, too. There was plenty enough money in Swiss accounts to set up a new life; the question was where. The world was full of repulsive foreigners—the main reason he didn't travel.

His eyes darkened as another thought occurred to him. He'd hate to think that Elyse had betrayed him. No, he doubted it. She wasn't smart enough for something like this. The blame likely fell at the feet of Jack Kendall, and he intended to make him pay for it—and Stacy Young, too.

Several agonizing minutes later, after seizing the cat and multiple boxes of his belongings, the police finally left the main house and went upstairs to search Anthony's apartment. Up until this point, Thad had felt relatively immune, but remembering Anthony's stash of OxyContin, it occurred to him that his fingerprints might be on some of the pill bottles in the apartment. Trafficking was far more serious than possession.

* * *

Trina shifted her weight on the branch and watched as

two more police officers came down the steps from Anthony's apartment carrying boxes overflowing with items—some of them hers. Had she left the wooden box open on the coffee table? If she had, it was too late now.

She knew they'd want to question her and was already working on her story. Without talking to her father, though, she wasn't sure what to say. Should she admit to knowing about the lab? As she waited for the cops to leave, she wondered where he was. Was he a fugitive, or was he simply wanted for questioning? Was he hiding in the panic room? Had he already spoken to the police? She meant to find out as soon as the coast was clear.

* * *

Ryan Solver's telephone rang for the fourth time in a row. To shut it up, more than anything else, he finally answered it. "If you're calling with more bad news, Bradshaw, I don't want to hear it." Leaving the room as dark as his mood, he pushed from his chair and shuffled over to the wet bar.

Peter chuckled. "Sounds like you've been hitting the sauce already. You can't tend to your patients when you're in the tank, you know."

Ryan set the whiskey bottle back on the bar. "What are you saying?"

"I'm saying the autopsy report shows that your wife suffered an ordinary stroke. A normal, everyday, ordinary stroke. You've been cleared of all charges."

Ryan squeezed his eyes tight. "Thank God." Leaving the bottle on the bar, he settled back at his desk. "What about my practice?"

"Just got the paperwork. They guaranteed your rate for another twelve months. You can go back to work tomorrow."

Ryan covered his mouth with a shaky hand. He could hardly believe it. If only Nita were here to share the moment.

"Ryan?"

"Yeah, I'm here."

"Your gamble paid off."

He finally let himself breathe. "It did, didn't it?"

"I'd still consider retiring, but that's just me. Have a good night."

"Thanks, Peter. Good night."

Ryan sat in the dark for several minutes, letting the news sink in. It was over. Did he dare go back into the ring?

The decision was his to make, and that in itself was price-less.

* * *

As soon as the last squad car pulled out of the gate, Trina used the light from her cell phone to backtrack to the road. She half-expected to find guards at the gate, but she didn't. She was a nervous wreck when she pulled into the courtyard, but every-thing was quiet. Grabbing the hidden key, she let herself into Thad's house. Leaving it dark, she made her way to the master bedroom and up the spiral staircase to Thad's study. "Dad, can you hear me? Dad?"

Thad's computer was missing, and the desk drawers were empty. As she looked at his desk, she noticed something she hadn't seen before—a small video monitor. She pressed the power button and was surprised to hear rap music coming through the speakers. That was odd. Her father detested rap music. When pictures of Anthony's apartment flashed on the screen, her eyes widened with surprise. Her first thought was that the police had torn Anthony's place apart, but as the frames clicked through their cycle, she saw a clear shot of Anthony's unmade bed and froze. "He wouldn't . . ."

Then she realized that the rap music was hers. She had left the stereo on. "Are you kidding me? He's been watching us the whole damn time?" She was so angry she was shaking. She felt sick and collapsed to her knees. "How could you?" she screamed.

"Because I didn't trust either one of you," Thad said as he emerged from the lab.

Trina nearly jumped out of her skin. She pushed to her feet and took a few steps back. "Get away from me, you freaking pervert!"

"Come now, Katrina. Stop over reacting."

"You watched us, didn't you? Admit it! You watched us!"

"So what if I did? You're the one guilty of incest."

"But I'm your daughter!"

"So you keep reminding me. Get over yourself, Katrina. You're nothing special."

Stung, she glared at him and then turned away.

"Now you listen to me, and you listen good. We've got to stick together right now, or we're going to jail."

"Ha! Like you really care what happens to me. You make me sick!"

Thad took a few aggressive steps forward, backing her towards the door. "If you hope to get any of my money, you'd better stay on my good side, and keep your nasty mouth shut."

"I have something you want, too. Remember? Your blue-blooded heir grows inside me, so you better stay on *my* good side, or you'll never lay eyes on him."

To her surprise, he laughed. "You've got Winchester blood in you all right. Decide now, Katrina girl. Do we stick together, or are you going it alone?"

"That depends," she said. "What do you have in mind?"

Her cell phone rang, making her jump. She pulled it out of her pocket. "It's the hospital."

"Don't answer it."

"They're not looking for me. Hello?"

Thad walked to the window and looked out.

Trina dropped her phone and fainted.

* * *

Too antsy to sleep, Jack decided to test his skill at getting past Bryant. When he stepped out the front door, Bryant stopped him immediately. "You know I can't let you leave," he said.

"I just need a few things from my car."

Bryant let him pass.

Jack's car sat outside the garage. He reached into the

back seat, stuffed his lab coat into the spy kit, and took it into the house. Fifteen minutes later, he sported a trim, grey beard, and dark-rimmed eyeglasses. With his hair frosted grey and his curls slicked flat, he looked like an aged business professional. He thought back on the caper he had pulled at La Bells restaurant and patted his name badge. His trusty lab coat hadn't failed him yet. He pocketed his false credentials and opened the bathroom door. The house was quiet. He looked out the living room window and saw Bryant pacing along the porch. Deciding that the back door was his best bet, he stepped onto the deck, forgetting that the screen door squeaked.

"Hey, where do you think you're going," Bryant said, coming around the side of the house.

"I was just—"

"Come on, Uncle Richard. Nanna likes to tuck me in by ten o'clock," Alexa said as she pushed through the screen door in her pajamas.

Jack could have kissed her.

"Hi sweetie, is this your uncle?" Bryant said, bending over to speak with her at eye level.

Alexa smiled. "He's my Daddy's favorite brother. Aren't you, Uncle Richard?"

"Absolutely," Jack said in his deepest voice.

Alexa yawned. "Can we go now?" She looked up at Bryant with pouty pink lips and sky-blue eyes.

Officer Bryant stepped out of the way. "Sure you can. Get a good night's sleep, okay, sweetie?"

"Okay," she said. She grabbed Jack's arm and led him to Daniel's truck. "Here are your keys, Uncle Richard. You left them on the kitchen counter."

Jack took the keys and helped her into the passenger's seat.

Bryant followed him around to the other side. "Forgive me for saying so, but isn't ten o'clock a little late for a child her age?"

"Don't tell her this," Jack said, "but she's got every last one of us wrapped around her finger."

Bryant chuckled. "Don't they all? Have a good night, sir."

Jack climbed into the truck and waved good-bye as he backed down the driveway. Relaxing his shoulders, he glanced over at Alexa, who was looking quite pleased with herself. "You're pretty handy to have around, you know that?"

"It's easy," Alexa said. "Stacy says men are suckers for pretty little girls."

Jack didn't admit it, but men were suckers for pretty big girls, too. "Okay," he said. "Where to?"

Alexa's eyes sparkled. "Ice cream!"

"How did I know? Call your mom and tell her that Uncle Richard is taking you out for ice cream. We don't want her thinking that you're missing again, especially not tonight."

Alexa clapped her hands. "This is so fun! I want to be a detective just like you when I grow up."

Jack rubbed the top of her head with his knuckles. "You better let me finish growing up first."

* * *

Thad rushed to Trina's side and checked her pulse. He patted her cheeks and tapped her hands. "Come on, Katrina, wake up. Tell me what's going on!"

* * *

Jack and Alexa ate their ice cream while admiring the fountain outside of Thalia Mara Hall—one of Alexa's favorite places. Jack swallowed a huge bite of chocolate ice cream and made a horrible face as a brain-freeze shot through his head. He covered his ears and waited for it to pass.

Alexa laughed. "That happens to me sometimes, too."

Shaking it off, he said, "It's nice to see you wearing pretty colors again."

"Yeah. Miss Stacy says if Daddy looks down from heaven and sees me wearing black all the time, it'll make him sad. Is she right, Uncle Jack?"

He took another delicious bite. "What do you think, Alexa?"

"I decided not to chance it."

"Good decision." His cell phone rang.

"Oh, no! Ignore it, Uncle Jack. Please?"

"I can't, Lexie. There's way too much happening right now. I'll hurry; how's that?" She gave him a doubtful look. He flipped the phone open and saw that it was Kevin. "How the heck did he find out?"

"Find out what? Who is it?"

"A buddy of mine. He's the Captain mucky-muck at the police station."

Alexa breathed an exaggerated sighed. "Better answer it then."

He braced himself for the riot act. "Jack, here." A few seconds later, he said, "What do you mean, he's in intensive care?"

After Kevin's call, Jack handed his ice cream to Alexa and pulled onto the street. "Get your mom on the phone again."

Alexa did as he asked, and handed him the phone.

"Hey, Jack," Christine said with a yawn. "Are you two finished playing *'fool the policeman?'* It's getting late for Alexa to be out."

"We've got a problem. Get Stacy and meet me in front of Union General Hospital ASAP."

"What? Is Alexa all right?"

"She's fine. Call Nora and tell her I'll drop her by. I'll be there in ten minutes."

"Rats!" Alexa said, pounding her fist on the seat.

"You're killing me, Jack. What's going on?" Christine said.

He stepped on the gas to keep from getting caught by the light. "Meet me in twenty minutes. That's Union General, Christine, not Dixie. I'll fill you in there."

"I've got it, but—"

"Hurry," he said and hung up.

Alexa pouted for real. "Why can't I go with you?"

"Sorry, Lexie. Not this time."

She frowned, but then a mischievous smile lit her face. "Then I get to eat the rest of your ice cream."

"You wouldn't dare." Keeping one eye on the road, he reached over and tickled her until she giggled.

Despite everything else, it was good to hear her laugh.

* * *

Thad felt both annoyed and put upon. Whatever Katrina had heard on the phone was important enough to make her faint, and he wanted to know what it was. Were the police on their way back? He continued to tap her hands and face. "Wake up, dammit."

He left her on the floor and hurried back to the window, but he didn't see any headlights.

Trina groaned.

"Thank heavens," he said and returned to her side.

She opened her eyes and stiffened. "Get back," she said in a stronger voice than he expected. "I'm all right. Just give me some space."

"Katrina, tell me what that call was about."

Her eyes hardened against him. "For your information, your *formula* is faulty. They've got Anthony in intensive care right now. He's alive."

Thad's knees buckled, and he had to sit down. "Holy Christ. What did you give him?"

Trina pushed to her feet, but she was weak. "How should I know? It came from one of your vials. He was supposed to shoot some detective with it, but it seems he shot himself instead. I'm going down there."

"Wait," he said. "We need to think this through."

"You think it through; I'm going to see Anthony."

Thad lunged forward and spun her around. "Wait a damn minute. There's a lot at stake here. We need to think this through." He could see by her expression that she wasn't as sure of herself as she pretended. He gestured towards a sofa.

She gave him a withering glare, but she sat down. "Make it quick."

Thad sat across from her, at a respectful distance.

"Anthony will be facing jail time if he wakes up, and medications make people talk. You understand that we can't let Anthony talk, don't you? We can't let him talk."

Trina gasped. "You want to kill Anthony?"

"Not me, Katrina girl."

She flinched as though he'd slapped her. "You're out of your ever-lovin' mind."

Thad rose and closed the distance between them. "We don't need Anthony now. He has served his purpose."

"Not according to you, he hasn't. Without Anthony, your grandson will be born a bastard, just like me, and we know how you feel about Winchester bastards. Don't we, Daddy?"

"Good point," he sneered. "How about this? You, the grieving, pregnant fiancée, beg the hospital Chaplain to marry you and Anthony so that the baby will have his father's name? Then you kill him."

"No! Anthony's the only person on this entire planet who's ever loved me."

"That's not true. Your mother loved you."

"Like hell, she did. She never missed a single opportunity to tell me how I ruined her life, and how you would've kept supporting her if it hadn't been for me."

"Your mother never wanted for anything—the ungrateful, conniving, little witch. I sent her money every single month until you moved out," he said, his voice growing louder with his resentment. "She's the one who wouldn't touch me after she got pregnant. So, you not only ruined her life, you ruined mine as well."

"Oh, that's just great. Now, I've ruined your life, too. I'm the one who got the short end of the stick, here. Do you have any idea how it feels to be called a bastard by your own parents? No, of course you don't. You're Thurston Oliver Winchester III. You were born with a shiny silver spoon in your mouth. You have no idea what you've put me through."

"Don't lecture me about privilege. Privilege requires sacrifice, but you wouldn't know about that, would you? I bought your first car. I paid for your college education. I've provided you with an allowance to live on. But no matter how much I do for you, it's never enough for you. You're just like your mother."

Trina hauled back and slapped him across the face. "I'm nothing like my mother!"

Surprised more than anything else, Thad stumbled back. He could see that she was trembling. He rubbed his jaw and glared at her for several seconds. Finally, he said, "I deserved that. Good for you."

Trina relaxed somewhat, but he could tell that she was wary and unsteady.

"Come on, Katrina, let's sit down and talk this through."

Trina glanced towards the door. "Only if you promise not to touch me. I don't want you touching me."

"Fine. I promise not to touch you. Sit down while I get you some water. Okay?"

Trina sat stiffly on the edge of the sofa.

Thad walked over and locked the study door. When Trina shot to her feet, he held up his hands. "That's just in case the police come back while we're working this out. You have my word; I won't harm you. You're carrying my heir, remember?"

She settled back on the sofa.

Good, he thought, he was finally getting through. He looked out the window and then took her a glass of water. Her hands were shaking so badly she needed both of them to get the glass to her mouth.

"All right, I have a plan," he said. "You have two choices. If you choose to let Anthony live—in whatever vegetative state he must be in—you won't get a dime of my money. Everything I have will go into a trust for your son, which will go to him upon your death. You won't ever see a penny. If you agree to let Anthony go, I'll take you out of the country and set you up in a house of your own. I'll pay for a maid, a full-time nanny, and I'll reinstate your allowance."

Trina blinked a few times and then met his gaze. "What are you saying?"

"I'm saying, why share your money with an invalid

husband when you can have a hundred percent control of it your-self? We can both get what we want."

Trina stared at him for several seconds.

For the first time, he wasn't sure what she was thinking. He found it a bit unnerving. She was more like him than he'd realized.

Finally, she said, "I want complete financial freedom. You put three million dollars into a bank account in my name, and I'll let Anthony go."

"Don't be ridiculous. I don't have that kind of money."

"I've been reading your account ledgers for years. Three million dollars amounts to a measly five percent of your assets. Do we have a deal?"

Thad poured himself a double Scotch and looked out the window again. "How much would it take for me to adopt the boy outright?"

"How about I disappear, and you never lay eyes on him?"

He shrugged. "You never know until you ask." He returned to the sofa. "Here's how it has to work, Katrina. You give Anthony the injection right after the preacher leaves, and then you leave, too. When the hospital staff discovers that Anthony is gone, they'll think that he fought to live long enough to marry you. Rather romantic, don't you think?"

Trina smirked. "Sure, why not? It's all about money for us Winchesters, right Dad?"

Thad smiled and relaxed his shoulders. "That's right, baby girl. At the end of the day, it's always about the money."

* * *

Christine's mother stepped outside the second Jack pulled into the driveway. She helped Alexa out of the truck and sent her inside.

"What's going on, Jack? I couldn't get Christine to tell me anything."

"Sorry, Nora. I'll fill you in later." He hit reverse and backed into the street.

* * *

Trina grew nervous as her father stepped back into the lab. She didn't trust him one bit. If it weren't for the baby, he'd take her out, too. She had no doubts about that. Her hand moved to cover her stomach. To her surprise, Thad returned with a loaded syringe and handed it to her.

"Feeling better?"

"Yeah, I'm great. Just perfect. My father wants me to kill my fiancé; the police have searched our belongings; and you're playing fugitive. I'd call it a stellar day, wouldn't you?"

"You've got a smart mouth; you know that?"

"Whatever," she said before she could stop herself. She knew it wasn't wise to provoke him, but her hormones, coupled with the extreme stress she was under, were wreaking havoc with her emotions. She took a deep breath and exhaled slowly. "If I can pull off the wedding, the next time you see me, I'll be a Winchester."

"Yes, thanks to your dear *cousin*," he said dryly.

Though she knew not to trust him, part of her still hoped their relationship would change once the baby was born. Would he honor her as the mother of his heir? She was annoyed with herself for caring, but she did. Pushing to find out, she got to her feet and opened her arms. "Care to hug Katrina Oliver goodbye?"

Thad made no move to hug her. She dropped her arms, hating herself for showing her vulnerability.

"I know you don't believe this," he said, "but all the hell I've put you through has made you a stronger person. You'll thank me one day."

"I'll thank you once I see three million dollars in my bank account, and not before."

He chuckled. "I never thought I'd say this, Katrina, but I'm quite proud of you. You have exceeded my expectations."

She was so surprised that she had to swallow hard to keep from crying. Making light of it, she said, "Does that mean I can start calling you Daddy in public?" Thad's mouth twisted with revulsion, and in that moment, she knew he'd never claim her. She might become a legal Winchester. She might be the mother of his grandchild, but in his eyes she'd always be a bastard—unfit for his inner circle.

"Let's leave that decision for another day, shall we?" he said.

Trina shrugged as if it didn't matter. "As you said, you never know until you ask."

"Oh, all right. Perhaps a hug is in order."

Trina eyed him warily, but when he opened his arms, despite everything she knew, despite everything he had said, she rushed into them. Tears rolled down her face as she clung to her father for the first time in her entire life, yet even in her joy, she was heartbreakingly aware that he had not wrapped his arms around her. This hug was a concession, not something he wanted. Rising on tiptoe, she whispered, "This is long overdue, *Daddy*." In one smooth motion, she uncapped the needle, jabbed it into his neck and pushed the plunger. Shoving back from him, she saw his shocked expression. "You have always underestimated me. Today, it cost you."

Thad dropped to his knees, and she bolted.

* * *

Jack spotted Christine and Stacy sitting in the main hospital foyer. "Are you two all right?" he said.

Stacy pulled back. "Who's askin'?"

Christine laughed. "Stacy, it's Jack."

"No way."

"I couldn't get out of the house looking like myself, could I?" he said, getting his usual charge out of fooling someone close to him.

Stacy squinted her eyes and looked closer.

He winked.

"Don't feel bad," Christine said. "The only reason I knew it was him was because he didn't cover that little scar by his eye tonight. When he does, forget it. He can fool anyone."

"That's way cool. I would have never guessed," Stacy said.

"Speaking of sneaky, how did you two get past Bryant?" he said.

"Oh, he fell asleep in his car while writing his report," Christine said.

"Ambien tea," Stacy said. "We gave it to him right after you left, so you'd have an easier time getting back into the house. Tell us what's going on."

Jack dropped to one knee in front of them. "There's been a mistake. The messenger— I mean, Anthony Winchester is alive."

Stacy gasped and covered her mouth.

Christine threw a protective arm around her. "I thought they did the autopsy already. You must be mistaken."

"What are we going to do?" Stacy said, drawing her knees up into the chair and wrapping her arms around them. "He'll come after us."

"Okay, you two, listen to me. I'm not trying to scare you, but Anthony *is* alive. Kevin says the coroner noticed his heartbeat at the last possible second and is quite shaken up."

"Well, he ain't the only one," Stacy said.

Christine shook her head. "But how can that be? You saw him, right? You said he was dead."

Stacy yanked a magazine open in front of her face and sank lower in her chair.

Following her line of sight, Jack spotted Thad's daughter racing towards the elevators. "Go out to the car and wait for me. I'm going to see what I can find out," he said.

"I'm going with you," Stacy said.

"Not this time, Lady Sherlock. Now, get out of here before someone sees you."

Christine and Stacy hurried through the sliding glass doors and out of sight.

Jack straightened his lab coat and strode towards the elevators. He leaped into one just as the doors were closing. "Does anyone know which floor ICU is on?"

"Six," three people answered in unison, and everybody

chuckled.

It felt like the slowest elevator ride in history as Jack waited through the exasperating exchange of patients, on multiple floors, on the way up. Finally, when the doors opened onto the sixth floor, he squeezed out before any of the four people waiting could get in.

He strolled down the hallway with pursed lips, glancing at the patient names on each of the doors as he walked by them. When he reached the central hub, he wasn't sure which way to go. A religious official dressed in black robes brushed by him and entered the third room to the left, down the west wing. Jack turned in the opposite direction and kept checking doors. About halfway down, he came upon two nurses who were whispering about something that seemed more serious than idle chatter. He bent over to tie his shoe, but they immediately stopped talking.

"Can you point me to Anthony Winchester's room?" he said, standing upright again.

"Oh, are you here for the wedding?" one of them said.

"I heard Anthony might pull through," he said, "but there's more good news?"

The women glanced at each other, clearly hesitant to say more. The second nurse, a heavyset brunette with a long ponytail, said, "I've never seen you before. Do you work here?"

"Look, ladies, I'm just looking for my friend. If you can't help me with that, then I'll find a supervisor who can. If my friend dies while I'm busy chasing down his room number, this won't be the last you hear about this conversation. Now, please, for everyone's sake, just tell me where to find Anthony Winchester."

The nurses looked at each other. The first nurse said, "I'm not taking any chances. His room is the third door on your right after the central hub."

"Thank you," Jack said and hurried the way he'd come.

* * *

Trina jumped up from Anthony's side the moment the minister came into the room. Two female members of the hospital staff entered behind him.

"I'm Reverend Collier," said the grey-haired man as he extended his hand for her to shake. "You must be Trina. I'm very sorry to hear about your fiancé."

Her legs were trembling, so she sat back down. "Thanks for agreeing to marry us. Anthony would be very happy."

"Are you all right?" Reverend Collier said, knitting his brow with concern.

Tears stung her eyes, as they usually did when people were kind to her. She nodded and brushed them away.

Reverend Collier pulled up a chair. Glancing up at the women who had come to serve as witnesses, he said, "Would you give us a few minutes, please?"

"We'll be right outside," one of them said.

Trina focused on the floor and wiped her eyes again.

"Never be ashamed to cry," he said softly. "Tears are a gift from God. They help to cleanse us from our pain and sorrow."

She bit her lip to keep it from quivering.

"Do you have any family here?"

"Just my father."

"Does he live in Jackson?"

"In Ridgeland."

"I'm happy to hear that. Will he be joining us for the ceremony?"

She shook her head and wiped more tears. She didn't want to think about her father right now. As relieved as she was to be rid of his hateful presence, she couldn't banish the memory of him sinking to the floor. She squeezed her eyes tight and reminded herself that the only thing that mattered right now was becoming a Winchester. She'd deal with the rest later.

"May I say a prayer for you?"

"For me?" she said, finally meeting his eyes. "But Anthony's the one who needs help."

"But he's not the only one, is he? I would guess that your entire world has turned upside down, too. Am I right?"

Trina looked down again. He couldn't know about her

father; he was talking about Anthony.

"Trina, there's no sugar coating your situation. If Anthony doesn't pull through this, you'll have the responsibility of raising your child by yourself. Will your father help you?"

She shook her head.

"Then your Heavenly Father will."

His words so surprised her that she looked up again. The love she saw in his eyes shook her to the core. "You don't understand," she said. "I'm not worthy."

The Reverend smiled and patted her hand. "That's what makes grace so beautiful. None of us are worthy, but God loves us anyway."

"Not me, he doesn't. I'm not . . ." She struggled for the right word. "I'm not good."

"Bow your head, Trina, and let me pray for you and Anthony."

Trina saw more concern on his face than she had ever seen from anyone. He wasn't judging her. He was building her up. If he only knew the truth, she thought with regret. She closed her eyes and bowed her head.

"Dear Heavenly Father—"

"Wait! Does it matter that I'm not Catholic?"

"I hope not. I'm not Catholic either."

For some reason, this struck her as funny, and she laughed. The more she thought about it, the funnier it was. Soon, she couldn't stop laughing.

After a moment's surprise, the minister laughed, too.

Suddenly, though, she was overwhelmed with fear, sorrow, regret, and shame. How dare she sit before a Godly man? Gut-wrenching sobs shook her body as all her painful memories exploded to the surface and came out in tears. She felt his gentle hand upon her bowed head.

"Please, God, comfort your innocent daughter in her hour of trial."

Trina wailed and cried even harder.

* * *

Jack backtracked to the central hub and saw two women standing outside Anthony's room. He started to walk past them but changed his mind. "Pardon me," he said and crossed in front of them into the room. Trina and the minister looked up. "Supply check," he said, and ducked into the bathroom where he rattled a few things, and then stopped to listen.

"And God, if it's your will, bless Trina's baby with two loving parents. Amen."

"Amen," Trina said.

"Are you ready to marry Anthony now?"

Jack stepped out of the bathroom and made himself look busy straightening things.

Trina sniffled and wiped her face with the back of her hand. "Yes, I'm ready."

Jack felt sorry for her. It seemed unfair that she was caught in the middle of all this ugliness when she should be a happy bride right now. He wet a washcloth and took it to her.

"I'm sorry for your pain," he said, his voice catching in his throat. "I hope everything works out for you." When their eyes met, he saw the depth of her sorrow, and it was heartbreaking.

"Thank you," she said in a stuffy voice, and then she buried her face in the cool cloth.

"Would you mind telling the ladies we're ready to begin?" the minister said.

"Certainly." Jack stepped into the hall and motioned for the women to go inside. He was tempted to stay, but he decided it wouldn't be right. Winchester's daughter had been through hell. She deserved to have supportive people around her.

He went to find the nurses he'd met earlier.

* * *

Stacy and Christine were waiting in the car when three police cars with lights flashing pulled beneath the porte cochere. Six officers climbed out.

Stacy and Christine looked at each other.

As the men grouped together on the sidewalk, Stacy

recognized Kevin, who appeared to be giving the men instructions. She jumped out of the car and ran towards him. "Captain Thomas," she called.

Kevin saw her and cringed. "Where's Jack?"

Realizing she'd made a mistake, but committed nonetheless, she said, "Wherever Anthony is, I would guess. Winchester's daughter is here, too. We saw her running towards the elevator about forty-five minutes ago."

"Thanks for the information. Now, get back in your car and go home."

Knowing it would do no good to argue, she walked back to Christine's car and got in.

"What did he say?" Christine said.

"We need to move the car."

* * *

Anthony faded in and out of consciousness, but he was aware of the voices around him. As the marriage ceremony took place, it reinforced his fear that he was going to die. He wondered what would happen on the other side. The possibility of reuniting with Angel and his parents, made the thought of dying easier to take, but he wanted to stay with Trina. He wanted to see their child grow into the kind of man he wasn't. Would he have turned out differently if his parents hadn't died? He believed so, but he had made many bad decisions along the way. During his first few years on the street, he had robbed and killed people in order to survive, but later, he had done it for the adrenaline rush. His list of wrongs was lengthy. He had never believed in hell, but now that he faced that possibility, it was a terrifying prospect. As the darkness beckoned him, he fought to stay awake. Were these his last moments on this side of death?

After his parents died, he had been angry and had cursed God for deserting him. Many of the homeless sought comfort in the churches, along with a free meal, but he saw man-made religion as a form of robbery. He didn't trust that its preachers and teachers were any better than he was, which was pretty damn sorry, yet the Reverend's prayer had touched him just now. He felt sorry for the wrongs he had committed and wished he could do his life over. The black man he had recently killed after selling drugs to Jermaine came to mind. The man had begged him for mercy, and he had denied him as if he had the right to make such decisions. He felt his heart being stabbed over and over as the images of people's faces flashed before him. How many lives had he destroyed? How many children had he left fatherless to suffer as he had suffered?

He thought back on the street ministers who had visited the places where the homeless gathered, and the prayers they had taught the people who wanted to be saved—prayers he had always rejected. Though he knew he was completely unworthy, he asked God to forgive him and save his wicked soul. Even before he finished praying, a warm and gentle breath blew over his body, making him tingle from head to toe, and then peace like he'd never known before covered him with love. There was no doubt in his mind that he had been forgiven, and the faith he'd thought he'd lost was suddenly reborn.

Just then, Trina said, "I do."

With more emotion than he ever remembered feeling, he said, "I do, too," in his heart.

* * *

"Right here," the minister said, pointing to the bottom of the marriage license. "Sign Anthony's name, too."

Trina scribbled both signatures and handed the pen to one of the female witnesses. Once the witnesses had signed, they quietly left the room.

"Congratulations," Reverend Collier said. "You are now officially Mrs. Anthony Winchester."

"Correction," Trina said, reaching for Anthony's hand. "I am now Katrina Kay Oliver Winchester, the first."

"Well, well, well," Thad said, entering the room wearing his lab coat and dragging his right leg.

For Trina, the room began to spin, the lights blurred, and

for the second time in her life, she fainted.

* * *

Jack caught up with one of the nurses just as she stepped out of a patient's room. "May I have one more moment of your time?"

The woman drew back. "Look, I don't know who you are, but my supervisor notified security. I'd get out of here if I were you."

"Perhaps another time, then." He did a quick U-turn. When he reached the hub, he took a right and jogged towards the stairway exit. The last thing he needed was to get arrested for impersonating a doctor!

* * *

The Reverend dropped to the floor beside Trina. "Somebody call a nurse."

"There's no need," Thad said. "I'm a physician."

"Thank heavens," Reverend Collier said, backing out of the way. "I have no idea why she fainted."

"From what I understand, she's been through quite a lot of stress this week." He picked up her wrist and checked her pulse. "Don't worry. I'll take care of her."

Glancing at his watch, the Reverend said, "If I didn't have to be somewhere . . . Wish her my best, won't you?"

"I will. Please, close the door on your way out."

* * *

Jack hurried down the stairs. When he reached the fourth floor, he stepped into the hallway and made a beeline for the nearest men's room. Finding one, he locked himself inside and began dismantling his disguise. After stuffing his glasses into his lab coat pocket, he ripped off his mustache, wincing as it separated from his skin. Next, he stuck his head into the sink and washed his hair with hand soap, returning it to its annoying riot of curls. After blotting it with paper towels, he turned on the hand dryer and bent over to dry his hair. It took nearly fifteen minutes, but when he stepped out into the hallway, he looked like his normal self. Even face to face, the nurses wouldn't recognize him.

Smiling, despite the stress, he rolled up his coat, tucked it under his arm, and headed for the lobby.

* * *

"Katrina," Thad said. "Wake up."

Trina opened her eyes and recoiled violently. "I thought—"

"Only a fool makes toxin without antiserum," he growled, returning to his feet. "I had some in my pocket when you jabbed me. Thanks to you, I know that the latest formula works better on humans than it does on felines. Once I perfect it, I'll have produced the first antiserum for one of the world's most deadly poisons. Think of it. My name will appear in every important medical journal across the globe. There will be documentaries to film and public speaking tours to manage—not to mention a Nobel Prize in Medicine. My legacy is all but guaranteed."

"Dad, did you bring antiserum for Anthony?"

"I'm not here to perfect your coup, you grasping little traitor. I'm here to make certain you fail—and don't call me Dad." He yanked Trina to her feet and pulled her towards the bed. Taking a syringe from his pocket, he jabbed it into Anthony's arm. "You see him, Katrina? This is your dead husband, and unless you do exactly as I say, you'll join him this minute. Do I make myself clear?"

Tears clouded her vision. "You are evil! I hate you!"

"Be that as it may, Anthony's heart will flatline any second now. When the nurse rushes in, you and I will slip out. If you so much as whimper, I'll stick you before you take your next breath. I'm quite capable of keeping you alive until it's time to harvest your child, so don't test me."

The alarms went off on Anthony's monitor, and the hospital staff came running.

"Step outside, please," a nurse said as she rushed by them to get to Anthony.

Pulling Trina along, Thad guided her out the door and towards a stairway exit, one he'd used many times during his twenty-year tenure. Seeing that his stiff leg was impeding their progress, he stopped at a service elevator and pushed the button.

"You need a key," Trina said.

He shoved her into the elevator. "Just so happens, I have one."

* * *

Jack was in a somber mood by the time he reached the first floor. Before Daniel died, he had never fully grasped how losing someone in death affected the living. He'd lost both parents when he was young, but that was when all of life was new. It was hard to identify, let alone separate, all the emotions of going through such an event. As much as he had missed them, he didn't remember feeling as devastated as Thad's daughter looked today. He had mourned for them, of course, but this girl . . . Trina's face before her wedding and Christine's face at Daniel's funeral had etched themselves in his memory. What he needed, he decided, was an ice-cold beer.

He saw the flashing lights beyond the entrance but thought nothing of it until a pack of police officers rounded the corner and walked by him. Curious, he turned around to follow.

"I ordered you to stay out of this, Kendall."

"Dang it," he muttered and turned around.

"I mean it, Jack," Kevin said. "Get out of here, or I'll arrest you for obstruction."

Aware that people were watching, and that Kevin's tolerance was at an end, Jack gave him a quick salute and left the hospital, but he was annoyed. If it hadn't been for that nosy nurse, he could've remained in disguise and Kevin wouldn't have recognized him. He could only imagine the tongue lashing Bryant would get for letting him slip by. He stalked towards the parking lot to look for Christine and Stacy. After several frustrating minutes, he pulled out his cell phone.

"Jack," Christine said, "Captain Thomas is here."

"Yeah, I know. He told us to go home. Where are you?"

"We're in the east parking lot. Want us to pull up?"

"No, I'll find you. It wouldn't be good for Kevin to lay eyes on the two of you right now. See you in a minute." He stepped off the curb and crossed into the main parking lot. The fresh night air and the brisk walk helped to steady his nerves. The day had run the full gamut of emotions, and he needed to sort them through.

Shielding his eyes from oncoming headlights, he stepped to the side to let the car pass.

There were so many things that needed his attention; he felt stymied. His homeowner's insurance company was demanding an incomprehensible mountain of documentation before they'd process his claim. He was stressfully low on money. He needed to finish building the kids' fort, cut Christine's yard, do the paperwork to close out Teresa's case, find out if the data on his hard drive had survived Anthony's attack on his computer, and the list went on. He hadn't even begun to think about what Anthony's recovery would mean for him and Stacy.

The word beer ran through his mind again. He dialed Christine. "Okay, I'm here. Where are you?"

"We see you. We'll be right there."

Jack stepped to the side to allow another vehicle to pass, but it hit the gas, swerved, and plowed right into him—propelling him over the hood and onto the concrete. As the car sped away, he saw the Jaguar emblem and then blacked out.

* * *

Trina punched Thad's shoulder. "What the hell are you doing?"

Thad checked his rear view mirror and saw Jack lying on the ground. "That was Jack Kendall, you idiot. Shut up and worry about yourself."

"Where are you taking me?"

"To the airport. The itinerary is in the glove box. Check the flight times. We are leaving the country tonight."

"But how did you . . ."

"I have arranged for a private jet."

Trina reached into the glove box for the itinerary and saw three loaded syringes wrapped in a rubber band behind it. She grabbed the entire pile and slid the needles into her pocket. Glancing over, she saw that Thad was concentrating on his driving and hadn't seen her take them. "Switzerland?"

"For starters," Thad said. "From there we'll go to England. There are way too many Germans in Switzerland for my taste." He pulled up to the main road and waited for the traffic to clear.

"Can we go back to the house first? There's something I need to get."

"No. We're going straight to the airport."

"But I need—"

"I don't care what you need. Shut the hell up and tell me what time our flight leaves."

Trina shoved her door open and climbed out. "I'm not going anywhere with you!" She sprinted towards the hospital.

"Suit yourself, you stupid bastard!" he yelled out the open window. When he stretched over the passenger's seat to pull her door shut, his foot slipped off the brake.

* * *

The crash was a horrendous cacophony of crunching metal, breaking glass and screeching breaks. Unable to turn away, Trina sank to her knees. It seemed like forever before the smoke cleared. Within seconds, people lined the streets, and medical personnel poured out of the Emergency Room.

Trina was beside herself. She tried to stand, but her legs wouldn't hold her, nor could she tear her eyes from the horrific scene on the street. All that remained of her father's car was a twisted piece of metal. Realizing he couldn't possibly have survived, she put her hands over her face and screamed, "Daddy!"

* * *

Jack was stable, but fading in and out of consciousness. Christine had gone out to Jack's truck in search of his insurance information, and Stacy went to see what caused the mass exodus from the Emergency Room.

Sensing danger, Jack opened his eyes to see Katrina Winchester staring down at him from beside the bed. He blinked a few times, but she was still there. She touched the scar beside his eye and said something he couldn't make out because his heart was beating so loudly. He wanted to call out, but the darkness was closing in. She held up a syringe containing yellowish liquid. In that moment he knew it was she who had administered the lethal injections. She was the missing link, the perfect cover for Thad Winchester.

"Please," he said, trying to rise, but he knew he couldn't stop her.

* * *

Cedric stood before the wall safe in his home library, transferring two hundred thousand dollars in Krugerrands into his trial briefcase, which sat open on the floor beside him. After shutting the safe, he spun the dial and rehung a gold-colored tapestry to conceal its presence. One more day and this would all be behind him.

* * *

"Don't!" Jack cried out in terror.

Christine jumped from her chair and was at Jack's side in an instant.

Stacy yanked the curtain back and called for a nurse.

Jack blinked several times and opened his eyes. "Where is she?"

"Who?" Christine said, glancing at Stacy. "We're right here."

A male nurse strode to the bed and took hold of Jack's wrist. "Hello, Mr. Kendall. How are you feeling?"

"Fine, I think. Where's Winchester's daughter?"

"You've got a nasty bump on your head. Do you remember the accident?"

"It was Winchester. I saw his car."

The nurse glanced at the vitals monitor and wrote down the latest readings. "Do you know what day it is?"

"I hardly ever know what day it is."

"That's true," Christine said with a smile. "He doesn't."

Jack was genuinely confused. Had he dreamed it? Had he imagined Winchester's daughter beside the bed? "When can I go home?"

"It shouldn't be too long," the nurse said. "We're waiting for the x-rays to come back."

"X-rays? For what?"

"It appears you fractured your leg." Turning to Christine, the nurse said, "I'll let the doctor know he's awake."

"Thank you," Christine said softly.

Stacy filled the spot where the nurse had been. "It's about time you woke up. We're starving."

* * *

Trina went to Anthony's apartment first. After gathering everything that mattered, including her favorite picture of Anthony, she took a last look around and trotted down the stairs for the last time. Once inside the lab, she went straight to the bookshelf. The last time she checked the safe, it had held only paperwork—his current financial records, his latest medical journals and the like. She doubted he left any money in there, but she had to check. Her hands were surprisingly steady as she dialed Thad IV's birth date, but the lock didn't click. She dialed again, but it still didn't open. Had he changed the combination?

She tried the date of his death, but that didn't work either. After trying her father's birthday and various other numbers, she was at a loss. "Dammit! You *would* do something like this!" How was she supposed to go anywhere without money? As a last resort, she dialed in her own birth date and was shocked to hear it click. The door opened, but the safe was empty. She sank to the ground and drew her knees up to her chest. What was she going to do? She had stopped at the bank on the way over here. All she had was five hundred dollars.

For whatever reason, the fact that he had used her birthday stuck in her mind. Why would he do that, especially for something as important as his safe? It made no sense. She laid her head on her knees and closed her eyes. She needed a plan. She needed more money. Suddenly, her head snapped up. She pushed to her feet and went back into her father's study. Taking a chair from in front of his desk, she dragged it before the fireplace and climbed onto the seat. Though she could barely reach the bottom of the portrait, she tried to lift it away from the wall, but it wouldn't budge. She needed something taller.

She glanced around and noticed the sliding ladders that led to the semi second floor, which circled the perimeter of the front half of the room. It had been years since she'd been up there, but she thought she might be able to reach the portrait from the far right side. She climbed the ladder and made her way towards the fireplace. The bookshelves stopped about six feet short of the portrait. She couldn't reach it.

Sighing, she had to acknowledge that it wasn't a likely place for another safe. He wouldn't have been able to get to it any easier than she could. There had to be another safe. The one in the lab was too small for a man of her father's wealth and ego. She just needed to find it. She leaned on the railing and looked out over the room. It had to be in here. This was his favorite room.

She thought about all the times she'd seen him pace back and forth to the window, but she couldn't see the window from here. That section of the wall was set back, which made no sense when she thought about the roofline from the outside. There could easily be a room behind the wall. That would explain the setback and the lack of other windows in the study. She started pulling books from the bookshelf and quickly discovered the lever. It was identical to the one that separated the lab from the study. As the door slid open, she saw a chain and pulled it. The light illuminated a long narrow room. Carpenter's shelves held numerous boxes of memorabilia consistent with what you might expect in any man's attic. But why conceal the entrance to a storage closet?

As she turned about, she noticed that the room was clean—no dust or spider webs anywhere. Glancing at the floor, she saw that she was standing on a seven-foot Persian runner. Stepping aside, she pulled it out of the way. Beneath it was an attic-type trap door. Her stomach tensed as she lifted the hatch.

The first thing that came to mind was that these were some serious stairs—not the rickety ladder she had expected. Spotting a light switch, she flipped it on and descended into a larger, cedar-walled room filled with stunning paintings, antiques, and family heirlooms that had been passed down through the generations of the Winchester family—her family. On any other day, these treasures would have awed her, but today she focused on the stainless steel vault, which stood against the back wall. This is what she was looking for. It had two combination dials. She took a deep breath and dialed in her half-brother's birth date. It clicked. Moving to the second lock, she dialed the date of his death. It also clicked, and the door opened.

She gasped. The vault contained stack after stack, row after row, of gold coins. She took a few steps back and cocked a brow, but it didn't take long to figure out why he'd left it. She now faced the same dilemma. She glanced at her watch. If she hurried, she could still catch her flight. Should she take only what she could carry and leave the country as planned? Or should she risk that the police couldn't prove she had administered the deadly injections? She stared at the gold. Was there another, better option? She pressed a hand to her forehead and blinked several times. What should she do?

CHAPTER NINETEEN

Just before 9:00 a.m., Cedric stood on the rotting, decommissioned bridge rehearsing the words he had composed for Winchester. Today marked the end of their so-called partnership. He was sick to death of being Winchester's puppet. After all, he had dirt on him, too.

Hearing an engine coming up the road, he squinted against the sun. It was a minivan, and it parked not ten feet from his Cadillac. Annoyed, he walked back to his car. As he reached to open his door, six uniformed police officers emerged from the minivan with weapons drawn.

"Hold it right there, Mr. Johnson."

"What's the meaning of this? I know my rights."

"We've got a warrant to search your vehicle. Unless we're mistaken, we're about to find a whole lot of money—your payoff to your illustrious partner."

Cedric's heart dropped to the pit of his stomach.

* * *

Sore, bruised, and wearing the same shirt as the day before, Jack stretched out on the couch to watch cartoons with the kids. Halfway through a repeat episode of *Scooby Doo*, Captain Thomas called. He answered but had a hard time hearing because of the TV. "Hey, Kevin, hold on a second." Pushing to his feet, he hobbled into the kitchen, still uncoordinated with his crutches. "Sorry about that. What did you say?"

"We picked up Cedric Johnson at Old Byram Bridge this morning. He had a boat load of gold coins in the trunk of his car."

"Two hundred thousand dollars' worth?"

"How the hell do you know that?"

Jack chuckled and maneuvered into a chair at the breakfast table. "Cedric's share of the settlement was forty percent. Assuming he split it with Winchester . . ."

"I'm only going to say this once. You're a far better detective than I ever gave you credit for."

"Thanks a lot," he said, making a face.

"Tell Miss Young that we found silver stationery in Winchester's desk. It perfectly matches the note Bryant picked up from Cedric Johnson. When we told Cedric we'd made the connection, he claimed Winchester has been blackmailing him into handling the Solver cases."

"Sure he was. Next, he'll say Winchester forced him to spend his half of the insurance money, too. I sat in his conference room; I looked into his eyes. Cedric Johnson is in it for the money. No one will convince me otherwise."

"Here's something else to stick in your craw. You were right about Doctor Solver being on the surgical team the night Winchester's son died. According to Cedric, Thad Winchester blames Solver for his son's death. That's why he targeted Solver's patients, to make it look like he's lost his professional edge."

"Ruining Solver's reputation along with his practice. Cedric's just full of information, isn't he?" Jack said.

"That's all we could get out of him. He's in the process of hiring counsel as we speak."

"Stacy had him pegged. He wasn't about to take the fall for this by himself."

Kevin chuckled. "Wait till he finds out that Winchester is dead. He'll be sorry he said anything at all."

"It is ironic, isn't it? Instead of ruining Dr. Solver's reputation, Solver will be exonerated, Thad Winchester is dead, and Cedric may go to jail. Still, that won't bring back their three victims, or heal the damage they have done." Jack plucked a grape from the fruit bowl in the center of Christine's table. "Any news on Winchester's daughter?"

Though everyone said he was dreaming, he was haunted by the vision of her standing beside his hospital bed, holding a syringe in her hand. He wasn't sure, but he thought she had touched the scar near his eye. He'd worn himself out trying to remember what she said, but it was gone.

"Not yet," Kevin said, "but Stacy was right about Winchester performing all three Solver-victim autopsies, and as much as I hate to admit it, your hunch was right also. Katrina Oliver—now Katrina Winchester—worked as a surgical assistant on each of the Solver surgeries. She was definitely in on it with her father. Our guess is that she administered the fatal injections."

A chill rose up his spine. Why didn't she kill him when she had the chance? Had someone interrupted her in the nick of time?

"In all three autopsy reports, Winchester pinned the cause of death on the anesthesiologist," Kevin added.

"Then Cedric settled the lawsuits, and he and Winchester pocketed the insurance money," Jack said with disgust. "Then on to the next victim, one step closer to ruining an innocent Ryan Solver."

"Yep. You and Stacy did an excellent job bringing this case to light. There's no telling how many lives you may have saved."

"You were pretty helpful yourself," he said, fully aware that without Kevin's patience, he wouldn't have been able to pursue the case at all.

"We've got an APB out on Katrina Winchester, but we figure she's financed well enough to settle outside the country. Still, I'd watch my back if I were you."

"Yeah, I'll do that. It's a lot to take in, isn't it?"

"There's more. Notes found in Winchester's lab indicate that he's been experimenting with biologically-altered puffer fish poison and antiserum, which apparently results in a prolonged paralysis that mimics death."

"Is that what happened to Anthony?" he said, thinking back on how certain they'd been that he had died in the alley.

"We're waiting on toxicology, but it would certainly make

sense considering the substance found in the syringe near Anthony's body matches the compound taken from Winchester's lab. Do you think it's possible he accidentally injected himself while you were fighting in the alley?"

"That's a scary thought. It could have happened the other way around."

"Presumably, that's what he had in mind," Kevin said.

"What's next?"

"I'll keep you posted."

After the call, Jack took a moment to contemplate the magnitude of what he had learned. So many lives destroyed on the altar of Winchester's vengeance. It was as mind-boggling as it was heartbreaking. He rubbed his chest to ease the tightness there and felt something in his pocket. He pulled out a syringe filled with yellowish liquid and wrapped in a ragged note.

> *I'm sorry for your pain. I hope everything works out for you.*

His heart slammed against his chest. He had spoken those exact words to Katrina Winchester when he handed her that washcloth, just before she married Anthony. Coincidence? It couldn't be. He turned the note over.

> *Peace.*

He swallowed hard. If there was ever a time in his life that he was glad to have been kind to someone, it was now. He dialed Kevin.

"Hey, you'll never guess what I just found."

* * *

It was nearly two in the morning, and Christine couldn't sleep. Granted, the financial pressure was off, and the kids had settled into a normal routine of daily activity, but for her, nothing felt normal. Her heart was still broken, and she was unbearably lonely. Having Jack and Stacy in the house kept her distracted, but she knew that wouldn't last forever. She'd soon be alone during the day while the kids were at school, and she didn't know how she'd cope with that. She had no interest in selling real estate, in seeing her friends, or in anything, really. She felt dead inside, and that frightened her for the children's sake.

Learning that Daniel had been murdered only made things worse. Knowing that someone had deliberately destroyed her family made her angrier than she'd ever been in her life, and she didn't know how to get past it. She hid it from the children, of course, but that only added to the feeling that she was living a lie. Nothing in her life felt real or genuine, except that she loved her children, but even that wasn't enough. As guilty as she felt for it, she didn't want to live without Daniel.

Wiping the tears from her eyes, she reached for a tissue and blew her nose.

"Mama? Can I come in?"

She wiped her eyes and said, "Sure, Jon. Come on in."

Jon's furrowed his brow as he padded across the floor and climbed into bed.

Christine smiled the best she could and wiped at the tears that fell, despite her trying to stop them.

"It's gonna be okay, Mama. God told me so." She nodded. Jon picked up her hand. "Really, Mama. It's going to be okay."

Unable to stop herself, Christine began sobbing. How her son could say such things was beyond her. Covering her face with both hands, she cried without holding back. She had longed for such words but believed herself unworthy.

"God," Jon whispered in his child's voice, "please help Mama forgive you like you helped me forgive you, and tell Daddy not to worry. Uncle Jack built me a really cool fort. Amen."

As Christine looked at him through tear-filled eyes, he smiled and handed her a tissue. Despite her pain, the love she felt so swelled her heart that she became aware of God's presence. In that moment, she understood that though her life would be different than it once was, that didn't mean she couldn't find joy and happiness again. She could, if she would allow it.

Her life wasn't over; she was beginning a new chapter.

As she accepted this truth, the clouds began to lift. She might not have Daniel, but someday there might be weddings and grandchildren. For the first time since Daniel died, she began to see a future. She began to have hope. She wrapped her arms around her son, looked heavenward and whispered, "Thank you."

CHAPTER TWENTY

After three weeks of being housebound, Jack was going stir crazy. He pushed the channel button on the TV remote repeatedly. At first, he had enjoyed the extra attention, but as the days wore on, and Stacy and Christine began leaving him alone for hours at a time, he grew impatient to get moving.

On the positive side, his forced confinement had given him ample time to catch up on his bookwork, including the insurance paperwork. He was anticipating a nice settlement check, which he planned to use to redecorate his house with the help of Christine and Stacy. By pleasant necessity, he had spent lots of time with the kids. School kept their lives moving forward and their days filled with interesting people and events. Alexa was smiling more, and Jon was all boy.

Christine had insisted he sell his Camry and accept Daniel's truck as a gift. They had argued about it for days, but he finally gave in. He needed the cash to pay his bills, and Daniel's truck was just too hard to resist. Kevin kept him informed as to how Cedric Johnson's case developed, but it would be months, if not years before a trial played out. Thinking of Cedric reminded him of Josh. He hadn't heard from him since Cedric's arrest, and he wondered how he was getting along. He made a mental note to call him later that evening.

There was still no word on Winchester's daughter, for which he was actually glad. Having seen the way Winchester treated her that night outside the morgue, and how broken up she was through the ups and downs of Anthony's death, he couldn't help but feel sorry for her. In all actuality, she had likely killed

Daniel, but still, he couldn't wish for her to be punished any more than she had been already. She seemed so fragile in the end. No matter what she'd done, she had lost her husband and her father on the same day. He couldn't imagine the heartache and regret she must be feeling. Maybe it was for the sake of her unborn baby, but he hoped she and her child would live a quiet life somewhere and put the horrible past behind them.

He pushed himself higher on the couch, glanced at the clock, and then flipped through the TV channels again. His stomach growled. Christine and Stacy had been gone all day. If they weren't home soon, he was going to have to raid the refrigerator for leftovers. Stacy was complaining the other day that he had *done been spoilt* by her and Christine's cooking. It was true, and he had no problem admitting it.

Stacy had been secretive the past several days, and he was beginning to think she might be seeing somebody—perhaps even Josh again. For some reason, he didn't want confirmation, so he didn't ask. He had to hand it to her, though; she was an amazing young woman. According to Christine, she had finished building the fort, and the kids clearly adored her.

One thing was sure; he was getting antsy for a girlfriend again. He had thought about contacting Elyse, but knowing she'd been with Winchester turned his stomach. Not that he expected her to live celibate, but Winchester? No matter how he looked at it, he couldn't reconcile that.

When he thought about the future, he saw it differently than he had in the past. If he had learned anything from Daniel's death, it was how precious the people in his life were, and how important it was to cultivate close relationships. He could finally see that material possessions are meaningless without people to share them. He switched off the TV and closed his eyes. As he drifted off to sleep, the remote control slipped from his hand and fell to the floor.

Sometime later, the doorbell rang. Reaching for his crutches, he made his way to the window and looked out. It was Elyse. Running a hand through his hair, he cleared his voice and opened the door. "Hey, you. I was just thinking about you. Come on in."

"I hope you don't mind; Kevin told me you were here," she said as she wrapped her arms around him for a quick, friendly hug. "What happened to your leg?"

"I had a minor tangle with a moving car."

"Oh, my goodness! What happened?"

"Nothing much. I'll be off these things before you know it. Have a seat."

Elyse appeared stiff as she waited for him to join her on the couch.

"I've been thinking about you, too," she said. "I was wondering if you still want to give us another chance."

Stunned, it took a moment for him to answer. "Elyse . . ."

"We could've been great together, if you had been willing to commit to our relationship. I know you cared about me."

He reached out and took her hand. "I still do, but you said it yourself, we've both moved on."

Elyse looked surprised. "Oh, I didn't realize you were seeing someone."

"I'm not," he said, "but that's just it. For the first time in my life, instead of looking behind me, I'm anticipating the future. I'll always be indebted to you for turning Winchester in, but . . ."

Elyse looked embarrassed and rose to her feet. "I see. I'm glad to hear you're doing so well. You know I wish you the best."

He followed her to the door, efficient on his crutches. "I wish the same for you, Elyse. I'll always be grateful."

"Daniel was my friend, too. It's hard to accept that Thad was responsible for his death."

Jack stiffened at the mention of his name.

"And to think that I was with him!"

"Please, Elyse, don't say any more."

Sadness and understanding registered in her eyes. "That's the reason, isn't it? You can't get past the fact that I was with him?"

"I wish I could, but I can't. I know it's not fair to you, but I can't."

Elyse sighed. "I understand. I do. There's nothing more to say then, is there? Nothing else matters."

He let her sentence hang. He hated to hurt her, but it simply wouldn't work.

She nodded. "As they say, then," she said awkwardly, "until we meet again." She kissed his cheek and turned to leave.

As Jack watched one of the most beautiful women he'd ever known walk out of his life for the second time, he knew he'd made the right decision. Once her car faded from view, he grabbed a beer and went outside onto the deck. As the sun sank lower in the western sky, he realized that for once in his life, he'd been true to himself. It felt good and right, and not nearly as difficult as he had imagined. He planned to make it a habit.

* * *

Two weeks later, Jack was free of his cast and feeling much better. Teresa had asked to meet with him at his office, so he parked his newly acquired truck as close to the door as he could and walked gingerly to the door. He paused when he realized he was looking at a newly installed security door.

The interior door opened from the inside, and Stacy stepped onto the front step. "It's about time you got back to work."

"What's with the new door?" he said as he walked past her.

A chorus of voices said, "Surprise!"

His mouth fell open. Not only was his office full of people, it had also been completely remodeled. "But who . . ."

Stacy leaned forward. "Teresa."

Glancing around, he saw Christine, her mother, Nora, the children, Josh, and a girl whom he assumed was Elizabeth, Teresa and Alan Lindsay, Lisa Colman, and Captain Kevin Thomas. His heart swelled as his friends gathered around to wish him well and to see what he thought of his new digs. After speaking briefly with each of them, he glanced around for Teresa and saw her standing off to the side with her husband and Lisa. He made his way over to them. "Teresa, I don't know what to say."

She gave him a wry smile. "I can't have my private detective working in a hovel, can I?"

"It was pretty awful, wasn't it? How can I ever thank you?"

Alan stepped forward and handed him an envelope. "By using this wisely."

"What's this?" he said as he looked inside. It was a check for thirty thousand dollars. "Holy cow! I can't take this."

Stacy tugged on his shoulder. "That's enough to hold us over while we develop our new clientele."

"What new clientele?"

"Jack," Teresa said, "we thought you might enjoy supplementing your income by working to reunite families who are searching for missing loved ones. God knows, someone needs to do it."

"I like the idea. It sounds much more rewarding than chasing after unfaithful spouses."

"Yeah. You're not too good at that," Alan teased.

Jack laughed. Turning to Stacy, he said, "What do you mean, our clientele?"

"You need help, Jack. And it just so happens, I'm available."

Josh, who had made his way over to the group, said, "Wait a minute. My new boss told me to hire an assistant. I was just about to offer you your old job back."

Jack saw her hesitate and held his breath.

"You'd be an idiot to hire me back," she said. "I'm part of the reason Cedric Johnson is out of business. Besides, Jack needs me more than you do."

"Yeah, you just like the excitement," Josh said as he extended his hand for Jack to shake. "Elizabeth and I are late for an engagement. It was great seeing you. Good luck."

"You, too, Josh." Jack waved to Elizabeth, who stood rigidly by the door.

Josh kissed Stacy's cheek. "Take care of yourself."

"You, too." She smiled and waved to Elizabeth, but Jack knew her well enough to know it wasn't sincere.

"Excuse me, everyone," Stacy said, "but I've got another surprise for Jack." She took hold of his arm and led him to the bathroom door where the kids stood guard. They giggled and stepped aside.

"Be careful when you open the door," Stacy said.

Jack gave her a sideways look and slowly opened the door. To his delight, out came two black and white, longhaired kittens. He immediately scooped them up. "Hey, guys. Who are you?"

"They were living in the attic. I coaxed them out when we were doing the remodeling. Now, they think they own the place. I figured you knew about them because of the food bowls beneath the sink."

"So these were the little noise makers I couldn't find." He remembered their mother and was pleased that he could give her little ones a good home. It seemed right, somehow, and made him inexplicably happy. "What should we name them?"

"How about Bandit for the boy," Jon said. "He looks like he's got a mask on because of the black around his eyes."

"Bandit it is," Jack said, handing him over to Jon.

"What about Bella for the girl," Alexa said.

"Bella's a stupid girl's name," Jon complained.

"Bella it is," Jack said, handing the other kitten to Alexa. "Watch over them for me, okay?"

The kids took off with the kittens.

Stacy snorted. "More like Bonnie and Clyde, if you ask me. Don't leave anything lying around or they'll steal off with it. Do you want them, Jack? If not, I'm sure we can find them a good home."

"Yes, I want them. We'll keep them here until my house is ready, and then I'll take them home."

"There are lots of feral kitties around here."

"Let's keep some food and water out back. I'm sure they could use some kindness in their direction."

"Thought you'd say that. I'm already on it," Stacy said.

Christine popped the champagne bottle. "Toast every-body!"

Stacy hurried to hand out plastic glasses while Christine poured the champagne.

Christine waited until everyone was ready, and then she lifted her glass. "To you, Jack, for being a faithful friend in my darkest hour. Daniel can rest easy knowing that you are looking out for us. Because of your hard work and dedication, justice is being served, and the children and I can concentrate on the business of living again."

"We love you, Uncle Jack!" the kids chimed in from across the room where they were feeding icing to the kittens.

"Several people had a hand in making those things happen," Jack said, "especially Stacy, Josh, and Captain Kevin Thomas, but I'm happy to be of service."

"Thanks to all of you," Christine said.

Everyone drank to that.

"Me, next," Stacy said. "To you, Jack. You went out of your way to help me when I needed you most. You believed in me and made me feel special for the first time in my life. Thank you, from the bottom of my heart."

"My turn," Nora said. "As you know, you are like a second son to me. Thank you for taking care of Daniel's family. I am eternally grateful."

"You're welcome," Jack said, but he didn't trust himself to speak beyond those simple words.

"I have something to add," Teresa said, raising her glass with the elegance Jack so admired. "I have many things to thank you for. Not only are Alan and I more in love than ever before, but we have an incredibly smart, beautiful daughter whom we never knew we had."

"And a granddaughter soon, too," Lisa chimed in, patting her rounded belly.

"Yes," Teresa said with genuine warmth. "Partly because of you, Jack, the four of us are a family. How can we ever thank you?"

"You already have. Look at my fabulous new office everybody. Compliments of Alan, Teresa, and Lisa Lindsay."

"Oh, my gosh," Lisa said. "I forgot that I'm a Lindsay."

Everyone cheered and took another drink.

Jack walked to the center of the room and raised his glass. "All right, everybody, I have something to say, too. Each of you has touched my life in various ways, and I am grateful. I am a far richer person for having known each and every one of you."

"Thirty thousand dollars richer," Stacy teased.

He chuckled. "That's not what I meant, but I'll certainly drink to that. To the new focus of my business—reuniting lost loved ones!"

Everyone clapped, and Kevin whistled. "Now, maybe I can get some work done without running into you everywhere I turn," Kevin said, but Jack caught the humor in his eyes.

While everyone sipped champagne, Jack lifted his glass one more time. "To you, buddy. I told you I'd figure it out."

A warm and wonderful feeling washed over him as he glanced around at the people who had gathered to celebrate his plans for a bright future—a future he hadn't seen for himself until this very moment. He wasn't alone in the world, as he had once thought. These people were his friends, and they very clearly cared about him.

As tears of gratitude pooled in his eyes, he was aware of his many blessings. Christine and the children were doing better every day. He was driving Daniel's new truck. The insurance company had paid enough to remodel his house. His office actually smelled good, and it looked like a two-room version of Cedric's office—from which he would be reuniting lost loved ones and working with Stacy. It was exciting to contemplate!

As he allowed himself to look ahead, he finally dared to believe that the best years of his life weren't behind him—they were yet to come.

COMING SOON

Pearl River Mansion
by Richard Swartz

The second novel in the Underdog Detective Series

Pearl River Mansion

As the only heir of Joan Chandler, Tyler Chandler stands to gain everything a man could want, including Pearl River Mansion—a 450 acre, post Civil War estate, that sits upon a ridge at the end of one of the many fingers of the Ross Barnett Reservoir. In exchange for receiving her wealth, his mother seeks to control his life—as she does everyone within her inner circle—but Tyler refuses her money, which always came with strings, and struggles to make it in the world on his keen intelligence, superior education, and exceptional good looks.

These good looks have won him the virtue of many hesitant females, including Sarah Richards, whose virginity he stole after making promises he had no intention of keeping. Six months later—the second time they had ever spoken—the equivalent of a shotgun wedding bound them as parents to a set of dark haired twins—a boy named Cody and a girl named Rachael—and all of this happened without Joan Chandler's knowledge.

When Joan learns of the wedding, she is furious. Sarah Richards, a redneck country girl, is not what she had in mind as a wife for her son, and she makes her sentiments known. As time goes by, it becomes painfully evident that Cody is Tyler and Sarah's favorite. Rachael is neglected and ignored. Joan, who has always longed for a daughter, is enchanted with her granddaughter and seeks to bring her under her care—no matter what she must do, or whom she must hurt to accomplish her goal.

But nature intercedes, and for the first time in her life, Joan Chandler sees a good use for the alligators that have kept her well away from the water's edge.

————

Stacy Young, Detective Jack Kendall's *assistant*, receives a disturbing call related to the Chandler case—a case that made national news but has grown cold for more than a year.

Jack and Stacy are about to receive the missing link, the key that opens the door to the most dangerous, complex, and emotional case of their lives.

Pearl River Mansion . . . a case you will never forget.